Per tugged hard on Dilani's arm, but she still moved forward, resisting him. Bey got his attention and pointed back, in the direction Per wanted them to go. A pack of ketos sped by, so close their armored skin nearly grazed Per's arms. Something small and bright darted after the ketos, passing so quickly that it was gone before Per realized that it was a projectile, not a fish. The sound of a whistle made him jerk his head around again. Half a dozen of the White Killers shot past, in hot pursuit of the ketos. The sound of their hunting whistles lingered like a contrail.

The Killers had almost passed out of sight when the last in line turned around. Per saw the pale, snake-pupiled eyes widen. The Killer turned toward them . . .

# TYPHON'S CHILDREN

## Toni Anzetti

A Del Rey® Book
THE BALLANTINE PUBLISHING GROUP
NEW YORK

A Del Rey® Book
Published by The Ballantine Publishing Group
Copyright © 1999 by Toni Anzetti

All rights reserved under International and Pan-American Copyright Conventions. Published in the United States by The Ballantine Publishing Group, a division of Random House, Inc., New York, and simultaneously in Canada by Random House of Canada Limited, Toronto.

Del Rey Discovery and colophon are registered trademarks of Random House, Inc.

www.randomhouse.com/delrey/

Library of Congress Catalog Card Number: 99-90607

ISBN 0-345-41871-9

Manufactured in the United States of America

First Edition: October 1999

10  9  8  7  6  5  4  3  2  1

# 1

Dilani swam outward from the edge of the world with long, strong strokes. The morning light still shone fresh and warm on the shores of the small island behind her. She swam through sun dazzle on tropical waves, but she pictured the darkness that lay below: the last tip of the beach sinking away behind her into the shelf, the slope, and at last the abyssal plain under the weight of the Deep's eternal night.

She envisioned her parents swimming outward, too, from their world into the night of the Deep above, coming to rest at last on Typhon as if on a lone atoll. All the first generation had made that crossing, yet they forbade her to swim beyond the reef, when the whole world lay beyond it.

A slight increase in turbulence and a quickening of light in the water told her that she had crossed the lagoon and was closing on the reef. She broke her rhythmic stroke to let her fingers trail across the dart gun at her belt. The reef crossing was the most dangerous part of the swim. She drifted into a glittering cloud of shilliks and moved lazily along with them, hoping the multitudinous shimmer of the round, silver fish would camouflage her from predators. Puffy pink monkey-faces and piku like crimson droplets of blood darted aside from her approach. She saw the intricate lacework of the reef passing below and felt cooler currents swirl around her as she approached deepside.

Lifting her head from the water, she couldn't see Per, but she knew he was out there, on the skipboard among the waves. She had seen him set out from the shore on another forbidden foray beyond the reef. He had refused to take her with him, as he always did, but she knew she could find him. She would show him that she, too, could take risks and explore the Deep. He would have to change his mind.

Suddenly the shilliks scattered and dispersed, faster than she could follow. From the deep blue below, a woven ivory crescent whipped gracefully outward. One of its edges, fringed like a frayed basket, encountered a clump of fish and knotted immediately around half a dozen of them. The tendrils blushed pink. The fish dulled and shrank till the sated tendrils allowed their husks to flutter downward out of sight.

Dilani froze in midkick. She hadn't expected tangleweed at this point on the reef. There had been none the last time she had ventured out alone. It was possible she might escape. The tangleweed had touched shillik last, so it wasn't attuned to her. It might pursue the fish, if she did not move.

With agonizing slowness, her residual momentum carried her over the reef. The tangleweed was a very large clump. She glimpsed lazily moving branches as big around as her waist. She averted her eyes.

Then she saw new shapes, beyond the fleeing shillik. Gray shadows hung in the deepening blue. Boogers! Her feet kicked in panicked reflex, before she could think, and the pale weed responded. An exploring limb whipped out and just brushed the sole of her foot. For a moment, she thought it would ignore her, but then the limb curled back and wrapped around her ankle. Her foot stung, then went ominously numb.

Holding still was useless once the weed had found her. So was fighting, but she struggled with all her strength. She reached for her knife and lashed about with it. The weed had a texture like tough leather and was almost impossible to cut. White limbs wove about her, immobilizing her left side, until only her right arm and head could still move. A casual tendril found her breathing mask and twisted about it, tearing it away, then discarding it as inedible.

A rush of bubbles feathered across her face. Now she had only the time it would take for her lungs to empty, and the weed would win. They had warned her not to swim out to the reef, and they had been right.

Numbness spread up her leg and across her ribs. At least being tangled didn't hurt, she thought. It was better than being caught by the boogers.

Air leaked from her lungs, trickled, then rushed out, and convulsively she struggled to fill them with the treacherous water that felt so cool and comforting on her face, but burned and stabbed in her throat. Her mind revolted against her body's actions. She tried to cling to the last few seconds of air, but a force greater than her will pumped her chest as she tried to breathe the water. Her fingers fumbled the knife and let it fall as her body went limp in the tightening grasp.

She no longer felt the weed's cutting grip. Instead, it seemed as if the water itself held her in its arms, pulling her deeper, trying to tell her something. She felt the water push against her ears with invisible fingers.

Then something awful happened, tearing her from the numbness. Something poisonously sharp and blinding exploded into the water around her, and her failing body convulsed again. The tangleweed whipped away, slashing her as it withdrew. Then she was gripped and pulled from the water. She found herself sprawled on the skipboard, vomiting and choking.

Without waiting for the retching to stop, Per rubbed her face and eyes with a spongy, strong-smelling wipe. He even forced it over her mouth and tongue. She fought against it until she realized that his rubbing stopped the burning pain of her skin. She was able to blink her eyes, and then to sit up.

The water pooling around her on the board's deck was pink. Abrasions on most of her exposed skin oozed blood, and her left wrist and ankle bore parallel cuts from the grip of the weed. Already the wounds ached. When the numbness wore off, they would hurt badly, but she could deal with that. What hurt more was that she had bungled her attempt to impress Per.

Per shook his fingers at her. *Should not, should not.* Always the same message. She spotted the harpoon gun lying where he had dropped it—careless, he might lose it that way—and pointed to it, curious about how he had driven off the tangleweed.

"Explosive head." His fingers worked deftly while he spoke. "Filled with something I cooked up myself, mostly ammonia."

Through the pain, Dilani was pleased that she remembered the name and that he didn't have to spell it out for her.

"You remember how tanglewood in the marsh withdraws if you piss on it? That's what gave me the idea. But I had to come up with a delivery system that keeps it from dispersing in water. You gave me a chance to test it, but you've ruined the rest of my day. Now I have to go all the way back to shore with you."

"What were you doing?" she signed, vainly trying to change the subject.

"I was lying in wait for boogers. Caught you instead," he signed, a wry smile playing across his face.

He stuck gel dressings from the survival kit on the worst of the cuts. Salt stung fiercely in the other abrasions as the numbness induced by tangleweed toxin started to wear off. He snapped a tether on her so she wouldn't slip from the board. She wasn't worried. Per had more skill with a skipboard than anyone. Taking a skipboard out beyond the reef was forbidden, as was swimming that far, but he did it all the time without paying any attention to the protests of the other adults.

Dilani crouched close to the mast to unbalance the board as little as possible while Per turned it toward land. Slow tears of shock and pain trickled down her face. She knew Per would turn her in when they reached shore, and there was no point in arguing.

The skipboard grounded with a shudder she could feel through the soles of her feet, and Per let her limp across the tidal flat alone while he wrestled with the mast assembly and a net bag that held writhing, slimy boogers. Their mean, triangular mouths worked as they tried to find something to rasp, and the caustic slime that coated their fat, muscular bodies seeped through the net. Per held them well away from his body. His arms were already spotted with healed and half-healed booger sores.

She waited for him on the beach and tried to take the mast from him. He resisted, but finally gave in and let her help. Far down the beach she could see Whitman Sayid waving at them. Even at that distance, she could see how angry he was. As they came closer, she could see his mouth opening and shutting, scolding away whether she could hear him or not.

More scolding, more bossing—that was all she had to look forward to, unless she could get Per's attention. In desperation, she dropped the mast in the sand and grabbed his free arm, shaking it till he looked at her. Then her hands moved insistently to her temples, as if she could pull the knowledge she needed out of the air. "Teach me!" she signed. "Take me with you; show me what you know!"

He put her off with an impatient gesture.

She planted herself firmly in his way. Her hands shaped her anger and her need in wide, slashing gestures.

"No! Stop! Listen to me! Nobody listens to me! Are you more deaf than I am? Who else will teach me if you don't? Nobody learns to sign but you, and you won't pay attention when I try to sign to you. What happens if you go out beyond the reef someday and die, like they all say you will? Who talks to me then? Who teaches me something besides cleaning fish? I'm alone!"

She saw Per lift his free left hand as if to reply, but his right was still burdened with the bag of twitching boogers. His shoulders sagged. She thought he looked defeated, but she couldn't tell if that meant he was giving in to her plea, or if it was something else.

"The Sayids sign. Teacher Engku signs. They teach you," he signed awkwardly, left-handed.

She stood her ground.

"Not enough! They can't teach enough. They don't know enough. They don't know anything! I want to know everything. Like you."

"You think that? Think I know everything?"

His face lost its weary look, and a shadow of his normal, mocking smile returned.

She shook her head vigorously.

"No! But you want to. Like those." She pointed to the boogers. The sign Per had invented for booger was finger-up-the-nose, but she was in no mood for jokes. "You keep looking at them. Why? Nobody knows. Nobody else cares but you. But they live here!"

Per dropped the net so he could use both hands.

"I don't have time to explain. They're mad enough already. Look—the committee doesn't want me to work this way. They won't let you work with me, if I want you or not. They have given you a work schedule. They're doing the best they can. I don't accept their decisions, but I'm an adult. I can make that choice. You can't." He signed in tense, jerky motions, close to his chest, showing his frustration.

Per was one of two adults in the colony who signed to her as if it were a language and not an awkward set of code gestures. She could read his heart in his hands, whether he liked it or not. The others moved their fingers stiffly or vaguely, then gave up, flapping their mouths and leaving her out of the conversation. Sometimes she felt like a sea creature gazing through the transparent wall of the surface into a world where she could never go.

"But they're wrong!" she signed. "You are right!"

He picked up the bag again and stepped around her, signing.

"Doesn't matter."

She followed behind, her arm aching badly again after the incautious motion. She knew she was in trouble, but stubbornly she clung to hope. At least Per had not dismissed her. He hadn't said yes, but at least he had talked to her.

Whitman Sayid was indeed very angry. He grabbed her and would have shaken her painfully, but Per stopped him.

When Sayid saw that she was hurt, he brusquely signed "sorry" and then started scolding her again.

"You had fish roster today! You run away again! Endanger community! Bad, irrespons—" he broke down in the midst of *irresponsible*. His signing was atrocious. On this occasion, that actually comforted Dilani a little. Usually it made her sad and angry. She had lived with Bey and Whitman since the bad thing happened, and Whitman still could barely speak to her. He lived on the opposite side of the transparent wall.

Per said something, and Whitman's scolding turned toward him. They argued while Dilani limped along behind, feeling faint and sick. The mast slid from her grasp, and she stopped, swaying. Finally Per turned around and saw her. There were more indignant mouthings and arm shakings. Then Whitman hurried on ahead while Per put down his net and helped her to the hospital.

There he eased her down onto one of the narrow cots and put a cup of fruit juice within her reach.

"Drink that."

He reached for the zips of her skinsuit and then frowned.

"I'll get Dr. Melicar," he signed.

The doctor was one of the people Dilani didn't mind, even though her signing wasn't nearly as good as Per's. Sushan Melicar's hair had gone gray. One side of her face was beginning to get wrinkled, but they were kind wrinkles. The other side of her face was more crumpled than wrinkled. The burning water had caught her and scalded her when the bad thing happened, and the treatments that might have restored her skin to perfection were unavailable on Typhon, as were the surgeries and implants that might have turned Dilani into a hearing person.

Dr. Melicar came over to her cot, and her hands were gentle as she peeled off the gel and began to scrub the cuts with antiseptic and neutralizer. She, too, hesitated at the fastenings of the skinsuit.

"Cut it off, only way," she signed. "Hate to spoil suit. Few extras."

Dilani curled her good arm protectively around the suit. It had been her mother's. If the doctor cut it up, she didn't know where she'd get another. She thought about pulling it off over the injured and swelling limbs.

"Leave it on?" she signed. "I'm not hurt underneath."

The doctor probed the hurt arm speculatively.

"If it swells, then I cut the suit. Guess it can stay till then."

Stoically Dilani endured the cleaning of her wounds. The only anesthetic they had was made from tangleweed toxin, and her body had already absorbed a dangerous dose. She understood why the doctor could not give her more. The numbness still partially prevailed, so it didn't hurt more than she could bear.

Finished with the painful task, the doctor smiled. Dilani could see that she meant to be kind, but she also saw how the lines deepened in Melicar's face. Dilani had brought the doctor more trouble by hurting herself again.

"Drink more juice, and sleep," the doctor signed. "If you feel short of breath, pull the cord right away and I'll come back. Going to dinner now."

Dilani lay back wearily and closed her eyes. She had a pounding headache. Tangleweed poisoning could make people really sick, though few got a chance to experience it. Usually, once the weed got hold of someone, that was the end. When encountered as tanglewood, which grew onshore in brackish water, it wasn't quite so deadly. It was easier to cut loose from it if you weren't drowning at the same time.

As she lay there, drifting, she felt again the relentless delicacy of the tendrils pulling her down, and jerked awake.

A series of thumps vibrated through the tubewood legs of the cot. Opening her eyes, she saw Bey Sayid trying to get through the door. It wasn't easy to push the wheels of his cart over the threshold, and she couldn't help him as she usually did. Bey's father was always talking about building a smoother-running cart for his son, but he never got around to it. That was another thing Dilani held against him.

Bey finally succeeded, without spilling the dishes he had balanced on his lap and gripped between his toes.

"Brought your dinner," he signed. "My father wouldn't let me bring any fish. The old no-work-no-eat blahblah. I brought you some spud mash. That's all we had. And stole you some chewynuts."

He tried to put them in her hand, but she waved them away.

"You eat them. I'm sick."

She fingered up a few mouthfuls of mash. Unadorned spud was about the blandest thing in the world. The grownups constantly complained about spuds and talked about potatoes and rice and fufu and how much better all those things were than good old spud, and then they scolded the young ones for complaining and told them how lucky they were to have spud roots at all.

In Dilani's opinion, the complaints came mostly from oldgens. Newgens had grown up on spud and liked it pretty well, boring as it was.

"Tell what happened," Bey urged. "I couldn't get it from Per and my father shouting at each other."

She sketched out the story for him, one-handed. She really didn't have the strength to tell it as it should have been told. The horror and magnificence of almost dying wouldn't come across with her there, flat on her back and one hand bandaged.

Bey understood anyway. He was about the only one who did, other than Per and maybe the doctor. The doctor never said much, so you couldn't tell about her.

Bey shook his head.

"You shouldn't have done that," he signed.

"Shouldn't! Shouldn't!" she mimicked angrily. "Only thing anyone says to me. Don't you start."

"If you died I would lose my best friend," he signed calmly.

She knew that was true, but she didn't want to answer it. She wanted Per to be her friend, but he wasn't interested, and meanwhile Bey had earned the title. He talked to her, translated for her, always stuck up for her, and protected her even when he didn't like what she was doing and wished she would stop. He had gotten in plenty of trouble for being on her side.

Bey's skin was a smooth, even brown, and his arms were long and smoothly muscled. He had shiny, curling black hair, and the most beautiful brown eyes on the island. Everybody liked Bey. He was perfect from the crotch up.

From the crotch down there wasn't much to him. His legs were the size of a baby's and curved out from his hips in a way that would never support his full weight. They weren't strong enough to have braces fitted to them. They ended in long, fin-like feet that boasted flexible toes that had originally been webbed together. Surgery had taken care of that, and though they weren't pretty, he made them useful. He could hold an object securely in his lap and turn it around with his toes while he worked on it with his hands.

He did the best fine handwork of anyone on the island, from net mending to fixing small machinery. His fingers had been webbed together too, and the scars still showed, but they worked all right. Bey was always working. Nobody ever said Bey was irresponsible or lazy, a danger to the community.

Dilani liked him too, but that was just the trouble. She felt as if everyone, especially Whitman Sayid, was watching her to see if they would get along. Sometimes she thought the only reason Whitman had provided her with living quarters was to secure a mate for Bey.

Of course, she should be grateful. She'd be a lot better off with Bey than with some of the other newgens. Nils Samerak, for instance. He had two legs all right, but his bones were huge and somehow misshapen, so his skull was too heavy for his neck and his eyes were sunk deep beneath ridges of bone. He walked, but he shambled, and his hands and feet were clumsy.

Then there was Bader Puntherong: he was nimble and lively enough, but he had been born with a gap in his lips and his teeth pushed forward like a prow. Surgery had given some function back and made him look more like a human, but he still had hardly any chin and drooled when he forgot to pull his ill-formed mouth shut. Bey said his voice did not sound like the others'.

Dilani wondered why Bader didn't sign instead. In private, she signed to him and he understood her, but if she did it when adults were watching, he looked pained and angry, and turned away to mouth flap with the others.

If she could have, she might have traded her deafness for the colored wattles of skin that webbed Selma's neck and shoulders. It looked funny, but Selma could hear all right. There was something else wrong with Selma, though: something that made her turn blue and gasp for air if she moved too fast. Dilani thought she would rather be deaf than turn blue.

Lila Skanderup had legs and a pretty face, but she also had something wrong with her spine, so she had to sit in a chair all day and didn't even go out in a cart like Bey. She wasn't in the running when people discussed possible mates, because although the Skanderups didn't talk about it, the word had gotten around that she could never have children anyway.

"Lucky," she shaped with her fingers, and then clenched her fist to cross it out. Sure, they all thought she was lucky. Her index-of-functionality score was really high. She had a body, arms, legs, eyes, ears, a brain. Never mind that she couldn't hear. Never mind that she was forever shut out from their discussions—of her and her future. To them she was nothing but a functioning body. It didn't seem to occur to them that she had feelings. She couldn't speak her thoughts, so they assumed she had none.

The room was beginning to get dark, though she could still see Bey by the glow of the nightlight.

"You go back to your father," she signed. "Don't get into more trouble."

She feigned a big yawn, even though she didn't feel sleepy any more.

Bey shrugged.

"Big meeting tonight," he signed. "Kids have to stay out of the way."

Dilani looked past him, through the open door, and saw some of the adults—those who had been on special duty and hadn't gathered for dinner—ambling into the big house. The lights were on inside, and the big sliding shutters that led to the veranda were open to allow the cooling breeze to flow through the crowded meeting room. She could see shapes silhouetted against the light and could tell the speakers apart by the way they carried their bodies and by the gestures they made.

"I can hear them," Bey signed. "I'll tell you if they say anything interesting."

They watched the figures move about for awhile.

"Uh-oh, poor Amina," Bey signed. "Melicar reports she has reached puberty. No lie!"

He waggled his eyebrows lecherously, and Dilani slapped his hand.

Bey strained his face in the expression Dilani had come to associate with the spelling-word *groan*. It meant he was uncomfortable and protesting against what he had just heard.

"Phillips Roon speaking."

Dilani had already seen Roon's tall, stooping form move to the center of the ring.

"Our genetic responsibilities again. He says Amina is the youngest left alive of the second generation, and no children have been born since the disaster. Soon the older women will reach menopause. Decisions must be made. If we want to give up and die out, we should admit it. 'This is essentially a suicide pact, it is mental cowardice, and as a scientist I refuse to play along with it any more.' " As he signed the final sentence, he mimed Roon's pompous stance.

Suddenly Dilani was acutely uncomfortable with Bey's presence in the darkening room. She knew what was coming next. Roon would talk about mating in all its possible forms, and she just didn't want to lie there, knowing what was in Bey's mind, and he knowing what was in hers. Admitting it to Bey would only make it worse, however.

The only escape she could think of was to go to sleep. She let her eyes close and breathed steadily, even when she felt Bey lean close to her and brush his hand against hers. After a while she felt the thumping rattle again, and when she cautiously stole a glance, Bey had gone.

He had left a glowstar on the table. Its luminescent limbs had curled back into its shell for the night, but they still glimmered faintly. Bey had filled her juice cup before he went.

She thought she had been pretending to doze, but her eyes wouldn't stay open now. She slid down a precipitous shore into the depths of sleep.

Per Langstaff was the only person who noticed Bey Sayid laboriously trundling his cart from the hospital building to the shadows at the edge of the veranda. That was because Per stood as near the door as he could get, as if to disassociate himself from the proceedings.

He didn't give Bey any encouragement, but he looked at the boy once and then ignored him pointedly so Bey would know that he, Per, had no interest in reporting Bey's presence. Per felt that if the young Sayid wanted to watch his parent make a rat's rump of himself, he was entitled.

A number of women, including Dr. Melicar, had responded angrily to Roon's speech, but he refused to yield the center of the circle.

"I am only stating the facts. A refusal to face those facts will not make our situation nicer or easier. Quite the contrary. I'd like to see those of you who object come up with answers. You of all people, Sushan, should know better."

Per, like everyone, knew that Phillips would gladly have maximized his genetic potential with the doctor. In spite of her injuries and her stubborn attitude, Roon considered her one of the more functional females remaining on the island. She had turned him down.

"Perhaps you're right," Roon said, his reedy tenor turning ponderous with sarcasm. "Perhaps we should remain passive, do nothing, allow the next generation to make the decisions. They will inherit Typhon. It's certainly true that we cannot keep them much longer in the position of minor children. They are physically full grown and will soon demand their franchise right. However, let me point out that they number a mere two dozen—twenty-six to be precise—and if we leave them to work this problem out for themselves, we are dooming them to a slow death by genetic attrition. They simply cannot sustain human life on Typhon, alone. They could not if they were healthy. The pool is too small. As it is . . ." He shrugged, the sentence unfinished.

"We've been through this before," the doctor said wearily. "It simply isn't fair to bring more children to life when we know they will be severely handicapped from birth. We don't have the resources to care for the colony members we already have."

"There are many possible alternatives," Roon said. "I've laid them out for you in some detail."

"Yes, we can all imagine alternatives," Melicar snapped. "Unfortunately they are all unpalatable, inhumane, or demented."

"I can't accept your characterization of eugenics as inhumane," Roon said stiffly. "It has been widely practiced throughout human history, by some of the most successful social groupings. Termination of an unviable neonate is no different in principle from fetal screening, which I trust we would all accept if we still had the equipment."

"I won't try to stop you from terminating your own offspring," Melicar said. "But I won't help you impose that protocol on the whole colony. Anyone who wants to go along with you can self-deliver their child. I won't assist. Furthermore, I doubt that many women will go through the mental anguish of repeated births only to turn the life or death decision over to you."

Rude noises signalled the agreement of most of the women present.

Roon's ears reddened, but he plunged on.

"We're dooming ourselves, as well," he said. "Without healthy offspring, there will be no one to care for us when we lose our faculties to age or illness. If you refuse to look for a solution, why not just euthanize ourselves at once and get it over with? You're deciding on mass suicide either way."

Whitman Sayid apparently realized that the discussion was getting out of hand. He stepped forward, put a hand on Roon's shoulder, and whispered urgently to him until Roon finally yielded.

"I hope there are alternatives that aren't quite that drastic," Sayid said, taking the floor. Per could see most of the members relaxing slightly. Whitman was blessed with a deep, mellifluous voice that produced a pleasant, comfortable feeling even when what he was saying was pure guano.

"I don't think any of us could argue that we aren't in trouble. Out of all those who arrived from Skandia, one in ten remains. Of course, we all hope and anticipate that a second ship will arrive from Skandia one day soon."

A chorus of jeers greeted this optimistic assertion, but he overrode them.

"It *is* still possible. We have no reason to be convinced that their silence implies anything more than a communications breakdown. Help may already be on the way."

"They'll be just in time to bury us," someone shouted.

"My friend over there has a point," Whitman continued, unperturbed. "Even though help from Skandia may be coming, we still must try to help ourselves, if we can. With all respect to you, Sushan, we're going to have to pick the least unpalatable alternative, make a face, and swallow. It's true that time is passing, and we don't have the luxury of waiting for a perfect answer."

"We've waited this long already," Melicar said. "It's been ten years since we finally admitted that it seems impossible to bear healthy children on Typhon. We've tried every combination among us, and nothing has worked. We've discussed this over and over again and found no solution. Why the sudden rush?"

"First of all, we have not made a scientific effort to try every possible genetic combination. It's been done on the basis of individual preference, and in a haphazard way. We should seriously consider organized, methodical attempts, perhaps by artificial means to avoid social disruption. But Roon is right: we would have to decide beforehand how to deal with our failures."

"But that's exactly why we haven't made a so-called scientific effort before!" Melicar said. "Because no one here is willing to bear children, only to discard them on the trash heap like so many spoiled omelets. We are human beings, Whitman!"

Sayid stretched out his hands in a quelling gesture as a murmur of argument began to rise from the group.

"Of course I realize that it must be an individual decision for the adult members, but I wish you would at least vote to discuss it."

Sayid paused, then continued. "However, the highest-priority reason for action now is the newgens. As of today, they have all reached puberty. In the past, there was no point in discussing it, but now it's essential to find out if they can reproduce. I know I'm talking about our children, and I hate to put it so bluntly, but I have my own son to consider and I can't urge this too strongly. It may be that the problem, whatever it is, will only carry through one generation. We owe it to them to find out as soon as possible. We should begin planned matings of the functional females immediately."

An uproar drowned out the last few words of his sentence. Dr. Melicar took his place in the center, only to be half pushed out of it by Olympia Haddad, Selma's mother, who in turn lost her place to Torker Fensila, the chief of fisheries.

Per watched silently. In the past, arguments had sometimes changed course when someone remembered Per's presence. Occasionally he had courted attacks to make sure no decision could be made. It looked to him as if this discussion had gone too far for that to work, but still he moved forward.

Before he could speak, though, Piping Melu pointed an accusatory finger at him.

"I see you, Per," she called out from the floor. "Langstaff stands in the corner listening as if this discussion has nothing to do with him!"

Piping had been pregnant four times, by three different fathers. The first two children had been stillborn, with deformities. The third had survived till age four, when he suddenly had stopped breathing. The autopsy had revealed a malformation of the pulmonary arteries. A fourth pregnancy had ended in a miscarriage. She had wanted to try again with Per, but he had declined her requests.

"What right do you have to speak here? You won't donate, you won't pair, and you won't get on a recreational roster. Are you one of us or not, Per?"

"My genetic material is my own." He had gritted out such discussions before. Though he understood Piping's reasons for reopening the question, he still found himself deeply angry. "If you're going to start forced breeding programs, we might as well be back in the Rationality. I have information for you, Piping: This isn't Skandia!"

Torker still held the floor, and he unexpectedly allied himself with Piping.

"Yes, what about him?" the fish boss said, addressing the group. "He hasn't contributed much lately, genetically or otherwise. He won't donate for a child, and he stays off the work roster most days, too. We need the fish pens enlarged. Instead he spends his time diddling around in the lab—or building pens for boogers, of all things. *Boogers!* Like we need more of them! Last month they got out and savaged the edibles! Does no-work-no-eat apply to everybody but him?"

Per welcomed the personal attack. It looked as if his attempt to change the focus of the discussion had succeeded.

"That was last rainy season, Tork," he said. "You must be losing your memory. There hasn't been a problem with my specimens in six months—unless you count the time some unknown person butchered my ramselfish and served them for breakfast."

Once again Whitman tried to defuse the situation.

"Per," he said in a confidential tone, as if they were chatting privately, "nobody objects to your running research in your spare time. In fact it's very commendable. But Torker has a point. There's all kinds of life-sustaining work that needs more hands right now, but you won't get on the roster. Furthermore, you're risking colony resources in unsanctioned ways. Just today you were out beyond the reef again, and look what happened."

"My dear chubs and monkeyfaces," Per said, addressing the whole meeting and not just Whitman, "nothing will sustain our lives if we can't find out more about this place we're trying to live in. All I'm bound to do by our compact is contribute to the building of the colony as best I can. I'm doing that. Impeach my compact and expel me if you don't believe it. Otherwise leave me alone. I have work to do."

"What about Piping's question?" Torker demanded. "Answer that!"

At that point, Per's strategy turned against him. Apparently Whitman felt things had gone too far. He shut down the debate by forcing a vote on a motion to form consensus groups, for the purpose of discussing reproductive options. After another hour of voiced opinions, they reached agreement to have group rosters made up on a random basis and to begin the discussion in the next evening free period. The meeting broke up without the usual friendly aftermath of chat. People were disgusted, tired, and full of misgivings, and they plodded off in small, grumbling groups.

Per accosted Whitman as soon as he found him alone.

"Are you out of your mind? I thought you agreed with me."

"From a scientific standpoint, Per, I suppose you're right. We shouldn't go on with this till we determine what's causing the problem. But I can't keep telling people that forever. It doesn't state in the compact that those who think they know best can run the show. If they reach consensus on some other form of action . . . Well, it's their colony. Our colony, I mean. I don't set myself apart in this area. I can't go on opposing the clear will of the majority."

"Even when you know they're wrong?"

"Per, we tried for years to find out why the newgens were born damaged. That was fifteen years ago, at the beginning, when we still had all the people and all the resources we brought from home. We didn't succeed then. Now, when we've lost so much that we once had, the task is probably impossible. Given that, I want to do the best I can for my son. I don't want to leave him here, helpless, if something happens to me. If even a few functional children could be born, it would be worth it. I know you don't share my views, but you have no children to consider; so please don't try to take this moralistic attitude with me. I'll do whatever I have to do."

He checked himself and smiled in a friendlier fashion.

"Of course, you still have my support as far as the work roster goes; don't worry about that. Torker is a boogerhead on this subject. You work twice as hard as most of his people, and your contributions have probably provided more food than you could have if you'd been out with a thrownet. I'll do my best to make sure you don't get choked off your research.

"About the other thing, though—" He paused, then continued. "You may have to at least donate. It's not so much to ask, is it?"

Depressed and in no mood for further battles over the same churned terrain, Per didn't answer him. He wondered how much of the discussion Bey had heard, and what he thought of it.

Certainly the young Sayid's eavesdropping would ensure that the second generation would know all about it, whether the adults saw fit to tell them or not. He was beginning to think again about refusing to teach Dilani. It seemed that no one else wanted the job. If the newgens were going to end up facing Typhon on their own, they deserved whatever scraps of information might help them. And at least Dilani had shown some interest in learning. It was more than he had received from his own generation.

Whitman walked briskly off toward his family quarters. Per suspected that all that good-fellowship hid some ugly feelings. Occasionally he caught a look in Whitman's eye that made him wonder just how trustworthy Sayid would be in an emergency. Maybe it would turn out that the public welfare required some pretty stern measures to be taken with Per Langstaff, a burr in Sayid's shoe for so long.

Per sighed. He didn't enjoy the impatient dislike directed at him from all sides. And any talent he might have had for making people like him seemed to have died with Sukarto. And Doi. And Sofron.

As he moved in darkness down the familiar path, he sensed someone waiting for him. It was Sushan Melicar; she stepped out and walked alongside him in a friendly way, as if to contradict his lonely thoughts.

"I wish you wouldn't stir them up," she said. "I worry for you. What would happen if they really did impeach you, and you had to live outside the compact?"

"Not a thing," Per said. It was an old conversation, and he took up the frayed thread of it where they had last dropped it. "They'd still need me. I could easily trade a living for myself, bringing in fish and usable materials. They'd end up having to give me my skipboard and my lab time no matter what. They complain, now, that I use those things, but who else wants to? They've all given up, Sushan. They're just waiting to die."

"Not Roon," she said.

Per made a noise indicating he chewed up Roon and spit him out.

"That ester-laden fart. He's just playing with himself to keep away the fear of death."

She breathed out the ghost of a laugh. "Aren't we all? There's a curious obsessiveness to the things we do. Torker thinks of nothing but catching fish, though we have as much as we can eat. Whitman behaves as if he's running for speaker of the Rationality. Roon and I argue and spit at each other, as if it matters who is right and who is wrong.

"Why can't we simply allow each other our delusions? Whatever happens, we won't be here much longer. On Skandia, another Typhon colony will be checked off as lost—if it hasn't been already. They're supposed to show up every five years! Why haven't they come to check on us?" The despairing note in her voice was unlike her normally calm and levelheaded manner. Per put his arm around her.

"What's the matter?"

"Oh—" She leaned her head briefly against his shoulder. Then she straightened up and spoke with clinical precision. "Realizing that Amina has reached menarche just reminds me once again that my girls will never grow up. It's becoming an obsession with me. Today, patching up Dilani, I was thinking, Why was there no one to save my children as you saved her? When I treat people and they get well, I almost resent them for living. I know we may not have many years ahead of us, but at least we'll have those years. I think, Why them and not Lesper? Why their children and not mine? It's horrible, isn't it? Yet I can't seem to stop."

"It isn't horrible," Per said gently. "It's only natural. It's only been two years. It takes people time to get over these things."

She laughed a little wildly.

"To get over it? Per, you're talking as if we're going to get well. We're terminal."

"I won't accept that." His voice was still gentle, but there was iron in it. "I won't listen to you if you're going to start talking that way."

"I'm sorry. I know: It can't be any easier for the parents who have to see their children every day and still wonder if they'll ever grow up. Amina's mother is probably crying tonight, wondering what's to become of her."

She pulled out a scrap of bark cloth and blew her nose loudly.

"Just walk me past the hospital, will you?" she asked. "I want to look in on Dilani before I go to bed."

A faint beeping noise from the desk showed that someone was in the office. Dilmun Elsker looked up and smiled as they came in. There was never any shortage of volunteers for the night watch, since the job carried with it access to free time on the hospital computer. Packed in a protective flotation cover, it was the only unit that had survived the disaster. Most volunteers claimed they needed computer time for special projects, but Melicar frequently found them playing childish games and pretended she hadn't noticed.

There was no need to pretend with Dilmun. Since she'd been injured in the worst of last year's storms, she hadn't been much good for fishing or gardening. She had chosen to make herself useful in the clinic, and Melicar figured she was entitled to play games if she wanted.

Dilani was sleeping soundly, though not peacefully; a scowl was fixed on her face. Her color and breathing were good, her kidneys and liver functioning well, and the level of toxin in her blood had dropped.

"Poor girl," Melicar said absently.

Per snorted. "Don't waste your pity on that one. She's tough as tangleweed."

"She worships you, you know."

"Oh, garbage. She'd pester the life out of me, if I gave her a chance. It's sheer boredom and teenage orneriness."

"She may be deaf," Melicar said, "but you can still wake her if you keep stamping around like that." She pulled him out of the room.

"Boredom and orneriness?" she said when they were alone on the path again. "Sounds like someone else I know. I wish you'd give her a little of your time, Per. She's much like you. I think she's made a kind of hero out of you. And why wouldn't she? You've saved her life twice now."

Per made no response. He didn't want to argue with Sushan, and he certainly didn't like the direction this discussion was going.

"You and Sofron were always such good friends with Dilani's parents," Melicar said wistfully. "I remember picnicking on the beach: Sukarto and Doi, you and Sofron, Lesper and me. It's all such a long time ago."

Still Per said nothing. Grief was omnipresent among the survivors, and there was nothing to say about it.

Melicar pressed just a little closer, the pressure evident only as an increase of warmth where their arms touched.

"Don't you ever feel the need for comfort?"

"No, I don't." He stopped in the middle of the path, letting go of her. "There is no comfort in this situation. Since I'm still alive without it, I must conclude that I don't need it."

Flipped abruptly from seduction to exasperation, she looked ready to sting him back. Instead she shrugged and let the moment go.

"You still think Sofron is alive somewhere."

"I hope I would be faithful to her memory even if she were not."

"You see?" she said. "Obsessions. We're showing all the twitches of a dying organism. Good night, Per."

## 2

Per let her go without regret. He knew she thought he was delusional, but it didn't bother him very much. His bond to Sofron had been his own private treasure, and it was nobody's business what he chose to do with the loss. If it was lost. The survivors on this atoll assured him it was impossible that any others had lived through the destruction of the first island. Per wondered.

He had built himself a shelter in a tree near the beach. He sometimes slept there when he wanted to avoid human contact. He swung himself up to the platform and stretched out under its canopy of flapping leaves. He reached into his pack and took out a hand light and his constant companion, his field notebook. The screen unfolded, and the text of the last session appeared.

Per stared into the soft glow of the screen, but his eyes refused to focus on his notes. He knew that reviewing his memories over and over, trying to retrieve and fix one more detail, was obsessive. But he surrendered to the compulsion, and as he did, raw data turned to vivid memories.

*He was grabbing Whitman's arms and screaming at him, but he couldn't remember what he had said. He had tried to find out from others exactly what had happened, but people didn't seem to remember much about those days. He knew that, like him, others had begged to turn back, to search for more survivors. But they preferred not to talk about it afterward.*

*The sea was terrifying. Waves were crashing halfway up to where the plateau had been. They were black, bursting into*

24

*incandescently white steam when they struck the chaos where the peak had disappeared. The waves rocked in different directions, at angles to each other, as if someone were shaking a boiling pot. The surface of the lagoon moved as water moves just before it boils.*

*Lava must have been rising from a crack in the sea bottom there. Sukarto had warned them they were living too near the rift. He didn't live to see how right he was. No doubt Whitman was right, too. They were half choked already by the fumes and ash. It would have been suicide to turn back and be suffocated in that boiling caldron.*

He knew that with his mind, in the present. With his heart he only knew that Sofron had been waiting for him. He knew where she had been: in the lab, in town, five minutes from the children's house. She had been seen there by others who had evacuated just in time. They got out, but she didn't. Neither did Lesper, or Koreng Lee, who was on duty with the children. Sofron must have gone with them, to help get the children out.

*I wish she had been at sea, or anywhere out of reach of the nursery,* Per thought. *Then, perhaps, she would have saved herself first. But she would have tried to help the helpless anyway, wherever she was.*

He imagined he heard her voice, as he had heard it so many times when he argued that she was taking on too much: *"But I knew I could do it, Per, and they needed me."*

On the day of the disaster, it seemed she had tried to do something no one could do.

*But maybe it was still possible,* Per argued with himself. *As long as she was with the children, they had some chance. Maybe there were survivors. She was the best small-craft sailor in the colony. She could have piloted a boat through that hell, if anyone could.*

That was one of the arguments he had screamed into Whitman's ear. He remembered that much.

Whitman only repeated what he had already said. *"Per, we can't go back. She's already lost. We can't risk the others."*

*Maybe he was right about the others,* Per thought. *But I would gladly have thrown my life after hers.*

He had tried. He didn't remember that part. Afterward, he had been told that people nearby restrained him, though no one would admit to having saved his life.

*We all did things we would rather not remember, on that day,* he thought.

He had one clear window of memory from that time.

*He was lying on the deck, exhausted, retching, seawater in his throat. Had he succeeded in throwing himself back into the sea? Had someone pulled him out? He still could not remember.*

*Dilani Ru was looking at him. Like most of the older children, she had been saved because she was old enough to be at work when it happened, not in the children's house with the little ones.*

*At some point, he remembered pulling her out of the water as he crossed the lagoon. She'd been making one sign again and again—the same one they had used when they'd had to tell her that Sukarto and Doi were gone. "In the water, in the water."*

*Was it because Per had tried to go there? Or had she somehow known what happened to Sofron?*

Per had lost consciousness then and had drifted in and out of awareness for the rest of their flight. When they had landed on the atoll—this tiny foothold of sand they called Refuge—his fellow survivors had assured him it was impossible that any others had lived through the destruction of the first island. They had told him that he had breathed deadly fumes and had almost died, himself.

No one blamed him, but he had never forgiven himself for lying helpless while others suffered and died. If only he had kept trying. If only he could have done something. He might at least have gained some glimpse, some hint of Sofron's fate.

The notebook still lay open on the platform, softly glowing like one of Typhon's noctilucent plants. Per lowered his face into his hands and tried to think of nothing at all for a few minutes. He had told the doctor that healing was a matter of time. In spite of those words, he didn't think he would ever outlive his own pain.

He rested one hand on the notebook and got some comfort from its cool, smooth surface. That it had survived at all was something of a miracle. The colony had lost nearly all the equipment they had brought with them. It had been self- or solar-powered, the batteries and miniaturized power sources good for a lifetime, carefully sealed against the aquatic environment. Probably some items were still working, on the bottom of the ocean. The others were charred and entombed in molten lava.

Some contingencies could not be planned for.

On the day of the eruption, Per had given no thought to his notebook. His field pack had stayed on his back through his swim to the evacuation boat, and the notebook had been in it.

Since that day, he had clung to it like a talisman. Most of the colony's history had been destroyed with the main computers. Predisaster records still existed in backup on the computers still in orbit, but with the uplink gone, that memory was no longer accessible. Fragments survived in other notebooks, in random files hastily grabbed for salvage, in the one complete system that had been installed in the hospital.

Per had taken it upon himself to assemble and recall as much as possible, and he added to it in a daily ritual. It was his link to a past that had died, and his only tie to a future that might not come. Whitman had tried to persuade him to donate the notebook and its contents for colony use, but he had refused.

He keyed the notebook to manual and scrawled his notes of that night's discussion across the screen. At first he jotted down only a skeleton outline. He was tired of reliving the same divisions, the same arguments.

Then he sighed, went back, and painstakingly filled in the outline with the details he remembered. He didn't know for whom he ultimately destined that report, but for his own purposes it had to be complete. His notes on his fellow humans were subjective and couldn't be as accurate as his observations of the natural world, but they were driven by the same need to pin down an elusive truth.

More rapidly and fluently, he recorded his encounter with Dilani on the reef. The success of his antitangleweed gun gave him the sort of satisfaction he doubted he could find in any dealings with the forum of Typhon colony.

That done, he looked out across the tidal flats, to the phosphorescent line of gently breaking waves. What he really wanted to do was plunge back into the dark water. There lay the answers he was seeking.

As he fell asleep, he could hear the faint whisper of the sea, trying to tell him something important—something that couldn't be heard over the din of human chatter and complaint.

Someone else was thinking and listening as Per fell asleep. That someone also willed himself to relax, to drift with the tide, and calm his racing thoughts.

The White Arms had trapped a new thing that day. At first sight, the creature seemed long and roughly cylindrical, perhaps a finless cousin of the Laughing Teeth. Long tendrils had whipped around one end of the body. He had watched while the White Arms had detached and discarded part of the creature's end. He hadn't been able to come close enough to see clearly, because of the Enemies hanging about, but he was almost sure the detached piece was a device. In his experience, Straight People carried no tools.

Then a shape had moved on the sky edge, and something had exploded into the water, driving away the White Arms and frightening the Enemies, as well. It had had a sharp, burning tang that reminded him of the fluid the Round People used to drive off those who would eat them. Was it a natural secretion of some creature unknown to him? Or could it be, as he wildly surmised, something deliberately made? Had he caught a glimpse of unknown intelligence?

He had wasted the rest of the light in searching along

the reef for a trace of the device, but without success. Either he had imagined it, or it had fallen among the White Arms, where he could not go.

Too late he had considered the shape that floated on the surface. He had never seen a thing like that before. His arms moved restlessly as he wished he had examined it more closely. What kind of material could present such a clear, smooth outline and move so noiselessly through the water? He acknowledged gloomily that it reminded him of the Laughing Teeth, and caused a fear that had made him reluctant to go closer.

His cowardice was partly redeemed by the fact that he had come so close to the forbidden Dry edge. But the only way he could completely vindicate himself in his own mind was to continue, to actually touch the edge and accept whatever curse or benefit it might bring.

So he had let the waves carry him closer, felt bottom intermittently as the sky edge rocked up and down. He got a firm feel of the mud and began to drag himself cautiously through the shallow water. His skin crept at the gritty feel of the Dry, but he continued. Ahead of him he saw shapes with simple edges, too still and stiff to be alive—he thought. He approached one cautiously, gasping air every few minutes.

He was completely in the Dry. His skin stung, and he could not stay there for long. He reached out and touched the strange object. It felt smooth and slick as glider skin, but it did not yield to his tugging. He could not taste any odor in the thin medium of air. He felt around the shape as far as possible, but could not grasp it as a totality. He could not tell if this was the same thing he had seen floating at the sky edge before.

Stretching up to the limit of his reach, he touched the upper edge of the shape and found that it was hollow on the inside, like a shell. He got another arm over the rim and pulled himself up and over with one fluid motion. Excitement burst within him till he felt faint in the inadequate breath medium of the Dry.

Objects lay jumbled in the hollow shape, and he fumbled over them impatiently. Their scents were nearly impossible to detect, revealing little. Their forms and textures were so smooth, and yet so asymmetrical, that he dared theorize they had truly been made for specific purposes.

One item caught his attention because it left a scent on his damp skin—one that he could perceive even without water to carry it. The smell was organic, not unlike the belt with attachments that he wore himself. Perhaps it was made from the skin of a Dry creature. As he tested the object again, he recoiled in reflex, though he stubbornly refused to release his prize. He recognized the pungent, painful odor that had swirled through the water to chase away the White Arms.

He was right. It had been a device, and it was associated with the Dry. He knew that much, though he had not yet found its maker. He wanted to spin with joy, but the gritty, sticky Dry and his famished lungs constrained him. Laboriously, he pulled himself up and over again, to land with uncomfortable force on the hard bottom of the Dry. He then crawled to the water.

There he sucked in great gulps of cooling, life-laden water. He could still taste the roiled grit of the shore in it, but at that moment it felt sweet as the silkiest sun-warmed top water of the open sea. He spun for joy, shooting up toward the sky edge and then plunging into the close-clinging welcome of the Deep.

It was dark. His night sight perceived the glitter of myriad lights on flights of little living things. Dim sparks showed above the sky edge, as if things lived and flew there, too. No brightwarm came to sparkle in the fractured wave fronts of the sky edge, but he felt as if brightness were bursting inside him.

He had discovered something *new*. He had proved false the claim that beyond the common space there lay the endless plains of endless night. The Dry edge had life, and if that was true, then the goal of his journey might exist as well. For the sake of that goal he had exiled himself from his lineage and bounds and given up his share in the common learning. He had journeyed as a solitary.

He sobered, finally, as he realized what those few moments in the Dry had taught him. There was no exile like the loneliness he had felt as he had passed through the boundary into the Dry. Even if Enemies had torn and eaten him, he would have been part of the great fullness of life. Not exile, nor even death, could be as lonely as the passage into the barren, breathless vastness of the Dry. Yet something lived there, unimaginably.

The last of his exaltation spun away and left him hanging, pondering. Slowly he began to weave the memory dance that would fix these events in mind, in case he ever had a chance again to converse with others of his kind. His body shaped precise, intricate gestures, while the colors of his skin flickered and faded in shades of meaning. He had been called Subtle, for the delicacy of his colors, though as he danced this dance he was nameless, for there was no one to receive his name.

Per dreamed he was on the deck again, and Dilani was looking down on him, her wide, dark eyes unreadable. "In the water," she signed slowly, meditatively. He felt her fingers touch the tears and saltwater on his cheeks. She traced the sign for *sadness* on his face. He had passed out then—but no, not in the dream.

In the dream he still struggled and cried out. The bitter peace of acceptance did not exist in dreams. Instead of fighting till he lost consciousness, he was doomed to fight until he regained it. He thrashed as if he could tear loose from the restraining arms that hoarded his life for him when he wanted to cast it on the water. His feet quivered as if they beat the water in flight to Sofron's rescue. Black waves received him and dragged him far under. Water filled his mouth.

He woke up with a grunt, choking on the black salt flavor of tears three miles deep, a weight of grief that could buckle steel plate and had certainly crushed the frail coracle of his heart.

*That was a mild one,* he thought, gulping air and waiting for his heart to slow down. His nightmares were usually far worse. He sat up and swung himself down from the platform. A haze over the sea obscured the lower stars. The breeze flagged, and the air hung heavily—too warm and damp. He waded out into the water and turned a somersault to clear his head. Even the water felt too warm and stagnant.

He waded back up the shore toward the fish tanks and the boats. He had no purpose in mind. He simply followed his habitual path. As he approached the boats, he thought he saw something dangling from the side of his skipboard. It was a dark, amorphous blotch. Had he left a netful of boogers hanging? He blinked, and the dark shape was gone. A moment later, he heard a faint but distinct splashing that soon ceased. It was too dark to see anything in the water.

He jogged a little way toward the boats, but the dew-damp sand clung to his feet. There was no refreshing breeze even at the water's edge. He retraced his steps, climbed back to his platform, and slept heavily, until the blazing fingers of sunlight reached under his leafy shade and touched him awake.

The force of the sun was tangible, like a hot liquid poured over his back. Something about the weather didn't feel right to him. He made a note to himself to check the accumulated weather data and see if the rains were delayed, or if he only thought so because he was tired of the heat.

As he wandered toward the dining hall to find something to eat, he met Bey Sayid laboriously pushing his cart along the path from the vegetable gardens. Bey paused to wipe sweat from his forehead with one hand, grasping the wheel rim firmly with the other to keep himself from rolling backward down the path.

"Good morning, Teacher Per," he said. Normally, scrupulous courtesy irritated Per, but Bey always seemed sincere. Per guessed that the boy used his voice to compensate for his body. He was incapable of springing to attention, standing up straight, or otherwise demonstrating the respect craved by elder members. He didn't want to be resented for always sitting down, so he took care to give each member due respect, and perhaps a little more than due.

"Where have you been so early, young Sayid?" Per said.

"Garden patch." Bey slightly raised the basket of bunched greens and tubers he held between his toes. "Fried spud and tangy greens for breakfast. And some of that fish spread made of those little red stripers."

*"X. Beta Chelonia hemichromis fensilii,"* Per said absently. All the sea creatures had been given scientific names, but most people continued to call them "red stripers" or "the bony one with yellow fins," and vernacular names were rapidly evolving.

"Yes, sure, Teacher Per."

"By the way, Bey, you didn't happen to hear of anyone going out to the boats in the night—you know, a newgen prank?"

Bey looked blank.

"No, Teacher."

"There's no trouble, you understand. I just thought I saw something out there last night, and it's puzzling me."

"Sure wasn't me, Teacher."

Bey lifted his golden brown gaze to Per. *Of course it wasn't him,* Per thought. *He can't walk.*

He was about to assure Bey that he wasn't a suspect, when he realized he was about to insult the boy. Bey had a ramp built on his cart that he could roll down to get to the ground. He must have done just that to dig the breakfast vegetables. Per pictured him with the basket in his teeth, hauling himself hand over hand back into his cart.

Bey went to a great deal of trouble to participate fully in the community. His dignity required that he be considered as competent a troublemaker as any.

"If you hear anything, you might let me know."

"Yes, sure, Teacher. I'd better go. They're waiting for me up at the kitchen."

Per continued down the beach and carefully checked the boats. There were no tracks in the sand above the landing place. He walked around each boat. The skipboard's hull showed some faint, circular marks, but when he touched them, they rubbed off. Apparently just dirt, though he wondered why the blotches were so regular in shape.

At first he thought nothing in the skipboard's storage well had been disturbed. He didn't remember leaving his equipment in such a jumble, though, but he had been in a hurry to get Dilani to shore. He straightened out the gear methodically as he checked through it. Then he saw that one thing was missing: the belt with his extra capsules of antitangleweed chemicals.

He retraced the path he had taken with Dilani. Maybe he had dropped it somewhere in the confusion. He was scanning the sides of the path, head down, when a flicked bit of tamal peel landed at his feet. He looked up. Dilani had managed to slip out of bed and leave the hospital, still wearing her old skinsuit and last night's bandages.

"What the hell are you doing here?" he signed.

She shrugged with one shoulder. "Bored. Hungry."

"Does Sushan know you're out of bed?"

Dilani nodded, unsmiling. "She gave up. Said, 'All right, you can walk, go.'"

He took a close look at her. He remembered her on the beach, the day before—all alone, singular, like a dark slash against the flowing colored maps of sea and sky. Her arms and legs were childishly thin and bony. Her skin was tanned to a deep brown where the old dark blue skinsuit, unevenly faded and patched, did not cover it, and her face, like everyone's, was patterned in light and dark where the sun had come through the webbing straps of the breather mask.

The smooth tan had been marred by countless nicks and scrapes even before that day's injuries. Now the skin at the edge of the bandages was dead white, her fingers and toes still swollen. Her eyes were bloodshot with irritation from Per's chemical bullet.

"You look bad," he signed.

"Thanks," she responded sarcastically.

A sudden thought struck him. If she was up now, maybe she had been up before.

"Did you take my antiweed belt?" he asked. He could easily imagine her deciding to go out and nuke the tangleweed in revenge.

"How the hell could I? Slept all last night. Ask Melicar."

Her sulky apathy couldn't have been more different from Bey's vigilant propriety. She looked really ill. The lost look on her face wrenched unexpectedly at his heart. He remembered her mother. Doi had been so lively, so curious.

"You and your mother—" he began.

Dilani saw his lips move and signed "What? What?"

He shook his head. "Come on. Breakfast," he signed.

She signed "Not hungry," though she went with him in perverse denial of her own statement.

He piled food on her plate anyway, and she chewed her way through it without saying thank you.

"If you see my belt anywhere, I wish you'd give it back," he signed. "I had to make it from off-list materials because it wasn't in the ration allocation. I used wingfin skin for the belt. I learned to make it stay pliable but not start to stink. Hard work. Without my underwater popgun, it's no use anyway. You know, you can't kill tangleweed with that, only discourage it."

"Sad troubles," she signed with mock pity. "Not my fault." She licked tamal juice off her fingers. The table around her plate was littered with peels and seeds, and their tablemates were looking at her disapprovingly. Tamals were rather a delicacy, and she had hogged a large number.

"You're being rude," he signed.

She concentrated on picking apart the membranes of her last tamal, making soft grunting noises as she usually did when she was concentrating. Pretending not to understand his sign was a good defense, since he couldn't exactly grab her and shout "Listen to me!"

That was Doi's child, the last remnant of his friends: a wild thing grunting over her lunch, oblivious to the fact that the adults were talking about breeding her like an animal. Doi's face came back to him very clearly, full of impish gaiety and intelligence. He could almost hear the sweetness of her voice. Her child could not speak.

Per was used to the pain of the past. But suddenly the present hurt him more than he could bear, as if tangleweed toxin had worn off, leaving him in the water with wounds full of salt.

He rose to his feet with a sweep of his arms that scattered peels and sent Dilani's cup rolling across the floor.

"Get up," he signed, his fingers rising past her chin, forcing her startled eyes upward. "I'm talking to you." His hands stabbed space inches from her face.

She rose as if an invisible line had hooked her. Her eyes were open wide. He didn't grab her, because he knew it would hurt. He turned and marched out of the dining hall, and she followed as if the invisible line still linked them.

"You throw trash around and sling your arms and legs without looking. People stay away," he signed. "Is that what you want?"

She gulped. "Stay away," she echoed, so tentatively he wasn't sure if she meant it as a question or a statement.

"You have no manners," he signed. "You're rude to people. You take yourself off work details without asking."

At that her face formed a good imitation of screaming, though no sound came out. Her spread fingers trembled briefly in the air, then made fists and smashed against each other. She turned her back.

He walked around to get her face-to-face again. Her curled hands pushed at the air in front of her in a gesture that must have come from babyhood. He didn't recognize it, but it seemed to combine accusation and defense, holding off something too mean to be tolerated.

"Go away," she signed, returning to coherence.

"No. I'm taking you to the fish boss. You're well enough to walk and make trouble, you can work. Do your job. No more running off."

Her thin shoulders slumped.

"I want to be with you," she signed, contradicting herself again.

"No. What I do is dangerous. My job. Do your job; stay out of trouble. Understand?"

She scowled at the ground, avoiding his eyes, but there was no sign of open rebellion.

"What roster today?" he asked.

"Fish." It was a dispirited and sickly fish her hand made.

"I'll take you to Torker."

She followed him as if the invisible string still pulled her.

Per stuck his head into the shade of the lean-to where Torker sat checking his nets.

"Here's Dilani," he said. For a moment, his own voice surprised him after so much silent conversation.

Torker grunted.

"Look, take it easy with her," Per said. "She really should be in the hospital. What have you got her listed for today?"

"Diskies. Out by the Finger."

"She shouldn't do diskies today, Tork. She shouldn't dive with these dressings on. Can't you get the diskies, put her on something else?"

Silence. Per's eyes had adjusted and could now make out Tork's considerable bulk hunched over the nets. The fish boss wouldn't even look up.

"Come on, Tork. Let her do something else."

"Tell her to fix the nets. And no fooling around."

Per interpreted. With a last, trapped flicker of her eyes, Dilani entered the shack and squatted, dragging a portion of the heavy net within her reach.

Per hurried down the beach toward his skipboard. Lingering would be futile and embarrassing. Torker would never speak to him again. That had been clear for some time. Yet Per couldn't deny that he had felt the temptation to linger. Torker had once been something approaching a friend.

Per cupped the wind in the skipboard's sail expertly, as if in the palm of his hand, and skimmed quickly out beyond the reef. He set out a sea anchor and made a few preliminary dives, examining this area of the outer reef for changes since his last survey. He was killing time until the object of his real observations appeared, and he kept popping up to the surface to look for that object.

He rose from the last of half a dozen shallow dives to see, instead, someone paddling toward him. Someone, Hell! It was Dilani again. She was riding astride a chunk of sponge-wood, bobbing precariously in the swells. Per hoisted himself up onto the board. As soon as she saw him, she waved her paddle, overbalanced her top-heavy float, and splashed into the water. Swearing, Per dropped his anchor line and steered quickly over to pick her up.

She sat on the deck dripping and grimacing while he recovered his anchor. He let the spongewood drift away—there was plenty more where that came from. He tried to control his irritation as he turned to Dilani.

"What the hell are you doing here? I told you to obey Torker and do your work."

She answered his question defiantly. "Fish boss turned his back, so I stole the net float and came. I can catch diskies. Show him!"

"Wish I could throw you back in and let you swim home!" he signed. "Now I have to waste another morning taking you back. Why are you doing this to me?"

"I want you to teach me," she signed stubbornly.

Per slapped his forehead in exasperation.

"I cannot teach you. There are reasons why—oh, hell." He lapsed into spoken speech and let his hands drop into his lap. "What's the use?"

She wasn't even watching him. She huddled miserably on the raft, obviously in pain, and stared at the horizon. She seemed to be scanning for something, but when she found it, she flinched violently and crouched down on the deck.

"What's wrong?" Per signed more gently. "You should not swim with those cuts. I told Torker that!"

Dilani shook her head.

"It hurts, but I don't care. I couldn't see the island. I thought it was gone. Thought I saw smoke."

She sneaked a look toward the shore across the barrier of a raised arm, as if she feared this island would explode like their other island.

"That isn't smoke," Per signed. "It's only a cloud. This island will not explode."

Not today, anyway, he thought.

"When I don't look at the island, I see it wrong. In here," Dilani signed, pointing to her head.

Per didn't understand.

"What do you see?"

"Mountain, mountain, fire, *fire*, mountain-fire!" Dilani signed, her gestures crescendoing to fortissimo like a chant or a dance. "Water-fire, air-fire. People running, people burning, houses falling. I see the island finished."

She bent and let the palm of her hand just skim the surface of the water. She lifted her hand and studied the water dripping from it, frowning, as if she were finding omens in the pattern of the drops. She touched the wet hand to her chin, to her forehead: "Mother, father. In the water. In the water."

She stared at the water and signed it again, slowly, sadly, questioningly. Per couldn't tell if it was longing or fear that fixed her gaze to the moving surface of the waves. He wondered if she still thought her parents might rise from the water.

"Very far away, over there," she signed, finally raising her eyes to the horizon, the faint smoke that stained it.

"Yes," Per agreed quickly. "Far away, by our old home, our home-finished." He made the sign, flicking it off, throwing it away, and gathered his hands back to his chest involuntarily. It hurt to sign *finished*. It seemed so casual a gesture, but it was so final.

Dilani looked at him questioningly, and shaped the S sign she had used for Sofron. "Sofron, in the water."

Per nodded. "Dead," he signed, and it felt like stabbing himself with his fingers. Dilani's eyes narrowed, frowning. She shook her head.

"In the water," she signed again.

"Yes, dead, in the water," he signed. This time, instead of pointing, he made the graphically brutal drowning sign, the feet disappearing through the hand-shaped water. Still Dilani shook her head, questioning.

"Yes, yes, yes," he insisted, choking out the words while he forced his head to nod. "Damn it, burn it, curse you, you stupid little monster, she's dead. Can't you understand anything?"

Then he was cursing Dilani, the sea, and the world itself with words no one could hear, and pounding the deck like a madman to keep himself from seizing Dilani and shaking her into immobility. He could still see her head stubbornly moving from side to side: denial.

Her hands were moving again. One swooped insistently from high to low, a sign he didn't know. She stopped, huffing deep in her throat, fingers working in search of something. "Boat," she finally signed, and rapped on the skipboard as if in imitation of Per's demented pounding. "Like this. Flat boat. Get tree leaves. Make a flat boat, mountain river, down *fast*." Her hand swooped again, and Per suddenly saw what she was talking about.

While the mountain had still been standing, the children who were physically able to climb it had played a game on its steep lower slopes. Many small rivulets coursed down its sides. The children had woven the broad, tough leaves of the giling tree together and had launched themselves down the slippery streambeds. The leaf boats went at tremendous speed, plunging through minor cataracts and shallow pools in showers of spray. Dilani was trying to describe the sliding game.

Per shook his head wearily. Sometimes Dilani acted like a much younger child. She must have retrieved an old memory of Sofron playing with the children. The game had been forbidden by parents as too dangerous, but Sofron might well have joined in just for fun.

"Playing in water, death in water—not the same," he signed. His hands hurt. He felt exhausted, and he was ashamed of his outburst.

Dilani looked as exasperated as Per felt.

She scowled fiercely, squinting as if trying to see the thing she was describing, far away. "Bright-colored. Yellow. Orange. Flat like a leaf. It was next to the children's house. Sofron could make a boat."

Per stared at her.

"Possible!" she insisted.

It was possible, Per thought. It was just barely possible. Dilani's description of the "boat" could have been an emergency inflatable, only partially inflated. Some extra equipment had been stored near the center of the village, after a colony member had pointed out that keeping all supplies near the beach was foolish. A typhoon might sweep them all away, yet leave survivors on the mountainside still in need of ocean survival gear. Sofron would never have given up while there was any option left. To escape the eruption by river slide was exactly the kind of thing she might have done.

"Sofron in the water," Dilani signed again. "Alive," she added defiantly.

Per recognized her expression. That was how he'd looked at the others when they'd insisted Sofron was dead. And now he was doing the same thing to Dilani.

"No one saw her alive," he signed.

"No," Dilani admitted. "I never saw her. I went into the water to look, but the water was bad. I saw fire."

She cradled her hands against her chest as if the sign had burned her fingers.

"You went into the water to look for Sofron?" Per signed.

She nodded, and then looked away, across the empty sea to the place where the island had been. She was trembling.

"Could be alive," she signed, but faintly, as if she were speaking to herself alone.

Per remembered pulling her out of the sea. She had been half drowned, choking and crying as he forced her to breathe air that was nearly unbreathable with hot, poisonous fumes. Even immersion in the writhing waves of the tortured lagoon had not washed off the sharp, gritty ash that had coated her.

She had gone into the water to find Sofron. Even though she had not succeeded, she had tried.

"I'm sorry," he muttered. Then he signed it, but she wasn't looking. Her sight was turned inward, and far away. Per closed his eyes, and the same vision broke over his head like a wave.

*Fire, fire. Mountain, fire. People running, people screaming, people burning. In the water.*

Oh, Sofron. Are you somewhere in the world still, somewhere in this vast, trackless, unmarked ocean?

Per hunched over his closed hands and cried. No one could hear him, so it was all right. But it didn't help. Fragments of old poems washed up in his mind. *I cast for comfort I can no more get/By groping round my comfortless, than blind/Eyes in their dark can day or thirst can find/Thirst's all-in-all in all a world of wet . . .*

When Dilani's thin, rough fingers clutched at his arm, he let them stay, and after a long time, he put his other arm around her shivering shoulders. Dilani never cried, but she clung to him like tangleweed.

Abruptly, she pushed away so he could see her hands.

"Father, Mother, Sofron, in the water," she signed. "I dream I fall in the water. There is no island. No one pulls me out."

Her nose was running, but her face was set again in her normal, stubborn expression. The question burned in her eyes.

"Where do I go then?"

Per drew a long breath. He felt as if he had just been pummeled by heavy surf.

"I'll teach you," he signed.

For once she seemed startled and at a loss.

"Teach me?" she signed. The gestures were sketchy, vague, as if she were afraid to be too specific.

"Yes. That's what I said. Now pay attention. You don't treat me the way you treat Tork. You show respect for me. If I tell you to do something, you do it. If you make a promise to me, you keep it. No lies. No more running off."

She scowled again, and he thought she was about to argue. Instead, she nodded once, punctuating with a clenched fist. "To everything," she added. Then she just looked at him, and he realized she was waiting for him to begin.

# 3

Per bent over and splashed his face clean with seawater before putting his mask back on.

"First lesson," he signed. "You need other people. Don't make them mad unless you can't help it." He made a wry face. "This is a hard lesson for me to teach."

She frowned at him, puzzled.

"You must go apologize to Torker."

Then he smacked his head in frustration.

"Damn! Torker!" he said out loud. He had forgotten his reason for anchoring by the rock they called the Finger. "If they come back while Torker's hunting diskies—"

Dilani was punching his arm for attention, her face thrust close to his. She could see his lips moving, and wanted to know what he was saying.

"Allfather, how do I explain this?" he said. He had to act, and he felt already how Dilani's persistent presence would hinder him. He was used to explaining only to himself.

Before he could do anything, he saw a distinctive black-and-silver fin cutting a perfect wake toward them from the open sea. His reason had chosen that moment to show up.

Dilani froze and pointed, making the *K*-in-the-water sign for *keto*.

The great, shining, shadow-patterned ketos were on the list of dangerous predators, third after boogers and tangleweed. The first island had been out of their normal migration route, perhaps because its waters had been too shallow, or poor in the ketos' preferred fish species. Whatever the reason, they

44

had seldom been seen in the first years of the colony. In the sea around Refuge, however, they were often sighted.

No one knew, of course, how many of the dead who were lost at sea had actually been victims of keto attacks, but there had been plenty of witnesses when the ketos had attacked and demolished the first frail fish pens. Everyone had watched their wild rampage through the captive schools of fish the colonists had been depending on for food. The ketos had looked as if they were enjoying themselves. They had killed wantonly, leaving slashed and mangled fish floating uneaten.

And everyone had heard the stories of a team of five who had been assaulted by ketos in open water. The ketos had bumped the team's boat until it had overturned, and had harassed the humans in the water, thumping them with powerful tails and ramming them. The humans had somehow made it to shore. Miraculously, none of them had been killed, but they had all been severely bruised and shaken, and some of them had broken bones and internal injuries.

Surfboards and floats had been found bitten in half, with toothmarks matching the keto pattern. Ketos were dangerous. Even Per would not deny that.

Dilani stared open-mouthed as the ketos approached, and Per made no effort to escape.

"Pay attention," he signed urgently. "I don't have time to explain now, but the ketos won't hurt me. I don't know if they will hurt you or not. Stay on the board. Please."

He didn't know what they would do to another human—he had never brought anyone with him to these clandestine meetings. One time he had stayed on the board, and the ketos had bumped it with their noses until it had capsized, spilling him into the water. He didn't think they had meant him any harm; they had only been impatient and curious. Still, he didn't dare stay on the board with Dilani, for fear they would knock him off it again, and Dilani with him.

He slid into the water and swam to meet the keto pod.

* * *

Dilani felt the board rocking gently under her feet and other than Per she couldn't see a single living thing from horizon to horizon. The island that had been her world looked flat and small, just a green shape hugging the surface of the water. She was beyond the reef, where she had wanted most to go, but she felt scared.

The board jerked as a great black-and-silver creature surged up from the water and submerged again in a blast of spray. Dilani saw Per's head bob up briefly, next to the animal. She was more than scared; she was terrified. She expected Per to be bitten in half at any moment. Then maybe the keto would crush the skipboard between its massive jaws and tear her to pieces.

The keto rolled, bringing Per up with it. He was grinning and clinging to the fin. It was true. He swam with the ketos.

Once she saw that, no fear could stop Dilani from joining him. Stiff with fright, she crept to the edge of the board on her knees, pulled her breathing mask into place, and let herself fall forward into the water.

The animal was huge, up close. It shook its massive head up and down, its mouth spread into a grin that showed teeth like knives, inches from her face. It seemed to be laughing at her. Its eyes seemed small in the shiny expanse of its face, but each black, slitted pupil was the size of her fist. It fixed her with one eye, as unreadable as the Deep. Some structure within the eye caught the light and flashed it back in a strange green-gold glow.

It pushed her with its blunt nose, and she was shoved backward so fast she raised a wake. She flailed her arms and legs, but she felt light as a floating fruit rind compared to the focused muscle of the animal. It pushed her again, and she rolled over and over. She had the mask on, but she still felt panic trying to seep in as her head was pushed under against her will.

The creature stopped for a moment, and Per bobbed up between her and the great body. He was stroking its fin and its nose, and by the way his neck and head moved, she thought maybe he was "talking" to it. The keto flipped spray at her with its nose, but it did not push her again. Instead it began pushing Per, and he seemed to enjoy it. He grabbed it behind the front fin and pulled, and then for a brief moment he was on its back, above the water. The creature leaped and plunged again, taking Per with it.

Dilani's heart was pounding, and her side hurt as if scalded all along the places where the tangleweed had slashed her. She was afraid that the great wild creature would carry Per away, leaving her hanging all alone between the sea and the sky.

She bobbed up above the surface again and glimpsed the silver flash of spray and sleek bodies. Briefly she spotted the red and black of Per's skinsuit arcing from wave to wave. A pang of jealousy shot through her. His head broke water next to one of the plunging bodies. He clung to a fin with one hand, and his head was thrown back, water drops flung in a shining arc from his wet hair. She couldn't see his expression under the mask, but the exuberant poise of his body made her think he must be smiling. He seldom smiled ashore. The swimmer shot up and dove again in a powerful surge of spray, carrying him with it.

*He likes them better than people,* she thought. *He loves them, and they're just fish animals.* Her hands moved in the water as she tried to shape a thing with no hands. The great bulk slid easily past her again, surfacing. As it threw back its head and bared its teeth again, she felt a kind of tingle run through her. It was a little like the feel of the skipboard grounding, vibrating through the soles of her feet, or the feel in her fingers when she touched a machine that was running; but the tingle ran clear through her flesh and bones, as if the creature had speared her with an invisible harpoon.

The keto was "talking," she knew. He and Per were communicating with each other, but it didn't mean anything to her. She wondered if Per understood the fish animal. *He tries so hard to talk to them,* she thought. *Harder than he tries with me. He can hear them. Is that so important? Are they better than me? They have no hands, so they can never really speak. But they make sounds. They make him come to them.*

The keto Per was riding circled back to where Dilani waited, and Per slid from its fin. Treading water, Per got his hands out where Dilani could see them.

"I told you to stay on the board," he signed.

Dilani thought about claiming to have fallen in, but decided it was safer to tell the truth.

"Afraid! Wanted to be with you."

She couldn't read Per's face under the mask, but he seemed more anxious than angry.

"These are my friends," he signed. "I hope they are friends. They have never hurt me. This one I call Slowbolt."

Dilani frowned.

"Slow lightning?" she repeated. "That's not a name. Makes no sense."

"Joke. Can't explain."

He paused, looking back and forth from her to the keto that was slowly cruising around them. She thought he signed *danger*, and fear darted through her, but it looked as if he meant "dangerous for *him*." Danger for the keto? How was that possible?

Per's signing was urgent. "Leave here now. Slowbolt must leave."

But the keto circled her slowly, brushing her again with his fin. The skin rasped painfully against her own; it was covered with little harsh-textured bumps. She could feel the power of the springy muscle under the skin. The great dark eye rolled back toward her, but she couldn't read the expression in it. The keto plunged, and she felt that strange tingling run through her again. The huge bulk slid by, just below her dangling feet. She thrashed in a panic, trying to get away.

Per bobbed anxiously beside her, trying to sign through her splashing.

"It's all right. It's all right," he repeated. "He's looking at you. He looks with his ears."

Dilani shook her head violently. That was stupid. Per must be teasing her.

"Yes, yes," he insisted. "He makes sound bounce off you. That shows him the shapes of things."

Dilani wrapped her arms around herself. Was that what the tingling was? Could this fish animal see right through her with his voice? She felt naked and furious.

The keto reared up in the water and briefly opened his mouth wide, as if to seize prey. Teeth extended like a rack of knives. The mouth looked big enough to engulf a human. Even then, Per seemed unafraid. He swam ahead of the fish, gesturing with his arm as if the fish could understand. "Follow me. Follow me."

Dilani felt a shiver in the water—not like the feeling of vibration coming from the keto, but a shock, as if something had happened. The keto twisted and leapt, with terrible power, in a motion very different from the smooth grace she had seen before. A rush of bubbles trailed in his wake. Per thrust himself toward the keto with powerful strokes, leaving Dilani without a backward glance. The bubbles looked funny: They were pink.

Per screamed in outrage as soon as his mouth cleared the surface. He had heard the harsh, broken whistling of Slowbolt crying out his distress, and knew that the keto's pain was being sent out to the others in a message beyond hearing. Per trod water frantically, trying to see the vapor venting from the keto's air chamber. It seemed still clear, untainted by blood. Per swam to Slowbolt's other side, looking for the injury.

A harpoon bolt of unmistakably human origin protruded from the keto's side. Pink froth rilled down his smooth hide as he rolled in the water. One of the colony fishing boats idled nearby, with Torker Fensila and a harpoon gun in the bows.

Per had no time to waste on his anger.

"Throw me the sling," he shouted.

"Get on board," Fensila shouted back.

"There's blood in the water, you idiot. The boogers will be here any minute. Get the keto out of the water or you'll lose him, and maybe us, too."

Fensila saw sense in that and threw down the sling. Per dove under the keto with the padded ropes, hoping that Slowbolt would allow him to fasten them. Dilani appeared at his side, and he motioned to the ropes. Her quick eyes took in his problem at once. She took over the first set of fastenings while he dove for the second strap.

Slowbolt lay passive in the water, hardly moving, as Per swam around him, but when he felt the straps tighten and begin to hoist him from the sea, he thrashed and strained against them. More blood dripped from the harness into the water. Per pulled himself over the gunwale and pressed close to the injured keto, stroking him urgently, wishing that he could communicate somehow to tell Slowbolt he was trying to save his life.

Ugly dark shadows roiled the clouded water as the boogers arrived and struck at each other, seeking the source of the taste of blood. A hundred yards off their bow, the other ketos leapt out of the water in agitation, their whistles shrilling on the painful edge of human hearing. Repeatedly they cut across Fensila's course as he circled, as if they were trying to stop him from carrying his catch away.

"What are you planning to do about the skipboard?" Fensila said. "You going to leave it out here all night?"

Per's fists clenched tight in frustration. He thought that if he left Slowbolt, Fensila might kill the keto.

"Could you do me a favor and tow it in?" he asked in a low voice.

Fensila laughed. "Sure. I'll report that I salvaged it after you left it in danger."

He cruised slowly past the skipboard, allowing Per to hook the anchor line and fasten it for towing. As soon as it was secured, Per hurried back to the keto's side. Blood oozed through the sling and splashed to the deck. Tremors passed through the creature's suspended body, but he could not move. Per didn't know how long the keto could survive out of water. He knew the keto had an external air vent, and he could see the opening move spasmodically, but he did not understand keto physiology.

"Get the first-aid box," Per signed to Dilani. "The box with the red cross—in there."

She followed his pointing finger instantly.

"Hey!" Fensila shouted. "Stay out of the cabin!"

Not hearing his words, Dilani paid no attention to his shaken fist. After a brief search, she returned with the kit. Per rummaged through the contents.

"Hell. I need pliers. What's the sign for that? Tool—like this—" He mimed what he wanted. Dilani watched, then scrambled for the cabin again. She emerged with a handful of tongs, pliers, and pincers. Per smacked his hands together in approval.

"Good job. One of these is bound to work," he muttered.

He had to drop the pliers again to sign to Dilani.

"Hold this until I ask for it." He handed her a tube of antiseptic, and another one of body glue. "First this one, then the glue." He held up a waterproof dressing. "Then pull the tab on this and slap it on." He demonstrated until she nodded. "Ready? Okay!"

The bolt had sunk deep in the flesh, and Per had to press the pliers into the wound to get a grip on it. The keto rolled his huge dark eye and writhed with agonized effort, but he could not escape. Per heard no cry, but the ketos in the water leapt and shrilled as if Slowbolt had somehow called to them. Per forced the jaws of the tool together, seized the bolt, and pulled. A gout of blood followed. He dropped bolt and pliers and smeared the antiseptic into the cut as Dilani squirted it on. She carefully applied glue while Per pushed the lips of the wound together, and at his nod, she slapped the adhesive dressing over the area.

Per's foot slid in the blood that had already gushed from the wound. A threatening sickness welled within him, but he fought it back. There was something else, some other reason why the blood was important. He ripped another dressing open, bent and scooped up the jellied clots and shreds of tissue, rolled the dressing tightly within its waterproof skin, and stuffed it into his belt bag.

Torker watched them from his place at the tiller and laughed.

"Mmm, that sure looks good," he shouted. "Why not cut off a steak right now? That fish is going to be barbeque sooner or later."

"He's not food, Tork. He's intelligent. I'm going to study him. We could learn—"

Torker laughed again. "Sure, study it. Study some recipes!"

He slowed the engines as he guided the boat into the harbor. Controlling the sling and hoist from the deckhouse, he lowered Slowbolt into an empty fish pen.

"Go ahead, take the sling off. I'll need it when I catch the rest of its buddies."

"Stay here," Per signed to Dilani. He had trusted her in the water with Slowbolt before, but he wasn't at all sure what the injured keto would do to her now. He wasn't sure what Slowbolt would do to him, either, but he had to take the chance. The keto needed his help.

He swung down the sling lines into the sea, treading water by the keto's side, waiting to see if Slowbolt could keep himself afloat. The keto wallowed sluggishly for a few minutes, then splashed and tried to dive. Per loosed the restraints and let him go. Slowbolt plunged and came up again, blowing spray. He swam around Per slowly, mouth open, as if taking a good look and thinking him over. Per wondered if he could get over the fence, in case Slowbolt decided to hold him personally responsible. A look beyond the fence convinced him that that wouldn't be a good idea.

The other ketos had pushed as close to the fence as they could, leaping and whistling, obviously calling to their fellow. Slowbolt hurled himself at the fence, rebounded, and backed off for another try. Per started toward the fence, turned back toward the boat, and then trod water in indecision. Fensila made up his mind for him by starting to hoist the sling aboard. Per grabbed the lines before they rose out of reach and swung himself back onto the deck.

Slowbolt's attempts to breach the fence and rejoin his friends grew more and more frantic. Most of the pens were built from fiber net and wood, and would soon have yielded to the keto's attack. Whether by chance or purpose, Fensila had lowered the keto into the secure pen, the one that had been reinforced with most of their scarce supply of wire.

"Tork!" Per called, wiping the water from his face. "Let him go. He'll ruin himself, or the pen."

Fensila leaned back lazily, watching, and didn't answer.

"The rest of the pod will rip that fence apart," Per said, still trying to speak calmly. "You don't need the aggravation. Let him go. They'll back off."

Finally Torker responded. "You're right; they will," he said. He started to turn the harpoon gun on its mount, pointing it toward the ketos beyond the fence.

Per bounded across the deck.

"No! You can't do that!"

"My boat, my gun—I'm protecting community property," Tork said, heaving at the heavy gun.

Per reached him and grabbed his arm. A warning pain shot through Per's head, but he held on.

Clutching the rail near the skipboard's tether, Dilani watched, alert for any clue to what was happening. She saw Fensila still aiming the harpoon gun as Per approached him. Whatever Per had in mind, the fish boss did not look helpful.

She expected them to make faces and wave arms at each other, but to her amazement, Per actually laid hands on Fensila. There was a brief struggle back and forth; then Fensila planted both hands on Per's chest and shoved him away. Per staggered across the deck and fell against the cabin while Fensila turned his attention to the harpoon again.

Finally Dilani understood. Torker wanted to shoot Per's friends. She ran toward him and her hands shot out in front of her as if she could catch and stop him, but she was too far away. Per jumped up and threw himself on Fensila, trying to drag the big man away from the gun. Fensila's weight was firmly planted, and he did not budge.

Dilani gasped; almost too fast for her eye to follow, Per's hand flashed out and struck Torker's head twice. The fish boss reeled back. He let go the harpoon gun and grappled Per. The two of them rolled over and over on the deck. Per clung desperately while Torker's blows rained on his back and ribs.

Dilani danced around them, mouth and eyes wide with

amazement. She had never seen a man hit another man. Children sometimes pushed each other, or struck with the hands, and then they were taken away and made to sit alone. She had never seen an adult strike another in anger. A painful, confusing excitement danced inside her and made her feet keep moving. She found the gaff tucked under the gunwale and curled her fist around it. She wondered if she could get close enough to hit, too, but she didn't know what she would do if she really had the chance.

Suddenly Per was on his feet and out of Torker's range. Fensila had clapped a hand to his ear. Red trickled between his fingers. He charged Per. His mouth was open and his teeth showed, like the ketos'. Dilani could have hit him then, but she was afraid to go that close. Per twisted away when she thought he was certainly done for. His eyes were wide, his lips working, but she could not read any of his words. There was blood on his mouth. She felt hot and sick.

Instead of defending himself, he used his hands for one frantic sign: "Out! out!" and pointed to the gaff. Then Fensila landed on top of him again.

Dilani danced from one foot to the other in agony. What did he want? What did he mean? She saw the keto leap again, like Per struggling out of Fensila's hold. He wanted her to free Slowbolt!

She ran to the side of the boat and leaned out as far as she could. It was no use. She couldn't reach the gate to the pen. She ran back to the stern. The skipboard was still tethered there.

She threw the gaff into the skipboard's cockpit, swung herself overboard onto the bobbing board, and cast off from the boat. She paddled quickly around the stern. She was on the same level with the ketos now. She could see the spray rise as they leapt from the water and beat their tails against it.

Before they spotted her, she hooked the gaff into the gate latch and pulled. The latch opened, but she couldn't pull the gate back. The skipboard slid on the water's surface, neutralizing her tugging. She dropped the gaff, grabbed hold of the gate with one hand, and held on to the mesh of the pen with the other, to stabilize herself. When she pulled again, the gate slid open.

At first Slowbolt didn't seem to see the opening. He kept throwing himself against the side of the pen. Dilani shook the mesh with both fists. The striped, shining face turned toward her then. She felt the skipboard rock as tons of muscle cruised past, turned, and passed her by again. The keto's mouth was open, his head to one side so the eye could look her over. He seemed to be deciding what to think about her. She held her breath. Then he sank into the dark water and was gone. She saw the backs of the other ketos hump out of the water briefly as they swam away.

Dilani could feel her heart pounding. She realized that she was still holding her breath. She let it out and gulped in another. Where was Per? Her angle of vision wouldn't let her see the deck. As she watched, a confusion of bodies slammed into the rail. From below, she could hardly tell what they were doing—still fighting, that was clear. She was trying to figure out how to climb back on board when one of the bodies broke free and tumbled over the side. At the last moment, it twisted to turn the fall into a clumsy dive.

Fensila leaned over the rail. His face was heavily bruised and dark with anger. The diver had been Per.

Per hit the water hard and went under. He wasn't sure which way was up, but he rose and his head broke the surface. He floundered, gulping water. The pain in his head had become so intense that he could no longer remain on deck without losing consciousness. For a moment, he was afraid that he would pass out in the water and drown.

He had to get away from the scene of the struggle. He paddled feebly forward and bumped against the boat's side. Finally he made his way around the bow and into open water, away from the fish pens. The inflowing tide gently helped him toward the beach.

He rolled on his back to float for a minute, panting. As the boat shrank into the distance, the pain diminished to a throbbing headache. His cuts and bruises stung in the healing salt.

His arms and legs felt weak and wavering, like rotted weed carried far out to sea. He was openly at war with his compact now; the first blows had been struck. And the ketos had seen what humans were. They might never come to him again. He saw again Slowbolt's agonized leap as Torker's harpoon sank into his flesh.

"I wish I'd killed him! I wish I'd killed him!" he muttered bitterly and let the pain lance through him like lightning from the distant sky. No one from shore could hear him, but even here it wasn't safe for him to say what he felt. The guardian in his mind heard him, and punished him. He plunged under the surface again and snarled a long string of bubbles through the biting kiss of saltwater on his cut lips. He swam with furious strokes, as if the effort could burn away his anger.

Dilani waited for Per to come up, but it seemed to take a long time. When his head reappeared, he was low in the water and moving sluggishly. While she scrambled to put the skipboard's sail up and get under way, she lost sight of him again.

There was no room to maneuver between the fish pens and the boat's bow. She cut around the stern and was relieved to see that Per was already some distance away, swimming for the beach with his normal stroke. She reached the beach first, grounded the skipboard next to the other small craft, and waited for Per to approach.

He lay in the shallows for a minute before dragging himself to his feet and stumbling ashore. His face looked bad. It was very white, except where the skin was cut or rubbed raw and oozing blood. He had a dark swelling around one eye, and his mouth was lumpy. She couldn't see under his skinsuit, but he moved stiffly, as if his ribs and back hurt.

Dilani ran to him.

"Wish I'd hit Torker, too," she signed. "I wanted to hit, but I was too far away."

Per started to shake his head, then put a hand to his temple as if it hurt him.

"Don't you ever," he signed. "Never. *Never* hit. This is my fight, understand? Not yours. You have to live with these people. If you hit, they'll say you learned from me. Take you away."

He stared at her, swaying a little, until she signed a half-hearted "Okay."

"Now take care of the board," he signed. "Leave me alone."

She saw that even his fingers were cut and bruised.

"Go to the doctor," she urged. "You look bad."

"Don't need a doctor. Need to be alone."

She watched him stagger away, hesitated for a moment, then shrugged and bent to pull the skipboard farther up the shore, to put away the mast and perform the other tasks she had seen Per carry out.

She kept thinking about the marks on his body. The old-gens were right. Fighting could hurt you. She had never seen it happen before. She felt a private and lonely pride. Maybe she hadn't fought, but she had helped him. Per had not tried to protect her, like some little kid. He had summoned her for help, without thinking about whether she could do it or not, and she hadn't let him down.

She hugged that fact. He needed her, even though he had pushed her away.


Per made it to his treehouse before he had to lie down. He sprawled gratefully across the platform and let the tree rock him. He closed his mind against the painful knot of events, thought about waves rolling in, and foam across the sand, and then about nothing at all.

He returned to consciousness after a few minutes, and found that he was able to sit up. Now he could feel the soreness all over his body, but the pain in his head had been pushed back to a manageable distance.

It was time to face the community.

First he checked the skipboard. Dilani had stowed the tackle and dragged the board safely beyond the high-tide line. She had done a good job. Per went over the equipment and removed anything that was his, or that was essential to his work, in case they tried to confiscate the skipboard. Then he headed for the community buildings. He might as well get it over with.

# 4

Dinner was already in progress when he arrived. He knew the meeting to censure him would not be held until the meal was over. He was hungry, and he ate as much as he could. In part it was an act of defiance; he wasn't going to fake the self-effacing penitence they wanted to see in him. Only Dilani sat at his table. He tried to ignore her, but it almost made him smile to see how she mimicked him, biting ferociously into slice after slice of fish as she glared at the rest of the colony.

After the tables were cleared, the mood darkened. No one wandered away from the dining hall; they had all heard what was going on. People sat down in a mixed array of living groups and work rosters. Only Per was alone. Whitman Sayid forced Dilani to sit near him, and Bey kept hold of her hand so she couldn't break away without being rude.

"Well, Per," Whitman said finally, "I guess everyone has heard what happened by now. Do you want to tell us your version?"

Torker Fensila pushed forward.

"Just a minute, Whitman. I'm the one bringing the complaint. I get to speak first."

"That's right," Sayid said mildly. "You are the complainant. How could I have forgotten? Tell me, do you want to run this meeting as well? If not, then please let me do it."

That lowered Fensila's volume a notch or two, but it did not stop him.

"He tried to open the gates to the fish pen to let in the pseudo-fish, monsters, ketos, whatever you want to call them. When I tried to stop him, he attacked me aboard my boat,

59

struck me, and lacerated my ear. Furthermore he left the skip-board to be brought in by a minor of impaired function—Dilani, there. She acted like she was going to hit me with the gaff, too.

"Then he made her open the fish pens when he couldn't do it himself. I want him punished, kept away from the fishing grounds, and prevented from having a bad influence on the newgens. Dilani was on my work roster before he got hold of her. I don't include her in my complaint. She doesn't know what's going on. But I think you ought to keep her under better supervision, Sayid."

Out of the corner of his eye, Per saw Dilani tugging at Bey's arm until he began to sign surreptitiously. She started to sign "Not true, not true" while he was still translating. But Per couldn't watch the end of their conversation and pay attention to the adults at the same time.

"Did you think at any time that your life was in danger?" Sayid asked. Fensila paused. Obviously he wanted to say yes, to make sure Per would be punished, but the full implications of such an answer were clear even to him. For deliberately threatening the life of a compact member, the penalty could be complete ostracism. Fensila wasn't willing to take that responsibility.

"No," he said, reluctantly. "At least, I don't say Per intended to seriously hurt me. But when I saw those critters with all their teeth showing, I sure thought I might be in danger. And being jumped on the boat I'm commanding is violence and insubordination, too."

"Do you have any explanation or apology to make?" Sayid said, turning to Per.

"Not an apology. An explanation, yes, I certainly do.

"You've all known me for years. Am I the kind of person who would attack Torker just for the hell of it? Do I look as if I'm crazy?"

"Get to the point, Per," Sayid said gently.

"It's true, I've been studying what Tork called the pseudo-fish. They definitely possess some kind of intelligence, and I'm beginning to make progress in understanding their communications so I can determine what kind of intelligence that is.

"Dilani and I were swimming with them out beyond the reef when Tork came up in the fishing boat and harpooned one of them. It was a pointless attack, and a dangerous one. If you want to talk about negligence, talk to him. He could have speared one of us instead. The blood attracted boogers, too. Dilani and I could have been chewed up in the water, along with the injured keto. We took the risk of securing the keto in a sling to get it out of the water, and we gave it first aid.

"I wouldn't have had a problem with keeping it in the fish pen under observation, but it panicked and started ramming the fence. The others in the pod were agitated on the other side. I wanted to open the gates to let Sl—the keto out, not to let the others in. They didn't want to come in anyway; all they wanted was their comrade back.

"Tork was about to fire on the other ketos. He didn't give me time to explain. I didn't want a fight with him. I just wanted to stop a senseless killing. He wouldn't let me open the gate, so I told Dilani to do it. If she hadn't, Tork would have killed more ketos, and the rest would have wrecked the fish pen.

"I apologize for any accidental damage to Tork. I didn't wish to harm him, and I didn't think it was very likely, since he has ten years and thirty pounds on me. I guess I got lucky, and I'm sorry."

"Is that true, Torker?" Sayid said. "Did you incite the attack?"

Fensila flushed a dark red. "I did not."

"Here we have two mutually exclusive stories," Sayid said. "I don't see any way to authenticate either of them, and therefore I—"

"Just a minute, Papan," Bey said clearly. "There's another witness you haven't questioned yet."

Sayid actually lost his self-control and looked startled.

"Bey, I don't believe you have standing." His voice started out harsher and louder than normal and quickly smoothed itself into its public tone.

"It's not me, Papan. Dilani was there. She has a right to speak."

Sayid looked more startled than ever.

"Bey, you know that's impossible," he said, lowering his voice as if Dilani might hear him. "She can't testify. She doesn't talk."

"Sure she does. She just needs an interpreter. I can do that."

"I object!" Torker said. "She's not an adult, and she's not fully functional. Besides that, if she talks through an interpreter, how do I know that Bey isn't—"

He realized a moment too late that questioning the veracity of Sayid's son might not win him any points.

"—that Bey hasn't misunderstood what she's trying to say," he finished lamely.

Melicar rose and came to the center of the circle.

"As the senior medical expert, and Dilani's doctor, I can certify that she does know the truth from a falsehood. Whatever her physical deficits may be, there's certainly nothing wrong with her intelligence. In my experience, she has never lied about any significant matter. She may be defiant, but she's not a liar."

"Well, she's lied to me!" Fensila exploded. "As a fishery worker, she was more trouble than a bucket of squid, and just as slippery."

"I can understand her sign, to some extent," Melicar continued calmly. "If Bey makes a major misrepresentation, I think I would catch it."

She sat down. Sayid frowned down at her, a resentful look. Per thought that Sayid had already worked out what he considered to be the proper disposition of the dispute. Testimony from Dilani would interfere with the smooth procedure of his plan. But there was no way to avoid it once the subject had been raised.

Sayid beckoned to Dilani.

"Tell what happened," he signed.

Bey wheeled himself forward to accompany her.

"She says Per is telling the truth and Torker is a . . . is not," he said, carefully watching her swift hands. "Tork—I mean, Teacher Fensila—he pushed Teacher Per on the boat and made him fall down. Teacher Fensila tried to kill the keto when it was swimming in the water with Dilani and Teacher Per. It wasn't hurting anything. Then he tried to kill the other ketos with a harpoon. Teacher Per only defended himself and the ketos, and afterward he told Dilani never to hit.

"She asks if Teacher Melicar remembers showing her in the rules where it says that smart beings have to be respected and no one should kill a smart being. It comes right before where it says no one can harm a member of the compact."

"Yes, I remember that," Melicar said. "I do a review class on obligations of compact membership when the kids reach puberty."

Dilani waited for Melicar's affirmative nod and then went on signing.

"She says Teacher Fensila broke the law first. He wanted to kill the keto. Teacher Per tried to save the law. Is that wrong?"

Whitman broke in. "We aren't talking about the ketos."

Dilani gestured emphatically—"Me, Dilani, I myself."

"She says *she* is talking about ketos. She says Teacher Per loves them, but you say they are not important."

He stopped speaking, though Dilani's hands were still moving. Per tried desperately to catch his eye, willing him not to continue. Per could see what Dilani was saying, and knew it would be a mistake. Bey hung his head until Dilani noticed that his mouth was not moving and punched a clenched fist in his direction.

"She says . . . she says, some of us are different from you, too. She says, 'I can't make noise. The ketos can. The ketos are not shaped like you. Some of us newgens are not shaped like you, either. Will you harm some of us because we are not enough like you? Which ones? I want to know.' "

Per was about to smack his own forehead in frustration. He should have realized that Dilani would insist on speaking, and coached her about what to say. But as he cursed himself, he saw Phillips Roon glance sideways, once, at Whitman. That look chilled him to the bone.

"Thank you for testifying," Whitman said smoothly. "You can sit down." Dilani tried to sign more, but Whitman overlooked her and continued to speak.

"Since there's some doubt about who initiated conflict, I recommend that Per not be censured at this time. As restitution for Torker's injuries, I suggest Per work on the fish roster for the next two weeks. I'd also like to propose that the ketos be left alone, pending further evaluation. We don't really need them as a food source, at this time."

After some discussion, those present agreed to endorse Whitman's proposal, and the meeting was adjourned.

"What a surprise," Per said sarcastically. No one appeared to hear him, or spoke to him as he left the hall.

He headed for the beach immediately, intending to soak the stiffness from his bruises in cool water. He thought he was alone, but a voice startled him. He looked around—and saw no one.

"Teacher Per," the voice said again, low to the ground. It was Bey, not in his cart, but supporting himself on his knuckles and his misshapen feet. He dragged himself forward laboriously, using the strength of his arms, the short, incurved legs serving only as props.

"We're having a fire tonight," Bey said. "Will you come? It's been a long time."

Against his will, Per was touched by the invitation, but he thought it would be a mistake to go. It was best for him to stay away from the newgens, and everyone else.

"This is a newgen thing," Bey said diffidently, before Per could raise an objection. "We won't be telling our parents about it."

A light wind fluttered the flames of the small fire in the center of the circle. It rattled the leaves of the tubewood trees and ruffled the newgens' hair. Their eyes gleamed and faded as the fire rose and fell, as if the newgens were shy wild animals drawn down out of the trees by curiosity about the new brightness near the water's edge. But there were no large mammals on Typhon.

The circle of half-hidden faces watched Per. He had often joined the newgens in a casual way, beginning when they were just old enough to light their own fires and to be out after dark. They liked his stories; they liked the small wonders he found in thickets or among the tide pools. He showed them shells and stinkbugs, and curly vines that wreathed around their fingers if they breathed on them. He found himself talking with them as he could not talk with their parents. He was neither a parent nor a taskmaster, just an odd wandering presence they sometimes welcomed.

Bey reached up and tugged at his hand. Dilani sat next to Bey, looking unusually thoughtful.

"Sit down, Teacher Per. Tell us a story."

"Story," Bader Puntherong echoed thickly, through his mutilated mouth. It was hard to recognize expressions on Bader's face, but Per thought he saw some irony there. "Story," Bader said. "About monsters."

"Well—" Per laughed, a little embarrassed. "It's been a long time."

The monster stories had been their favorites, when they were little. Per liked telling them. He had improved them, and made them more and more horrifying, until someone had nightmares and told the parents, and the telling had had to stop. Sometimes he still told them, though. Sometimes he heard the newgens retelling bits of them to each other. Per had told monster stories so often that the guardian in his mind had become lax and let them slip out without punishment. In Per's telling, the stories hadn't happened to him anyway, but to someone else, a long-ago boy the guardian could not recognize.

"In a time that was and was not," he began, "there was a boy who lived on an island in the great black Deep. It wasn't an island like this one. It was an island of steel and kemplex. It would have been like a boat, but it was too big to be a boat. It had plants and lakes of water, like an island."

"Were there people on this island?" Lila asked. Someone usually asked that.

Per used to think very hard about that question, hoping to recover some fragment of memory, but nothing ever came to him.

"The boy couldn't remember," he said reluctantly. "He seemed to be alone. He thought that once there had been people, but he never saw them, and he could not remember them.

"The ship island wasn't like this island. Inside the ship island, you could never see the sky."

At that point, as when they were little, the newgens drew together more closely, knowing that the frightening part was coming soon.

"The boy lived in tunnels that never ended. He could never go outside. He could see pictures of the outside, but it was always dark there. It was sometimes dark in the tunnels, too, but as the boy walked along them—" He paused and frowned. Now that he thought of it, he did not remember walking.

"He flew. He swam in the tunnels. It was like swimming, I suppose."

There was a stir of interest among the newgens. This was new. He had never said that before.

"Swimming in air? Is that possible?" Lila asked.

Per shrugged. "It was possible there. Anyway, as he moved through the tunnels, some of them were always light, but some were dark ahead and behind, and lit up only when he arrived. And some were dark forever, dark like the great Deep outside. Their lights had failed.

"All over the ship, things had failed and gone wrong. It was a very old ship, old and dark, and full of things that were sleeping, or broken. Full of things that might have died, or had never been really alive."

The newgens leaned closer together, even at their age.

"The boy didn't remember any people, but he knew there were others living on this big, half-dead island. There were ruks who were twice the size of an ordinary man. Their legs were like towers. Their hands were like animal traps—like keto jaws, I mean. They could tear a boy's arms off like the wings off a bird—or the legs off a frog. Sometimes they were friendly. Sometimes they were mad with stupid rage.

"There were vacuum jox with leathery skin and flat eyes and mouths like saws, and hands with sticky cups that could cling to the smooth kemplex skin of the ship's hull, outside, in the dark. There were toxicants with red-pocked weeping skin. If they breathed on you, you could dissolve and die. Their breath was so poisonous they had to wear suits and airhoods even inside the ship or they would poison every living thing. The boy saw them sleeping in their airshrouds down in the . . . in the place where things were cold."

Per held his hands out to the fire. The air was warm and sweet in this rocky hollow, but he felt cold inside. He remembered a place where people slept in shrouds of ice, where their breath frosted into crazy cracks until it froze into stillness. *Where was that place?* It was nowhere, they had told him—nowhere but in his mind.

"Maybe worst of all—" He lowered his voice, and the newgens shivered."—worst of all was the sinue. The sinue had been turned loose in the tunnels long ago, and the boy didn't know any more what they were for. Maybe nobody knew. They must have started out small, but they grew. Their bodies fit within the tunnels. They flew easily, but they could never walk. They had no legs, and their arms seemed pitifully small, their mean, clawed little fingers only good for gripping prey. Their eyes seemed small in their swollen faces—small but horrible, as if human intelligence lived on, madly, in a body that was all beast and all belly.

"Their mouths were the ugliest part of them. When they were closed, they looked like long zippers ringing the flat, wedge-shaped heads. But they could open. The small ones could open wide enough to swallow an arm or a head, and the boy thought he had dreamed or remembered a man dying with his head engulfed in that mouth, while his legs kicked outside.

"But the big ones—the really big ones—" Per himself shivered.

"Maybe they were created to run the tunnels and keep them free of vermin and debris. Maybe they had once been messengers, or guardians. But now their purpose was to eat—and only to eat.

"One day—or one time, for there was no day or night on the dead ship—the boy was flying through the tunnels like a fish spearing through water. His arms were at his sides, his feet were straight behind him. The lights turned on just ahead of him and blinked out behind him.

"And suddenly, ahead of him, the lights flashed on, and showed him not a smooth, curving tunnel but an open maw so big its jaws touched the tunnel's sides. Within that maw lay another tunnel gaping to receive him—a tunnel of churning, flexing muscle, pink and dirty green, glistening wet. He was flying like a spear point, headfirst into the belly of the sinue. Its mad little eyes showed above its stretched lips. He never forgot their look of glee."

No, Per thought. He had not forgotten that. Those little eyes had demoted him from a person to merely something to eat. But what had happened after that? They wanted to know, so he tried to think it out.

"He could not stop, but with a frantic contortion of his body, he pulled himself into a ball and spun till he was feet-first. He kicked out, and his feet smashed into the mad red eyes and the bone around them. Then he was arrowing away again, in the opposite direction, and the sinue shook its tail against the tunnel till the walls boomed.

"It chased the boy, but it was half blinded and it couldn't catch him. He heard it shrieking like a vapor leak in the blackness that swallowed up the space behind him. Ahead, the light revealed a blot of black, the mouth of a tunnel that might be too narrow for the sinue to enter. The boy caught a cleat and swung himself round so hard the skin split from his palms, swung himself and plunged feetfirst into the narrow opening. And the sinue thrashed on past. He thought he heard it moving in the dark for a long time—long after it was gone."

There was a pause while the newgens listened to the rattle of leaves in the twilight. They had wanted him to tell a story for some reason, Per thought, but the story had distracted them from their original goal.

"This really happened?" Nils Samerak said in his slow, deep voice.

"Things like this really happened," Per said. But he wasn't sure who it had happened to. A boy. The boy might have been Per. Per felt a ghostly pain in his palms and calves as he thought about it, as if he remembered the pain of cramped legs crouching in the dark, cramped fists clenched on split and bleeding skin. He remembered a smell that was indescribable, because it existed nowhere outside lost memories of a dead ship and the cold stink of a monster.

Per made stories of fragments that worked up through the layers of his mind, fragments that might or might not belong to him.

"Who made the monsters?" Nils said.

"People, I suppose. Maybe the people who were on the ship before."

Bey leaned forward from the shadows where he had been interpreting for Dilani.

"Why did they want to make monsters?" he asked, and a sigh of appreciation went around the circle. They were back on the trail of what they wanted. No one had asked Per that before. They had been children, wanting scary stories at dark, and he had pleased them—and himself—with the broken shards of the past, the sharp splinters lodged in his mind, the things he was forbidden to remember. He had eased his mind, and thought he was doing no harm.

Now he was worried. He had given the children dangerous toys.

"Why?" Bey urged, and the waiting eyes shone. Per knew he had been called before them as a witness this time, not as a teller of stories. *Why not?* he thought finally. *They've had their parents' version—why not mine? It's all fragments, anyway.*

"There was a war," he said, after a long pause.

Heads nodded around the circle. Yes, the war. They had

been told about that. It happened long ago in the bad days —
something shameful and vague, described in technical terms
to take the thrill and the obscenity out of it. The people had
come to Skandia, fleeing from that war. The good, peaceful people had separated themselves from the bad, and that
was that.

There were no wars any more. The war makers had killed
each other long ago, among distant stars.

"The monsters were made for the war. They didn't start
out as monsters; they started out as humans. But they were
changed before they fully reached the human form—maybe
as pre-embryos, maybe in the genes themselves. Each was
made for a purpose: the ruks for heavy work and hand-to-
hand fighting; the vacuum jox for the great dark outside the
ship, where there is no air; the toxicants to poison and terrify
the enemy. Even the sinue had some use on an armed ship of
war."

"And that is why we must never tamper with human
genes," Lila said primly. "Mutations lead to monsters and
war."

"Yes, that's what they teach in school, isn't it?" Per said.
"But they never talk about *why*. Why did the people from Sol-
Terra and the old worlds want to do something so bad and
dangerous in the first place? Why did they start?"

Lila put up her hand as if she were in class. "Because they
were arrogant. And they didn't have social responsibility like
we do. They let everybody do what they wanted—scientists
and war makers, too."

"They were evil," Bader said heavily.

"Maybe they didn't think so," Per said. "Maybe they started
out trying to do something good. Maybe they saw people suffering and thought they could stop disease and crippling,
right from the start. Maybe they wished for their children to
be better than they were."

"Then how could things go so wrong?" Lila asked.

Per rubbed his hand through his salt-stiffened hair. *What
would be a true answer?* he wondered. *Arrogance, evil, near-*

*sightedness? Or just the fact that nature is always one step ahead of our understanding, laughing at us?*

"It has to do with the nature of the genome," he said.

They fidgeted. That was one of those words from their social-ethical classes. They associated it with boring, pious lectures.

"I know what they teach in social-ethical," Per said. "It's the same thing they used to say back on Skandia. Well, the genome isn't some sacred object; it's simply a very long list of codes for making amino acids. In our case, about three billion base pairs. At the beginning of the Flight Era, humans on Sol-Terra were beginning to unravel it. At the time of the wars, they had the ability to create armies of monsters, all built on human genes. They always promised that soon we would be creating a new and better kind of human. But it hasn't happened."

The children stared at him blankly while Bey tried to explain to Dilani what Per was talking about.

"See, it wasn't so hard to make monsters. They only wanted the monsters to do a few specific tasks. But it turned out to be harder to make humans who were really better in all ways.

"Even in the early Flight Era some biologists suspected that each gene might affect many others, rather than coding for one specific thing in isolation."

Per realized that he was losing the newgens. This wasn't their vocabulary. He was going to have to oversimplify, and that wasn't *his* specialty.

"I'm trying to think of an example. Let's say you wanted a human with pink eyes. Well, there used to be a gene that made your eyes pink. But it also made your hair white and your skin pale, so your skin burned if you went out in the sun. This gene causes a lack of an enzyme that helps creates skin pigment, and it affects everything, not just your eyes."

Dilani signed something, shoulder turned to him so he couldn't quite see, and the children snickered behind their hands.

*Pinkman*, he thought. *That's what she said. They think* I'm *a mutation.*

"Anyway," he continued, "lack of this enzyme also affects the optic nerve—the nerve to their eyes—so they can't see as well. So if you want to keep the pink eyes, you have to fiddle with something else to try to fix the skin that burns and the bad eyesight. And when you fiddle with that, you create another problem. So when they tried to reengineer people, they ended up with a mess. Our genes are like a tangled net; whatever string you pull on creates a knot somewhere else.

"If you're working with animals—or monsters—you can just kill the ones that don't work out. But that doesn't seem right with humans. So most of the old worlds agreed to ban human engineering till we had the kind of comprehensive understanding we needed to reshape humans through direct genetic manipulation.

"But it was too late. The monsters were out of the box, and the wars came." *And that wasn't all,* Per thought. His head was beginning to throb warningly, but he groped for the debris of memory that had surfaced, trying to catch the fragments before they sank again.

"There was more to the story than monsters and soldiers," he said. "They made people as delicate as flowers; dancers and acrobats who could almost fly; people with brilliant minds; people who were seven feet tall and the color of obsidian; people with cinnamon skin and golden eyes.

"The group who called themselves Original Man untwisted the mixed strands of human history and called up the races that had existed when humans were trapped on one planet—pale men and dark men, tall thin desert men and short stocky men of the snow. Not all of them were healthy or even sane, and not all of them lived long, but they all had their own kind of beauty."

The newgens listened, enthralled.

"But it was still wrong," Lila said stubbornly. "Maybe the sinue think *they* are beautiful, but whether they're beautiful or ugly, they're still monsters."

Per sighed. "We judge the makers through a distant lens,"

he said. "Certainly it was arrogant to make them; perhaps it was evil. The people who made Skandia thought it was evil, and they put a strict ban on genetic tinkering with humans. But they still wanted their children to be better than they were, so they used the old-fashioned ways. They tried to weed and edit the breeding stock in hopes of gradual improvement through the offspring.

"If you were still on Skandia, your genes would have been mapped long before you reached this age. Then, before you could have children, your living group would decide if your offspring were likely to fit in with the genetic profile they wanted for the group.

"It's not just physical things, either. Many social behaviors have been shown to have roots in your genetic structure, too, so if you were considered antisocial, you could be turned down for that reason."

He grimaced. He could still remember sitting in the gene doctors' office at home in Nordstrand, listening to their verdict on him.

"Have you got anything to drink?" he asked abruptly, changing the subject. They nudged each other and whispered. A stack of shells appeared, and one was passed into his hand. They poured it full of a dark liquid that looked like giling juice but smelled sharper. He sipped and stared at them in disbelief.

"Where did you get this?"

Bey wriggled his shoulders. "We made it. We tried various things. First it was spud mash with a yeast starter. That was bad. This is tamal juice supercharged with giling sap and distilled in a kettle. We stole the kettle."

Per grinned. "I'll be damned," he said. "You newgens are sharp."

"You're not going to tell?"

"Not if you give me a drink every now and then," Per said. He sucked the shell dry and held it out for more. The squall line of pain in his head receded somewhat, temporarily.

"If they all wanted their children to be better than they were, then why did we come out the way we are?" Bey said.

The circle held still. He had come to the most important questions.

"You should ask your parents," Per said. "They can probably explain it better than I can."

"That's just what we don't want," Bey said. "They tell us what they want us to know. We want to hear it plain."

"I wish I could tell you," Per said. "No one knows. Other colonists have been sent to Typhon, but they never lasted past the first generation. This world is as beautiful as paradise, but it kills people.

"When we arrived here, there was no trace of the last set of colonists. We thought we were holding our own—until the babies started to be born. You. And every one of you had some kind of congenital anomaly."

He spelled it out for Dilani, but she just shook her head, anger reflected in her face. The others understood what he meant, but she refused to accept it. She refused to accept herself as damaged.

"No mistake. I'm fine," she signed. The happy-face expression that normally went with the hand sign for *fine* wasn't there. She glared at Per, and her fingers were stiffly flexed. It was like hearing somebody shout, "I'm not angry, damn it!"

The newgens who sat next to her patted her shoulders soothingly, to coax her to stillness so Per could continue.

"Many of the babies didn't even survive till birth. Some died too early for us to know why; the others all had problems, too."

"But why?" Lila said. "Were our parents bad? Was something wrong with them?"

"At first the medical staff thought the parents might have been damaged by radiation as we traveled. Records from other colonies showed this was a risk, but only one case recorded had been so severe. That colony did not survive. They had passed through a major solar flare. We did not. I never believed that was the reason.

"And the doctor, Lesper Rogier—he was Sushan's partner, before he died—he didn't believe the problems were due to radiation damage, either. If that had been true, the defects should have been more randomly distributed. They aren't. They cluster in certain areas, hot spots, as if some mutagenic agent targeted those areas on your chromosomes. That points to something in the environment: some toxin or infection."

Per sighed. "That's where I got into trouble. Whitman Sayid couldn't accept that theory. Because, you see, it meant we were doomed. It meant there was something in the environment that would never permit us to live here. Gene damage from the trip could be fixed, dealt with, but what about an unknown—something that attacks all over again every time a woman gets pregnant? So Whitman kept arguing about it, trying to turn research in some other direction, as if a majority vote could affect reality."

He checked himself. There was no point in criticizing Whitman in front of his son. Let the boy work it out for himself—if Typhon granted him time.

"Well, Whitman had support. Lesper and I, and the others who were working with us, couldn't get permission for some of the things we wanted to try. Plenty of people thought we were climbing the wrong tree. Others, though, came to us through the back door, and begged us to do just what the forum was forbidding.

"One of our theories was that the problem might be a virus native to Typhon. There are records, going back to the pre–Flight Era, of viruses that attack the fetus at certain crucial points, even though the mother might not feel the effects. We knew there were plenty of viruses on Typhon, but we didn't know which one might be causing the problems.

"However, we created an antiviral agent, and hoped it might have a generic effect on a range of Typhon viruses. After much brain racking, we decided to test it on several of the women who had volunteered. Fensila's partner, Norit, was one of them. She and Torker said they had confidence in me."

Per paused for a minute. He had described the results with detailed accuracy in his journal, but he didn't like to recall that whole, brutal sequence of events.

"Did it work?" Selma Haddad asked.

"Of course it didn't work!" someone whispered loudly. "Look at us!"

Selma looked away, fingering the discolored flesh that hung from her neck.

"No, it didn't work," Per admitted. "We don't understand what happened. Probably our intervention triggered a mutation in the virus. Anyway, it only made things worse. The gross physical malformations became less pronounced, but certain aspects of the babies' metabolisms were so screwed up that none of them lived more than a few minutes after birth.

"What was worse, whatever we did apparently made it possible for the virus—if it was a virus—to affect the mother as well as the child. They experienced tremors, convulsions, and finally went into a coma. In spite of everything we could do, they all died. Norit Fensila was one of them.

"Torker never forgave me for that. There was a big community hearing about it. They couldn't really do anything to Lesper except give him the cold shoulder. He was the chief of medicine, and they needed him. They voted to censure me, and denied me access to any of the medical equipment. I went back to concentrating on fish after that."

He had been staring down at his hands, twisting them tightly together. At some point he had forgotten to sign, and had left the translation entirely up to Bey. He straightened up and faced the children defiantly.

"I'm not sorry we tried. It could have been one more step toward understanding, even though they died. But we didn't pursue it. People who were brave or stupid enough to get pregnant went on, hoping they'd be lucky, and the rest of us gave up on ever having children. I was left with that mark on me—unauthorized experimentation, just one degree short of murder, in their minds."

It seemed to him that the newgens' eyes were fixed on him accusingly.

"You gave up," Bey said. "Not just you—all of them. You shouldn't have let this happen. You should have done *something*."

"I agree with you," Per said in a low voice. "But I can remember what things were like before, and maybe you can't. At first we had all the equipment and most of the people we brought with us. But the babies weren't the only problem we had.

"The big disaster wasn't the first, you know. We had three minor eruptions in the first five years, and they all killed people and did damage. Each year there was typhoon season, and people got eaten and poisoned and lost at sea, and died of random illnesses and accidents. Like Dilani's parents: they went out beyond the reef to make some routine observations and never came back."

"Like my mother," Bey said softly.

"Yes, like your mother," Per said. Bey had been lucky; he'd had two parents until he was ten. Then his mother had died, stricken by a brief, sudden fever.

After a moment, Per continued. "We were struggling for our lives, even then. And now, since the disaster, we've nearly lost everything. We can't fix things for you. I'm sorry."

He felt their eyes on his, still silently accusing. He couldn't blame them. What he was saying might be true, but it still amounted to nothing but excuses for their parents' impotence.

"They created us," Bader said laboriously. "We are monsters. What will they do with us?"

"You're not monsters," Per protested, shocked.

"The oldgens think so," Bey said. His hand rested protectively on Bader's shoulder. His handsome face was pinched with thoughts too old for him.

"Not your parents, surely. They care for you."

Bey just shrugged. "On Skandia they would never have permitted us to be born," he said. "You told us that. I'm sure our parents have thought of that, too."

"They don't tell us, but they talk about us," Bader said. "They talk—what to do? You've got to help us."

"Look, you have to realize that I have no standing with the other adults," Per said. "They censured me once. The only reason they didn't censure me again today was that Dilani somehow put grit in Whitman's engine. The next step would be to expel me from the compact. That doesn't mean very much, practically speaking, since we're all stuck here together no matter what, but it means that the other adults of Typhon colony have no patience with me and are tired of putting up with me. Associating with me will do you no good. It will only make things worse."

"We don't expect you to argue with them or change them," Bey said. "We just want you to listen, and warn us what they are planning to do. We deserve to know. Will you do that much for us?"

Per weighed his answer. Bey appealed to his sense of fairness. It seemed only right that the newgens be given full information, like other members of the colony. Yet Per wasn't prepared to make a promise that would bind him against his own better judgment.

"I'll try," he said finally. He was thinking of the look that had passed between Phillips and Sayid. He wanted to find out what that meant; he would decide later whether to share its meaning with the newgens.

"We'll trust you, Teacher Per," Bey said. "We have no choice." He propped himself up on his hands for walking. "It's late," he said. "We should go, before they begin to wonder."

The newgens made their way back down the beach in a group, helping one another as needed. Bey was the slowest and the last. Per walked along with him; the others went ahead at their own speed, except for Dilani who looked back and waited for them. Bey sank back on his haunches to free his hands.

"I want privacy," he signed rapidly. "Do you mind?" Dilani made a face at him. She strolled along beside them, looking out to sea and not at their hands and faces.

"Is that why my father looks at me the way he does?" Bey said without preamble.

"What? I don't understand."

"Sure you do, Teacher Per. All those things you told us about Skandia. How important it was to them to have perfect children. I've seen my father looking at me like he doesn't know where I came from."

"I'm sure your father is proud of you," Per said stiffly. He had never thought he would find himself defending Whitman Sayid.

"Garbage," Bey said. It was the first rude word Per had ever heard from him. "We came to you because we thought you would tell us the truth. If I wanted to hear polite lies I could ask someone else."

Per wondered if Bey would be able to make any sense of his father's past; he had never seen a city, a factory, or a polling station. Per wondered how much to tell him.

"It doesn't really have anything to do with you," he said. "Whitman was a rising star in the political heirarchy back home. Even an antisocial type like me was familiar with his smiling face. Then he announced he wanted to pair up, and it became known that he carried a gene complex that can be associated with metabolic disorders if it becomes dominant. Of course, the chances of that happening were very small, but it was enough to disallow reproduction. His career was ruined."

"His career? What does it have to do with his career?"

"On Skandia, being 'clean' is so important that you lose prestige if you're disallowed. Whitman lost status. He could have succeeded at a lower level, but he couldn't accept that. He ended up being sent here.

"You could have been his vindication—a perfect son to prove to the Skandians that they were wrong about him. When he looks at you, he sees his own fears about himself, in the flesh. That's what he's rejecting."

"Stupid," Bey muttered, doggedly drawing himself through the sand. He looked up. "Is that why you reject Dilani?"

"What do you mean?" Per said. For a moment he panicked. He looked reflexively at Dilani, feeling that somehow she must have heard him, though he knew that was impossible. She strolled on, drawing lines in the sand with her toes.

"I mean because she's not perfect enough," Bey said. "It's the same way my father looks at me."

Beginnings of sentences sprang to Per's lips—explanations, justifications. He refused them one after the other. After a minute, Bey spoke again.

"Dilani needs someone: one person she can depend on."

"That seems more like your business than mine," Per said. "I'm hardly of a suitable age."

Moon shadows hurried over Bey's face as a look of weariness and anger crossed it. Another look too old for his age.

"That's not what I meant," he said. "Can't you oldgens think about anything but mating?"

"I'm sorry," Per said, as if to an equal. "It was a stupid joke."

"She needs a friend."

"Well, aren't you her best friend?"

"She looks at me and sees my father, too: rules, work, consensus, the colony—everything she doesn't want. You're outside. She wants to be outside with you."

"I said I'd teach her. But she is not 'with' me. Nobody is with me. I can't be responsible for her."

Bey toiled on in silence for a few minutes.

"Why did you come here?" he said suddenly. "Are you disallowed for reproduction, too?"

Per almost gave him the answer that lay waiting, but a stab of pain behind his eyes stopped him in time.

"They no longer wanted me on Skandia," he said. "I'm antisocial. I don't cooperate well. I always think I'm right, even when the group is against me."

Gentle waves lapped against their bare feet, nearly as warm as the balmy air.

"It's different there," he said. "The oceans are small and frigid. Without a warmsuit from head to toe, you'd die in minutes. A single pinprick in the suit lets in water so cold it burns like fire. And the shore is cold and rocky. Fish don't jump out of the sea, and fruits don't fall from the trees. You struggle for your food and shelter.

"But at the same time, it's easier in a funny way. Everything's controlled. Living groups and work rosters link smoothly, like the parts of a machine. But there's not much space there, between all those smooth-running parts. The machine doesn't tolerate grit.

"There's not much they can do with someone who won't accept discipline. Even in the polar fisheries and the northern mines, where they can use people who want to feel tough, they need good citizens who follow the rules.

"I got sent to camp when I wasn't much older than you. It's a wretched place where you have to work on your own, live on a survival level, out in the woods hunting animals and chopping down trees. No skinsuits or heaters or food rations. It's supposed to make you feel miserable, scared, and lonely. After a summer of that, you're supposed to be overjoyed to return to the security of your compact."

Bey glanced up, briefly smiling. "It didn't work, did it?" he said.

"No. It was the happiest time I'd had on Skandia. I would have gone back the next year, but I knew that no university would take me with two camp seasons on my record. So I tried to make them believe I had learned my lesson.

"I learned it all right. I learned I would never fit in on Skandia."

They had reached the edge of the path that led to the cluster of dorms and public buildings. Per tried to smile through his blinding headache.

"Anyway, Typhon is a paradise for a marine biologist," he said. "I like it here."

Bey nodded. "This is where we turn off. Goodnight, Teacher Per. And thanks."

"Thank me when I've done something," Per said.

He heard the shuffling sound of Bey's progress into the dark, faster once he reached the hard-packed path. Per turned the other way, toward his own isolated shelter.

# ☙5☙☙☙☙☙☙

*Once again I saw the strange ones,* Subtle danced in the night-blue water. *On this time 574,519 of light-and-dark, time 9,532 of light-and-dark of Subtle the Round One.*

*The brightwarm had passed two-thirds of the sky edge when I saw them in the water. They are straight, not round, but not watersmooth like the Laughing Teeth. They are split, once at the end and once on each side, and the split limbs are crooked but not broken.*

In dancing it, the full ugliness of the new creatures came over him. He felt awkward and broken himself as he found a way to express it. But the greater the strangeness, the greater the admiration and ecstasy would be when others saw it gathered into his limbs for them to experience.

*They carry madethings with them—wonder: head masks? not Deep united, not water one at all but native to the Dry?— even most-precious metalthings. AND: senseshock! swimming with the Teeth, touching with crooked limbs, riding the wake of those-who-eat, uneaten!*

*Again I saw the watersmooth shape, now sure it was made, not live—by them? Unknown. Churning water/confusion. From the shape came a mademetal tooth that swiftly dove and pierced the Laughing One itself. No longer laughing! I heard the paincry. Like a hatchling he piped distress, his defeat made known to all the Deep, the great killer begging in his pain. From the shape came madelimbs, and lifted the Tooth away. Shock! OUT past sky edge—O admiration! Possible??—and the Split Ones with him. Beyond the world!*

Then came a pause, clearly not an end, for Subtle's colors

82

stirred and writhed with the changing hues of powerful feelings. After the suspense, his limbs stirred again to explosive life.

*Still the shape touched our skyward edge, and I followed as it moved swiftly toward the Dry edge. Powerfully water-smooth it cut the sky edge, leaving turbulence behind. Powerfully Subtle swam, deep breaths of water surging through him, wake hot with effort.*

*Barrier! Course blocked, in front-four and both front-side-twos of direction. Mademetal, fine-thin and regular, a net of shape-of-four from sky edge to bottom. The very diagram of potential intelligence! Geometries in metal.*

*Clouded water, hard to see through. Here comes the pack of Teeth! All attack the barrier, tearing, butting with heads until blood in the water endangers all. The artifact defies their berserk strength. Their Deepsong carries fear and rage, hysteria of the baffled pack. Brief triumph for the Round One, who dances, watching.*

*Fear and amazement, like effervescence in the water. The barrier moves. Not torn by Teeth, but moving smoothly as if willed by invisible power. The barrier is moved by something or someone beyond, beyond . . .*

Here the dance stammers and is incoherent—*Is it beyond the sky? from the Dry itself? or only beyond the comprehension of Subtle watching? This dance cannot be finished till he knows.*

*And the Laughing One who was taken is returned.*

*Somewhere in the water, when it is too late, Subtle senses the traces of the Split Ones again. The Teeth go mad with rage as if they see their enemy. Their song speaks of biting and tearing a wounder of their kin. But there is confusion in the song, and the pack departs, and Subtle, with the courage of the Ancestors, touches the metal and tastes it.*

Who could believe such a story?

*Taste the water. Sincerity bathes me, undeniable as the astringent, painful savor of metal wire.*

*Skin is truth. Taste me and behold.*

\* \* \*

He brought the dance to an end and hung exhausted in the water, allowing his limbs to trail in the aimless currents. The dance was half finished, a rough sketch, a framework. He floated within his own aura; the exhalations of his body spoke exhaustion and frustration, but married inextricably to those scents was the flavor of discovery and absolute sincerity. No one who could see his dance—if anyone ever did—would doubt him.

He half hoped that a wandering godbit might be drawn to his strong aura and carry some fragments of the tale back into the shared waters. But it was the wrong time of year and the wrong part of the sea for godbits. Perhaps when the dance was finished, Subtle would carry it home himself, or perhaps his life would end before that could happen.

He only knew that his way still lay outward, toward the Dry. He must see the Split Folk and learn if the metalwork was theirs, if they carried speaking minds within those crooked, water-unsmooth bodies.

He rested for a few minutes. He was hungry, and should drop toward the bottom to search for food. But curiosity, a more powerful hunger, drove him toward the shore.

Weariness descended on Per as soon as he was alone in the darkness, like the weight that drags the diver's heels as soon as he comes ashore. He walked the narrow path without a hand light, stumbling occasionally. Fortunately, the tricky part where it was easy to step into the tide pools was illuminated by colonies of glowstars. His persuasions had worked: a little irrigation with nutrient-rich waters, and a breeding program to improve their tolerance for low salinity. They clustered along the margins of his path, outlining it in a pale greenish glow not quite bright enough to read by. He began to consider ways of increasing their luminescence.

For the time being, though, he still needed nonbiological lights. His oil lamp, topped with a glass chimney so it wouldn't blow out, gave a flickering glow as he entered the dark house. He lit the others, and was annoyed for the hundredth time by the clustering shadows they cast. But before long, his half-formed thoughts of possible solutions gave way in favor of more pressing concerns.

Sushan would have stored the keto tissue samples for him. That was important. He suppressed an impulse to go back to the hospital and check for himself. Sushan had promised. She was reliable. If he went back to look, he ran the risk of meeting other colony members and stirring things up, instead of giving them a chance to calm down.

Even if he met only Sushan, he would confirm her assertions that he tried too hard to control everything, and that he believed he could trust no one but himself.

But it was the simple truth, he argued. He'd had ample proof recently that not all of his fellow colony members wished him well. And he was pretty sure that Whitman was hiding something from him. He thought again of Dilani's incautious statement at the meeting, and the glance that had passed between Roon and Sayid. What was going on there?

His mind was churning in confusion.

He whirled around and squinted through the flickering, unsatisfactory light. He thought he heard something, a splash perhaps, from the direction of the pools. After a moment of tense listening, he shook his head and began to chuckle. Oh, indeed he was indulging in paranoia. Too bad Sushan wasn't here to share the moment: Per Langstaff afraid of a fish. He was far too tired to do any useful work that night—might as well admit it. He blew out the lights, sprawled across his hammock, and fell into sleep.

He was too sore and stiff to sleep deeply. Aches and pains and dream fragments kept him moving restlessly. Finally, as he wriggled in search of a more comfortable position, he noticed that it was starting to get light. He gave up and rolled out of the hammock.

His bruises and abrasions hurt more than they had when he first received them, but at least the headache had gone away. He limped to the freshwater jug and took a long drink, then negotiated the smooth stone terraces of his tidal shelf garden and carefully pissed on a tangleweed. The bone-white fronds were beautiful in theory, but it gave him a lot of satisfaction to see them shrinking away from him.

"That's right—fear and worship me, the giant from another world," he muttered.

The sun hadn't cleared the horizon. Possibly he would still have time to pick up his samples before Sushan arrived at the clinic. He splashed his face with another handful of freshwater, ran his wet fingers through his hair, stepped into his skinsuit—wincing as he pulled it tight over bruises—and hurried down the path.

When he came to the tide pools, he stopped abruptly. The water was low, and many of the glowstars lay quiet, with their spiky fronds folded together until the water returned. But large clumps had been torn from the colonies. The faded shells of the little organisms lay scattered over the rocks. Something had torn them from their bases, sucked out the tender interior, and discarded the hard, spiky tendrils.

Per's first angry thought was that some human had done it maliciously, but if that were true, why would the human have gone to the trouble of ripping out the interiors and carrying them away? Glowstar meat was inedible to humans. It had an unpleasant bitterness that induced vomiting after just a few mouthfuls. The beach was too rocky and gravely at that point to provide clues in the form of footprints. It looked very much as if an unknown predator had attacked his carefully tended colony. He remembered the splashes he had heard the night before.

*Live and learn*, he thought sourly. *Never dismiss paranoia. It's a very useful call to action.*

Doubletide was going out. The current was strong enough that he was able to fall into the water as if into his hammock, and allow the tide to carry him most of the way from his house to the point near the clinic. There he had to work to swim out of the current before bumping into the fish pens, but by then the pleasant touch of the water had eased his stiffness a bit.

\* \* \*

Another being also found joyful ease in returning to the water.

*This darktime I, Subtle, have eaten the changed food of intelligent creatures from the Dry.*

Subtle made a brief, elegant dance fragment out of it. He wasn't ready to create a complex, convincing pattern freighted with evidence and carefully weighed conclusions. However, he *was* very pleased with his own daring and enjoyed repeating the body memory at intervals throughout the brightness.

He had found beds of twentyspike-small-shine-in-the-darks in a place near the Dry where they should not have been able to grow. Shinies liked places where the water tasted strong, but the water there had been feeble, like water that flowed into the Deep from the Big Dry, or water that fell from beyond the sky edge. The shinies had tasted weak, too, like the water they grew in.

Perhaps they were a new kind of shiny that had come to the edge of the water and changed by themselves. But he did not think so. He had followed the clusters of shinies along the edge of the rock, and had come to a place where the rock was smooth and washed by the sea. He had been able to climb there easily and explore.

It was his second time in the Dry. Still it burned him when he tried to breathe, and rasped his skin, but the sensations were easier to bear because they were no longer completely new. He knew now that the Dry would not kill him—at least, not right away.

On the smooth rocks were many smells that were strange to him. And there was more changed life. He saw short growth like stiff weed, but dry, with hard stems like coral. His senses reeled with astonishment when he found thin twists of mademetal among their branches.

His senses did not work as well in the Dry, but a trickle of water running across the stone brought him the warning signature of the White Arms. In the same moment, he tasted the powerful substance that had driven off the White Arms by the reef. He dared to approach. The White Arms stretched toward him but could not reach his place on the rock. He quivered with fear and excitement at staying so near to it and remaining untouched. The arms were short, too short to snare him, and all around them was the powerful smell. It stung his eyes and skin, but it was a smell of intelligence, a smell made by creatures that changed other beings. Something—some*one*—had planted shinies that could live in weak water, had put metal on plants, had planted the White Arms and then imprisoned it and kept it small.

His dance degenerated into messageless emoting, but he did not care, for his fellow scientists were not there to mock him. *Rejoice, rejoice, rejoice, says Subtle of the Round People!*

Per found the clinic deserted. The beds were empty of patients. The night aide had gone to sleep in Melicar's napping hammock. Per went to the cooler and found his tissue samples.

He divided them carefully, labeling portions and storing them in the tiny freezer, then preparing other portions for the centrifuge. He checked to make sure the centrifuge was fully charged up. He placed other solutions in the incubator. His moving about in the back office awakened the night aide— Dilmun Elsker, one of the original engineering crew. Per stuck a DO NOT DISTURB sign on the incubator.

"Tell Sushan not to touch this," he said to Dilmun. "It's very important. Understand?"

Dilmun nodded, yawning, and hitched herself laboriously out of the hammock. A tree had fallen on her in last year's worst typhoon, crushing her pelvis, femur, and two vertebrae. Though Melicar had not been sure she would ever get out of bed again, today she could walk, in a halting, sidewise fashion. Per knew that she would not report him for unauthorized use of medical equipment. He had helped to dig her out from beneath the tree trunk.

"I'll be back for these around lunchtime," he said. He decided against stopping for breakfast in the dining hall, and trudged back down the point to his own house.

He prepared his gel sheets—that at least was easy to do, using gel made from the wide variety of sea plants—but it didn't take long. He opened his notebook and recorded the discussions of the previous night, making his observations from memory. That took longer, but he still had some time before his other materials would be ready.

He wandered down to the water's edge. Doubletide going out had exposed a large bed of the bladdermoss he used to make one type of gel. He plucked up a few handfuls, picked them over to remove the tough bladder pods, and chewed them by way of lunch. They had a strong flavor, not unlike caraway, and were fibrous but fairly nourishing. He felt a brief stab of sadness; Doi Ru had been the first to analyze the qualities of the moss.

Several patterns were working to clarify themselves in his mind, but he could no more hurry them than he could hurry the sorting process taking place in the centrifuge. He went back into the house to get his pouch of tools. Then he forced himself to sit calmly on his garden terrace until his eyes adjusted to the scale of the miniature grove before him. Only a hint of the beauty he imagined for it had yet appeared.

He had gathered his first set of trees on the mountain cone of the first island, the one they had assumed to be dormant, as he had climbed with Sukarto Ru. Even now, the sight of the salt-wet foliage on one narrow-leafed tree plunged him back into memories, and he reached for his notebook, never beyond arm's length. He did not need to unfold it to remember the exact date recorded there.

He had accompanied Sukarto on a three-day climb up the peak. The forest that clung to the steep slopes had astonished him with its beauty. Per had loved the northern forests of Skandia, but in those woodlands, one type of conifer alone might cover hundreds of square miles, with a mere scattering of undergrowth clinging to the thin soil. Such forests had provided Per with no vocabulary to describe the variegated richness of Typhon's shining glades, floored with moss and fronded bushes. The forest shimmered with as many shades of green as the sea boasted shades of blue.

The diversity of fauna had been remarkable, too. Per had seen hundreds of different forms of snakes and spiders, more than he had ever imagined. He had even glimpsed several slow-moving creatures that appeared to have fur, and carried young in a manner reminiscent of marsupials. He had been anxious to examine one of them, but Sukarto had been eager to press on up the peak. He hadn't seen any predators large enough to threaten a human—not then, at any rate. The slender, fan-shaped trees had held a multitude of emerald, crimson, and yellow tree frogs and lizards, their colors bright and wet as fresh paint.

He had glimpsed all these riches only in passing, as he stumbled up behind Sukarto, trying simultaneously to keep his footing, record pictures, and clip specimens of foliage and flowers. He had found a few odd moments to take notes and catch his breath when Sukarto paused to examine rock formations—at least, when Sukarto wasn't in need of assistance to belay him while he hung out over a cliff face chipping out samples.

As always, Sukarto had lectured breathlessly as they went along. He had never been able to accept that other people might not find rocks fascinating. Per had been amused, but he had listened carefully. In a colony so small, useful knowledge had to be shared.

Sukarto had explained to him that the cone of rock that formed the foundation of their island was largely composed of rocks called ignimbrite and tephra. Per had watched him slide down a steep slope and disappear into head-high vegetation to examine a fan of rubble. Sukarto had emerged triumphantly with some samples of what he announced was pumice.

Per smiled at the memory. In the process Sukarto had dislodged half a dozen bright-colored snakes. Per hadn't had a chance to find out if they were venomous or not, since they fled precipitously from the geologist's thrashing about.

Once Sukarto had recovered his composure, he told Per that the composition of the rocks confirmed his theory—that the island chain was a series of arc volcanoes. When Per had asked him what significance this held for the colony, Sukarto had sobered up a little.

Per could still remember the exact look of Sukarto delivering that lecture while they stood on the rocky path with the sweat cooling on their shoulders. Sukarto had tilted his head and blinked at something off to the left, the very model of a bemused expert trying to think how to explain to the layman.

"Well, first of all," he had said, in his best "I'll make this as simple as I can" tone, "first of all, and quite obviously, Typhon follows the same tectonic pattern as Skandia. In fact, Typhon is closer to Sol-Terra–normal. Skandia is small, cold, and perilously close to the lower limit of sufficient crustal movement to create Terraform life conditions. Typhon is *very* active volcanically. Although the land-to-sea ratio is smaller than Terranorm, much smaller than Skandia's, volcanic action is constantly building up land masses.

"So! This island arc is volcanic, and is perched in a zone between a spreading rift on the sea floor and a subducting trench, where a portion of one plate sinks under the edge of another. Such zones are known for their violent potential.

"Now, secondly, such volcanic action as there is on Skandia is mainly geothermal—hot springs and so forth. And the lava in those areas is mainly basaltic."

At that point, Sukarto had digressed into a discussion of the chemical composition of rocks, and Per had nudged him back to their particular island. It turned out that basaltic lava, like that on Skandia, tended to flow freely, with few of what Sukarto called "pyroclastic effects."

"These islands where we are, on the other hand—" Sukarto had continued with some relish. "—the volcanos that formed *them* spewed rhyolitic lavas. These are sticky and form plugs that explode with tremendous violence, as proved by these rock samples. Ignimbrites are formed by the fusion of pyroclastic fragments, red-hot bits of rock that fly through the air like rock shrapnel, or surge downslope in incandescent clouds of fragments and gas. Same for this bit of pumice—lightweight rock like this forms when gas bubbles expand within the lava under tremendous heat. Then—*pow!*"

He had made an expansive gesture like a child playing meltdown.

"You might say these islands are solidified clouds. But red-hot clouds, laced with lightning and black ash, not nice fluffy white clouds."

He had been packing up his samples. At that point, he had started to scramble upward again with fresh enthusiasm.

"Is there a danger that this peak might explode again?" Per had called after him, trying to catch up on legs that had stiffened during the pause.

Sukarto had shrugged.

"Depends on how old it is, how long dormant, how far it's drifted from the original hot spot. I want to see the caldera before guessing that."

In Per's recollection, the slope had become near vertical as they continued. They had climbed part of the way on ropes, but Sukarto had halted at the first good ledge. Per had never been an expert climber, and Sukarto knew when to be cautious.

They'd rested, had a bite to eat, and then scrambled around until they found a notch in the lip of the caldera where an old flow had poured out, leaving a lower and less steep route to the caldera's interior. They had made their way up that handy ramp, and had finally perched on the top looking down on a sight that had inspired awe.

The caldera had looked old to Per. Grown over with vegetation, like the lower slopes, it had been a little pocket world, a cupped hand holding a toy garden up to the sun. Per's mind had raced in circles at such an excess of riches. He had been wild to explore the differences in species that might be observed within the walls of the caldera.

Before they left, late in the afternoon, Sukarto had showed Per through the scopes how a trail of white vapor vented from somewhere down below and mingled with the mist.

"Our island may be old as volcanoes go," Sukarto had said, "but there's still fire hidden deep down inside."

Fascinated, Per had tried to persuade Sukarto to go down to the floor of the crater, but Sukarto had insisted that they concentrate on taking samples near the rim. They could come back with a larger party, he had said. After all, there was no hurry. They had the rest of their lives to explore.

"The rest of our lives," Per sighed. For Sukarto, that had been a very short time. It was hard to realize that that richness of fauna and flora had been completely destroyed. Nothing remained of that mountain garden but a smoking stub of volcanic cinder.

Per's carefully nurtured miniature forest had gone with it, of course, but that loss had been insignificant when compared to the others they had suffered. If the new set of trees lived, he might name one of them for Sukarto, and try to preserve some hint of the qualities of his friend in his shaping of the tree.

His eyes took refuge in the subtle variations of color and leaf form. He ran his hand over the saltmoss beneath the trees, velvet soft and dewed with spray, and calm deepened around him like a rising tide. The angle of a shadow clarified an idea for him, and he reached for his small clippers and a bit of wire. The branch could curve *so*—

A footstep grated on the stone terrace, and he turned quickly. The clipper blades snapped together as his fist clenched.

"Sorry. I didn't mean to startle you."

It was Melicar.

"Good morning, Sushan," Per said grudgingly.

The doctor peered curiously over his shoulder.

"Do you mind if I look at your trees?" she asked.

"Yes, but I suppose you're going to do it anyway. You're interrupting me. Don't you have some work to do?"

"Yes," she said calmly. "I was planning to run some blood tests, but you have preempted my centrifuge. I see it's set for a long run, so I'll have to recharge it before I can use it. I have nothing better to do in the meanwhile. I wish you would ask me first."

"That would be making you an accessory to my misconduct," Per said. "I'm forbidden to use the medical equipment, remember?"

"You'd better let me know next time, anyway. Or you could find that I've thrown out your project. I'm not afraid of Whitman and the committee."

"Speaking of Whitman, what is going on between him and Roon? I saw them cozying up at the trial last night."

"You overdramatize. That wasn't a trial; it was just a hearing. You did lacerate Torker's ear rather badly. Poor man! There's obsession for you. You should try to avoid conflict with him."

" 'Poor man'!" Per said. "He was crushing me."

He tried to turn his shoulder on Melicar and return to the trees, but the moment was gone. He fumbled with the wires. He knew what he wanted to accomplish, but approaching it with the right attitude always seemed to affect the outcome.

"What are you doing?" Melicar asked, leaning over his shoulder again to watch.

"Persuading the trees. Back on Skandia, I could have accomplished this by snipping and restricting the twists of the tree's DNA. Now I have to do my snipping with a pruning knife and bit of wire."

"But don't you hurt the tree? Damage it?" Melicar asked.

"No. I'm helping it. From genes that are essentially the same as any other tree's, I help it reach this unique expression. I help it become something marvelous, something normally beyond its reach. This is its highest form."

"According to you. What gives you the right to change its destiny?"

Per smoothed the curve he had just wired.

"Maybe I have no right. Maybe I stand condemned as a torturer of plants, a disturber of the natural order. As I see it, I only copy what the winds and weathers do: create a few shapes like this, shapes we see as beauty. Joy in invention, in variation—is that completely out of harmony with the scheme of things? I hope not. I hope there's a margin on the edges of the great pattern for decoration, for experimentation. For play."

"Oh, I see. So you're playing with their lives. Yet you reject any attempt by the community to reshape *your* habits."

Per laid down his clippers.

"Playing with sharp instruments today, are we?" he said. "You think I'm clay that talks back to the potter? As I recall, that parable was told of a man who mouthed off to god. I'm afraid I decline to place the compact in so lofty a position. If they wish to exercise their pruning hands on me, they had best spend as much time and effort to study me as I have spent on this plant."

He heard other footsteps coming through his house. The feet sounded heavily and unevenly, making no effort to be unobtrusive. It was Dilani.

"Hell!" Per exclaimed. "What is this, a convention? Is this still my house?"

"I asked Dilani to bring over your materials when they were ready," Melicar said.

Per slapped a hand to his forehead in consternation.

"Don't worry. I told her to be very careful," Melicar said as Per accepted the package from Dilani. "I thought you were going to teach her. You might as well teach her about lab technique."

"Thank you *so* much," Per said, keeping his temper with difficulty. "Now will you please go on back to your clinic so I can get some work done?"

"No, I will not," Melicar said calmly. "As you pointed out, you are implicating me in your misbehavior. I insist on finding out what you're doing."

Per shrugged. Perhaps she anticipated a fight, but she wasn't going to get one.

"There's no reason for you to be suspicious. This is purely investigative."

He moved to the small table where he had set up his equipment, and tested to make sure that the current from his solar-powered generator was full and steady.

"As you can see, I've already prepared the gel," he said to Melicar. He spelled out *g-e-l* for Dilani—it seemed easier than inventing a sign—but *electrophoresis* made him pause. He finally settled on *electric-current-carrying*.

"In this solution—this water—" he said, showing her the vials of separated components, "there are tiny fragments of body and blood, too small to see. I put them in here—" He dropped each solution carefully into its well. "—and I run electric current through the gel. Current in water pushes big things partway up the shore, little things farther, doesn't it? Big pebbles here, little pebbles there, then sand?" He drew the striations for her with his hands. She frowned and then nodded. "Electric current does the same with things too small to see. Lines them up, sorts them—here, in the gel."

Dilani looked closely and shrugged. She couldn't see anything happening.

"Now we wait," he explained.

While they waited, they passed the time wandering around Per's terrace.

Dilani pointed questioningly at the tangleweed.

"Yes, tangleweed," he signed.

"Kill it," she signed decidedly.

"No, no," he signed, laughing. "That is my tangleweed teacher. I learn from this tangleweed how to kill weed out in the sea. This tangleweed helps me."

A wandering beach fly buzzed too close to the delicate white tendrils, tasting them to see if they held edible sap. With a snap, a cluster of fronds closed around the insect. It buzzed furiously for an instant, then fell silent. Shortly the fronds opened again, dropping a small winged husk.

Melicar kicked sand in the weed's direction.

"That's disgusting."

"On the contrary," Per said. "Tangleweed is so ingenious. I find it fascinating. It's already given us the crude toxin extract for anesthesia, and its chemical compounds are so complex, I'm sure we'll find dozens of other uses, if not hundreds. Organisms dangerous to humans often are so precisely because they have made such clever use of their inherent resources, and for that very reason they are likely to present us with great opportunities.

"At the moment, I'm still working on discovering the weed's weaknesses—and on how to control it. Once I reduce the danger factor, I'll be able to see how it can help us. It was sheer luck that I found out how to dwarf it. That makes it much easier to study."

"You've turned this whole tidal shelf into an experimental garden," Melicar said accusingly.

"Not quite."

"What happens when the typhoons come? Won't this all be destroyed?"

"Well, think about it, Sushan. The typhoons come every year, and somehow the atoll still carries a rich burden of life. Either the organisms are very resistant to typhoon damage, or it may even be beneficial to them in some way. I hope to observe its effects here, where I know just what I've planted, and even out on the reef, in areas where I've carefully recorded what grows naturally.

"I should get some answers there, too. For instance, I know how much force it takes to pry various molluscs off their rocks. I've encouraged a carefully graded series to take up residence here, starting below the lowest tides and continuing up the rocks past the highest point I expect the storm surge to reach. I'll be able to find out what force the waves have along the point. I hope. Once it would have been a simple matter of measurements with instruments, but now that the instruments are gone, I have to get the world itself to tell me these things."

Sushan stayed until the first set of gel sheets were finished. She watched Per set up a second set and begin to fix the first results on synthetic membrane.

"I made this myself, too, obviously," he said. "This is just one of the many reasons I don't have time to waste on work roster assignments."

"I can see you're working wonders in a prehistoric sort of way," Melicar said. "But what's the point of all this?"

"I know what I'm hoping to see. The actual results may not

be ready till the end of the week. I'll come down to the clinic
and show you, if you don't think letting me use the computer
will implicate you in too much misbehavior. In the meantime
I believe Dilani and I will go fishing. So you can tell anyone
official, if you see them, that I am hard at work as ordered."

## 6

Dilani liked working at Per's house, though she didn't understand why he wanted her to do certain things. The work was clever. It involved following steps in order, measuring things exactly, and making things fit together neatly. It took concentration.

Everything Per did had a reason behind it. She didn't mind following his orders, because they usually led to an interesting result. When other people failed to explain things to her, it made her furious. They just didn't want to be bothered with her. However, she accepted it when Per said he couldn't explain. She had seen other adults puzzled by what Per said. He really did know things that were hard to explain. Possibly if she imitated him well enough, she would come to understand those things as he did.

When she signed that she was hungry, he didn't scold her; he gave her things to eat. They were strange things, and some of them tasted terrible, but they were interesting: pink worms from under the sand, shiny grubs from under the bark of trees, scalloped fungus, bladdermoss, fish eggs, creeper buds. The island was like a cupboard full of peculiar snacks. It was no wonder that Per seldom bothered to show up at the dining hall for spud mash and fried fish.

Sometimes Dilani put her hands over her eyes and wondered if Per had done something to them when she wasn't looking. She saw things everywhere that hadn't seemed to be there before.

Between times of intense work in Per's house, she spent hours with him in the water beyond the reef. They set out bait and even lured and speared several large, meaty deep-sea fish, but Dilani knew Per wasn't really interested in fishing. He was looking for the ketos.

Dilani followed him into deep water, the true Deep. They went down past the sparkling surface, with its myriad of tiny creatures shimmering in changing golds and greens overlaid on the water's blue, into the darkening twilight where shadow and solid were hard to tell apart. There was no sandy bottom there, no comforting landmarks of coral, like houses full of bright-colored neighbors. The Deep was everything. Dilani felt its power surge around her. Subtle pressures swayed her, like invisible fins of a great beast that only tested her before exerting all its strength.

Sometimes she stared into the indigo depths. They frightened her and compelled her, and they reminded her of the day the mountain had burned. There had been something in the Deep then. Secretly she called it a "voice" because it had come to her from outside, but she had not seen it. She was sure it would give her knowledge, if only she could understand it.

One day Per found her floating motionless, staring into the Deep, and he had to shake her repeatedly before she responded. He wouldn't let her go into the water for two days after that, and even then he watched her closely all the time. He tried to explain to her that there was danger in deep water, something that would get into her blood and maybe kill her or cause great pain. But she didn't really believe him. It seemed implausible; she had been in deep water before, and he had never acted frightened. He was afraid to see her "listening," she thought, so she kept it to herself after that, and felt smug that there was one thing she did that he couldn't understand.

They fished in every place Per had ever seen ketos, but the creatures did not appear. Per wondered if they had left the area forever. He continued his work with the tissue samples. If a smear of blood was the last he would ever see of the ketos, he didn't want to waste it.

One morning he asked Melicar to meet him in the hospital early, before the others were up.

"If I may use your computer for a few minutes, I'm ready to show you the final assembly of the analysis you found so suspicious earlier this week," he said when she arrived.

The request was pro forma. In fact, he had been using the computer since moonset, long before dawn. He waited while a copy of the results printed out on reusable sheet. It showed a series of vertical bands striped with different densities of color.

A single glance at the distinct stripes told him he had found what he was looking for, though he wasn't sure exactly what it was.

"Yes. Yes!" he said softly, holding the sheet so tightly that it crinkled. Melicar tried in vain to see around him.

"What is it?"

He laid it on the table, still unwilling to let go of it.

"It's a hybridization analysis," he said.

"Well, I can see that," she said impatiently. "Congratulations. But what's the point?"

He took a deep breath.

"I digested DNA samples with a restriction enzyme—"

She interrupted him. "Skip the methodology lecture. Just give me the results."

"You won't believe it unless I walk you through it."

"You can tell me later, after I decide if it's worth my time."

"Worth your time?" He came close to raising his voice. "All right, bite on this: That sheet demonstrates that we have DNA sequences in common with the ketos."

"You've gone to a lot of work for nothing, if that's what you're so excited about. We already know there are quite a few analogies between us and the Typhon fauna. We have to have proteins in common or we wouldn't be able to eat them, and vice versa. I hope you're not trying to imply that we came from the same evolutionary sequence, because I'd be forced to conclude that you really have gone crazy."

"Come on, Sushan, use your head! Look at this and tell me what you see."

She frowned at the sheet.

"Tumor viruses. It looks like a standard diagnostic test for a retrovirus."

"Exactly!" Per said with satisfaction. "I used samples from newgens and those blood and tissue samples from Slow-bolt that you saved for me. Newgen and keto DNA shares the same viral inclusions. I've finally found something definite that is present in the environment and in the damaged newgens—and that could theoretically have caused the damage."

"How is that possible? Are you thinking that the ketos somehow infected us? We hadn't even encountered ketos when the first children were born. And your keto isn't genetically damaged, is he? How could one virus be responsible for so many separate effects?"

"I can't tell you—yet. I don't think Slowbolt is abnormal, and I haven't seen any damaged ketos—or any keto offspring, for that matter. When Lesper and I were working on this during the first years, we tried to match the newgens' DNA against many different viral samples from the environment. We never found any correlation.

"We assumed that what we were looking for would be found in something close to us. I don't know how our genetic problems could be related to ketos, but you see my results in front of you. Maybe there's a third source of infection that contacted both groups. But the point is, we have a step forward!"

Melicar nodded, but she didn't look as stirred as he had expected.

"I understand your excitement. But it's still a very theoretical step, isn't it? I can't see the application, unless you think you can find a way to block the virus. Frankly, that's pretty unlikely, since we don't even know what it is or where it comes from. All we've got here are its traces, long after it has penetrated the body."

"Of course there are all kinds of questions," Per asserted. "But they can be answered. If we put all our remaining resources into pursuing this—"

Melicar shook her head.

"That's even more unlikely. If you spent more time with the community, you'd know that they're looking for short-term solutions. You know I'm with you, but look at it from their point of view. They may not be completely wrong. Building a vaccine for the ovine dystrophic virus on Skandia took five years, even with the entire medical industry working on it, and OVD is relatively simple. We may not have even that long."

"You don't know how difficult it will be till we've tried. I don't know why you hesitate. Do we have an alternative? Show me an alternative solution!"

She stared at the sheet, apparently preoccupied.

"Where did you get your human samples?"

"I used an assortment of the newgens. I tried to pick a variety of conditions, to see if the same virus would be present in all of them. I've only included half a dozen in this series, but now that I know I've got results, it would be easy to test the others. Easy, but pointless. This is the cause, I'm sure of it."

Her lips were pinched together by an unpleasant thought.

"All right," he said. "I know I violated their privacy by stealing samples. I apologize. It's easier to apologize than it is to get permission."

"That's not what I was thinking about," she said absently. "Did you take any samples from adults?"

"No, I didn't." That question caught him by surprise. "I assumed that it couldn't have affected the adults, because none of them showed any symptoms."

"Never assume anything," she said. "Run some tests on adults. You can check me and yourself, of course. I'll get you other samples."

"Sushan, you don't have to get involved. You should at least wait until I get permission from the forum."

"What can they do to me? I'm the only doctor they have left. Just do it, Per."

He looked at her more closely.

"You have something on your mind, don't you?"

"I don't want to prejudice you," she said, "so I'm not going to tell you until you've had time to draw your own conclusions. But I'd like you to find out as quickly as you can."

Another general meeting was scheduled for the following week. Per had been skipping his discussion group, as usual, and heard about the meeting through Melicar.

"You really should try to spend more time with the group," she said. "How can you hope to get their cooperation when you treat them as if they aren't worth talking to?"

"I'm busy scoping their DNA," Per said. "That's as intimate as I want to be with them."

He worked hurriedly to learn as much as he could before the night of the meeting. He was tempted to stop doing Torker's fishing work, but he didn't want another complaint brought up against him at that particular meeting. So he continued to fish and look for the ketos with Dilani during the day, and he worked late into the night on the hospital computer.

He was surprised and disturbed to find that adults in the colony seemed to have been contaminated with the virus, as well. Melicar had given him numbered samples without names, but it did not matter which sample belonged to whom. All showed similar stretches of inserted genes.

That only made him more determined than ever to present his findings at the meeting. Perhaps there was a secondary site that determined how expression of those genes would affect the organism. Perhaps the virus targeted fetal tissue, or was restrained by an adult immune system. There were many possibilities, and he would need a concerted effort by the rest of the colony in order to explore them.

The night of the meeting was stuffy and overcast. Looking up at a starless sky, Per felt uneasy. The stars were always visible, except during storm season when it rained so hard that no one looked for them.

The weather had been strange all day. Storm clouds had

arisen in the afternoon, as they should, and had towered above the island as the heat grew tyrannical. But instead of the expected downpour, a restless hot wind had come and pushed the towers around the sky till sunset, when darker clouds closed in for a stifling, humid night.

Per reminded himself that two years of observation at this location hardly constituted a valid statistical base. He had spoken to Henner Vik, the meteorologist, and Henner had only shrugged and said that she expected rain any day.

Per had gone to the trouble of digging out and putting on a faded pair of shorts and a vest that still bore the official logo of the Typhon Exploratory Team, with the seal of the Rationality of Skandia appended. He passed the hospital and noticed that it was dark for the first time he could remember. Apparently word had spread. No one, not even a night aide, would be missing the meeting. Melicar stepped out of her tiny living quarters as he passed. She stumbled as she crossed the boardwalk to the sandy path, and he caught her elbow.

"Are you all right?" he said.

"More or less. I'm tired, and my scars are bothering me, I think. The adhesions inflame periodically and I lose mobility in my joints. It seems a bit worse than usual. My balance is off."

She sighed. "Maybe it's the weather—this perpetual feeling that the storm is about to break. I dread the storm season, but I wish we could get it over with."

"Doctors shouldn't treat themselves," Per said. "What would happen if you got sick?"

"Oh, I suppose Dilmun could nurse me. She has spent enough time filling in at the clinic that she at least knows how to distill and inject tangleweed."

"Yes, but what you need is a doctor. Haven't you ever thought of training a successor?"

Melicar waved a hand listlessly.

"You're right, of course, and Whitman is always on at me about the same thing. But really—do you see a medical academy around here? How can I even teach the basics of anatomy? We haven't the most rudimentary scanning devices."

"It isn't my specialty, but they had doctors in the pre–Flight Era, so there must be something we could do to heal ourselves, even after our supplies run out."

"Perhaps we need not worry. At this rate we will run out before the supplies do," the doctor said.

When they reached the dining hall, it was already crowded. They pushed their way to the back to find a seat atop one of the tables that had been moved against the wall.

Per's forehead crinkled in a puzzled frown as he mentally checked off faces. Torker Fensila's bulk was notable in its absence. Miko Narayan and Kee Benksen were also missing

Before Per had time to count up the other absentees, Whitman stepped into the circle. Per listened, hoping he would find an explanation there. He expected introductory remarks, followed by tedious reports from the focus groups. However, Whitman began in strained tones that were unlike his usual soothing manner.

"I'm not going to call on group leaders tonight. I've been receiving reports from the discussion groups all week, as have the other members of the steering committee, and we've decided that a consensus is clear enough to warrant closing down the discussion. Making a decisive commitment to action is imperative now—more important than further voicing of opinions.

"The steering committee and its scientific advisors have reached a decision which we now present. Phillips?"

Roon moved into the circle next to Sayid, his tall, stooping figure overshadowing the chairman. Listeners shifted impatiently as he cleared his throat and peered at a notepad.

"Please bear in mind that I am reporting facts to you, not expressing my opinion," he said. "Statistical analysis of the population shows that we are on the edge of an irrevocable slide to extinction. If the rainy season brings continued attrition to our population at the average rate—I am, of course, excluding the year of the disaster, though it should be borne in mind that disaster could reoccur at any time—we will lose even the possibility of maintaining our numbers within the next five years. We must reproduce now, or resign ourselves to losing our foothold on this planet."

As a murmur began, he raised a hand to forestall interruptions.

"Yes, I know that reproduction is problematic. But in the face of certain death, we must take action, however low the probability of success. It is the consensus of the steering committee that we must go ahead with the action proposed at the last meeting, and proceed with planned breeding as soon as possible."

A hubbub broke out immediately. Angry compact members lunged for the speaker's ring, and others held them back. Roon held to the center, raising the notepad like a shield. His face was heavily flushed and perspiring, and his fingers trembled visibly as he clutched the pad. He continued to read from his notes.

"Volunteer group leaders have been selected to oversee the process. You will be contacted by your group leader, who will explain further procedures."

Uli Haddad waded through the crowd to stand nose to nose with Phillips.

"We're not going to put up with this," he shouted. "What do you think you're doing? The steering committee can't push this on us without our consent. We'll resist—with force, if necessary."

They were so unused to force that Uli didn't even know how to make a fist, Per thought ruefully. He and Torker were the only two men on Refuge who had ever raised hands to each other in anger, and they might be the only ones for whom a fight would have been possible.

He looked across the room to the far door and saw Torker himself framed in the opening. In one big hand he carried the harpoon gun. Pain stirred warningly in Per's head.

Whitman Sayid stood up on a chair to get his head above the crowd. They were so accustomed to listening that even now they quieted to hear what he would say.

"We knew this would be a very stressful and conflicted

time," he said. "Naturally we all have profound misgivings, but we are convinced this is the only way to save our colony. We wanted to ensure that no one would do anything he or she might regret, under the stress of the moment.

"Uli speaks of using force. We don't want others to become hysterical and hurt themselves, so we have taken the precaution of collecting all items that might possibly be used as weapons. Those that also serve as tools will be handed out at the discretion of the steering committee, under supervision from one of the peace officers you now see stationed around the hall."

He nodded toward Fensila, Narayan, Benksen, and other large, strong individuals, most of whom were carrying potentially lethal fishing gear.

"If you find yourself in conflict with other compact members, you can appeal to these officers for help," Whitman said.

Per saw Torker's eyes pause on him for a moment. Torker was smiling. As soon as his gaze had passed on, Per slid off the table and began to worm his way through the crowd toward the front.

Bader Puntherong's father had already joined Haddad.

"You dare to bring weapons in here, to a forum meeting?" he shouted in outrage. "I demand you disarm those men and tell them to sit down."

He took a step toward Torker. The fish boss raised the harpoon gun automatically.

"They wouldn't dare fire on us," Uli Haddad shouted. "And if they did, they couldn't hit us all. Rush him!"

Others nearby were too confused to join in; only Haddad and Puntherong rushed for the door. Torker looked confused too. He backed away, but continued to aim the gun. Per's head now throbbed so fiercely that it was hard to keep his balance, but he kept working his way through the crowd.

Writhing through the packed front rows, he burst through at the same time as Haddad. He saw the look in Torker's eyes and tackled Haddad just as the gun went off. The harpoon bolt tore a gash in Puntherong's arm and shot through the hall just above the heads of the crowd, to bury itself in the far wall. The *thunk* of its impact was clearly audible in the sudden, frozen silence. Puntherong's grunt of pain followed immediately.

"Let me through," Melicar cried. She was applying pressure to the wound in seconds.

"The gun misfired," Torker said. "I didn't mean—"

"Run to the hospital and get my kit," Melicar ordered. "In the cabinet, on the center shelf."

Torker laid the gun down and ducked out.

"It's not serious," Melicar said. "But it could have been!" She glared at Sayid. "Clear the weapons—yes, I said weapons—out of this hall immediately. Are we going to be reduced to the level of killing each other? Better extinction than that!"

The big men had stepped down from the doorways, spearguns and gaffs dangling uncertainly from their hands. The tension was defused for the moment.

"Apologies for this very unfortunate incident," Whitman said, his voice trembling slightly. "I think it demonstrates graphically the need for unusual measures. I will now read the list of volunteer group leaders."

Per slipped out of the hall amid the ensuing confusion, and walked back to the hospital, which now stood open with the lights on and the door ajar. The wind had continued rising, but it wasn't blowing the clouds away. They seemed to be piling up, darker and deeper. Per left the door open and gulped the slightly cooler air. If he made his mind a complete blank, the pain diminished somewhat. He hoped Sushan would come back soon and that he could talk her out of a couple of Skandian painkillers. And there was something else he had to do.

Sushan arrived, finally, carrying the emergency kit as if it were very heavy. Her face was drawn with exhaustion. Usually Per saw the expression in the undamaged half of her face and ignored the scars. That night, the scar tissue seemed to be dragging down the unharmed side.

"You were right," he said as soon as she was in hearing distance. "I should have spent more time with the group. I should have seen this coming. Hell, what sheep they are. They'd let Whitman walk on their heads and bark if he told them it was for the good of the compact."

"Just hold the diatribe for a minute," she said. "I need to sit down."

She limped to the cooler, poured two glasses of fruit juice, and sat down heavily.

"There's nothing you could have done even if you had foreseen it," she said. "Whitman is a genius of consensus politics. The Rationality really missed out when they sent him here. They'll go along with him not because he is forcing them to, but because he has discerned what they really want and is making it easier for them. They could never have come to an agreement about it through discussion, but they're relieved to have the decision taken out of their hands. Once they get over the shock, there will be no significant opposition."

"What about you?" Per challenged her. "You can't believe this is all right. Are you going to lend your services to this cattle-breeding program? Are you going to euthanize Roon's 'nonfunctional' offspring when they come along?"

She looked up, and when he saw her clear-eyed despair he felt a little ashamed.

"This ship is going down, Per," she said. "I'll do my best to save what I can. Perhaps Whitman is right, and we will have another generation to care for. At any rate they'll have a few months of hope. After that, it may be taken out of my hands."

"What do you mean?"

"Your retrovirus. Whether it's responsible for the newgens or not, can we be sure it hasn't affected the adults? There are many examples of slow viruses that eventually damage or kill. I'm no longer sure that the weakness and discoordination I'm feeling are the result of my injuries alone. I think there's some kind of neurological problem.

"And Torker—after he hit you, I began to watch him more closely. He has outbursts of irrational anger more and more frequently. That could be psychological, of course, but I wonder. He's always been an angry man, but in the old days he would never have used violence. I'm keeping a file of minor complaints that people report to me, and that I can't find any cause for. It's a thick file now, and I'm beginning to see that the problems circle around certain areas, just like the newgens' problems."

It took a moment for Per to focus on this entirely new set of questions.

"You mean that some of what's happening here may be the result of brain damage?"

Unexpectedly, Melicar laughed.

"That's an oversimplification," she said, when her laughter died away, "but yes, it's possible. Paranoia, megalomania— the problem is, those are fairly common human behaviors, as well as symptoms of something gone awry in the brain chemistry."

This wasn't what Per had come for, but she had given him something new to think about.

"Brain chemistry . . . If you're right, could these changes affect memory?"

She looked alarmed. "Why? Are you experiencing memory loss?"

"No. More the opposite. I'm remembering things best forgotten." He brushed the questions aside. None of them could affect his decision.

"I came to say goodbye," he said abruptly. "After tonight, I have no choice. If I stay, I'll have to participate in Roon's breeding experiment, and I refuse. My life and my body are my own. I'd rather give them up entirely than submit to use them at Sayid's behest. Or Roon's! Allfather! The compact has a right to require my work, but the committee doesn't own me. I'm going."

He added something he hadn't meant to say.

"Want to come?"

But he knew Melicar's answer before she shook her head.

"I can't leave people who depend on me, and who may be sicker than they know. It would be desertion. And just where in Hell's kingdom do you think you can go, anyway?"

Per took a deep breath.

"Out to the open sea, to find the ketos."

"I thought you would just sail down to the next atoll and wait till spring! That would be risky enough. Why on Typhon would you head out into the Deep?"

"I've wanted to do that ever since I met the ketos. They migrate. To get a complete picture of their life, I have to find out where they go. I might learn how they reproduce, and get some clue to the origin of the virus. I put off acting on this because I wanted to present my findings to the forum and get permission for an expedition. Now that I have to leave anyway, I may as well do that as anything else. You can tell them after I've gone, if you like."

He hesitated; there was more that he could tell her, but he wondered if it was really necessary. He was tempted to go away without saying anything. It would be easier. His head still throbbed, making it hard to think. If he went back to his own house without speaking, it would stop. While he hesitated, someone tapped at the door, and then entered without waiting to ask permission.

The group that shuffled inside was small, no more than five or six, but enough to crowd the small room. Uli Haddad seemed to be their spokesman.

"We've been looking for you, Per, because you're the only one who can stand up to this," Uli said without preamble. "You refused to give in to violence from Torker in the past. You know about saying no and using force to back it up. We need your help."

Per was waving his hands before Uli had finished.

"I can't help you."

"You can! We know about your past, Per. You were sent to camp when you were young. You have a long history of social disobedience. You can show us how to create resistance."

Per pushed himself up out of his chair.

"I cannot. And I don't mean will not, I mean *can't*. Yes, I did go to camp. I've used physical violence long before Torker. And that's why I'm telling you that it's not possible for you to choose that kind of resistance. Most compact members have no idea how to use force effectively, and wouldn't want to. You have to be willing to kill. Are you?"

Haddad looked shocked.

"Surely it won't come to that! Whitman set up those 'peace officers,' but I don't believe he intends to kill anyone."

Per shrugged.

"Whitman has cleverly picked out the few who have a suppressed wish to impose force on others. They've spent their whole lives denying their drive toward violence, and now he gives them a chance to hurt people in support of the 'greater good.' Unlike trained police, however, they have no rules to go by, so they'll be very unstable. They're complete amateurs, excited and with guilty consciences. So they're likely to overreact to whatever you do, and be sorry later. Someone will get hurt.

"You can't stop them unless you're willing to kill first, and that would tear the community apart. It's an impossible situation, and I don't see how I can help you."

Someone in the back said "But, Per—" and then stopped.

Haddad looked at the floor. "Well, when you put it that way," he said uncertainly.

"Do me a favor and think about it for a couple of days," Per said. "Discuss what actions you would consider justified and how far you're willing to go. We can talk about it again."

Haddad looked relieved by that suggestion.

"We will," he said. "We'll come back when we have a specific proposal for you. Thanks."

They left, and their soft footsteps diminished in the sand.

"They won't be back," Melicar said. "You've stopped them—just as Whitman did. They'll start discussing the problems, and each one will have a different viewpoint, which will horrify the others, and pretty soon they'll see that you were right—they can't possibly attack as a unified body. Per, you've got to change your mind and stay. You're the only one with the force of mind to stand up to the consensus. And the newgens trust you. You have a responsibility to them!"

Per thought of the harpoon bolt flying through the air,

tearing flesh as it flew; a stab of pain made him press one hand to his head involuntarily.

"What's wrong?" Melicar said, instantly alert.

"That's exactly why I can't stay," he said. "I can't fight them. I don't want to find out what happens if I do."

"I never thought of you as a coward," Melicar said. "You're brave enough when it suits you. Is it true what they've said— that you just don't care about the rest of us?"

"I'm telling you what I just told them," Per said, struggling to keep his voice low. "I said I *can't*. I wish you'd believe me, Sushan. I haven't lied to you."

She was about to reply when Whitman opened the door without pausing to knock.

"Sushan—privacy, please," he said brusquely, with no hint of his usual tact. "Now!" He held the door open until she had passed through, and then let it slam.

"So you're giving orders now?" Per said. "Boss Sayid, is it?"

Being shut in the same room with Sayid doubled his anger, and with it, the pain. There was a foul, metallic taste in his mouth, and he had to swallow hard against nausea. "You're becoming quite an aversive stimulus, dear Whitman," he murmured. But Sayid took no notice.

"What were you doing with Uli and his gang?" Whitman said. His face was pale, and his movements were hurried and nervous. If he hadn't just taken control of the colony, Per would have thought he was frightened.

"I was just advising them that violence was impractical," Per said drily. "Some people are angry about what you did tonight."

"That's what I came to talk to you about," Whitman said. "Violence. We're trying to avoid it. I was impressed by you tonight, very impressed. I'm grateful to you for avoiding what could have been a very unpleasant accident. The difference between your reaction and Torker's was very clear. Your ability, your reaction, was far beyond his. You could teach us a great deal."

He had recovered most of his composure, and his voice was once again soothing and sincere.

"I don't understand you," Per said, though he was beginning to.

"I think you do," Whitman said. "You don't have to pretend with me. I know where you come from."

"Then you know more than I do."

"Don't waste time, Per," Whitman said. "My position on Skandia gave me access to quite a lot of interesting information—including records of salvage in Skandian planetary space. I've viewed all about the finding of the *Langstaff*. If it had been up to me, the disposition of that matter would have been different. I thought it was madness to throw away such a tremendous potential resource. And there were many with similar views who weren't as vocal about them, and they are still on Skandia. I'm sympathetic to your situation. I hope you'll be equally sympathetic to mine."

Per said nothing. It seemed the safest course.

After waiting a minute for a response, Whitman said, "I have a proposal for you."

He continued. "I know you were requested to say nothing about your early experiences, nor your background before you were rescued. I know that your adoptive living group hoped you would be able to suppress your unusual tendencies and live as if you had been born Skandian.

"But I believe the time has come for you to follow a different path. We need the full abilities of every member of the compact. If you could work with us, you could put *all* your abilities to use. You'd be free to recover every memory and every skill you can find."

Per struggled to keep his mind a blank. Pain pried its way in with the thoughts.

"Whitman, I can't discuss this," he said. "I can't even consider it."

"We're not on Skandia anymore," Whitman said. "You don't have to fear punishment. I know what you are. If you're working for me, I don't care."

Per finally lost his patience and struck out, heedless of the consequences.

"Put it simply, Whitman," he said. "You hope I'm a monster, so you can use me to intimidate my fellow citizens. You don't care if I hurt them as long as I make them do what you want. You're as bad as the men who made the wars in the beginning. If you know my files, you should know that I can't remember, and I *won't* remember, for you. Go away."

He got to the last words before retribution crashed into him like a thunderbolt. Whitman's image blurred and doubled before his eyes as the pain twisted in his brain. He only hoped that he could hold on until Whitman went away. He was afraid that his condition showed on his face.

Whitman stepped back; he hadn't lost his composure, but he was angry.

"I came to you in good faith, Per," he said. "I bent the rules a little, to give you a chance to think this over before the community makes a decision about you. You will be a part of this process, Per; you will be asked to donate, and this time we won't take no for an answer. You can participate as a trusted, responsible associate, or you can do it the hard way. Think about it."

He left, and Per doubled over, clutching his head. He knew that once the pain reached this level, it would not recede on its own. He needed solitude and silence.

Melicar returned almost immediately. She didn't look reproachful and angry now, only curious.

"You heard that," Per said between clenched teeth.

"Of course. I'm sorry about your privacy, but I couldn't pass up a chance to eavesdrop on Whitman."

She looked out into the darkness to make certain Sayid was gone, and closed the door carefully.

"So you're the boy the satellite techs picked up in a lifeskip. I grew up on South Island, near the launch port. That was a big story on the newsflash—for about two days. Then the story died instantly. Truthfully, I've wondered for some time if that might have been you."

The pain in his head was a living entity now, squeezing him like the jaws of a sinue.

"Do you have any Skandian painkillers left?" he asked abruptly. "Tangleweed won't do it and neither will ordinary pain blockers. They have to be high-level mindmods, or I won't be able to go on talking. I'll pass out."

Understanding dawned on Melicar's face. "You've been remediated," she said. She didn't curse or raise her voice; the simple words sounded bitter enough.

"Yes," Per gasped. "Please. Give me something now."

"I have it in rapid release," she said. She went into the next room for what seemed like an interminable time, but returned and pressed a smooth white button against Per's neck. After a moment, the pain, bright as blood by this time, dimmed a little.

"Another one," Per said.

"I don't think so," she said. "This is a heavy dosage already."

"Do it!"

She applied a second dose.

"Thank you." Per found he was able to unclench his teeth.

"The trouble with pain as a modifier," he said, pausing to catch his breath between words, "is that one simply can't remember certain levels of agony. Before you step over the line, you think, 'Well, how bad can it be?' And then afterward when it's too late, you're thinking 'Oh god, now I remember! Make it stop. I'll do anything.' But it's not effective as a deterrent."

"Can you tell me what you did?" Melicar said cautiously.

"I didn't do anything. Nothing I remember. I was remediated because—" He shut his eyes and pushed the words out in a rush so the pain couldn't stop him. "They didn't find me on a lifeskip in orbit. I was on a ship—a really big one, a ship of war. They said I was in cold sleep, the only one, and they took me off and pushed the ship into the sun."

He stopped and panted. "Give me another one."

"Per, I can't! It could kill you."

"It won't. I've done this before. Not often, but I have done it. Abuse of restricted medicines. One of the minor reasons for sending me here."

She gave him the medication. He let himself sink out of the chair to the floor, and crawled over to the wall to prop himself up. His hands and feet seemed a great distance away.

"If anyone sees you like this, I'm in trouble," the doctor said. She pressed a sensor to the artery at his neck and grimaced at the results.

"What are they going to do? Send you to Typhon?" Per said. This seemed very amusing to him, and he laughed. But he remembered that he had put himself into this fix for some reason. In fact, he remembered many things. He wished that he had time to tell Sushan about all of them.

"The monsters were real," he said. That seemed important. "They tried to tell me that I dreamed it all. I was in cold sleep and I had bad dreams, and then they rescued me. But they lied. I didn't dream it. There was a time when I was on the ship, and I was awake. I saw things that were real. They whispered to me in my sleep that none of it was real, but I know I was on a ship. They made me take the medicine, and they shocked me because I couldn't forget. I am a shiptroll."

"How old were you?" Melicar said.

"I don't even know. They assigned me age fourteen. But I could have been on the ship for a long time."

"What about your parents? Wasn't there anyone else on the ship?"

"I don't know. They said I was the only one. Maybe they lied about that, too—pushed the others into the sun. I can't remember. I don't know what things I forgot and what things they made me forget. I'll never know now what's true and false. They installed the pain so I couldn't think about it or talk. But they couldn't stop the dreams, and the dreams made my head hurt so much I stole the mindmods. Then I started to remember things again. Round and round."

"Who did these things to you?"

"I don't know. Ministry of Remediation. They looked like doctors, but maybe they weren't. Their faces go all to pieces when I try to recall them. When they were finished with me, they fostered me out to a living group in Nordstrand, up by the Polar Sea. They came around each year to look at me. I think I was an experiment. They never meant for me to stay on Skandia. They just wanted to watch me for awhile. If I hadn't come here, I think I would have been terminated. You know the kind of report—'lost his sanity and euthanized himself so he wouldn't be a burden on society.' Sad."

"Don't talk if it hurts," Melicar said. She laid a cooling hand on his sunburned forehead.

He pushed it away irritably. "Talking is the whole point. Otherwise why bother? Think this is fun?"

He paused to collect himself. "Don't interrupt now. Sofron knew this. I told her. She didn't care. She even wanted to risk having children.

"On Skandia I was totally disallowed. They told me there was too much damage from radiation and the cold-sleep process. I don't believe that was the reason. They think the people on the ship were Original Man from one of the pale clans. That's why I'm so white. They think I was an Original Man child and maybe engineered for some war purpose. So they watched me, all the time. Everything I did was under suspicion. It might be some troll trait about to come out.

"That's why I can't fight. Not because of their stupid conditioning. It hurts, but what I'm afraid of is, What if they were right? What if something in my head waits for them to push the right button—then it jumps out and kills people? Just like the ship monsters. I saw them kill. I am a monster. Whitman wants to use me. It's better for me to go away."

"I'm sorry," Melicar said. "I'm sorry I said you were a coward."

"Then there's Whitman's other plan," Per continued. "You see now why he wants my monster genes? He hopes they're different enough to resist harm from Typhon. The fact that Sofron and I couldn't successfully have children might have discouraged him at first, but now that we're desperate, he'd try me in every combination.

"It's funny, isn't it? I'm shipped off Skandia to stop me

from reproducing, and now Whitman and Roon want to reproduce me against my will. And if the results live to be born, I get to watch while those two decide if they should live or die."

"Per, it's just your genetic material," Melicar said. "Don't take it so personally."

"It is personal," Per said. "I can't let this happen. I'd kill Whitman and Roon first. I have to leave. I wanted you to know why, so you wouldn't think I was running away."

"I wish you didn't feel this way," Melicar said. "Dilani needs you. We all need you. Are you sure that Whitman would really do this against your will?"

"Think about it," Per said. "Listen to him. You'll be sure."

Dilani's name had reminded him of one more thing he should say, perhaps the hardest of all.

"Dilani. I want you to watch out for her."

"Of course I will. You don't have to ask me that."

"Shut up," he said. "Listen. Sofron and I wanted to have children, and they didn't make it. Maybe that was my fault, not even because of Typhon. Maybe the remediators told the truth. But Sofi wouldn't try with someone else. We wanted only each other, for always. People told her I was crazy, and I wondered if they were right. Maybe that feeling for just one person was more conditioning from the ship, from the bad old days."

Pain brought tears to his eyes, but it wasn't the installed pain that lived in his head. It was a different pain, from somewhere deep inside him.

"I can't remember what I was taught," he said. "I don't know who made me the way I am. I only know how I feel. Sofron was in the clinic after the last of the babies died—remember?"

"Yes, I was there with her that night."

"You sent me home to sleep. I couldn't sleep. I walked up and down the beach and cursed myself for being a shiptroll. And Doi Ru was walking on the beach as well. I met her in the dark. She asked me about Sofron, and she was crying. She and Sukarto couldn't even get pregnant. She took my hand, and she was crying."

"Oh, Per." He couldn't bear the compassion in her voice, as if she understood his pain. No one could understand it.

"You don't have to tell me this," she said. "I know how things happen. Most people would say it was only natural, that you were only kind, that what you did was right, not wrong. Sofron would say the same. Only your own mind blames you. Does it matter now, when everyone is dead? Can't you be glad you comforted her, and leave it there?"

"How can I leave it there?" he said. "It's with me every day. Doi and Sukarto couldn't even get pregnant, and the next year, Dilani was born. Almost perfect. Tall like me, angry like me."

"Oh," Melicar said, this time as if something had just become clear to her.

"Watch her, Sushan, please. What if the monster lives inside her, too? I don't know what can live in the genes of a shiptroll. I had to tell you so you would understand why she was important. I can't tell her; it would only do her harm. But watch her, please."

Per had to stop for breath; he had done everything he came to do, and he was tired. But the drug still held the pain off. It hovered like a gleaming swarm of meteorites off the port bow. It seemed a pity to waste this opportunity.

"I wish I could tell you," he whispered. "There were beautiful things on the ship, too. Not everything was broken, not in the beginning. There were gardens with no sky—pocket gardens like in the crater of our old island. They gardened by starlight and by shipsheart light. There was a well like a silver mirror surrounded by green mossy mountains only as high as a boy's head. And the trees—there were tiny trees there, too. I wish I could make you see it."

Melicar touched the sensor to his neck again. "Maybe you should sleep now," she suggested. "I'll keep an eye on you."

He roused himself. "No. I want to go home. I have to be alone."

"Per, you can't."

"Yes, I can. I've done it before."

He pushed himself to his feet, leaning against the wall until he could get his balance. He paused at the door, swaying slightly.

"Try to remember some good of me," he said. "I did my best to be human. They made me forget so much. I want someone to remember me."

If she answered, he did not hear it. He staggered out into the night. The warm sand and the fitful wind from the sea received him like friendly arms. He had to go slowly, with occasional rests in the sand. Once he fell asleep for some time, and woke up to find the sand and himself lightly beaded with cold dew. Eventually he made it to his own quarters.

He added a few personal items to the survival gear in his field pack. He wanted to post a list of instructions for the garden, but they kept slipping from his mind. He decided to do it in the morning. He wandered outside to take a last look at his trees. There was little chance now that he would create one suitable for naming after Sukarto.

The wind was still freshening. Greatmoon showed as a faint smudge of light, and he could see, far out, the faint flashes of white where waves dashed against the reef. He left the matting rolled up so he could still see out, and finally collapsed into his hammock and let the dreams and fragments sweep him away, like the foam over the reef.

## 7

The water danced uneasily with Subtle. So near the sky edge it was warm, too warm, prompting him to flee to deeper, colder waters, to safety.

When the water warmed, the big waves came soon. In the Deep, they were not so dangerous, and could always be avoided by diving deeper yet, but Subtle was too close to the Dry. Even the Laughing Teeth could be washed helplessly ashore by the waves when the unexplained perturbations of the sky edge made the water leap and roil. Observers from the Round Folk had reported seeing mangled bodies of fish and Straight Folk and stranger creatures from the Dry all mingled together in the wrack after the big waves and the water from beyond the sky edge had ceased.

Already the water pushed Subtle toward the reef, pushed and pushed without letting up, until he had to seek a crevice to hold on to, to avoid being flayed against rough coral.

It was time to turn from the Dry, but Subtle moved restlessly from side to side, expressing his indecision. How could he leave the strange creatures he had just discovered? The big waves might tear them from the Dry and destroy them, and he would never learn their secrets. Or, if they were truly intelligent, they might have a way to protect themselves and their works. If Subtle stayed, he might see those wonders. If he fled, he would never know. He kept a good hold on the rocky crevice while he talked to himself with his other limbs.

The decision he finally made was not prudent, he knew, but he chose a form for it that expressed bravado and daring rather than folly. Then he chose his wave carefully and let it slide him over the reef. The shallower waters within the reef wall would become a thrashing death trap when the waves came, but for the time being they were calm.

Subtle swam purposefully toward the place where he had last seen the oddly split creatures who might be intelligent— the long thin one with the Enemy-quelling device and the shorter one with the dark tendrils. He could not flee to the Deep without trying for one more sight of them.

Dilani had been waiting in the damp sand outside Per's house since before dawn. It was hard to say just when the sun had risen, for thick, scudding clouds still covered the sky. They moved fast, driven by a wind high up. Low to the ground, the wind was damp and hot, and blew in restless gusts, though it strengthened by small increments and never truly slacked off.

Close to the sand, where Dilani sat, she could see small grains leapfrogging each other to tumble down in tiny dunes that crept ever inland. Gradually the sand grains leapt higher and higher, until they no longer tumbled visibly back to earth but flew through the air to sting her cheeks and hands. She turned her back to the wind but stubbornly stayed put. Per would not leave his house without her knowledge.

Late in the previous evening, Bey had awakened her. He had been excited and upset. The faint light of night-blooming flowers had shown that sweat gleamed on his arms and face. He hadn't been sweating only from the heat; Dilani had wrinkled her nose at the sharp smell of tension. She had been disappointed when she learned he wanted only to tell her about the latest of the oldgens' dreary meetings.

As he signed to her what had happened, however, she felt her own palms growing damp.

Bey had left her in a hurry, without his cart, to creep down the line of living quarters and contact all the newgens he could find. Dilani had immediately risen from bed and headed for Per's house. She had stopped along the way to provide herself with a lapful of fruit for drinking and eating. She had dozed a little since finishing off the fruit, but never for long. She wanted to talk to Per.

Finally the door opened. She jumped to her feet as quickly as she could, finding that her legs had stiffened with the wait. Per started to brush past her as if this were any ordinary day, but she moved around him, always in the way, until he had to stop.

"No lessons today," he signed. "I'll be busy."

She saw that his field pack was on his back, as usual, but it was stuffed out fat and stiff. Per must be planning something unusual, and he hadn't planned to include her.

"Need to talk to you," she signed.

His shoulders went up, then down, and he let a stream of air out through his nose.

"About the meeting?" he signed.

She nodded. When it came to the point, she felt an empty, fluttering feeling in her stomach, a burning as if she had stayed down too long without a breath. It was like being afraid, but she knew that couldn't be the reason. What was there to be afraid of?

"Whitman, Phillips, the whole bunch of them," she signed sketchily, omitting the honorifics. "Bey says they will arrange matings for functional females. My index is very high." She had little idea what that meant, except that she could walk and follow instructions, but she had encountered the phrase often enough that it came automatically. "So I think they want me to have a baby. Is that true? Can they make me do that?"

The wrinkles around Per's eyes deepened as if he had a pain. That alarmed Dilani. Did he think this was a bad thing? Bey hadn't liked it either. Melicar liked babies, though; Dilani knew that.

Per nodded.

"They can."

"You are very smart," Dilani signed. "Can I mate with you?"

She had hoped he might be pleased. She had expected that at worst, he would stare into the air as if examining some unseen object, and would sign "Interesting, let me think," as he did when she asked him a question he liked.

She was completely unprepared for the fierce wild-eyed look he gave her, and the way he stepped back, signing, "No, no!" as if he were shaking something bad-smelling off his fingers. Her mouth dropped open in disbelief and pain. She clutched at his arm. She had to make him understand.

"Whitman picks?" she signed rapidly. "Roon picks? Don't know. Who? Don't know." Inside her chest, something hurt. It was the look on Per's face that made it hurt. She tried to imagine a baby, and could only see a pink, puffy thing like a monkeyface with a head that was sometimes Roon's, complete with protruding ears, and sometimes deformed like Bader Puntherong's.

Her fingers flew incoherently. Per made out "Don't want, don't want," but not the thing she was trying to describe. "Thought you would help," she signed clearly at last. "Don't care. Hate you, too." Then she ran furiously away down the beach. Per rubbed his forehead.

"As if I don't have enough problems," he said to himself. Then, "She's a child. She'll get over it."

But his conscience, or his stomach, or something inside him hurt, as he thought of what lay in store for her. Forced pregnancy, ending in spontaneous abortion or in a child so deformed it would be taken from her and killed. Even if, by some miracle, the newgens could bear functional offspring, Dilani would not understand what was happening. She would certainly never get over it.

"What do you want me to do?" he said to the empty beach. "Whittle a fish spear and murder Whitman and Roon and a dozen others? Sure! That would be great for the newgens—kill their parents. And then die—maybe next year—and abandon them. What a creative solution."

For a moment he closed his eyes and gave in to the luxury of despair.

But not for long.

"Teacher Per! Teacher Per!" It was Bey's voice, breathless and hastening closer.

Per's eyes snapped open. He saw Bey's pointing finger, and took in the source of Bey's alarm even before the boy could explain it.

Dilani had put out to sea on the skipboard and was already scudding swiftly across the lagoon. Per cursed and began to run toward the beach. His thoughts caught up with him as he ran. He was going the wrong way. None of the boats on the beach could catch the skipboard in a fresh breeze. Only the motorized fishing vessels, moored to buoys by the fish pens, had more speed. He stopped dead, ready to turn around. But if he ran back to the pens, then swam out to the buoy—no, there was no way to reach her before she hit the reef.

"The lifeskip," Bey called from behind, still trying vainly to keep up. "Get the lifeskip out."

Per veered inland without slowing. The lifeskip sat in the stores shed above high tide. Bey was right; it was the only craft within reach that was fast enough to give him a chance of catching Dilani. Per shouted to every able-bodied person he passed to help him run the lifeskip down to the beach. In the few minutes it took to lift out the light, well-balanced craft and carry it to the water, Per ran his eye over it, checking for any obvious problems.

It was apparently in perfect condition—one of the surviving bits of their Skandian equipment. The hull, bright orange for visibility, was made of a composite that was almost impossible to shatter. At least, Per would have thought it impossible before encountering Typhon. But so far, the hull seemed unblemished.

He jumped into the cockpit as the others shoved the keel free of the sand. A quick glance showed him that Dilani had nearly crossed the lagoon in the time it had taken them to get the boat from the shed.

"What's the big worry?" one of the fish crew called to Per. "She's been out before."

Per didn't pause to answer. Bringing the skipboard to harbor in a calm sea was one thing. This helter-skelter flight toward the Deep was something else. The skipboard took expert handling. The weather was bad, and getting worse. Dilani had to be brought back before she hurt herself.

The little battery-powered motor could not pour on much speed, but it hummed steadily. The lifeskip carried its mast folded and stowed in a slot astern of the cockpit. Per could raise sail automatically, with the touch of a button. The lifeskip had been designed to rescue and sustain five or six people, even if they were too weak or badly injured to handle sail or steer automatically. In the worst of weather, the cockpit could be sealed to create a watertight bubble.

For now, Per stood leaning over the coaming, allowing random waves to splash over him into the open cockpit. He tried to keep his eye on the bobbing dark shape that was Dilani. It was agonizing to wait as the lifeskip slowly gained on her, but Per decided against raising sail. The wind was against him. Using the engine alone, the lifeskip skimmed straight across the waves. Dilani had to slow as she reached the reef. She was tacking back and forth, looking for a channel.

*She doesn't know the reef as well as I do,* Per thought. *She'll have to slow down, and I'll catch her.*

Water was pouring over the highest point of the reef. The surf was much heavier than normal for this tide. The waves might be forerunners of a storm surge. Dilani tacked again and headed straight into the line of foam.

"No!" Per shouted, as if she might hear him. He couldn't believe she would choose a course so willfully stupid and reckless.

For a moment it looked as if she might get away with it. By luck or good guessing, she went over the reef on the high back of a breaker, avoiding the coral. But she misjudged the waves on the other side. She disappeared from Per's sight for a moment, hidden by spray. Then he saw the skipboard leap into the air and tumble back. He could no longer see Dilani.

He hammered the coaming of the lifeskip with his hand, in a fever of haste. The little engine whined as he maneuvered through the coral. He searched the restless crests and troughs for some trace, but saw nothing. That was all right; if she had her mask on, she could be underwater and still be fine. Did she have her mask on? He couldn't remember seeing it.

He would have to dive for her. He cursed himself for a fool with a one-track mind. He should have brought someone with him to stay on the boat. He might lose Dilani, skipboard, lifeskip, and all. He put some distance between himself and the reef and set the sea anchor to slow the lifeskip's movement back toward the reef. Then he closed his mask and somersaulted into the water.

The water was milky, flint-colored: cloudy with froth and stirred sand. Per lunged toward every shadow, only to watch each one dissipate as he plunged through it. Then it occurred to him that there might be things other than Dilani in the water.

His head broke the surface again. The wind was definitely rising. Long waves rolled regularly against the reef and broke noisily over it, pouring into the lagoon. Gusts of wind flung occasional trails of spray from the wave crests. In the sky above, clouds piled one atop another like the breakers. Per knew that he ought to be afraid, and that soon he would be, but the knowledge still seemed detached from his body. Reality was the struggle with the water, the constant alertness for some sign of Dilani.

He hadn't thought to whistle for the ketos. He had assumed they would not come to him in such weather. He dove after another shadow, one that seemed more solid than the rest, and darker, more like Dilani's skinsuit, and bumped against a rough yet yielding surface that felt nothing like skinsuit material. He cried out in fear inside his mask—an absurd, smothered croak—as the shadow bumped him back.

It was one of the ketos, but he couldn't tell if it was one he knew. With slightly opened jaws, it poked at him, as if impatient, sending fresh twinges through his injured ribs. Was it a wild one, hostile, about to take a bite of him? Then it rolled, showing its pale underside, in a gesture he remembered.

*Maybe it's trying to verify my identity,* he thought. *The skinsuit covers the places where the human body normally emits pheromones. It could be trying to get a smell of me.*

The keto butted his neck. His throat, exposed between mask and skinsuit, suddenly felt very fragile. If the keto's teeth punctured the skin, even by accident, he could be killed. He ducked his head and tried to swim away, but the keto followed, butting him relentlessly. The blows jammed Per's mask painfully against his face. The seal slipped, and water leaked in along the sides. It seemed almost as if the keto were trying deliberately to smash the mask from his face.

The keto stopped butting briefly, only long enough to roll again, showing its belly. The powerful body brushed past Par, too close and too fast, scraping him painfully against abrasive skin.

Per struggled to stay afloat, to keep thinking. Why was the keto doing this? If it wanted to kill him, it could easily do so. Per pushed himself to the surface again, but he couldn't see anything. Wave crests struck him in the face. Even without the keto's interference, his chances of finding Dilani were small. He had to make it stop attacking him.

The keto surged briefly above the water, and Per got a glimpse of its markings. He was almost sure it was Slowbolt. It cruised past him, rolling fin-up, as if offering a ride. But when he tried to catch hold, it eluded him, only to turn and pass him again.

The keto leveled out and bobbed its head vigorously up and down, mouth slightly open, nosing Per again. He flung out his arms to fend it off, and it rolled again. Not the fin—it was offering him its flank. He bobbed next to the keto, searching its sleek side. It held still. He must be on the right track. His fingers found welted scar tissue—this was Slowbolt. The dressing was gone, but the scar exuded a thick slime that stuck to his fingers. A way to keep telltale blood sign out of the water? He didn't have time to think about that now.

The keto undulated impatiently, bumping against him. Where the torso began to taper toward the tail fin, he found skin that was slick and did not rasp his fingers. He felt a nub embedded in the smooth skin. As he touched it, it extended from the skin folds enclosing it. He pulled his hand back, afraid of touching some sensitive organ and enraging the keto.

Slowbolt spun with amazing speed and bumped Per's head again, so hard this time that he was dazed for a moment. He gasped for air. He felt complete frustration. He could not guess what Slowbolt wanted. Somewhere, Dilani might be drowning, and like Dilani, he was blocked at every turn by creatures he could not understand.

Something brushed his back. He turned, and again he was pushed from behind. He was surrounded by ketos. His mask was leaking. He had to keep swallowing seawater to keep from choking.

*Pay attention,* he told himself fiercely. *This is no time to give up!*

Slowbolt rolled once again, and this time one of the other ketos butted him. The other keto nosed at his side, where Per had touched him. It reminded Per of something. It looked like a kid goat butting at its mother.

The other keto dove and disappeared, and Per felt himself shoved toward Slowbolt again.

*They can't mean that,* he thought.

He took a deep breath and ripped his mask open. Underwater, he groped for the nipple and bit down on it. A pungent, oily, overpowering taste rushed into his mouth along with the bitter sting of saltwater. He gagged, but gulped it down. He drank until the need for air drove him to the surface. He gasped and sucked in foam along with the air, and choked. He fumbled for the mask but couldn't get it fastened again.

Then a supporting fin slid under his arm and hoisted him above the spray. He clung to Slowbolt's back while he sealed his mask again and sucked in deep lungfuls of air. The bitter, oily taste still coated his lips and throat. It seemed to be in his nose and lungs as well, as if it had rushed instantly to fill every part of his body.

The keto surged forward, paused as if to make sure Per had a good grip, then swam powerfully. Per had time for his first coherent thought since he had jumped into the water.

*They're helping me now. Does that mean I did what they wanted? Do they know where to find Dilani?*

Slowbolt dove with him; Per's ears popped. He swallowed, and his ears popped again. The keto leveled out. Per caught a glimpse of a shadowy shape out of the corner of his eye. It was Dilani.

She wasn't moving; her arms and legs hung limp, but Per's heart jumped with relief as he saw that she was wearing a mask. Per kept one hand on Slowbolt's fin as he reached for the floating body. Even that far below the surface—twenty feet? thirty?—the water was turbulent and he could hear the roar of the waves battering the coral rock. He pulled Dilani toward him. Did she stir slightly, or was it only the turbulence?

Suddenly she twisted in his grip like a snake and struggled blindly to swim away, to swim down. His fingers sank into her arm till he seemed to be gripping the bone, but still she strove powerfully toward the bottom. He crooked a leg around her waist and managed to immobilize her arm against his chest. She thrashed and kicked, but could no longer swim.

*Why didn't the keto go?* Per almost let go the fin, to seek the surface alone. Finally Slowbolt raised his great head and drove upward. Dilani reverted to limpness, and Per worried that he was cutting off her air. How long had she been down, and how deep? he wondered. He had lost all sense of time. He feared that raising her so abruptly would cause decompression sickness, but he could see no choice. He couldn't pause on the way up to decompress—not in that sea.

He had given no thought to how he would get to shore with an uncooperative and possibly unconscious cargo. He clung to Slowbolt's fin and wondered where they were going.

When they reached the surface, Slowbolt stopped and seemed to be waiting for something. When Per continued to hang, unmoving, from the keto's fin, Slowbolt suddenly leapt straight up, shaking Per loose from his hold. Startled and frightened, Per found himself treading water with one arm around Dilani.

*What now?* he thought. Slowbolt shot past them again, his

fin raised in a familiar gesture, and Per groaned. *You don't understand,* he thought. *I can't! Not now!*

But he didn't think the keto was giving him a choice.

Dilani had run to the Deep because there was nowhere else to go. She had been looking for the thing in the Deep that had called to her on the day the old island died. Maybe if she could find that feeling, she would know what it meant to "hear." Maybe the water would communicate with her, as people could not.

She'd floated down deep, to get away from the smashing spray up above, and had closed her eyes to concentrate on the feelings that came from the water. She'd been able to feel the low vibration of the waves grinding against the reef, and when the ketos had come, she had felt the trembling in the water that seemed to pierce right through her, that meant the ketos were seeing her with their ears. She had felt them coming closer. She'd kept her eyes closed and tried to guess where they were.

Then someone had grabbed her. She'd kicked and fought reflexively, like a child dragged out of sleep. It was Per again, always Per. She was glad to see him, but she was still angry, and wished she could punish him for what he had done.

The ketos were with him. His favorite, the one he called Slow Lightning, was right in front of her face. Dilani could see the finned slits along the sides of his throat flickering open and shut like a bird's wings in flight. His mouth hung slightly open, showing the fearsome teeth. The rest of the pack leapt and surged in the churning water. Another keto broke from the pack and shoved Per with its nose. It jostled and buffeted Per, then turned to her.

The great snout was smooth and resilient, but firm enough to bruise, and it pushed Dilani back again and again, till she felt smashed between the force of the keto's onslaught and the resistance of the water at her back. She flailed with her arms, reaching for Per, or anything to hold on to. The pack seemed to be circling her. The keto turned again, pressing against her as it passed. The rough skin scraped her bare forearms and left slime sticking to her hands. Panicking, she beat against it with her hands, but only hurt herself on the rough, protective denticles. She was trying to swim out of its way, but it wouldn't let her. It pressed against her again, insistently.

Then Per was there beside her, signing something. Dilani saw "off, off" and "drink." That couldn't be right. He couldn't be telling her to take the mask off and drink seawater.

Then, without further warning, Per seized her and pulled off her mask. As her mouth opened in shock, he pushed her face against the keto's side. A fold of dense, rubbery skin slid between her lips. Per slapped her back, hard. She started to inhale, choked, bit down, and found herself gulping a mixture of bitter saltwater and something else with an awful, oily taste. Then she was thrust powerfully to the surface and burst into the air, choking.

Per held her up while something propelled them through the water. Blindly, she struck at him. He was a traitor. She hated him. He was trying to kill her. Her mask was still off, and waves slapped her in the face. Per kept pulling her along and wouldn't let go. He pushed her, and the keto joined in. She hated them both.

Unexpectedly, she felt herself rolled onto a solid surface. She wiped water from her eyes to look, expecting to see the skipboard, but somehow Per had boosted her aboard the broader deck of the lifeskip.

She considered jumping off the other side to get away from him, but she needed the solidity of the deck too much. She struck at him as he pulled himself aboard. He stopped her hands with his open palms.

"Look, look," he begged. She didn't know what else to do. They were too far from land. While he was signing, he couldn't grab her again. So she watched his hands.

"I'm sorry," he signed first. "No time to explain. Ketos wanted us to drink. It's like milk, but not milk. It's special liquid made in their bodies. It makes them smell the same to each other. All ketos in the pack smell the same. They wanted to make us smell like them. They were trying to make you drink."

He had to stop and grab the gunwale to get his balance. The rising waves tossed the little boat like a chip of wood.

"I'm sorry," he signed again. "Are you all right?"

He offered more apologies than she could ever remember. People never said "sorry" to Dilani. She was supposed to be the sorry one. She sat up with as much dignity as she could. It triggered another spasm of coughing, and she spat into the water.

"Tastes awful!" she signed.

"Till today, I did not know for sure about this," Per signed. "I saw them bite each other, without blood, but till today, I did not guess what it was.

"Slowbolt knows we helped. He wanted to help us, make us friends, but we didn't smell right. As soon as I tasted the stuff, they took me to you—all of them did. I knew they would help you if you drank it, but you wouldn't understand me. Too scared."

"I understand now," Dilani signed.

She thought she did. She was glad the ketos wanted to be friends and didn't want to hurt them, but she was still angry. Ketos were too big. They pushed her and shoved her, made her do things she did not like. She didn't like them. She spat in the water, and spat again. An oily taste burned at the back of her throat.

Dilani no longer looked as if she would jump back into the water, so Per turned his attention to the urgent task of returning to shore before the surf rose too high. He took a last look around for the skipboard, but didn't see it. If it hadn't smashed against the reef, it was probably upside down in the trough of a wave, wherever the currents had taken it. Hauling in the anchor while he looked, he started the engine and steered for the reef channel.

The first heavy impact against the bow knocked him loose from his grip on the tiller. At first he thought he had run into the reef, but more blows thudded against his little boat. The heading arrow on the display swung around. Something had changed his course for him. Peering through the spray, he saw the ketos leaping around the lifeskip. They rammed the bow until it pointed straight out to sea. Slowbolt made a wriggling leap of approval, and his wake splashed over the coaming. He forged ahead of the lifeskip. To Per, the keto's curveting gestures seemed to say *Come with me* as clearly as he had ever seen.

Per turned the lifeskip back toward shore. Again the ketos changed his course, more brutally this time, as if impatient with his stupidity. It cost him an effort to turn back.

He could have gone. The open sea would soon be a maelstrom of towering waves and blinding spray, but the lifeskip had been designed for secondary use as a submerged diving platform. He could fill the ballast tanks and seek a level below the turbulence. He could ride out the storm with the ketos. But he wasn't alone.

So he held to his original course. The other ketos dropped away, submerged, and disappeared. Slowbolt leapt across his bows again and again, trying to turn him back. As the lifeskip neared the roaring line of breakers along the reef, Slowbolt turned, rolled one last time as if in farewell, and was gone.

Per heard the hull grate on coral as he crossed the reef chest-deep in foam, but he didn't capsize, and Dilani held on. Once in the calmer waters of the lagoon, they were safe.

When they grounded, Per leapt out to tug the lifeskip up the beach, away from the mounting waves. Dilani staggered to shore without his help.

A small crowd of people had gathered on the beach. As far as they knew, it had just been Dilani, acting up again. They were curious to see what the excitement was about, but most of them didn't seem much concerned.

"Tie that boat to something solid," Per said to them. "The weather's getting worse."

Bey was in the group, so Per had some hope they would carry out his request. He steered Dilani toward the hospital.

"What happened this time?" Melicar said as the door closed behind them.

"Ask her, the bloody little lunatic," Per growled. It had just begun to sink in that he'd lost the skipboard, probably forever.

Dilani coughed weakly. Her nose was running, and her face was pathetically white, with big circles under her dark eyes.

"Are you all right?" Melicar signed. "What happened?"

"Fine," Dilani responded lethargically. "I went in the water."

"Hell, we know that," Per said.

"Why did you do it?" Melicar asked.

"Per said he wouldn't mate with me, so I ran away," Dilani signed. Her expression was matter-of-fact, though Per wriggled in embarrassment. Instead of sympathizing, Melicar looked at him reproachfully.

"A little patience, a little kindness, " the doctor murmured.

"What do you expect me to do? Sleep with her? Get her pregnant?" Per shouted.

"Of course not! But you could have explained it to her, calmed her down, said no without setting off this adolescent outburst. Speaking of outbursts, try to behave like an adult yourself."

She listened to Dilani's chest and passed her fingertip through a scope to check the blood gases.

"I don't think she has inhaled any water," Melicar said. "And the nitrogen saturation seems well within normal levels. She's fatigued, but that will pass soon."

"But she seemed unconscious," Per protested, "or in a trance. I thought it must be some kind of narcosis."

Melicar turned to Dilani and waited till she had the girl's full eye contact.

"Dilani, it's important you tell us exactly how you felt in the water," she signed carefully. "When you looked unconscious, what happened? Do you know?"

"Not unconscious!" Dilani signed indignantly. "I knew everything. I was in the water. Till he came and pulled me out."

She didn't seem particularly grateful.

"So what were you doing?" the doctor signed.

Dilani scowled at the floor, as if she preferred to evade the question.

"The Deep talks to me," she signed reluctantly.

Melicar leaned forward. "Talks? You mean, you hear something?"

Dilani squirmed and shrugged. "Yes. No, don't know. I feel it. It calls."

"What does it say?" Melicar signed, fascinated.

"Go in the water. Go down."

She shook her head when they pressed for more.

Melicar sent her to take off her skinsuit and get dry, and started to warm a drink for the three of them. When Dilani didn't come back, Melicar looked into the back room and saw that she was asleep on one of the cots.

"Now I've lost my skipboard," Per said. "I don't know what I'll do without it. Build a canoe, I suppose. Waste of time, those sentimental goodbyes. I can't leave anytime soon."

He stared down at his hands, wondering how long it would take to build another boat. Storm season would arrive long before he could finish.

"Sushan, you don't think Dilani is suffering neurological damage, on top of everything else?"

"I don't know," the doctor said. "Have you noticed this kind of behavior before? When did it start?"

"She has sometimes acted strangely during the last few weeks," Per said. "Swimming down, not up. Claiming to 'hear' something."

"Maybe it isn't a delusion," Melicar said. "We don't know the exact extent of her deafness. Maybe she senses the grinding vibration of the waves on the reef and imagines that's what we do when we're hearing. She badly wants to be like you, Per. It might lead her to claim that she hears, like us, but in some special way."

"I think it's just a quirk in her mind," Per said. "When her parents died, some fool told her they were in the water. For months, she threw herself in the ocean every chance she got. Do you remember that? I can't tell you how many times I pulled her out—always struggling, thrashing, trying to bite me.

"Finally one day she got away from me, and it took me a little too long to get her out again. She got some water down her throat and found it wasn't fun, drowning. After that I guess she believed me when I said her parents were dead. She never said any more about it from then till now."

"I had forgotten those days," Melicar said. "Well, maybe you're right. Maybe it's just Dilani. I just wish I knew what was going on in her head."

"Good luck finding out," Per said, getting stiffly to his feet. "Would you mind letting Whitman know where she is? I don't feel like talking to him today."

"I'm just going to let her sleep," Melicar said. "She's had a hard day. She can go home when she wakes up. I'll tell Whitman she's here."

She watched Per shoulder his heavy pack.

"You might as well stay here, too," she said. "There's an extra bed if you feel like having a rest. I don't like the looks of this weather. I'd feel better knowing you were here."

Per shook his head automatically, but then paused. He had closed up the house. He had no experiments running, no particular reason to go back. He was tired.

"I guess I will," he said. "If you can keep Whitman off my back. You're right about the weather. If I were you I'd start float collaring essentials now."

"Thanks, Per. I think I can manage," she said with gentle sarcasm.

"Sorry. I'll come help you in a bit, but I could use a few minutes' rest, now that I think of it. Come and get me if anything urgent comes up."

"I'm going over to the dining hall to get something to eat before I do anything else," she said. "Do you want me to send you something?"

He started to refuse again, and again changed his mind. "Hell, why not?

"Hey—thanks," he called belatedly after her.

* * *

A kitchen helper brought over a leaf tray piled with moon-fish steaks and spud mash, still warm, a mess of root vegetables fried in spicy oil, and cooked fruit. The rich smell of frying made Per's mouth water. Looking back, he thought it must have been a couple of weeks since he had tasted anything cooked, let alone hot.

He was grateful that Sushan had not returned to eat with him. He'd told her his stories on the previous night because he hadn't expected to see her again. He no longer felt comfortable with her, now that she knew, now that she had seen him in that condition. But he was grateful for the food. He cleaned the tray down to the bare leaf.

Then he sprawled on the spare cot, noticing how much softer it was than his wooden platform. The unusual sensation of a full stomach kept him awake for awhile in spite of his tiredness. He smiled ruefully as he realized that he was thinking how much easier it would be to live like a compact member again: to line up for meals and to sleep in his assigned bed. But that wasn't an option.

The real question was what to do about the loss of the skip-board. He had planned to take the board and leave, the next day if possible. He'd felt no unease at taking the board; no one else used it anyway. To take one of the other boats would feel too much like stealing. Each vessel was part of the colony's dwindling resources. He had no right to deprive them of something they might need.

Yet, if he waited to build a boat for his own use, he would be trapped on the island for the rest of the storm season. If he stayed, more efforts would be made to force him to conform to the new directives.

It wasn't a problem he could solve with five minutes' contemplation. He fell asleep.

He woke with a jerk; he had heard the door bang, and a memory from his sleep told him someone had been shouting at him. It was very dark. He felt disoriented. He'd gone to sleep in the afternoon. Was it the middle of the night?

He heard the rattle of tubewood in the next room. The storm shutters were down. That was why it was dark.

Dilani was already gone. The hospital was deserted. When he opened the door, wind rushed in and slammed it back against its hinges. Outside, it was daytime, but he couldn't tell the hour. The sky was dark, and darker yet out to sea, where he could see a continuous shimmer of foam about the reef. A long and powerful surge beat a slow, relentless rhythm against the shore. The storm had finally arrived.

A gust of rain splattered in through the door; he stepped outside and was about to wrestle the door shut when a second thought stopped him. He ducked back inside and seized his pack. Anything left behind might be lost forever.

Peering through wind-driven rain squalls, he saw most of the colony scurrying around their living quarters, lashing down shutters and removing irreplaceable items for storage above the high-water line. A chain had formed and was passing supplies from the stores building to higher ground. Already drenched, Per made his way toward the nearest group, and found Henner Vik among them.

"What's going on?" he shouted near the meteorologist's ear. "You said we might have rain. You didn't say anything about this."

Henner ducked her head under the pelting rain. "The weather broke without warning," she said. "I had a bad feeling, but I couldn't predict—it came so fast and hard. This is a big one, Per."

Per stepped into line and joined in heaving watertight canisters uphill. He wished he had gone back to his own house after all. Judging by how far up the beach the water had already risen, his terrace would be awash, the little trees perhaps already poisoned by saltwater. And he guessed that the storm surge was nowhere near its peak. When it crested, all the structures the colony had built with so much toil would be underwater. They had guessed wrong.

Henner had known the water temperature was high, and the conditions were right for storms, but she couldn't have predicted this, Per thought. Was that just incompetence?

Should we have known? Perhaps the eruption had had an effect on the weather. But it should have cooled the air, not heated it. Maybe it had created a greater temperature differential somehow, a shift in the wind patterns.

Or maybe this is normal, and our experience earlier was a period of mild weather we just happened into. We had satellite reports back then. Henner's used to receiving data. She's blind without her instruments, like me. We're all blind to this world, deaf to its messages.

He wondered if the highest ground on the island would be high enough. It might be that the storm would wash completely over the atoll. He wished he had spent more time studying the land. He might have been able to tell from the growth of the plant species how long it had been between such events, but it was too late.

It was also too late for him to leave the community. As long as they needed his help, he couldn't desert them. Though it was impossible for him to live with them, he might end up dying with them.

He was sunk in his thoughts, and in the rhythmic effort of shifting the stores, when Melicar hurried past the line.

"Hey, Per," she shouted, leaning close to make herself heard. "I sent one of the kids to wake you. We're moving the newgens up to an emergency shelter. Then we have to finish moving the hospital, too."

"Good," Per said. "The beach area will be leveled. Get the kids into float vests, too."

"Thought of that," the doctor said. "We already float collared as much equipment as we could."

"Tell them to use wood and bladderweed if they run out of floatables. The water may go all the way over. It's five meters past doubletide already. I'm afraid we'll lose the boats, too."

"Torker's working on that."

"Hope so. Where's Dilani?"

"Told her to meet me back at the hospital. Help pack."

Per watched as the doctor disappeared into the blowing rain. He decided suddenly that he should have gone with her. He broke from his place in line and shouted after her, but the storm swallowed his voice. He tried to run into the wind and found that he could move only in a jerky stagger. He waded more than walked toward the beach.

It looked as if the lifeskip would be lost, too. No one had brought it in. It was afloat, straining at the anchor line and surging jerkily inland with each wave. That made Per angry; the lifeskip was a sweet piece of technology, something they'd never have again, and it was going to be sacrificed for a few more bundles of rations.

He made a lunge for the line, but couldn't reach it. Surf rushed up to his thighs and nearly pushed him over, then sucked the sand from beneath his feet as it dragged off down the shore. Per looked around for help. It seemed that everyone had moved up and inland; the storehouse stood empty with its doors swinging in the wind.

He struggled back toward the hospital, shouting for Melicar. He could hardly hear himself; the wind carried his breath away. He saw several men coming up from the buildings, but they carried along the last of the hospital stores. Hunched over their burdens, they didn't see him waving. Someone saw him, however, and let the wind push her into him, like a skiff ramming the wharf. It was Dilani. She tried to sign something, but he didn't have time to pay attention. He grabbed her arms and squeezed as if he could plant her like a post in the ground.

"Stay here," he signed emphatically. "Don't move!"

He got into the lee of the dining hall, where it was slightly easier to move, and was able to walk a little faster. He reached the hospital. The storm shutters clattered wildly, but could hardly be heard over the roar of the wind. He could see for himself that the building was empty. Melicar was gone, and the computer had been taken, as well.

Plunging through the weather outside, he spotted Dilani on the beach, and in a few minutes he was beside her again.

"Let's go," he signed, but she stayed stubbornly planted. She signed insistently something that began with a B. A name sign, he realized. *Bey.*

"Where?" Per signed. He saw no one. All the other adults had fled to higher ground.

"Not with the others," Dilani signed. The wind made even signing difficult, but it was easier than speech. "That's why I stayed behind."

At least she has a float vest and her mask, Per thought. He tried to look around for Bey. Even turning his shoulders was hard and nearly made him lose his balance. He could barely see through the rain.

Dilani slapped his shoulder to get his attention, and pointed. He wiped his stinging eyes, and finally made out a shape in the lee of the trees, a dark shape huddled near the ground. Per fought his way through the sand, with Dilani clinging to his arm. As they drew near to Bey, Per could see that the boy was trying his best to close the gap between them, but his arms weren't strong enough to drag his body against the wind.

When they reached him, Bey was panting so hard he couldn't speak at first.

"I had Lila in the cart with me, and Kee was helping push," he said between gasps. "Wind blew down the rooftree of Skanderup's house. Smashed the damn cart, and Kee. I tried to help Lila, but—" His face distorted into an ugly mask.

"Lila's dead, too?" Per shouted.

Bey nodded. "Now she is. She breathed again for a couple of minutes, but then she quit."

He squinted toward the sea.

"You and Dilani go on. I can't move fast."

Bey spoke calmly, but an icy jolt went through Per when he looked where Bey was looking. The sea was heaving itself slowly over like some massive creature with a hide of marbled silver. The waves were so big that it seemed to take them forever to fold over and break. Then they hit the beach, and the water began to rush up, faster than Per could run.

"None of us can move that fast," he yelled. He looked around in vain for a refuge. He thought for a moment of climbing the trees, but he had no lines to secure them, and the trees themselves would probably go soon.

"Go," Bey urged, pushing at Per's legs.

"It's too late," Per mouthed at him. "Too late; can't get to the shelter," he signed to Dilani.

The water was pushing the lifeskip farther up the beach. The little craft was down at the bow. *The anchor must be dragging,* Per thought. Soon it would snap, and the lifeskip would batter against trees and rocks till the hull finally sprang a leak and it sank.

But it could still save them, if only they could reach it. "The lifeskip!" Per shouted to Bey, and saw understanding dawn on his face. Per shook Dilani by the shoulder and pointed. "Hold me tight. Swim. Get in," he signed, and she nodded.

Crouching, Per put on his mask, then got Bey's arms around his neck and hoisted Bey onto his back. The extra weight made him stagger; Bey was heavy even without legs. Dilani hooked an arm through the straps of Per's pack. Together they waded, beating slantwise upwind toward the lifeskip that jerked and bucked at the end of its tether.

Per tried to gauge the moment when the lifeskip would be farthest inshore, but he couldn't seize the best opportunity, because he couldn't move fast enough with his burden. The backwash dragged the sand from under his feet, and he felt himself toppling. For a moment they were all tossed helplessly in the foam, and he thought it was ended, as simply as that, in one misstep.

Then his hand struck something narrow and rigid as iron: the anchor line, drawn taut to the edge of tolerance. He felt his skin rip as he clung to it, but his grip held.

He flailed with his other arm. His hand glanced off the rail, but he got his elbow over it on the next try.

Per's body bobbed up like a cork as Bey let go and pulled himself into the lifeskip. Bey braced himself with one hand on the rail and reached over with the other to help Dilani in. Per put a hand under her knee and heaved; then she was in. When the next wave struck, Per felt his legs fly up and his head go down; for a moment he thought his back would snap, but no, not yet; the wave would drag his hands off the lifeskip and then break him in half. *At least the kids are in the boat,* he thought.

Something hooked the strap of his mask and pulled, choking him. He was pulled loose from his death grip on the anchor line. His body was heaved up again and rolled over. It took him a minute to realize that Bey and Dilani had kept hold of him through the passing of the wave and had rolled him into the lifeskip.

They had a few seconds before the next wave, precious seconds to do the correct thing and save themselves. They had to belt in, but Per didn't have time to take off his mask to tell them. He could only hope they knew what to do.

He drew his utility knife, leaned out perilously over the bow, and cut the line, freeing the lifeskip to be sucked back toward the sea. Per flung himself down in the pilot's position and let the belt snap shut around him. He closed the canopy and nosed the lifeskip under till he felt it grate on sand, and gave the little engine full throttle.

As the next wave came in, the boat was carried backward toward shore, but not as far as the waiting tree line. Breaker by breaker, they continued to fight their way toward deeper water.

Per felt some slight lessening of the pounding against the hull, though the turbulence continued. He dared to twist his head around and look for the monitors. He found the little glowing screens; in fact, his nose was nearly jammed against them. The depth line receded reassuringly; they had made it out of the breakers and into the lagoon.

He piloted the boat with more care now, watching the monitor closely. The water was so high over the reef that there was little danger of going aground on it, but a freak wave might lift them and smash them down with tremendous force. He tried to keep a cushion of depth under them to prevent that.

At last the bottom dropped away steeply; they had escaped into deep water. Per took the lifeskip down a few more feet. They were away from the wind-stirred caldron of the surface, but they still tossed and rolled among the powerful roots of the waves. Per turned on the pump to drain the water that had splashed into the lifeskip before he had closed the canopy. He found storage lockers at his side and hunted through them for antinausea patches. He felt queasy himself, and a telltale odor told him one of the others already had thrown up. He knew the storm might continue for days.

Bey had donned a mask. He opened it now and looked around.

Per sat back, on the port side of the lifeskip's enclosed compartment. Bey was on his left, in the middle, and as Per rose on his elbow to search for the patches he could see Dilani, strapped down just beyond Bey. They were laid out like small fish in a pan.

"It's all right to open the mask, but you might as well keep it on," Per said. "I've activated the air exchange in here, but I'd rather we were all prepared to be dumped, in case of emergency. By the way, thanks for holding on to me," he added.

He saw Bey's quick smile flash as the boy adjusted his mask.

"Returning the favor," Bey said.

"What will we do now?" Bey added after a moment's silence.

"Ride it out. We're safer here than on shore. After that, we'll see where we are. Would you have a look at Dilani? I can't see over you very well."

Bey twisted around; Per could see that he was signing, but not what he said. The bubble they were strapped into was lit only by the glow of the screens. Their faces showed as greenish highlights, but the rest of the space remained in shadow.

"She's all right," he reported. "She threw up already, but she's better now."

"Ask her if she saw the doctor leaving the beach," Per said.

Bey turned back to him, shaking his head.

"She didn't see. I didn't either. I thought she left with the last group of newgens, but she might have gone back when Lila and I didn't show up. I hope not."

"No. They wouldn't have let her do that," Per assured him. "She's safe."

The words came awkwardly to his lips, because he didn't really know if they were true. It was possible that she had risked her life to look for them, and that they had left her to die on the beach. There was a long, strained silence in which they all had plenty of time to wonder about everyone left behind. His mouth felt dry and sour, and he reached for the water.

"Take a big drink," he said, handing it to Bey. "Tell Dilani. Don't worry about running out of water. The boat has a desalter, and so does the membrane in your masks. It's important not to get dehydrated."

After another long silence, Per saw Dilani's arms rise up, her hands flicking upward from her chest. He could read that sign all right; she was calling repeatedly for light.

Well, there really wasn't any good reason why not, Per thought. The lights were rechargeable. He fumbled for the controls and turned on glowing lines, too bright at first, then lower. He was surprised by how comforting the light was. It warmed and soothed, almost as good as food, though there was nothing to see but the dim bulk of his companions and the gray curve of the canopy overhead.

As he stared up at the canopy, however, he began to notice other things. At first they seemed like something floating in his eye. Then he realized that minute organisms were crawling over and clinging to the smooth canopy, perhaps attracted by the glow. Soon there was a layer of tiny, fragile-looking shapes, like gelatin capsules—eyeballs with arms and legs, or transparent, mobile bunches of grapes—all stuck tenaciously to the transparent window.

Per wondered if he should worry. He hoped all the creatures attracted by the glow would be small and harmless. He didn't think they were deep enough to encounter light-sensitive predators, but they knew so little of the Deep beyond the reef. Perhaps it would be better to turn off the light and stay under cover of darkness.

In the end, the pleasure of watching the tiny creatures led

him to put off a decision. As he watched, more and more of their transparent fellow travelers began to glow, too, as if in imitation. The window became a twinkling starfield, or a sky full of fireflies. Fragile as they appeared, the creatures were hanging on, undisturbed, while the hurricane raged. He couldn't help thinking of them as friendly.

Subtle felt the pulse of the waves rolling over him with steadily increasing force. It beat with warning rhythm: *Leave the reef.* Still, he inched stubbornly from crevice to crevice, alert for other signals that would tell him the strange ones had returned. The Deepsong fuzzed and blurred under the assault of the storm with its shifting winds and currents. The strangers' shapes were unfamiliar and their sound signatures intermittent. Soon the noise level of the storm would rise so high he would not be able to perceive them. He risked being torn to pieces if he stayed that long.

If the strange ones truly had intelligence, they, too, would flee. Perhaps they had a hiding place so deep in the Dry the water never reached it. Subtle's deepest colors crept and glowed as he tried to imagine such a place. Even with the waves washing relentlessly past him, his skin prickled with the memory of dryness.

No—it wasn't memory. It was the distinctive, rapid tingle of fast-traveling Laughing Teeth bouncing messages off each other. Subtle instantly assumed the protective color of the surrounding coral. A pack of Teeth swam toward him, almost straight on. He was amazed. It was too deep into the longerlight/warm-water time for Laughing Teeth. They always left before the summer storms arrived.

A cluster of strangenesses seemed to be budding around this unremarkable coral clump.

Subtle crawled laboriously down the reef wall toward the bottom, until he could let go of the coral without being tumbled into the lethal surf. He swam toward the Deep, far enough down that the Laughing Teeth would not bother to come after him—he hoped. The sea quaked unsteadily around him, roiled even that far down.

He twirled himself for a full-circle eyescan of the rocking sky edge above him, looking for the Teeth, and involuntarily shot up several limblengths in surprise at what he saw. It was one of the strangers, with long, weedy growths writhing from its top end. It moved uncertainly in the water, twitching its stiff, awkward extremities, and then hung quietly, gathering itself into a straight shape. It looked for all the world as if it were trying to orient itself to the lines of the Deepsong.

Subtle rebuked himself; he was reading too much into the stranger's posture, assuming that body shape had any meaning for the creatures.

Then he furled himself in dismay. The Teeth were nearly overhead. A reckless urge surged through him, and he nearly shot up to them, to give battle. But caution and curiosity urged him to wait. What did the Teeth want? Would they eat the stranger? It had an unappetizing, inorganic smell.

The Teeth circled the stranger. They bumped it, but no blood ensued, no struggling of the prey or piercing sounds of terminal fear. A companion stranger appeared. Subtle was almost sure it was the same he had seen before. The creature's body patterns were very simple and seemed to remain the same. Of course, it was possible that a whole school of them might keep the same pattern, like fish from the same egg batch.

The stranger-creatures intertwined. Were they mating? Surely not in the presence of so many of the Teeth. They swam with the Teeth, and then vanished from the water. They had gone up past the sky edge again.

Subtle heard the whining power sound he had heard before, by the net of geometrical metal. It moved toward the reef, then over it, and he could no longer hear it. The source of the sound came from beyond the sky edge. Subtle shot across the bottom in a zigzag expressive of great frustration. He couldn't see what they were doing. Above him the Teeth vanished and reappeared, penetrating the sky edge, but he could not do the same.

The power sound passed through a notch in the coral. Waves pounded and roared through that narrow passage. Subtle would be shredded against the wall if he dared to follow.

He jammed an arm into a crevice and clung there, through the pounding that drenched all his senses with the same, monotonous tone. He needed all his strength to hang on, and had no freedom left for weaving messages, but his limbs knotted and relaxed in a message to himself: I hold on till they return, and if they do not return, I hold on till I die.

The water grew darker. No lights showed in it. The luminescent children of the Deep kept their brightness to themselves as they fled the storm or huddled into refuges to wait it out. Subtle let himself sink into a resting trance, while minimal awareness kept him gripped to the coral. His limbs twitched as, in trance, the patterns of his memories unfurled around him.

*Hold on,* he danced in the memory. *Hold on.*

He was dancing again with Redheart, his friend, and to his everlasting indigo sorrow, his mate. He danced *Hold on* wildly, every segment of his skin undulating with the brights and darks of warning. The Teeth were cruising in the coral forest, and Subtle was caught with his friend. Casually the Teeth dove and passed them, one by one, each with open mouth and fins cocked to sweep the cowering Round Ones from the coral. It seemed a game to them. Perhaps the winner would eat the victim, but Subtle doubted it. More likely the Teeth would leave the lifeless remnants for Enemies and clingfish to clean up, while they soared off carelessly. Who could tell why the Laughing Teeth did anything?

Already Subtle's torso oozed blood from a dozen near misses. A direct hit, even with a rough fin instead of a razor tooth, would kill at once, and bring the Enemies to tear apart the survivor. Yet, if they waited, the treacherous messages of the blood would bring the Enemies sooner or later. Subtle despaired. It seemed there was no other course but to hold on, and hope the Teeth would leave before the Enemies arrived.

But to hold on was never Redheart's way. In spite of her unusual choice of friends and occupation, she was a true female: big and powerful, great-hearted and reckless, an exuberant dancer and a mighty hunter. Her years of scholarship had not dulled her edge. In spite of Subtle's desperate pleas, she loosed her grasp on the sheltering rocks and launched herself in a swift arc toward the nearest of the Teeth.

She wrapped herself around his gill slits, clinging and smothering. His air chamber would give him enough oxygen to prevent him from suffocating, but he would be frightened and slowed as she cut off his breath. Then, using the leverage gained by clinging to his body, she stabbed and tore at him with her mademetal blade.

Ah! Subtle heard the panic that shrilled through the pack of Teeth then. They had not known they were attacking armed scholars. They had thought the pair were simple Round Folk of the murky floor. Now the Teeth were bitten.

Redheart slipped from the Laughing One's torso, leaving it deep-bitten with countless scars from her hold and from her knife. The other Teeth of the pack let her go, foregoing vengeance as they shouldered to their wounded mate, rubbing its wounds with their body slime to stop the blood so they could escape the Enemies.

And sure enough, the Enemies came, but by then the two Round Folk had fled deep into a crevice in the coral, blocking the way with stones and shells. They heard, from a distance, the echoes of a tragedy as the Enemies tore the Laughing Ones to pieces. Long after the sounds ceased, the water brought them somber flavors of the deaths of their tormentors.

Subtle had never loved Redheart more than in that final moment. At rest, her colors of agitation faded into the steady glow that gave her her name. Her skill and decision, her bright spirit and cool thought, had saved them both. Subtle was happy in spite of the soreness of his wounds, till he felt the unmistakable touch of her mating limb, and with it, the cold current of death.

He tried, vainly, to twist away from her, to escape contact.

*You swore never to mate,* he danced as well as he could in the cramped space. *You promised me we would always live as partners. You swore not to throw your life away for the sake of a string of eggs. We agreed it was behavior not becoming a reasoning being.*

*I did not understand then,* she swirled in return. The colors of her mantle were like the brightwarm swirling in the sky edge at the height of longlight. Her dance shook through her in warm, intimate ripples like the flutter of breathing. *I knew nothing. I was a fool. How could anyone resist this joy, this glory? You will feel it too, Subtle. You must! All study, all length of days are nothing. A food scrap, set against this bright edge of life and death. This is everything. Our vows, our studies, they were bright grains of sand that children swallow before they know the smell of food.*

*Then leave me. Go,* he thrashed in agony. *Mate with some other, not with me! Do not make me the agent of your death!*

Her limbs danced close to his skin, caressing as they signified. *Sweet Subtle, I would be continued with you—with you my cherished workmate, not a stranger. It is life we taste together. In the greatlife we will live ever united.*

She breathed over him a mouthful of body-warmed water carrying a full charge of mating scents, and his head was swimming in brightness. *It's the chemical motes,* he told himself frantically. *It's only chemical. Think. Think against it.* But she was right. He could not. Thought was a chemical process, and his thoughts were scattered in the water like bright dots of light scattered among the refractions of the sky edge. He fully tasted the truth of her dancing. Mating seemed the right thing, the only right thing, and all other rightness faded like a paled membrane withering in the grip of the White Arms.

The joy of their dance went far beyond any message he could remember afterward. No pattern he could shape with his limbs had ever given him more than a faint hint of what they felt together. For once there was no difference between the signed and the intended, the inner and the outer, the skin-scent and the limbshaping. Subtle experienced their mating as the ultimate truth, and he knew that never again would he be able to dance in such harmony.

And if there was death in the water, bitter beneath the sweetness of the mating scent, it only served to buoy up their joy, as the vast deserts of the Deep held up the light and warmth of the sky edge.

But then the dance ended. All the glow was quenched from Redheart's skin. Turned inward, ashen, upon herself, already brooding, already loosening her hold upon the world, she turned from Subtle, too. He could still feel the loss, the anguish, as her limb had slipped from him, and no straining of his could grasp her again.

*Hold on. Hold on,* he danced, again and again, in vain. She slipped from him and sought the vast slide where the roots of the reef went down into darkness, and she flung herself down willingly, as if Subtle were not there at all. Long he waited on the brink, dancing her name and sending out the motes of his call, till he was exhausted and could no longer create even a shadow of her scent.

Long he searched, daring ever deeper and deeper into the inky night of the Deep. But she had done everything well, and this last thing of all she had done perfectly: to hide herself until the eggs were brooded, far from any eyes. No one had ever seen her again.

Subtle waited till the brooding time had passed, and it was certain that she had perished. No matter how big and daring the female, she never outlasted the brooding. She fasted in the dark, keeping the eggs from harm, and died as they were hatching, to be their first food and fuel for the dangerous journey back to the light.

Subtle waited long past the time, but in the end he was forced to acknowledge the truth.

At first he vowed to bring clay, and smooth it, and carve a shadow wall with the shapes of her story. He spent weary lightless days dragging together a heap of the finest clays, but in the end he found himself hovering aimless upon it, like a female building a nest, but sterile of any glimmering eggs of thought.

Then he wished to die, but withheld himself from that, knowing that if he did, her memory would perish with him.

Several of the old solitaries journeyed laboriously to see him, and to try to comfort him. *We told you it would happen,* they pointed out. *Females cannot avoid the mating urge, however strong in mind. Therefore male and female can never work together. Let them hunt in their appointed circles and we in ours. It was against nature, what you did, and now you experience pain as nature rectifies the crooked limb.*

He was comforted, of course, for when the motes of comfort float within the water, one must swallow; but he rejected their wise shapings. Against nature, was it? A wish that mating and love might go with limbs braided, that continuance might not mean death?

*The Great Folk went against nature,* he danced to the old ones, daring greatly. *They changed themselves, their own nature. Everything in the Deep, they tasted and changed, and spat out different. The record of their deeds and the power to change still live with god, in the library.*

*I will go there, and I will submit myself to god. If he consumes me and changes me, I will ask for a life where female no longer dies to breed, where male and female can hunt together. And if he consumes and destroys me, so be it. Redheart's bright memory then will live forever in the memory of god, along with the price I paid to preserve it.*

Then the great solitaries began to argue among themselves, most saying that god was a myth, and even if true, impossible to reach. But a few, and Subtle's old teacher among them, said that the records of the Great Folk clearly spoke of the god, and the undoubted existence of godbits and other messengers of transformation in the water testified that god was still active and could be found.

So Subtle said his few goodbyes, donned a traveling belt, and set out for the edges of the world.

The whine of the power sound cut into Subtle's trance. He let go his grip before he thought, and was immediately tossed up and around by the swirling water. His head actually broke through the sky edge at the top of the wave, but he saw nothing. In panic he pulled his limbs in tight to his body and dropped as fast as he could, spilling the last ounce of buoyancy and jetting for added propulsion, so fast it dizzied him.

Glimpses of the coral rushed by, but he reached a safer depth without being flung against them. His mind spun with the sudden leap from trance to action, and he half thought he had flung himself down the steep with Redheart. The water seemed nearly dark enough. No, it was not Redheart he sought, but the strangers. How would he ever find them in such turmoil? He dared not go to the sky edge where they always swam.

He rose part of the way. The grinding of waves against the reef deafened him. He spun in search of other sounds, and heard the faint whine again. Storm noise cut it off, but spinning more slowly, he found the direction again. He struggled toward it, but the waves tossed him up and down, and distorted sound so he could not tell if he made progress or not.

Straining his senses upward, he suddenly felt the vibration beneath him instead. He looked down in astonishment, and saw the watersmooth shape of the strangers' floating madething. Subtle had just wit and strength enough to furl and drop upon the thing and cling to it as it passed slowly beyond the reef and outward toward the Deep.

## 8

The storm swelled to fill the world. In Per's mind, it ceased to be an event and became an eternal condition. There was a chronometer in the lifeskip, but he kept forgetting what day it had been when they started, so the little green numbers changed without meaning.

Once or twice he tried to ease the lifeskip up to the surface, but the turbulence got worse, Dilani whined tonelessly inside her mask, and even Bey looked over toward him, too polite to complain, but wanting to. So he tried to keep them level, using minimal power, and stayed below the surface.

He let Bey and Dilani unbelt, to stretch and wriggle, but they couldn't fully sit up in the cramped space. They all experienced muscle cramps from lying in the same position, and began to itch under their skinsuits, but could not scratch. Per tried telling them stories, but the monster stories made him uneasy in that tight space.

He ended up translating selected portions of his notebook into sign as best he could. He was still missing many technical words, and Bey couldn't help him with those. It was a strange kind of signing, hands stretched up over his head, but talking to the newgens for many hours improved his fluency. He found that Bey and Dilani used many signs that were faster and more allusive than the ones he had learned. He realized that he had been signing slowly and stiffly, like an old fogy.

After what he thought must have been several days down, he began to worry about their health. All of them became lethargic and irritable. He felt thick and slow, as if he wasn't

157

getting enough air. Without recharging in sunlight, the filters couldn't function at peak efficiency.

Cautiously, he nosed upward again. The luminescent organisms still clung to the canopy, even when waves began to break across it. Per couldn't get a good look at the outside world through the coating of organic jelly. So he warned Bey and Dilani to strap in and have their masks ready, and he retracted the canopy.

The lifeskip pitched and rolled, but in a regular, repetitive rhythm, not the chaotic motion of the hurricane. The sky was gray, and no longer embattled with burgeoning white towers. Waves raced, hissing, across the lacy gray sea, under a mist of foam. Far off on the horizon, Per thought he saw a softening, a brightening, as if the clouds might be breaking up.

"All right, kids, you can come up," he said to Bey. "It's over."

Seeing Per gesture, Dilani stood up immediately, lost her balance, and sat down hard. She pulled herself to her feet again more slowly, holding one hand to her head as if it hurt her.

When they had climbed out of the hold, Per slid the deck plate back over it. They sat by the gunwale, abovedecks for the first time in days. The wind seemed very cold after the enclosed atmosphere below. The autopilot kept the lifeskip heading up into the wind. Waves crossed the sea as straight and regular as if they had been lined out with a ruler, and the little boat spanked across each one with the same leap and nod.

There was no land in sight.

There was nothing in sight anywhere but the waves receding to the far horizon, and the gray sky with its matching lines of cloud. Between them flew the invisible wind, etching its wake on sky and sea alike. Dilani stared at the water flying by; absently, she licked the salt from her lips. After a long time she turned her eyes from the sea to Per and signed "Where?"

He could only spread his hands and shrug. He had no idea.

\* \* \*

Subtle clung to the surface of the madething as it ascended toward the sky edge. He saw the edge dimple silver around the tips of his limbs. Then the silver dimple enlarged around him, vanished, and he lay flattened and gasping in the emptiness of the Dry. He pressed closer to the smooth surface under him. He felt that if he loosened his grip for an instant, he would fall away into the searing gray void.

He wondered if he had gone blind, for he could find nothing to fix his eyes on. But when he focused them close, he could see his own limbs, and something that thinned and thickened, colorless when thin and then with a vague silver-bluish color where it thickened. It came and went over the surface, and after watching it, Subtle suddenly connected it with the feeling of cool wetness coming and going across his body, and realized that this was what the Deep medium looked like when you were out of it. When the Deep was brought into the Dry, it pooled together into a thing with color and surface and changing shape. That thought shuddered through him with strangeness.

He looked farther along the surface and saw something colored and solid. He could not smell it in the Dry; the scent motes penetrated through the Dry too slowly, and there was no wet to bring them to his gills. It stuck to the surface like the foot of a mollusc, but then it flexed and lifted and stuck itself down again. There were two of those things, each with a thick stalk that extended upward. Subtle stretched himself to see farther. The two stalks joined at the top, into a bulk that seemed too great for them to support out there in the Dry. From the bulk, more stalks split off, but those hung down and wavered about as if they floated in the Deep. Above the place where the down-hanging stalks split off, a small bulbous mass rose up. It was shaped like a limb bud on a flowermouth.

At that point Subtle experienced another shudder of shocking thought. The bud mass was encircled by a thing like a thick membrane or folds of fin, a thing Subtle suddenly thought he recognized. He also thought he recognized the color pattern of the bulging torsolike mass below the bud. It was black and red in curved stripes, till part of the way down the stalks, when the color changed to a pale, fleshy pink. The thing shifted its foot surfaces again, and he saw another creature behind it. That one seemed to have collapsed, so its feet and stalks could not be seen, but it had the trailing fronds around the head. The surge of joy would have sent him spinning if he had been in the water.

He had succeeded; he had found the strange creatures from the Dry.

A moment later he was terrified. The being with the fronds around its top end unfolded suddenly, revealing two footed stalks and two dangling ones, like the other, and it began to lurch toward him, shifting each foot in turn, but in an unnatural way—lifting them alternately right off the surface, not sliding them along it as a mollusc would. His vision began to blur. He needed to breathe. He wanted to stay and meet the creature's examination, but the need for breath motes was too great. He slid from the surface into the sea, but he kept one limb pressed tight to the madething. He had come too far to lose them.

"By hell, it's an octopus," Per exclaimed. "Careful, it's an octopus," he repeated impatiently in sign, as Dilani moved toward the stern.

Dilani pushed past him to see it. He realized that the sign he had used meant little, because she had no associations with *octopus*. To her, he had merely stated the obvious: that they had found something with tentacles.

The creature slipped off into the water, apparently alarmed by Dilani's approach, but it did not swim away. One tentacle still clung tightly to the stern of the lifeskip. Once it was unfolded in the water, Per could see just how big the creature really was. The tentacles moved and twined so much that he couldn't count them, but he thought there were more than eight. Their full spread looked bigger than a human's height— over ten feet, maybe fifteen.

He heard a splash. While he had been counting tentacles, Dilani had jumped into the water.

He shouted her name without thinking. Then he turned and

snapped on his own safety line, grabbed hers, and jumped in after her. The water was still moving fast. Anyone who was separated from the lifeskip might never find it again.

Per found himself in the midst of the tentacles; they wove curiously around him. He forced himself to focus on the sensation alone, not the panicky overdrive of his imagination.

The tentacles touched him gently, but he could feel their power: all muscle, like a snake. No, no; not like a snake. Per didn't like snakes. They had the same springy muscularity as the ketos, but without the harsh texture of the ketos' studded skin. The skin of the octopus felt silky and deceptively soft over those flexing cables of muscle.

He looked at the body and suddenly caught sight of an eye three times the size of his own.

*Allfather, it's looking at me,* he thought. His mouth went dry with fear. The eye was yellowish, and seemed to have a round pupil that dilated and constricted as it fixed on him. Within the iris—if it was an iris—grains of color seemed to flow and shimmer. The eye seemed to have no lid, but as he watched, a membrane swept across it. Then the creature's gaze shifted from Per to Dilani.

The tip of one tentacle moved around Dilani's head. Per noticed with fascination the delicacy and precision of its movements. It wound itself around a strand of her hair and pulled. She jerked away, clutching at the tentacle with both hands and squeezing. The octopus let go of her hair and twined its tentacle tips around her fingers, separating them and feeling over them one by one.

*It's a dodecapod,* Per thought, *not an octopod.* He had counted twelve tips. The creature continued to examine Dilani's hands, like a mother counting a baby's fingers and toes.

The creature still kept one or two limbs curled around Per, not threateningly tight, but as if it wanted to assure continued contact. Per dared to reach out toward the body, a mass about as big as Bey's torso. The skin there wasn't smooth like that on the tentacles, but ribbed and stippled. When Per touched it, the skin puckered, and a rainbow of colors rippled across its pores. Purple and white flickered across it, and the dodecapod seemed to pull itself together in a violent contraction.

Startled, Per pulled back his hand, his heart pounding. He and the creature stared at each other.

It moved away from them, still clinging to the stern of the lifeskip. It didn't touch them again, but its arms moved over and under each other in a ceaseless rhythm that Per found vaguely sickening to watch. Dilani seemed to be fascinated by the motion.

She hung still in the water, and then began to move her arms and legs as if in imitation of the dodecapod's fluid motions. It looked as if she were trying to sign, but in a wider space, one that went all around her body instead of occupying a window in front of her face and chest. Per took advantage of her concentration and the creature's withdrawal to swim behind her and fasten the safety line.

He thrust his hand in front of her face to get her attention and signed, "Get back on the boat."

She shook her head, frowning, but he pointed to the deck, where Bey stood guard with a speargun. As soon as Dilani saw the gun, she swam to the side and pulled herself out of the water. Then she tried to grab the gun from Bey.

"You must not shoot him," she signed. "He's friendly."

Per followed and sank down on the deck, realizing too late that he was in a puddle created by drips from his wet suit. The water had been warm, but the wind was cold.

"Friendly? No!" he signed wearily. "It's a dangerous wild animal. It could kill you, and we know *nothing* about it. Keep away. Understand?"

Dilani scooted along the deck toward the dodecapod. It was still holding on to the stern. Even though they were out of the water, they weren't beyond its reach. Per didn't know how strong it might be out of water. Sol-Terran cephalopods had no interior bony structure and collapsed out of water, though they could manage to breathe for some limited time. The skeggorm on Skandia was more like a snake; though it appeared tentacular, it had a rigid skeletal frame within. Skeggorms were dangerous in or out of the water, as Per knew from experience. He caught Dilani by the collar of her skin-suit and yanked her away from their unwelcome companion.

"I said keep away," he emphasized.

She shot him a venomous look. To distract her, he asked, "Why do you think he's friendly?" He kept shivering, and his hands felt clumsy as he signed. He wanted to be wrapped in something dry. He wanted hot food.

She scowled. "He's strong," she pointed out. "He could have hurt us, but he didn't. You like ketos, and they *did* hurt us."

"That was an accident," Per signed, interrupting, but Dilani stuck out her chin and pushed his hands down.

"You like ketos; I like the octopus."

"Fine, you like him. But don't touch him."

Bey had gone through the lockers in search of a net and had set it off to the side of the boat.

"I thought maybe some fresh food, Teacher Per," he said.

"You can stop calling me Teacher," Per said. "We're not in Typhon colony anymore, and if we ever get back, you'll be an adult."

"Sure, Teacher, if that's how you want it." He made careful adjustments to the net lines. "You really don't know where we are?"

"Well, I know roughly what direction we were going, and at what speed. So I have some idea what area of the ocean we're in. My best guess is that the currents will have carried us farther along the island chain, so there may be some land nearby. But I don't know exactly which way to go—nor how to get back to where we were. I don't know the currents and the winds here."

Bey's face was serious, but he concentrated on checking the net. It was hard to tell if he was worried or not.

"Well, it's not like we'd be safe if we could get back to the island, is it?" he said finally. "So we're in the water. The whole world is water."

The net already contained half a dozen pale golden fish of a species Per had never seen before. Bey knocked their heads against the deck, then skinned and gutted them. He threw the entrails overboard before Per could warn him not to, for fear of predators. The dodecapod—Per was already tired of the cumbersome name—saved him the trouble. It neatly corralled the tidbits and tucked them into a mouth somewhere beneath the swirl of tentacles. Dilani reached for one of the fish and flipped it to the creature. She signed "fish" to it.

"Don't feed it," Per signed. "It will never go away."

"I don't want it to go away," Dilani responded.

"At least we know that it eats these fish," Bey said.

"I don't know what that tells us," Per grumbled. "We don't know what's good for an octopus. It might easily eat things that would poison us."

Bey sniffed the firm, slightly translucent flesh of the fish.

"It smells all right. There aren't enough rations in the boat to get us home, if we're as far away as you think. Besides, I'm sick of rations."

He put a piece in his mouth and chewed. They waited, and nothing happened. The dodecapod put out a questing tentacle in search of more fish, and Dilani slipped it another one.

"All right, all right," Per said irritably. "Give me some, before Dilani's friend gets it all."

They followed the meal of plain fish with a suck of warm, flat-tasting water from the boat's distillery. Then Per made them inventory the lifeskip carefully, checking the supply of food and medicine, going over sheets and sails. He himself swam beneath the hull and examined every inch of it.

He had not expected any damage, and he didn't find any, but he saw that the tiny organisms that had covered the canopy had attached themselves to the hull.

He tried to scrape them off with a gloved hand, but they only clung briefly to his hand, and then migrated back to the hull. He was sorry he had touched them when a small clump drifted to his bare forearm and attached itself to the skin. He felt a prickly, crawling sensation, like being stung by ants. He brushed the clump off, hard, and backpaddled away from the hull. He climbed back onto the deck, wondering if he had been injected with some kind of venom, and if so what its effects would be. He felt a little shaky, and his arm stung for half an hour, but nothing serious happened.

He warned Dilani and Bey to be careful around the jelly creatures. He felt stupid. He had assumed the creatures were harmless simply because he had enjoyed their light during the long night of the hurricane. As a result, he had been stung, and now he was stung by his own foolishness, too.

He felt chilled again, and squeezed his belt surreptitiously, wondering if it was heating properly. He couldn't feel any warmth. He kept his hands pressed close against his sides, and eventually the chilled fingers began to warm.

Bey silently handed him a sweetbar. Mentally he calculated how many bars they had left, and knew there wouldn't be enough if they kept eating them at the rate they had been. But he accepted the bar and bit it anyway. He was alarmed by his own weakness, and didn't want the children to notice it.

He looked at his arm; the skin was marked with tiny, regular circles of red dots, as if pricked out by some tidy tool. Within the circles, the skin was bruised and slightly raised, as if something had been sucking on it. It looked as if the jelly creatures had taken a little of his blood.

*Well, it would be no worse than bloodfly in the High North, on Skandia,* he thought. *Anyway they can't bite through the skinsuits—I don't think.*

Subtle could hardly contain his agitation; he stretched himself into the water as far as he could while keeping one limb-tip on the madething. But he could not quite let go.

He had seen godbits! More astonishing still, he had seen the godbits taste of the stranger. He scanned the water all around him, and at last, in mouth direction, toward the backward side, he saw them gathering.

The first became visible, glimmering out of the dark below as a circlet of tiny points of blue light. Those were eyes, twelve of them. When they came close enough, Subtle could see the outlines of the miniature limbs fringing the opening below the eyes. Then came a dome of linked globules whose function none of the Round Folk fully understood. Within one of the globules, Subtle saw a bubble of red. If, as he guessed, that globule was a sample stomach, then the Dry creatures who had just been sampled had red blood, perhaps similar in structure to Subtle's own.

More godbits drifted outward from beneath the curve of the madething. While Subtle gazed in wonder, they linked together to form a drifting ring. God had sent its emissaries, and they had tasted the strangers. Now, surely, if Subtle followed, he would find god—and his quest would be fulfilled.

But he could not leave his discoveries. Here, in the open sea, he might never find them again. Conflict tore at him.

The godbit ring had completed itself. Subtle could not keep still any longer. He had to seek contact with god. He loosed his hold on the smooth madestuff and glided on a breath toward the ring. He extended his palping limbs toward it, the most honorable of the limbs. He hardly dared, but he let just the tip penetrate the opening of the ring. He quivered with excitement as the ring brushed his skin and then contracted around his tentacle.

He felt the sting, and watched as a thin thread of red moved around the opening to pool in another globule. He had been right; those structures were sample stomachs. The ring stretched, moved up his limb, and again he felt the sting, but not as strongly. The third time, he felt nothing; the godbit must have attuned itself to his body, as tangleweed did. It was injecting a substance that killed the pain as it sampled.

The ring parted to form a straight line and glided up Subtle's body to re-form as a crown circling the vulnerable spot between his eyes. He did not feel anything; he could not see the godbit any more, but he knew it was there.

Suddenly blue-white sparks bloomed in his eyes, and vanished as suddenly as they had come. Clusters of scents and sights expanded and faded before he could attach any meaning to them. A mixture of exaltation and terror filled his scent pores. He guessed that the godbit was sampling his mind as well as his blood.

The roil of restimulated memories slowed and quieted. He tentatively raised the tip of one limb and found that the godbit ring had gone. Weak with shock, he let himself sink slightly, beyond the waves' tugging, into calmer water.

The ring was gone. If there was another in the vicinity, he could not sense it. But as he let soothing breaths of water ripple through his gills, he tasted a strange flavor in the water nearby. It tasted familiar, like himself, but with something foreign and stronger added, something that stimulated yet repelled investigation. It was the taste of the godbit.

Though these were strange waters, Subtle hung motionless and tried to sense the direction of the waves. He could distinguish the wind-driven surface movement from a deeper crosscurrent. That deep current moved in a way that showed it had been blocked and turned aside by some tremendous object rising from the sea floor ahead of them. The godbit trail went in that direction.

He sensed distant water messages, probing tentatively in thought along the godbits' path, and was suddenly overwhelmed by a message that was close and demanding. It was as if it had been injected into his own blood. He had not just been sampled—the godbits had seeded him with motes and memories that clung, that drew, that demanded.

He could no longer choose to follow the dimming path of the godbits. He *burned* to follow it. He had been godcalled, and all other purposes fell away.

He had always thought that, if this moment ever came, it would be a glorious one. But dread flowed as a dark, cold current beneath the amazement. He saw himself now as a single mote in the Deep—no longer free to come and go, to plan and decide, but caught in an irresistible tide, like a grain of sand swept from the Dry over the steep shelf and into the abyss.

Without thinking, he began to jet away in the direction of the call, but the call itself stopped him. God had not summoned him alone. He had a mission. He must bring the strangers to the place he yearned toward, the place where they all would see god. He did not know how, but it must be done.

He broke surface again, and was relieved to find that the strangers had not journeyed far in the time he had been preoccupied. He reclaimed his position at the end of the floating thing, and continued to watch them. All the while his limbs stirred in thought. If only he could speak to them and explain how important it was to follow the godbits! If only he could find out what they were doing in these seas. Perhaps they too had a quest.

There could be cooperation, if only he could find communication.

Dilani saw that Per felt bad from whatever had bitten him. She was sorry for that, but it didn't stop her from edging along the hull toward the twelve-foot as soon as she saw that Per had closed his eyes to rest for a minute. She didn't think Per was right to call it "the twelve-foot." Those weren't feet; they were hands. She had felt them touching her.

The ketos could "hear," so Per said. They had no hands, and they had big sharp teeth. The twelve-creature probably had teeth, but she had not seen them. Its touch was gentle and clever, unlike the blows of the keto's blunt snout. If all twelve limbs were hands, it had more hands than she did. Even if each tip was only a finger, it still had two more than a human. With so many clever fingers, surely it would have a language.

"Twelve," she signed to it, but the big round eyes goggled at her without reacting. *Not too surprising if it doesn't know how to count,* she thought. A puddle of water lay on the deck near Twelve; Dilani dipped her fingers in it and laid them against her lip in the water sign. Twelve should know what water was. But still it did not move or blink. Dilani tried to pick up one tentacle tip and dip it in the water, but the tentacles were surprisingly strong and resistant. She could not get the creature to cooperate.

Subtle watched as the creature with the dark tendrils dragged itself toward him and touched him with its upper appendages. At this distance, he could see that it had eyes—or at least, it had organs that resembled eyes. They were positioned on the front side of its top bulge or bud—or at least, what he thought was the front side. That was the side it presented first, anyway. Each eyelike spot appeared to have a pupil that responded to light, though the surrounding iris appeared static and unresponsive, always the same dark color. The eyes appeared small and somewhat flattened, so that Subtle wondered how they managed to focus enough light for seeing.

He was surprised when the creature touched him. He remembered that the other one also had placed its appendage against his skin. The touch was unpleasantly dry. He curled his limb around the creature's and tugged. If he could get it to come back into the water, it would be easier for him to examine it.

He was surprised again when the creature appeared to understand, and slid over the edge of its floating platform into the water. It still wore the attachment on its head, but the face area—if it was a face—remained visible, and the device had not closed over it.

The creature had a protruberance below its eyes whose function Subtle could not guess, and below that was an opening that looked very much like a mouth. It had lips like a fish mouth, though it did not seem to be taking in water for breathing. To have a mouth on the front side of the face, so close to the eyes, seemed vaguely disgusting, as well as inefficient.

However, it was the appendages that most intrigued Subtle. The limbs were straight, and awkwardly attached, capable of bending only in a limited and narrow range of motion. Yet, at the end of each upper limb, there was a cluster of smaller limbs. They mimicked the larger limbs in that they were straight and bent only at certain joints, but their motion seemed defter and more flexible.

The creature appeared to have a complete lack of sensitivity to scent ambients, exhibited no apparent sound-sensing organs, and seemed to possess an awkward and limited range of communication. Subtle wondered how it could survive at all. He felt a proprietary compassion for it. Certainly these creatures were not dangerous; his earlier panic at their approach seemed ridiculous. Yet there was still the puzzle of their association with the Laughing Teeth. How did something so defenseless swim with the Teeth without being eaten? They might still surprise him with hidden abilities.

In any case, this wasn't solving the problem of whether or not the creatures could communicate. Subtle twined a greeting and breathed out a scent message of good intentions. Scholars had determined that the main components of the peace message were chemicals that indicated a lack of hunger. Subtle couldn't imagine how one would begin to eat such a thing, anyway. All bones and unpleasant thin skin, wrapped in a nasty-smelling garment of madestuff. He quickly stopped himself from thinking of eating, lest the traces show in the water.

The creature watched him without moving. He did not catch any responsive scents. When Subtle let his limbs trail at random again, the creature began to move, and Subtle's skin crept with excitement.

The creature lifted one appendage and placed all its tiny limbs together—Subtle saw that they looked like a flipper when it did so—and brought them to a point above its eye, then waved them outward. It didn't look like communication to Subtle, but the creature did it again. Was that random?

A shimmer of gold passed between them, interrupting Subtle's concentration. Those fish were tasty, but he did not want them now. The creature spun and looked. It put its tiny limbs together again, and pushed the resulting fin through the water, wavering from side to side. *A poor strategy for fish catching,* Subtle thought. Then it puckered its small limbs together and pushed them against what Subtle surmised to be its mouth. It was almost like the real gesture of eating.

Excited, Subtle launched himself into the midst of the school of fish and seized one. He thrust it at the creature. It pushed the tiny limbs through the water again. Subtle folded his limbs together and tucked the fish under him, into the mouth concealed beneath his mantle. If the creature was intelligent, it would see that he had just eaten in front of another in a most mannerless way. But that hardly mattered at a time of such importance. He hardly tasted the fish as he gulped it and swiftly focused again on the creature. It put the tips of those strange, straight, awkward little limbs against its orifice again and tapped them insistently. *Fish. Eat.*

It was talking!

Subtle jetted upward and spun in ecstasy. He had spoken to the creatures from beyond the world. *They were intelligent.* They could talk. His spinning limbs danced the growing of the brightwarm, the surging of rich waters from the bosom of the Deep. Then, in grandiose gestures, he equated those events with this great day and the thing that had just happened.

*On this day, I, Subtle of the Round People, spoke with a stranger from beyond the world. On this day, a new world began. Grasp this day in memory, and hold on.*

Subtle wove himself a swift, if extravagant, memory dance for the observations and the immediate moment of discovery. Then he calmed himself. *Fish* and *eat* were all very well, but there were still a thousand questions to be answered. Where should he begin?

He tried the sign for *identity/this self*. It seemed obvious enough: With a graceful, encompassing gesture, he used all of his limbs simultaneously to create a spherical volume around himself, spinning the body one complete turn at the same time, and finishing in the starting position. As he finished demonstrating, Subtle let a wash of blue-gray gradient patterns pass quickly over his skin, demonstrating his own skin name.

The creature's response was pathetic, but it gave him some hope. It tried to imitate him, but it had only four limbs, and the lower pair would not curve and extend in harmony with the others. Still, Subtle was almost sure that the upper limbs had tried to copy his gesture, and the creature did manage to spin, though it had to break the sign in order to thrash with its upper limbs, to move itself. Though he watched closely, Subtle saw no color changes taking place, nor could he smell any alteration in the surrounding water.

Subtle and the creature exchanged the sign several times, until he was sure the creature was truly trying to imitate him.

Then he asked for its identity, extending his palping limbs carefully, then retracting them before the gesture could be mistaken for an attempt to seize and eat. At the same time he let his skin subside to a neutral color, and released another dose of not-hungry signals.

The creature tried, but all it could do to copy him was to extend its scant two, broken-looking limbs, and pull them back again. No hint of its own identity followed, or none that Subtle could recognize. He waited, unsure how to clarify the situation.

Shortly, he realized that the creature was gesturing again. Such small, jerky movements it used! It hurt his eyes to focus so closely, while his other senses went begging. It put two of its tiny limbs atop another two, the rest of the limb bunch folded under. Then it put one appendage up to the side of its head, with just one tiny limb protruding. Could that be an identity sign? It seemed so petty, so barren of skin significance.

He played his colors again, but the creature could not respond. It made the sign again. Then it reached toward him. Instinctively he recoiled, but then he made himself float quietly. The creature had to use the same limbs for palping, grasping, signing; it could not indicate its intent by limb choice. Without scent indications, surely these creatures must always run the risk of initiating hostilities, even when they wanted only conversation. *Treachery and mistrust must be very common,* Subtle thought.

But he let the strange limbs touch him; it was not so unpleasant when they were wet. The creature tapped him, then withdrew and flicked two of its tiny limbs upward.

Subtle was almost insulted. Did the creature intend that as an identity for him? Or perhaps for all the Round Folk? He flounced his mantle and vented a stream of water slightly colored with internal dye, to show confusion and exasperation.

The creature seized his limb-tip again. This time it held up only one tiny limb. It gathered another limb-tip, and held up two tiny limbs. Subtle transformed from irritation to excitement again. It was trying to set up mathematical equivalence. It was counting for him. He became confused when it held up three tiny limbs again for six, but then realized that they were a different three. Configuration counted as well as strict equivalence.

Comprehension burst on him. Of course! The creature had only ten tiny limbs, where Round Folk had twelve large ones. Base ten was quite possible to use, Subtle knew; it just wasn't as convenient as the normal system.

When the creature reached the last limb, it again made the flicking-up of two tiny limbs, and then Subtle understood. The creature's name for him was *Twelve* because of his limbs. Or perhaps that was its name for all the Round Folk. It hardly mattered, since Subtle was the only one present.

Subtle decided that he could not go on calling it "the creature," especially since it had named him, however inadequately. He let one limb-tip delicately play among the tendrils on its head, and then brought his four front limbs together and rippled them to sign *Seagrass*. It was a name without color, the kind of name one gave animals, but he could hardly sign them for their color, or all three would be *Plain and Tan*.

Seagrass brought one bunch of tiny limbs together, at the side of its face where it had signed, and tried to ripple them. *It has accepted the name,* Subtle thought.

He jaunted a little way to front-syphon-side and back again toward front-plain-side, a little jig of approbation. *Now we're getting somewhere.*

At that very moment, the conversation was interrupted. A thud and a rush of bubbles indicated that something had jumped into the water. As the water cleared, Subtle saw that it was one of the other creatures, the one that wore red-and-black madestuff and was a mottled pinkish color around the edges of the red and black. On the spur of the moment, Subtle named it *Pinky*. It seized Seagrass, who seemed to struggle. Then it pushed Seagrass back toward the floating chip.

Subtle already felt protective toward Seagrass, and he

wanted to continue trying to communicate. Ripples of agitation passed over him, but he restrained himself. It would be rash to interfere between members of the same kind without knowing what the consequences would be. However, he followed them and made sure to get a good grip on their floating chip. He wasn't going to let them get away.

Dilani was furious at being interrupted. She struggled vigorously. The water slowed her down, but she could feel Per wince as her elbows connected with his ribs. On the deck, she started to sign angrily as soon as she had wiped the water out of her eyes. But Per ignored her and began signing just as furiously.

"I told you to stay out of the water! You disobey me as soon as I go to sleep! You promised to obey me."

"The twelve-foot signs. He signs," Dilani insisted. "He is friendly. He wants to talk. He *signs*."

"That thing in the water could hurt you. It—" Per broke off as what Dilani was telling him finally penetrated. "It does what?"

"Signs," she repeated. "I showed it a fish, and the *eat* sign. Then it told me a name, but I can't show it. It gave me a name sign. Like this." She repeated the finger rippling.

"I don't believe it," Per signed.

"Go see!"

Per shook his head vigorously. "It's dangerous."

"Twelve has no teeth," she signed. "You swam with the ketos. They have teeth."

She felt the same hurt inside her that she had felt on the beach when Per recoiled from the idea of mating with her. She didn't know why it felt so bad.

"You think Twelve is not smart because he can't speak," she signed. "Why don't you believe what I say? Do you think I'm stupid too? If you found me in the water, would you try to talk to me?"

Per lowered his hands, looking defeated. "All right," he signed. "All right, if it's still there tomorrow, I'll try to talk to it. But not tonight. I'm cold. It's getting dark. Now pay attention—I do not think you are stupid. *But*—even smart people are wrong sometimes. Understand?"

"You're scared," she signed, but he chose not to see her.

As the brightwarm withdrew and the dark swept after it, and the living lights of small creatures began to swim beneath him, Subtle held to his post with one limb and talked to himself with the others.

It seemed most unlikely that the creatures could grow more limbs, and even if they did, they would still be lacking the other senses needed to understand the language of the Round Folk. Subtle could perceive their way of communicating, but his separate limbs had a hard time reproducing the shapes of the bunched tiny limbs. It was axiomatic that the higher form had to be the one to learn how to communicate with the lower.

The only real question was which limbs to sacrifice. The palping limbs were the most sensitive and best supplied with small muscles, but he decided he could not risk them. Finally he settled on his front grasping limbs. He might experience a small handicap in hunting, but the limbs should retain their strength above the tip.

He found the bladder of White Arms' venom in his pouch, and carefully anointed the tips of the selected limbs with it. He had to block the pain messages to his nervous system, or his body might seal off and drop the damaged limb. Then he slipped the keen, narrow blade of metal, his scholar's weapon, from its sheath and tried to decide where to cut. He needed to leave enough bundles of muscle fibers in each segment to make it usable. The water moved his limb gently and made it hard to cut precisely until he thought of bracing the limb against the strangers' floating chip. That moved too, but at least it provided a flat hard surface. Carefully, yet swiftly, he made four incisions in each limb.

He squeezed in droplets of a solution containing mote creatures programmed with instructions to encourage growth of muscle bundles. Those particular instructions had been borrowed from a radiant arm that could regenerate any segment of its body. Normally, the Round Folk used it only in response to severe injuries, where part of the body had been actually torn away, but Subtle thought it might work also for adding tissue where none had been before.

The solution blocked the reaction of Subtle's own body chemistry that would have worked to seal the cut surfaces quickly. Just enough blood leaked out to attract the attention of the tiny jellies that disposed of dead tissue and encouraged skin growth. Once they had attached themselves, they would consume any blood that continued to trickle out.

Subtle put the knife away carefully. Though there had been no pain, it was somewhat stressful to damage himself, so he put himself into a resting trance that would last until the brightwarm came back.

# 9

Per had molded a bubble blanket tightly around himself and had finally warmed up enough to enjoy his first comfortable, unbroken sleep in a week. He was awakened unpleasantly by Dilani waving something cold and wet in his face.

"Look, look, it's a fish," she signed, inches from his badly focused eyes. He made a face that he hoped would show disgust and nausea, and tried to roll himself away from her, but she slapped his shoulder insistently.

"Twelve gave me the fish," she signed. "And he has fingers now."

Per sat bolt upright at that.

"Bey, will you tell me what is going on here?" he said aloud, but Bey didn't answer.

Dilani had seen his lips move.

"Bey is in the water," she signed. "And it's not polite to speak to him in front of me."

She must have seen the alarm on Per's face, for she added "He's fine. He can swim."

Anxiously, Per scanned the water around the boat until Bey surfaced. Something else was in the water, too. The water roiled around Bey, and then the dodecapod lifted its head for a moment.

"Stay here," Per signed, without much hope that he would be obeyed, and jumped into the water.

He soon saw that Bey was perfectly all right, and felt somewhat foolish. Bey's net bag was already full of assorted fish. The dodecapod did not appear to be hurting him, but the sight of its tentacles writhing in the water still gave Per the creeps. Reluctantly, he approached to within arm's reach of it.

"Good morning, Teacher Per," Bey greeted him breathlessly. "Twelve catches fish like magic. Wish I could maneuver that fast. I'm going back on deck to fix breakfast."

He turned to the dodecapod and signed "Thanks for the fish."

"Wait a minute. You believe it talks?"

"Sure," Bey called back as he swam for the lifeskip. "You'll see."

"Hey! If this thing tries to strangle me, for heaven's sake shoot it," Per shouted after him.

An ambiguous answer drifted faintly back.

"Don't worry."

The dodecapod flounced backward a few feet, to hang facing Per with its limbs stirring gently in the current. Slowly, it raised one tentacle to a place near its eyes, then waved it outward.

*A greeting?* Per thought. Then he focused on the tentacle, fascinated by what he saw. The limb no longer narrowed to a whiplike tip. Instead, there was a cluster of stubs, pressed tightly together. As he watched, they separated slightly, like digits. Paler, smoother skin showed on their inner surfaces, the kind of difference that, on a human, might have indicated new growth. Per's gaze flicked to the matching tentacle on the other side. It, too, had the new ending. All the other tentacles looked as they had the day before.

Dilani was right, Per thought incredulously. It has fingers. He knew he had not seen them the day before. Had the dodecapod been hiding them somehow? It hardly seemed possible that it had grown new appendages overnight.

His incredulity grew as the dodecapod brought the two limbs out in front of it and signed again. Carefully, it placed two of the stubs across two from the opposite limb.

"Name Twelve," it signed.

A wave of amazement passed over Per. He was face-to-face with a new intelligence, with thought that took a different form.

For centuries, humankind had gazed into the clouds and waters of other worlds, and had found only mirrors, reflecting their own lonely images. Per could hardly believe that luck or fate had made him the first to find a stranger's face looking back.

Then he remembered that he was not the first. Dilani had been the first. He grinned, thinking of the ridiculous name she had given him. It would be the first word he spoke to the alien race, and somehow that seemed very appropriate.

"Pinkman," he signed. "My name is Pinkman."

He rubbed the skin of his arm and signed *pink* again. Bits flaked off; he was sunburned, as usual, and long exposure to saltwater had frayed his epidermis, too. He didn't know if the dodecapod would understand that the sign meant a color, but one had to start somewhere.

Twelve—if that was indeed its name—moved about restlessly. It—he?—seemed to be seeking more words. It counted its tentacles for Per, using the correct signs. *Dilani must have taught it that,* Per thought ruefully, *while I was still insisting that it was unintelligent.* Then it delicately extended a tentacle, not one of the fingered limbs, but one of a pair of slightly smaller, more slender arms that attached to the top portion of its body, near the eyes. With the tips of those tentacles, it touched Per's fingers, while counting them, first with its own digits, in human sign, then according to some method of its own, involving combinations of tentacle tips pressed together.

When it withdrew, Per fumbled in his belt pouch, and pulled out a handful of small, colored floats used for securing nets. He swam closer to the boat and began to lay the floats out in groups on the water's surface. Twelve extended the tips of its tentacles to touch them, and in the exchange that followed, Per discovered that the dodecapod could manipulate abstract symbols, understood place value, used a base-twelve system but could convert to base ten, and knew about prime numbers.

Per had also glimpsed a waistlike narrowing of the dodecapod's rounded body, partly concealed by its mantle.

Around that narrower portion, it seemed to be wearing a belt much like his own. On first sight, the pouches and sheaths had appeared to be organs of some kind, but Per became convinced they were artifacts. He touched his own belt and tried to open discussion, but Twelve seemed to be agitated. The dodecapod bunched its tentacles together, then shot them outward, moving back slightly. Clearly, the gesture was deliberate, but Per wasn't sure what Twelve meant by it.

A call from the lifeskip interrupted him.

"Per! Want breakfast?"

"Fish. Eat." Per signed to the dodecapod, and began swimming slowly toward the boat. "Come," he signed, as the dodecapod began to follow him. Suddenly Per had an idea. "Go," he signed, and then moved in another direction, away from both the boat and Twelve.

Twelve hung motionless, watching, apparently puzzled. Per acted the little scene again, but the dodecapod didn't respond. Per thrust himself above the surface as far as he could.

"Bey!" he shouted. "Send Dilani here."

"The fish is getting cold," Bey complained, but moments later, Dilani swam out to them.

Per apologized extravagantly as soon as he saw her, smacking his chest vigorously with his fist in addition to the usual "sorry."

"You were right," he signed. "I am stupid. But please try to talk to me anyway."

She looked puzzled, then remembered their earlier exchange and smiled. For a moment, her face held no trace of a scowl. She spread her arms, then pulled them in tight and spun in the water like the dodecapod.

"I need you to help sign for Twelve," Per signed, when she was facing him again. "Teach him 'go' and 'come.' "

Dilani nodded; Per signed "go" to her and she swam swiftly away from him. He beckoned, and she swam back. When he repeated the signs, Twelve gathered up its limbs and jaunted along with Dilani. Then the dodecapod repeated its own gesture: It bunched its tentacles and shot them forward, moving itself slightly backward. Then it launched itself away from them. Coming to a standstill, it stretched out the grasping arms and waved them in a movement analogous to Per's beckoning. Dilani swam to it. Twelve bobbed up and down several times, then spun in apparent glee.

"Come," Per signed again, starting toward the lifeskip. "Fish. Eat!"

Now that communication had been established, Subtle's one burning desire was to follow the godbit traces before they vanished completely. However, the Dry creatures insisted on the need for eating. They ate very often, Subtle reflected, though not in great quantity. Perhaps their digestive systems were as rudimentary as their communications. After his digit-building exertions, Subtle thought his body could use more nourishment, so he didn't mind sharing their food.

He nearly spat it from his mouth when he discovered that it was heated. Older scholars had told him of encountering dead fish in the aftermath of undersea eruptions. A short time after the eruption, the flesh was coagulated but still edible, even though the fish was dead. Normally, the Round People did not touch dead food, but it was said that dead, heated food stayed edible for some hours.

Conquering his reflexes, he ground the food in his beak and gullet and swallowed it. He detected no traces of decay. The urge to regurgitate was strictly cultural, he told himself sternly, and unsuitable to a scientist. The food lacked the delicious, invigorating juices of live food, however, and he jaunted briefly away from the floating chip to find live fish to cleanse his gullet. He felt better after that, and his revulsion was replaced by heightened respect as he realized the strangers must have some controlled heat source concealed on the chip. He wondered if he might dare, in time, to crawl aboard and investigate.

Before that, however, he needed to convince them to follow him in his quest for the godbits. He had memorized the direction the godbits had gone, relative to the underlying wave patterns of the area. He aligned himself with the waves, and when he was sure of his course, took hold of the floating chip at its front end. He hoped it was the front end, anyway; the chip always seemed to move with that end first.

"Go. Go," he signaled, in their language, and then, more forcefully, in his own, with all limbs working save the one it took to hold him to the chip.

"It's trying to tow us, I think," Bey said, gazing over the bows into the water.

"Yes, it's signing just as it was in the water with us," Per signed. "Only it's signing 'go.' Do you think that means it wants us to go away?"

Dilani shook her head.

" 'Come *with* me,' same as go," she signed. " 'Come *to* me' is 'come,' our way. Twelve wants us to follow him."

"Should we?" Per looked to the newgens for opinions.

Dilani nodded emphatically with her fist. Her eyes sparkled.

"Sure," Bey signed laconically. "We have nothing better to do."

"What if it's taking us home for dinner?" Per asked.

Bey thought about it and shook his head.

"It's strong. If it wanted to eat us, it could have eaten us already. The way it plays in the water and shares fish—I think Dilani's right, and it's friendly. Curious. It seems happy when we understand it—that spin thing it does."

"So you think we should trust it?" Per signed.

Bey shrugged. "Nothing's safe, Teacher Per. Isn't that what you've tried to tell us? But it won't hurt us on purpose. Our job is to be careful."

"Well, maybe their idea of dinner conversation is different from mine," Per signed, "but I myself—talk about prime numbers with somebody, then eat him? No, never. All right, let's try it."

He ran the sails up, and set a course in the direction the dodecapod seemed to indicate. It was a tedious process. He tried to set the autopilot to hold their course, but Twelve kept dropping off the bows to swirl itself in the water. When it reattached, it would show a slightly different heading. It was more trouble to reset the pilot than to steer by hand, so Per sat by the tiller hour after hour.

By midmorning, he could feel his skin crisping in the unrelenting sun that had burned off the last rags of storm cloud. He asked Bey to rig him a shade. They went slowly. The wind was light, but the lifeskip was capable of making good way in the lightest airs. The problem was Twelve; if they went faster than it could naturally swim, it would drop off again to reorient itself. Per surmised that the bow wave might interfere with the dodecapod's direction-finding method, whatever that was.

They glided over long, easy swells all day, and saw nothing that would give them a clue to their location. The sea spread around them like an opalescent disk of blue shell, and they seemed fixed in its center. Bey and Dilani took their watches at the tiller. Per tried to sleep, but found it difficult. Curiosity nagged at him; he wanted to talk to Twelve again. Finally he checked his safety line and slid into the water with the dodecapod.

But he was disappointed. Twelve seemed preoccupied and didn't respond to Per's efforts to open a conversation. Nevertheless, Per stayed in the water with it. Several times, he watched Twelve stop and spin itself slowly, and wondered if the dodecapod had organs that allowed it to sense magnetic lines, or some other directional clues.

At sunset, Dilani pointed in the direction they were traveling—into the darkening eastern sky. Per turned; he had been watching the furnace glow of the sunset and wondering what was happening on the atoll far behind them. His eyes slowly readjusted to the dim shades of nightfall, and he saw that the dark motes darting about the horizon were bird flocks swarming about some invisible point. His heart lifted with hopes of an island, and he steered on with greater confidence in Twelve's pathfinding.

As darkness fell, Per let the young ones steer and returned to the water. Its gold and green shadings faded with the sunlight, leaving it a ghostly blue gray. The dodecapod's skin rippled with matching colors till it almost seemed to disappear in the shadows. A myriad of tiny lights began to shine in the depths below them, and then in the waters around them. Occasionally, tiny beads of light paused for a moment on Per's hands and arms. These didn't sting, but they weren't easy to brush away. They clung until they felt like moving, then floated off like bubbles. Looking down, Per saw that his feet were outlined in luminescence.

Several hours of the night had passed before they reached the distant place of birds. The birds no longer flew. A few stubs of rock showed as dark shapes against the light-sprinkled water. The smell of guano drifted across the waves, and Per heard the soft, constant shifting of the resting flocks.

"Dilani wants to know where the island is," Bey called to him.

"I'm afraid it's underwater," Per said. "This looks like a guyot or a seamount. Either it never rose above the surface, or it's been worn down below the surface. I'd guess it's a seamount because of those rookeries still sticking up."

It occurred to Per that they should anchor till morning, whatever the dodecapod thought. Even if the island was completely submerged, Per wanted a chance to look at it in daylight, and if it was partially above water, he didn't want to risk running aground in the dark.

"Bey, down sail and drop anchor," he called.

The light but steady pressure of their passage through the water ceased, and Per felt the up-and-down rocking of waves over the sunken island. The dodecapod loosed its hold on the bow and submerged slightly. Suddenly, its limbs jerked together in a convulsive motion that seemed to lack the fluidity of its ordinary gestures. Before Per could try to get its attention, it began to drop through the dim, pearl-shot water.

Per looked down. His own feet no longer glowed bright against dark, but showed as shadows against a pale blue light gleaming up from below, like a moon beneath the sea. Twelve's curving limbs showed clearly against the light as the dodecapod sank directly toward its center.

"Bey! Throw me a dive line," Per called urgently.

Bey's face appeared over the side.

"You're going down there? Now?" he said. "What if you don't come up? Then what do I do?"

"I'm not going far," Per said. "I can't wait till morning. The light down there is shining now. If that's what Twelve has been leading us to, I want to know what it is."

Bey disappeared briefly, then came back and threw the line into the water.

"We'll give you twenty minutes," he said. "Then Dilani and I come down after you."

"Absolutely not," Per said. "I want you to stay in the boat."

"Sorry," Bey said. "That's our decision. We agreed."

*Treating them as adults has its disadvantages,* Per thought. But he couldn't be both underwater and above it, enforcing his orders. He grasped the line—which almost immediately was outlined in dots of light—and let the weight carry him downward.

At fifteen meters, he found he was gaining on Twelve. Somewhere between fifteen and thirty meters, he saw a rough surface behind the light. He still couldn't see what caused the light itself; it glowed too brightly.

Twelve seemed to be hovering, and Per paused just above the dodecapod. Gradually his eyes adjusted, and he followed Twelve, the two of them inching downward.

The bulk of the seamount extended below him, and stretched out on either side to some unguessable distance. The visible portions were layer on layer of dead coral rock. Some kind of cleft or fault showed as a line of dark shadow in the blue glow.

He continued to descend till he hung only a few feet above the topmost coral fragments, and then he could see where the light originated. The cleft in the seamount's summit was lined with oval shapes, as long as Per's body. They appeared to be bivalve shells, but all were open, and within those caskets he saw fantastic shapes, like soft antlers, like rounded fern branches, like multiple fingers in fringed gauntlets. The muscular forest swayed and rippled softly and emanated a bioluminescence almost bright enough to read by.

Twelve paid no attention to the display. The dodecapod had moved past the row of guardian shells and was gazing at something else, swaying about its own axis in a way that looked to Per like rapt amazement. Per swam slowly over the glowing guardians, careful not to brush against them, until he floated directly above Twelve again.

For a moment, he thought his eyes must be mistaken. Within the fault line, there was a smooth, flat, vertical surface, different from the crumbled convolutions of the dead coral. As Per watched, Twelve's tentacles reached out to caress that space. Beneath the moving limb-tip, Per saw figures, carved into the wall, picked out in low relief by the blue light cast upon them.

None of the shapes seemed familiar to him. They marked the rock in ordered rows, evenly spaced: too orderly, he thought, to be an accident, and too diverse to be explained as tracks of some kind. His eye followed Twelve's tentacle, and suddenly he saw a shape he understood. Twelve caressed the outline of a dodecapod.

At that moment, Per saw something familiar emerge from the shadows of the trench. It was a compact, transparent dome fringed with glassy tendrils, each of which glowed with a tiny pearl of light. It drifted over to the dodecapod, opened like a bracelet, and closed around Twelve's tentacle. Indigo and deep purple formed concentric rings on the dodecapod's body, flowing up from the place where the jelly banded it. Twelve hung motionless; its questing tentacle slipped from the carved wall.

Then the ring re-formed into a dome and began to swim, with a bobbing, twirling motion, toward Per. He drew back, remembering the sting from the last time he had encountered such an organism. He grasped the line to ascend, but he was too late. The bracelet of fringed lights closed around his wrist.

He felt the sting again; his skin seemed brushed with fire as the ring moved up from wrist to elbow. He thought that he should move quickly to get rid of it, but a curiously detached sensation had come over him. He watched his other hand come up slowly and fumble at the living bracelet. He could hear his heart beating, with a hollow rush like water pouring into a cavern.

A sudden warmth rushed through him. Without warning, he felt unbelievably good. His hand floated away from the organism, and his head floated back, relaxing as if the water were a pillow. The sting felt better than any mindmod.

*I should be able to resist this,* he thought dimly. He puzzled over his lack of fortitude, and convinced himself that he could resist it if he wanted to, but he couldn't seem to find a reason for resistance. He noticed that the living bracelet seemed to be moving up his arm. That was nice; he enjoyed watching it come closer to his eyes so he could see it better. It was made up of many smaller envelopes of clear plasm, each containing transparent or colored shapes that moved within the bubble like unicellular organisms in a microviewer.

The bracelet moved out of sight; he wondered where it could be.

Then the question was swallowed up in a sudden burst of fragmented memories—vivid, random samples of his own past. The part of him that floated above the experience wondered if the bubble creature was causing changes in his brain chemistry. The rest of his mind experienced lava fire; the wash of surf; warm, dry skin contact; a sudden snippet of Sofron's voice that jolted him like an electric shock and then vanished.

The sampling moved rapidly backward in time until he reached the moment of first splashdown on Typhon. Over and over he relived that impact. Then, as if that had broken through some barrier, he fell through it into a different splashdown. The shuttlecraft lurched and thudded, and the locks opened to show him a gray, ice-cold world where hard gravity clawed at his shivering body.

For the first time since it had happened, he remembered arriving on Skandia. His lips moved in slow, soundless protest.

"Nnrh." He heard himself moan inside the mask. He saw the dome with its fringe of glowing dots dancing erratically away into the darkness. The euphoric feeling seemed to go with it, but the slowness persisted. He felt a bumping, scraping sensation and realized that his belt weights must have carried him slowly downward while he hung in the trance of the jelly creature. He bumped against the rough coral. A small cloud of gritty sediment rose around him. His hands flailed clumsily as he tried to pull himself upright, and a fragment of rock broke off in his grasp.

The dodecapod's limbs agitated the water above him, and Per felt vaguely sick at the sight of their writhing. From that angle, he could see something that resembled a mouth working at the center of the limbs. Helpless to withdraw, he had to keep watching, and he began to see that Twelve was not moving aimlessly.

The limbs made patterns. They separated and crossed in changing combinations, three against two, five on seven, then two sets of three as Twelve rose a couple of feet and sank again till it was eye-to-eye with Per. But Per could not grasp the message, and the dodecapod let its limbs falter and float. He seemed defeated.

Then the limbs moved forward in concert again. They stretched out and closed gently around Per's body, forming a sort of cradle. He cringed at the cool, warty texture of Twelve's skin, but the feeling of being supported wasn't entirely unpleasant. He felt himself moved upward in a jerky glide. A strange dotted line of light crossed his field of vision.

It was the weighted line. He recovered enough to reach for it and hold on.

Twelve tugged at him gently, but when he resisted, Twelve stopped and waited, still supporting him in the water. He remembered to check his armband. The timer recorded a safe twenty-five minutes. He pressed the depth gauge for a maximum reading and got forty meters. He was safe; he could go up, but his grip loosened before he could check the timer again, and he felt himself drifting downward.

Twelve's tentacles gently stopped his fall. He was shoved upward and bundled over the gunwale of the lifeskip, where human hands met him at last.

Dilani pulled his mask open and signed to him, but he couldn't keep his eyes focused. He heard Bey's voice.

"What happened? We were about to come after you."

"I saw—" Per croaked, but he couldn't get any farther. "Wonderful." He waved his hand, trying to show the magnitude of his discovery, and found his left fist still clenched around an object, some fragment of the seamount. He opened his fingers with difficulty, and the fragment clattered to the deck. Bey picked it up and turned it over, holding it where Per could see it. It was a curved shard of clay, the rows of carved figures still fresh and clear. Per's eyelids floated inexorably shut.

Subtle dropped back into the light and spread his limbs across the wall as if to print its carvings on his skin.

The godbits had brought him here. Even in its marred condition, the wall told of the Great People and held clues to the location of their god. The curve of the currents told him of more high places within the Deep. The rock fins stabbing up past the sky edge marked the way. He could speed to his goal, if only he did not have to guide the Dry creatures. The godbit call that filled him with energy and excitement seemed to weaken them. He did not understand why, and it disturbed him. He waited impatiently for them to return.

Per awoke with the sun in his eyes and a raging thirst. Dilani crouched anxiously beside him, and started to question him as soon as she saw his eyes open, but he signed for water and turned his head away.

As he raised the cup she brought him to his lips, she grabbed his wrist so that water spilled over his chin.

"What's that?" she signed.

Per saw that his arm was ringed by a circle of scarlet pinpricks.

"Something in the water stung me," he signed, setting down the drink. "Will you just *wait* a minute?"

Bey held out a tray for Dilani to carry over to Per. "Eggs," he said, grinning. "I swam over to the nearest perch and lifted a few. Phew, it smelled awful, but the eggs are all right. Try to think of it as fish that luckily tastes like fried eggs, instead of eggs that unluckily taste like fish. Eat and tell; I'll translate."

As he devoured his omelet, Per described the night's adventure.

"It seems there was intelligent life on Typhon in the past," he concluded. "I wish Sukarto were here. I have no way to determine how old those rocks are, or when the carvings were made. Of course, the real question is, where are the makers now?"

He polished his tray with a scrap of pressed rationbread.

Dilani held up the clay fragment. "This is more important," she signed.

Per examined it carefully. Like the wall carving, it was enigmatic. Most of the figures meant nothing to him, though he recognized a few marine creatures.

"Twelve can read it to us," Dilani signed. "We can learn more words."

"What makes you think Twelve can read it? I don't suppose its race created that wall."

"Why not?"

"Well, Twelve seems too primitive to have come from a race that old. It swims around naked except for some kind of belt, and it eats raw fish. Furthermore, why does the carving have to be writing? It might be pure decoration."

"I want to see it," Dilani insisted.

Per looked over the side. By daylight, the changing colors of the water clearly mapped the area. Fantastically eroded stubs of rock reached up into the air, but their sides plunged straight down, and they did not join above water. There was no dry land. Flocks of birds again wheeled about the rock eyries, plunging occasionally seaward to seize a fish. Apparently the hunting was rich in this area.

He rolled the cuff of his skinsuit back and scratched the flaking skin. He would have given a good deal for a rinse in fresh water. He was getting salt sores where the suit rubbed. Staying here wouldn't help them toward the landfall they needed.

"What about those stings?" Bey signed. "Is there something down there that will go after us?"

Per tried to remember the details of the incident.

"I don't think so," he signed. "I only saw one. Like last time. But whatever it injected me with, the effect was much worse. The thing looks like a small, dome-shaped jellyfloat with a ring of luminous organs around a central opening. In daylight, it would be almost invisible. If you see it, give a warning and get out of the way."

"Did it hurt Twelve?" Dilani asked.

"I don't know," Per signed. The question surprised him. "The jelly attached to Twelve's tentacle, and Twelve flashed some colors, but I don't know if that meant pain or what."

"It's still down there, by the wall," Bey signed. "I looked while you were sleeping."

"Go down," Dilani signed emphatically.

"We need to move on."

"Learn more words," Dilani signed.

"She's right," Bey agreed. "If we could communicate, explain, maybe Twelve could take us to land. Maybe there's a whole civilization in the Deep somewhere. We can't just sail away from him."

"Not so fast," Per signed. "I believe Twelve is intelligent, but it still isn't human. How do we know it thinks like us?"

"Twelve isn't a thing; it's a boy," Dilani signed, and Per understood what she meant: *Twelve is not an it, he's a person.*

"Teacher Per," Bey signed, "I don't know biology, but I know people, and I know Twelve is one. Maybe he will change his mind. I guess you're right; he could do that. But right now, he doesn't want to hurt us. And he is the only help we have."

Per relented, and they spiked the anchor line to one of the rock eyries, then secured a line from the stern, as well. They took the floodlight and the speargun with them and descended slowly toward the area Per remembered from the night before. Twelve met them as they descended and accompanied them back down.

The water was clear, and visibility was still good at that depth, though the color had faded to shades of ghostly blue.

The luminous growths were quiescent, withdrawn into half-closed shells, glowing very faintly now. In the more diffuse light of day, the wall carvings didn't show as clearly, but it was possible to see the full extent of the formation, rather than just one illuminated area. The flat, carved wall extended at an angle to the seamount's surface for at least fifteen meters. At the far end, the darkness that Per had at first thought was a shadow turned out to be a dark cleft or fault in the surface. Twelve, with his flexible body, squeezed easily into the darkness and disappeared.

In a few minutes, Twelve reappeared and joined them by the tallest portion of the wall. Twelve moved back and forth across the wall in methodical arcs. Eventually Per realized that the dodecapod was clearing algae and sediment from the carvings, using a jet of water from his syphon. The force of the jet also moved Twelve backward, until he coiled a couple of limbs around Per, trying to use him as an anchor. Per found that the touch of Twelve's tentacles bothered him less now.

He was surprised by the force of Twelve's water jet. It rocked his weight as well as Twelve's. He leaned out and grasped a projecting horn of fossil coral to steady himself until Twelve was finished.

Twelve stopped, seeming to rest, and then his tentacles caressed the carvings, moving slowly from one to the next, as if reading by touch.

Dilani floated to the wall and placed her fingertips next to Twelve's. His tentacles felt cool, deft, soft, and powerful. She tried to imitate their swift, circular movement, but she couldn't keep up with them. They didn't move like anything human, and the water moved along with them, creating a moving echo of their shape, elusive and subtle.

Touching the wall produced a thrill of another kind. Someone had made that, someone who wasn't a human. The surface was smoothed, but still felt grainy under her fingers, as if the clay it was made from contained grains of coarser sediment. She could see that it was grooved and pitted with tiny tracks and holes. Through the years it had existed, small things had crawled over it and colonized it. With her mask inches from its surface, she thought she saw a faint gridwork of parallel scratches, as if the original surface had been smoothed with a tool of some kind. Or an appendage of some kind—it could have been a fin or a foot.

The symbols on the surface had been cut delicately and in detail. Their edges were slightly undercut, so they stood out clearly from the wall. Some were crosshatched or detailed with patterns that looked as if they had been stamped with a shaped punch. She didn't recognize any of the shapes. Around the edges of the wall, like a decorative border, she found markings that made more sense to her.

At first the area looked like a dense stripe of curlicues, but on closer examination, it broke down into a complicated design made of stylized carvings of plants and animals. Broadshelled molluscs with branching bodies, like the ones growing near the wall, were prominent. Excited, Dilani yanked on Twelve's nearest tentacle to get his attention. She rubbed the carving and guided his tentacle to it. Then she pointed to the living version near the wall. Twelve did not seem to understand her at first. She had noticed before that pointing did not get his attention as it did with a human. She swam over to the half-closed shell and touched one of the fronds waving lazily from its rim.

She recoiled, wringing her hand in pain. Had it stung her? When the pain subsided, she checked for bite marks, but did not see any. Yet pain had shot through her, jarring her to the bone and convulsing her arm. Per and Twelve both jetted over to her, uniting their limbs to drag her away from the harmless-looking gray shell. Both of them were signing furiously. Per signed, "Electricity, electricity." *How embarrassing,* she thought.

Twelve jerked all his limbs together, like a swatted insect. Dilani wondered if that meant *electricity*, or if he was only miming what had happened to her. She had drawn his attention to the molluscs, anyway. He raised the strange, fingerlike ends he had on two of his tentacles and clapped them together in an open-and-shut motion. Dilani copied him, wincing, and swam awkwardly to the wall to touch the carving again. Her fingertips were still numb from the shock, but she forgot that when Twelve's tentacles joined her hands on the wall. She had learned another of his signs.

Their communication accelerated after that, though they often ran into barriers when Twelve signed a definite word for a carving that meant nothing to the humans. Sometimes the dodecapod could clarify the sign by miming, but more often the meaning remained obscure. They began to build a small common vocabulary, though the content was heavily weighted toward sealife and simple artifacts, lacking abstractions and technical words.

They realized that it was late when the light faded till they could hardly see the carvings, even with their noses an inch from the wall. Per checked his armband. He had known they were overstaying their limit, but it was worse than he thought. They would have to spend time in decompression, hanging on the line like bait. He silently berated himself, but there was nothing to be done.

The giant molluscs began to glow, dimly at first, and then with a swelling brilliance, as if someone had pressed a switch. Per tapped Dilani.

"Time to go up," he signed.

"No, please, just a little longer," she begged, keeping her eyes fixed on the intricate line of symbols. "There's enough light now."

She turned back to the wall, and then bobbed abruptly upward several feet. She shoved herself back down by pushing her fingertips against the wall, and reached out to seize Per's arm.

"Look! Look," she signed excitedly, following the sign with movements Per recognized as Twelve's language. She clapped her hands in front of the dodecapod, sending a surge of water toward Twelve's front side. That seemed to get the creature's attention.

"What is it? What is it?" she signed, dancing up and down in the water.

Per peered at the wall, and then pressed his hands against

the carving before he could stop himself. He had to touch it to believe it was real. The wall showed a four-limbed, upright shape, the limbs divided at the ends into six small, jointed extremities. The torso was topped by an oval shape with two circles part of the way up, and beneath the circles, a vertical slit and then a horizontal one. It could have been human, but for the fanlike appendages pictured around the neck and ankles.

He turned to Twelve. The dodecapod hung with its limbs trailing. It moved back and forth vaguely, as if reluctant to communicate. Finally it signed: first the spin that signaled identity, then a movement that stretched eight tentacles straight down, twined together in two bunches, and two on each side, held straight out—an imitation of a biped? The sign gave Per no more information than his own sign of *octopus* had given Dilani.

"Where?" he signed, or what he hoped was *where.* Twelve appeared not to understand. The dodecapod again performed the uneasy swaying movement that seemed to indicate indecision. But it did not sign *no*. Perhaps that meant that it didn't know where the beings were, or might know, and was reluctant to say.

Suddenly, the molluscs on their right dimmed to an ashy gray. As they turned in surprise, the glow from the molluscs failed all down the line, and the shells snapped shut, leaving the quartet in darkness that seemed absolute.

Per swept his arms through the water, trying to reach the others without changing his own position. He blinked hard, willing his eyes to readjust, but he still couldn't see. At last he touched something that felt live. It jerked instantly out of his grasp, then reached for him again, and turned out to be Dilani's hand.

Something seized his ankle, and he kicked out in a panic until he realized that it was Bey. A cool, flexible tendril twined around his arm, and he grimaced in revulsion. *It's Twelve. It's only Twelve,* he told himself, while his skin crawled.

He wanted to plunge upward to sight and air, but they had

been down too long. Where was the line? He couldn't find it and keep hold of the others. Why was it still so dark?

The tentacle shifted from his arm to his waist, and Twelve pulled at him. He resisted in vain. His back scraped against a rough surface. Still he could see nothing. An acrid, oily taste seeped into his mouth from the surrounding waters.

At last his sight started to come back; he could make out a pale form, moving in the darkness. The form seemed to glow with its own light—not the bluish illumination of the molluscs, but a bone-white pallor that penetrated only a few inches into the gloom. By the pale light, Per discovered that the gloom was the result of dark billows—like clouds all around them. Could Twelve have created those clouds? Was he trying to conceal them from an enemy?

As that thought flicked through Per's mind, he finally got a clear look at the approaching form, and he felt as if the water around him had turned to ice.

The thing was bilaterally symmetrical; it had two arms and two legs. The skin was bone white, pulled tight over sharp bones that clearly showed its inhuman anatomy. A lipless mouth, hard-edged like a lizard's, opened to show rows of pinpoint teeth and a thin tongue that coiled and uncoiled, ceaselessly tasting the water. There was no nose, only a ridge guarding sunken pits covered by a membrane.

The wide, flat face had little chin, and was dominated by orbital bone and the creature's eyes: They were wide, round eyes with only the faintest tinge of yellow in their white irises, and dead-black slitted pupils like a snake's. They flickered restlessly from side to side, the pupils expanding and closing.

The eyes scanned, and Per felt himself shrinking from them. They fixed on his face. A spiny ruff flared upward around the creature's neck, and its arms shot forward, brandishing a long, saw-edged spike of a weapon that gleamed like a tooth. Just as it began a dive that would have carried it within striking distance, Per felt the tentacle around his waist slide free. Twelve's limbs lashed out, whiplike, through the inky water, and coiled around the creature's neck and torso.

The creature slashed at Twelve with the weapon it carried; the mouth snarled soundlessly, showing more teeth. Clouds of blood puffed from Twelve's cuts.

Per felt Dilani grabbing at his belt and remembered his knife. He brushed her hands away, drew the knife himself, and launched himself toward the creature. He stabbed at the torso, but did not know where to strike. The first blow grated against bone. The second sank into leathery, resistant blubber and apparently touched nothing vital. Then Twelve's tentacles lashed around Per, pinioning his arms and wrenching the knife from his grasp. It flashed once as it tumbled into the darkness below.

Twelve shook the creature, twisting at its neck, crushing the spiny folds behind its head. The creature's mouth gaped; then the light that surrounded it faltered and faded, leaving a broken gray thing that Twelve sent spinning away into darkness. The dodecapod seized the three humans by the first limb he could grasp and dragged them away.

Per wanted *up*. The mask worked as well as ever, but he felt choked. He wanted light, air, the safety of the lifeskip. Yet he knew they could not rise without waiting to eliminate the gases that saturated their tissues. He was afraid Twelve would drag them to the surface, killing them without meaning to.

They emerged from the ink cloud into normal darkness. Per's starved eyes gratefully drank in the small lights of night-glowing sealife. Some of those lights should have attached themselves to the line by that time, marking it with their glow, but still he couldn't see it.

Twelve kept swimming—towing them along in jerky, powerful darts—until he brought them to one of the rock stubs that protruded above the water. But the dodecapod didn't seem to have thought of escaping above the water. Twelve attached himself to the coral rock and crept over its surface till he found a crevice. Compressing himself amazingly, he drew inside, leaving only parts of the tentacles outside.

Per held himself steady by tucking a foot under a projection. Signing inches from their faces, he hastily reminded Bey and Dilani that they must not rise yet.

Twelve reemerged, as if reluctantly, from his little fortress. Wrapping them carefully with his tentacles, he seemed to urge them to take advantage of the hiding place. When he saw that they were incapable of tucking themselves into so small a space, he remained outside with them. He pressed them gently against the rock, as if emphasizing that they should remain hidden. Bands of violet and white alternated swiftly across the dodecapod's body.

Per glanced at his armband. They would have to remain at this level for at least twenty minutes more; half an hour would be better. If the bone-white marauders found them again before that—

"My knife," he signed to Twelve. "Why did you take my knife?" He realized Twelve did not understand him. He recalled the sign for the glyph that had looked like a knife. He could sign that in Twelve's own language, but he could not remember the sign for *why*. "You—my knife," he signed awkwardly, feeling inept.

But it seemed that Twelve understood that time, for the dodecapod broke into a flurry of signing. Per understood "kill" and "eat" and "blood," as well as a repeated negative sign. Piecing the communication together, he guessed that Twelve had not wanted him to cut the marauder. Something about the blood.

Of course—the blood attracted boogers. But Twelve had already been cut, so why not cut the marauder, as well? Per looked apprehensively at Twelve's injured tentacle, but it seemed to have clotted over already, and telltale blood no longer seeped out into the water.

Dilani and Twelve jerked attentively, almost at the same moment, turning in the same direction. The white and violet bands on Twelve's skin moved so quickly they seemed to shudder; then they vanished, and Twelve turned as dark as the rock behind him.

Per turned to look too, but saw nothing. For a moment, he thought he felt a curious kind of flutter of the water against his skin, as if he were feeling a vibration of some kind. It faded, then returned more strongly. He could only describe it to himself as a dull muttering in the water. He wasn't sure why, but it reminded him of something moving fast and purposefully, and it gave him an uneasy feeling.

A moment later, he understood why. For the first time, he saw a pack of boogers at close range. Numb with fear, he couldn't turn his eyes away.

The boogers moved swiftly, thrashing their fat, powerful tails in rhythmic motion. The pack maintained a dense, arrow-shaped form while each individual member changed places constantly with others in the roiling mass. *Like maggots on fast-forward,* Per thought, his stomach churning. A few outliers swam at a slight distance from the others, on all sides, though they, too, changed places constantly. Occasionally the main mass of the pack would flow toward the outliers, and they would be engulfed in the change of direction, while new outliers appeared on the edges of the new course. Per guessed that the outliers' job was to check the surrounding waters for chemical traces that could guide the boogers to their prey, like hounds on the scent.

Within seconds, the pack came level with the cowering humans. Suddenly the water darkened around them again, and an acrid, stinging taste, more intense than before, seeped around the edges of his mask. Twelve must have exuded some kind of scent defense. Per hoped it worked even better than his own makeshift efforts had against the tangleweed.

The pack moved away.

They waited for the pack to reappear and swarm them, but the boogers did not return. Per heard sounds again: a high-pitched, urgent whistling, followed by sucking and crunching noises that continued unendurably, punctuated by more whistling. The whistles weren't modulated like a human scream, but listening to them, Per felt sickened as he would have at the sound of human agony. He knew that he was listening to death—other white creatures had been following them. The boogers had bypassed them and had been drawn to the blood of the pale creature; his stabbing blows had done some good after all.

The sounds ceased, and the water remained quiet. Twelve's

ink gradually dissipated. Per glanced at his armband. Plenty of time had passed; it was safe to rise.

The surface waters were calm. Per popped his mask open and took a deep breath of warm, salt-laden air, rich with scents of weed and guano. Greatmoon rode high in the clear sky, silhouetting the dark stub of coral in a pool of silver. Per experienced a moment of disorientation. Where was the lifeskip? He must have surfaced by the wrong rock.

He swam farther from the shadow of the coral pinnacle and looked around again. Still no lifeskip. When he turned back to his waiting companions, he saw that he had surfaced at the correct point after all. The lifeskip lines were still spiked to the rock. He pulled an end out of the water; the fibers had unraveled during their immersion. But the line was tough, difficult to cut—even deliberately. It didn't seem likely that it had frayed on the rock in such calm weather.

He chafed the frayed end between his fingers, as if that could help him understand. Their hope of returning to Refuge had been slim before; it was gone now.

In theory, as long as the masks and desalters worked, they could live in the open sea. In reality, without the protection of the lifeskip, their chances of survival were small.

Bey swam over to him, splashing carelessly in his agitation.

"The lifeskip—it's gone?" he asked.

"Yes; it looks as if something cut the rope," Per answered.

"It can't have drifted far! Come on, let's look for it." Bey immediately swam off around the pinacle.

"Wait; take Dilani with you. And don't go farther than the next rock. We mustn't get split up. There could be more of those things around, or more boogers. Be watchful."

Per helped in the search, but he swam slowly and deliberately. He held no hope of finding the lifeskip. Clearly, it was gone.

After nearly an hour of fruitless, repetitive searching, they gave up and floated face-to-face in the moonlight. While they had been searching, Twelve had been alone in the shadow of the rock, weaving and spinning by himself. When they stopped, the dodecapod also ceased his solitary dance and joined them.

"What happened to the lifeskip?" Bey asked, speaking and signing at the same time.

"Floating chip, gone where?" Dilani echoed for Twelve, clumsily using the dodecapod's own gestures.

Before Per could respond, Twelve began to answer. He assumed the position that seemed to mean *biped*, with limbs twined together. Then his shifting bluish hue turned to a uniform bone color as he repeatedly signed, "Kill without eating."

"White killers," Per said. "He's signing 'White Killers.' He thinks those white things took the lifeskip."

"What are we going to do now?" Bey said. His eyes and Dilani's searched Per's face expectantly. They had no doubt that he would think of something.

Nothing came to mind but a line from another long ago poem: *Alone, alone, all, all alone, alone on a wide, wide sea . . .*

*Twelve,* he thought. *He's our only resource.* He tried to think of how to say "We need dry land," and ended up pointing at the unwelcoming spires of black coral. He had a discouraging feeling that he had only succeeded in saying something like "I want/eat big rocks."

Twelve didn't seem to be paying attention at all. His skin alternately ghostly and pulsating with white and purple alarm, he continued to dance in agitation.

"He says the White Killers will come back," Dilani signed.

"How can they? The boogers ate them," Per signed.

Dilani signed to the dodecapod, and he lashed his limbs in a violent negative.

"He keeps saying, 'No, no, many, many,' " Dilani reported. "I think he is afraid. And he keeps talking about something that is small with eyes that make a light. He says we will go with it to a big thing that is made of small things—or maybe the big thing that is everything? I don't understand him."

Per was afraid, too. What Twelve was saying about the

white things made sense. Whoever had taken the boat hadn't necessarily been around when the boogers attacked, and was just as likely still alive and dangerous. And like Dilani, Per didn't understand the rest of what Twelve was trying to say. He wondered if she was interpreting accurately.

Twelve stopped agitating, and his colors flowed back in a lovely iridescence that started at blue and continued down the spectrum. His tentacles formed symmetrical arches above and below his body. He floated calmly, motionless but for a rhythmic rippling of his syphon as he breathed, and the swirl of pigments in his huge golden eyes. Per found himself breathing calmly as he fell involuntarily into the rhythm. Whatever Twelve was trying to communicate, the dodecapod now radiated peace and security.

Abruptly, Twelve snapped back into active mode.

"We go there," he signed briskly.

Per shrugged, and turned to Bey and Dilani. "We don't have many options," he signed. "We might as well go with him as tread water here. But I want you to be very careful. We no longer have the boat. Any accident, any mistake, could be the end of us. We follow Twelve—*carefully*—and hope he takes us to a safe place."

*I, Subtle, feel great surprise at the strange split creatures.* Subtle fidgeted his limbs and released tiny amounts of the scent indicating shock as he prepared to descend. He could have sworn they did not know what he was talking about, yet they had responded to his final, desperate presentation of the great sign *god*.

He let a little sourness of self-doubt trail behind him, replacing the shock. Perhaps it was false to promise he would take them to god. For all he knew, he was leading them to their death.

Assuming the god sign had calmed him, though, and he was able to stop thinking like prey and once again experience many-sidedness. If it was their fate to be resumed into the greatlife, then he would not have lied. That, too, could return them to the infinite library of forms that was god.

Subtle flexed the limb that was still healing, feeling again the awe of seeing the White Killers with his own eyes. He had tasted their death threat in the water, yet he still lived.

The White Killers had always been the stuff of tales told when he was small and soft. They had been described as deadly parodies of the Great People, a lethal white shadow flung off in the Great Ones' unending search for diversity. It seemed almost wrong that he, Subtle, a mediocre and vagabond scholar, should have throttled such a long-storied being and flung it to the abyss like so much stale fish.

Perhaps, left to himself, he would have hung foolishly in the water until the White Killers had pierced him. The need to protect had swelled his limbs with rage before he knew what he was doing, or he might even now have been heroically returned to the greatlife. The chance for such a remarkable death did not come every day.

*Still, I do not wish to know truth from the inside of a White Killer's belly,* Subtle thought. *Perhaps opportunities for still more remarkable deaths lie ahead.*

The euphoria ebbed, leaving him refreshed and energetic. He swam downward, limbs streaming behind him, and the strangers followed, till once again they floated beside the carved wall of the Changing People.

Subtle moved purposefully, but he did not really know where he was going. He knew only that he must continue in the direction the godbits showed, and he had last seen them here, by the wall.

His colors paled with disappointment when he reached the spot. No godbits were evident, and their traces in the water had been stifled by a heavy overlay of blood and death.

## 🕊10🕊🕊🕊🕊🕊

Per wondered what Twelve was waiting for. He stared into the dim waters for any hint of predators, but perceived no movement except the slow coruscation of light from above. Suddenly a tiny ring of blue-white sparkles appeared—for a moment he thought it was an illusion. The ring approached; he swept a hand before his face to fend it off and found that he had misjudged the distance. Another ring appeared, and yet another.

Per's sense of perspective returned; the rings of light were emerging from within the dark cleft. That was why they seemed to appear out of nowhere. With a sick feeling, he recognized them. He tried to elude them, but they encircled him.

The jellies closed around his wrists like a series of jeweled bracelets. He rubbed at them fiercely, trying to push them off. They rolled beneath his fingers and re-formed as soon as he stopped. This time the stings sent tendrils of fire deep into his veins. He had a moment to feel panic before the euphoria struck.

Then his eyes rolled back, and he was floating in a warm lagoon watching leaf shadows blow against a succession of sunsets, noons, and dawns. But no—he floated in air, not water, and the flickering edges weren't leaves, but thin metal shutters closing over a bar of blue-white brilliance. The air whistled strangely past his ears, and he felt that he must somehow respond, but he couldn't move. He gave himself up to the flicker of sensation that passed through his motionless body.

\* \* \*

Subtle saw the godbits forming around the stranger's body, and he involuntarily released tinted motes of extreme astonishment. At last he drank in understanding. The godbits had not been seeking him; it was the stranger they hungered for, all along.

But why? Why this alien being from the Dry? What gift for god could he possibly bring? And why, of the three strangers, must the god choose this one, the impulsive one whose language was limited to a few rudimentary postures? Why not choose the smaller, dark-tendriled alien, the one who almost achieved grace at times, the one with a scholar's determination to communicate? Surely that one was more worthy to be received. Even the third, the one whose truncated shape seemed more natural in the water, could communicate better than the pink-patched alien.

Subtle tasted the truth darkly seasoning the water: disappointment, anger, ah, bitter taste of the shed skin of dreams! Plans long-cradled in the limbs, slipping over the edge in a mud slide to vanish far below!

He gave himself up to the lashing dance of rage. *I, Subtle, hunted god. I chose the dangerous way, the hungry way, darting between sharp teeth. I sharpened my wits like a scholar's knife, gathered my life and prepared to lay it before the god as a gift. My thought, my danger, and this stranger darts in and seizes my prey out of my mouth. Without me, it would be dead!*

As he shaped this thought, the anger ebbed. He had, after all, brought a gift for god, and it had been accepted. What did it matter why the godbits had come? They were there, and he would follow them—to the place of transformation.

As his limbs relaxed, he heard the ghostly whistling again. He hoped, for a moment, that he had not. Surely it was currents, swirling through crevices in the rock. Then it came unmistakably nearer, and still the godbits clung to the Dry creature as he hung limp in the ecstasy of being sampled. Without weapons, without refuge, one companion useless, there was no escape.

Subtle swelled with rage. *Bones will decorate the floor of the abyss,* he danced. He drew the scholar's knife; it would fall into darkness painted with the blood of his enemies. He twined several of his limbs securely around the unconscious pink-patched one; he would defend the alien to the death. He felt regret that the pink one could not yet know he would live forever in the library of god.

White Killers descended upon them from above, and closed in from all sides. The Killers crisscrossed in a deadly net formation. Their whistled hunting cry sounded from all sides, enclosing them in a confusing globe of sound. *Redheart, I come to join you,* Subtle danced in his mind. His limbs, held ready for battle, only rippled with the faintest hint of his thought.

The Killers surrounded them now—wait, on all sides but one! Mouthside, Deepside, still lay open, empty. Subtle edged toward the steep slope where the underwater mount fell away and plunged into the abyss. Then, with the speed of the thought, Subtle grabbed the others, folded his limbs, and hurtled over the edge, pulling the strangers with him.

Per returned from his many-colored trance to the dark waters, and felt himself descending. He couldn't move, but he was able, with great effort, to turn his eyes toward his left arm. Something had a firm grip on him, but he could not see what. The darkness was complete.

Then he saw one of the glowing jelly rings, still clinging to his wrist. At last he located the luminous armband that registered depth and time. The numbers kept moving. He couldn't read them, but he knew there was a good reason why they shouldn't keep moving that way.

He heard the whistling around and above him, and knew they were plunging downward to get away from it. Pressure increased; the dark water squeezed him, and he tried to swallow, but his throat wouldn't cooperate.

Suddenly he understood that they were being pursued by the white things again, and that Twelve must be dragging them downward to escape. He vaguely remembered that some forms of Sol-Terran cephalopods were found as far down as the abyssal plain. Twelve couldn't know that humans would be crushed long before they reached that depth.

Why didn't Dilani struggle? Why didn't Bey try to explain? Per tried again to move his arms. One finger twitched faintly.

That seemed extremely funny. With massive effort, he twitched again, and heard himself giggling inside the mask. *It's rapture,* he said to himself, chuckling. The gases forced into his tissues were making him spacy. The others were no more in control than he was. Their fate was in Twelve's hands, and Twelve had no hands. Per laughed out loud.

The sensation of sinking no longer alarmed him; it had become a pleasurable vertigo. Stately chords of music seemed to march slowly through his mind, in rhythm with his fall.

A huge bulk rolled up beneath him and then sank away. It seemed greenish gray in places, then a slick smooth black like keto hide. The greenish patches had a rough, pebbled texture, and they made a faint light that gleamed on the blackness in between. Per decided that he was flying over mountains, and wondered if the green patches were trees or lichen on stone. The mountain heaved beneath him again, close enough to touch, and the eerie music sounded all around him. He liked it better than the whistling he had heard before.

When he felt Twelve's encircling arms pressing him against the moving surface, he didn't try to resist. To stay close to the musical mountain seemed like a good idea. To his surprise, his arms moved, so he wrapped them feebly around a rough protuberance. *Give good old Twelve a hand,* he thought, beaming happily at his own wit.

The hunting whistle of the White Killers had masked the Deepsong of the Guardians when Subtle first began to fall, but as they drew closer he felt the Song reverberating through his whole body. It resembled the migration song of the Laughing Teeth, but slowed and deepened.

When Subtle finally glimpsed the great, encrusted side rolling up beneath him, he was surprised to realize that he felt almost calm. He had spoken with strangers from beyond the sky edge. He had been sampled by godbits, and hunted by the

White Death. Why should he not also behold the Guardians of the Deep? The Guardians were less mythical than the White Killers, since they had been seen by Round Ones. But they came seldom, and they never communicated.

The Guardian was awesome to behold, but Subtle's scent turned toward irritation, mostly; he had no time to cope with one more strangeness in the last few moments of his life.

Then illumination changed his scent. Perhaps he had been granted one more chance to save himself. Towing his string of helpless aliens, he put on a desperate burst of speed, pumping with all his might, until he was dizzy from the rush of water. He whipped out his longest limbs and clamped their sucking surfaces to the rough encrustations on the Guardian's hide.

The great singer was moving with deceptive speed. Subtle felt his limbs nearly torn away, and begged his internal systems not to sense a trauma great enough to justify jettisoning the injured tentacles. They held, and so did the limbs he had wrapped around the strangers.

He tucked the creatures closer and dragged himself by tiny increments across the giant's body till he reached a fin that would provide a secure mooring place, and that also protected him from the force of the water as the Guardian swam on. Subtle held the strangers as securely as he could, hoping they would soon reawaken from the trance into which they seemed to have fallen. The fin twitched once or twice, but the Guardian took no further notice of the riders, as far as Subtle could tell. The song continued, greatly intensified as Subtle pressed his body to the giant's back.

Subtle wasn't sure if the Guardian could outswim the White Killers; they could attain tremendous speed. But he hoped that by keeping close to the giant he could conceal himself within the Guardian's scent and sound signature. As the whistling faded and died, he rejoiced. He had succeeded; the Killers had given up. Nonetheless, he continued to cling to the great back. The strangers were still unresponsive. If he rose to the surface, he did not know what he would do with them.

At least, with the Guardian, they were traveling, though he did not know where.

The deep vibrations surrounded him as tightly as an embracing tentacle. He felt songs joining in from many directions. The Guardian spoke with its own kind, and directional signals resonated within Subtle's body. He began to recognize a pattern. Some of the song elements resembled keto phrases, vastly slowed and skewed.

The Guardians sang of a great thing made up of many tiny things. The motif formed and re-formed beneath the repeated directional checks. Subtle hoped he was interpreting correctly that they might be singing about god.

Per slowly awakened, only to discover that his bad dream was the reality. The euphoria had passed, as before, and left him feeling weak and sick. He could move his arms and legs again, feebly, but he was still fixed in place by Twelve's powerful grip. The moving mountain, he assumed, was some enormous life form of the Deep. Satellite surveys had reported such creatures, moving in small groups through the open sea, but if any human on Typhon had seen them, an account of the sighting had not survived.

Per felt the bulk beneath him humming like a huge machine. The music vibrated painfully through his body. Some of its notes were too deep for his hearing; others set his teeth on edge with pain.

Fully awake, Per knew despair. He didn't know how deep they had gone. Already he was lightheaded and confused. That could be the result of the unknown toxins, but it could also be the onset of pressure sickness. Human beings weren't designed to function at such depths, and neither were the masks. If they rose, they needed to decompress, but he had no control over their rate of ascent.

He tried to reach Bey and Dilani; as he stirred, he felt the full weight of the water on him, and moved with great caution. They didn't respond to his touch. He thought they might be unconscious.

He couldn't sign to Twelve, nor could Twelve communicate with him, since the dodecapod's many limbs were fully occupied. He desperately wanted to explain the dangers to Twelve: the masks could fail, suffocating them; the pressure could cause nerve and brain damage; they could die in convulsions if the leviathans breached suddenly.

Still, they were alive. His mouth stretched out in a grimace that would hardly have been recognized as a smile. They had been sure of death before, when the White Killers attacked, yet they were still alive. If they died, they would die seeing and feeling what no one—no human, he corrected himself—had ever experienced. It would be an interesting death.

He took a long, cautious breath against the tight band that seemed to enclose his chest, and strengthened his grip for the ride.

After long hours of isolation, Per noticed a change in the note of the cyclic song, and in the angle of the great bulk beneath him. He stirred and groaned; he had sunk into a stuporous state, and as he roused himself, his head hurt fiercely. He wondered dully if carbon dioxide was seeping back into his air.

The dark water around them grayed, then acquired a tinge of blue. He clutched the fin in helpless dread; they were rising, and the night had passed.

The water warmed around him, and the light grew. He could see again, but tears blurred his vision as stabbing pains in his head, his joints, and his belly doubled him over. His nose ran like a faucet, disgusting inside the mask.

"Down," he wheezed. "We have to go down!"

He was close enough to Dilani that he could hear muffled grunting from inside her mask as she thrashed around. Bey, held only by the end of Twelve's tentacle, pushed hard enough against the leviathan's side to pry himself away and float, enclosed by one curl of the tentacle. He gestured widely.

The next thing Per knew, he was floating free, the leviathan speeding past him like a mountainside past a falling climber. He fell back into colder, darker waters that felt like death, but the pain eased until he could straighten his body and look around.

His mouth opened silently, and he hung spread-eagled, staring. Still towed by Twelve, they were descending toward something that looked like a city seen from the air, a spider-web network of avenues outlined in lights. The lines were straight, the walls and contours geometrical. Per realized almost at once that the lights were bioluminescence, but as they came closer, he could tell that what had appeared to be walls and buildings were just what they seemed. This place, whatever it was, had been created by someone who had developed architecture in the same way as humans. Almost the same way, Per amended. The straight lines were interrupted at intervals by clusters of curved structures that looked like smashed wasp's nests or broken honeycombs. The result was a different aesthetic, but the whole great pattern had obviously been built to some standard that was also pleasing to human eyes.

Per remembered, belatedly, to look at his armband. If the depth gauge was still working, they were about thirty meters down. Looking up, he could see sunlight filtering down through clear water. Somewhere around fifty meters, they touched down among the shattered walls and floated, their gently sculling feet puffing up small clouds of sediment and scatters of tiny swimmers.

Per grasped Dilani's shoulder and peered into her mask, but it was too dark to tell if her pupils were normally dilated.

"Are you all right?" he signed urgently. "Do you have pain in your head? Fingers? Belly? Anywhere? Can you breathe?"

She pushed him away with the familiar irritable gesture.

"I'm fine," she signed. "Hungry. Where are we?"

Per sighed with relief. For the moment, she seemed normal.

"When we started to come up, did anything hurt?"

Dilani shrugged.

"Head hurt some. Snot from my nose—yuck!" she signed graphically.

Bey nodded.

"Pressure," he finger-spelled, and tapped Per's armband. "I signed to Twelve, 'Go down.' Lucky he understood me. Do you still feel bad?"

Per shrugged in turn. He felt a persistent ache in his joints and sinuses, punctuated by occasional sharp pains. He could only hope that the symptoms would gradually ease, if he stayed down long enough, and that his mind would stay clear. He also hoped that he wouldn't develop an embolism—if that occurred, he could die instantly. It was a lot to hope for. He kept his worries to himself.

"What about you?" he signed to Bey.

"No problem. I didn't feel anything."

Maybe not having proper legs helped, Per thought. Perhaps Bey had absorbed less gas into the tissues, without the big arteries and muscles of normal limbs. Or maybe he had been born with greater resistance to pressure sickness. That happened—though it was dangerous to presume on natural resistance, because you never knew when you had crossed the line.

Twelve hung nearby as they talked, not participating. He was a color Per had never seen before.

"What is this place?" Per signed to him. The dodecapod's answering gestures seemed unusually diffident, almost timid, yet the strobing patterns of alarm were absent.

"This lair belongs to—" Twelve signed, and then a gesture Per thought might mean "far away, distant." Then Twelve assumed the pose for a biped, the one he had used by the carved wall. His skin retained its delicate, shimmering hue. Twelve hung for a long time in that shape, as if caught in a trance, then burst into a flurry of signs that finished by again assuming the symmetrical arching shape he had shown them once before.

Per hadn't learned how to say "I don't understand." He could only respond by signing, "Again."

Twelve snapped out of the pose into a tight spin, and signed briskly, "Come. Use eyes." He spread his mantle and set off gliding through the streets of the drowned city, and the humans followed.

They passed dark openings that might have led to dwelling places, wide spaces that might have been assembly sites, scattered artifacts half buried in sediment. Twelve swept heedlessly on, his mantle flapping behind him like a cloak. They passed repeatedly over one particular type of structure: a broad, sunken circle with a spiral ramp coiling its way down from the rim. Each street had several. Per wondered what they could be.

It was like flying through a dream full of unexplained wonders, a dream where there was never time to ask for meaning.

Soon the well-preserved patterns broke up into heaps of shattered clay tile. Deep cracks bisected walls and split streets. The underlying rock heaved up into chaotic sequences of humps and ridges. The delicate city began to remind Per of a model pounded to pieces by a malicious child.

Ahead of them, the sea floor began to rise in a long, gentle sweep. On their left, however, Per felt a current of colder water. The city slumped away into deepening darkness on that side. Per wanted to follow the rising slope, but Twelve turned insistently toward the dark.

There, the city was truly in ruins. Walls and structures had been shaken to pieces, like a dropped cake, and slid toward the abyss in unrecognizable windrows of debris. The debris itself vanished under mounds of a smooth, dark substance, different from the porous texture of coral. The sight of it gave a cold twist to Per's stomach, as if it were something evil. He remembered where he had seen those smooth, dark ridges before.

*Coils of dull black surged, snakelike, toward the water. The skin cracked and bulged, revealing a viscous, glowing red that moved in sluggish spurts, crusting over with black, only to break out again. Tongues of darting steam hissed, and flames flickered where the red-black coils gathered and crushed the life in their path. Buildings crumpled, then exploded in flames, and the abandoned belongings of small, fleeing creatures were swallowed by the red maw of the advancing lava. Even through the heavy medium of the water, Per thought he could hear the remembered shrieks of living beings crushed beneath a mountain's weight of fire. He saw the destruction of Typhon Colony superimposed in garish color over the silent relics below him.*

The dead city, built in spirals like a delicate shell, had been destroyed by some ancient eruption, and now lay buried under the cold lava. The long-dead inhabitants had met the same fate as the humans who had rashly built on Typhon's unquiet mountains. A kindred sadness crept over Per's heart, along with a dull disappointment. He had cherished some wisp of hope that there might be an intelligence on Typhon that could help them, but it seemed there were only ruins. This must be what Twelve had meant when he signed that the inhabitants of the city were far away.

Twelve turned upslope again. Per's bones throbbed warningly, but he followed Twelve a little farther. It was far enough. The coral organisms had been diligent since the lava cooled. The slopes were ringed with a series of terraces, each with its own proliferation of fans and branches. Gazing longingly uphill toward the sunlight, Per could see faint hints of color in the warm, shallow zones. Even at this depth, the reef had a somber beauty, like a winter garden.

Twelve floated westward, where the rock below the coral wall plunged straight down, and the coral itself rose up sheer as a battlement. The dodecapod moved in little darting sweeps, as if searching for something. Suddenly, he stopped dead, his mantle swirling about him as he gathered his limbs together in surprise. The coral wall next to him was marked by unusual shapes protruding from its normal crop. Per approached cautiously and looked. He too stopped dead, sculling his hands and feet to hold himself still. Bey and Dilani bumped gently into him from behind.

He thought for a heart-stopping instant that he was face-to-face with more White Killers. A long, bony form seemed to float free from the dusky bulk of the reef; others hung behind it in irregular, shadowed ranks. He couldn't count them all.

But the shapes didn't move. No eyes gleamed from the dark hollows of their skulls. Twelve's skin didn't show the colors of alarm. It had darkened to the deepest indigo. The dodecapod flattened itself into a disc-shape, its limbs curled close to its spread mantle. It seemed to be making itself as small as possible, as if in abject awe.

Per allowed himself to float closer. A nearly imperceptible current moved him, as if the wall itself drew him. He reached out and touched the figure's gleaming, high-arched skull. It wasn't alive, as he had thought at first, but it wasn't bone, either. Perhaps it had been bone at one time, but it had developed a smooth, iridescent surface like colored porcelain.

The fleshless face leaned out from the coral, bony gums parted as if ready to speak; the feet were tangled in the reef, and coral intertwined with the ribs and shins. A spined, lacy ruff, no more than eggshell thick, fanned out from the creature's neck. The shape closely resembled the White Killers, but the bones were elongated, the rib cage less dense and stocky. The mouth held no teeth.

Those bones, when living, had been taller than Per. There was no way to tell if this being had been savage or beneficent. But as Per gazed at the stripped planes of the face before him, he couldn't believe that this being would tear his throat out if it could be returned to life. It might have come from the same species as the White Killers, but it was of a different kind.

He moved down the wall, gazing in awe at the throngs entombed in the reef. They came in different heights and proportions, with different ruff forms, different faces, but all were of one kind. With time to study them, he might have learned whether they had two sexes, and perhaps how they reproduced.

One thing puzzled him: he saw no children. Smaller forms intermingled with the others, but their shapes were different. They seemed to go on all fours, and they had tails; their skulls were long from front to back, and instead of ruffs they had mere frills where a mammal would have ears. Those skulls were large enough to hold intelligence, though. Per wondered if they were pets, or a subordinate species. They had been close enough to the larger ones to accompany them in death.

Per turned to Dilani. She was carefully fingering over one of the small, tailed beings, stroking its skull and tracing the cavities where the eyes had been. Per touched her, and she looked up.

"Ask him for the name," he signed. "Who are they? Ask him how this happened."

Dilani didn't touch Twelve in his absorbed state. She swept water toward him with long, circular strokes of her arms. After a few minutes, his color lightened somewhat and began to pulse with a more lively rhythm. Once he uncurled, she swam closer to him and rubbed the palm of her hand against the stippled skin above his syphon. Only then did she begin to sign.

Per watched Twelve's answering movements. He didn't understand their content, but he could see that they were deliberate and sweeping. When Dilani turned to Per again, her signs seemed brusque and sketchy by comparison.

"He says they are the builders of the city; their name is the sign that is like the sign for the White Killers, only with good colors, not bad ones. He says the tiny builders who make the reef have built something for the big builders, to make them last long."

She tilted her head forward to see better as Twelve twirled himself and extended his arms again.

"I think he's talking about those jelly circles with eyes," she signed. "There is—something—something about them here."

She shook her head.

"To him I am like a hearing person. Like you signing. I miss things. He signs with his skin, not just hands. I think if I could take off this mask—" She tugged irritably at the strap. "—I could taste his sign in the water."

Per seized her hand in alarm.

"Don't touch that!"

She peered at Per from the shadow of the mask's rim, but her expression was unreadable.

"The water tries to talk to me," she signed. "I feel it but I cannot hear. I am deaf in air, deaf in water. I could feel the mountain fish talking. I want to take this mask off and be like Twelve."

Per groaned inwardly. Of course she had felt the powerful vibrations of the leviathan's song. Had she deluded herself into thinking she would hear if she took the mask off?

"*Don't* touch that," he signed vigorously. "You'll *die*."

He controlled himself with an effort. Orders never worked on Dilani. They only made her more stubborn.

"Already you understand Twelve better than me," he signed. Awkwardly, he reached out and touched her shoulder. "Keep the mask on. I need you here to interpret, not swimming away like a fish."

She gave a small, pleased shrug. Per still worried. He knew that she never let go of an idea, once it had settled in.

"I don't think his name is Twelve," Dilani signed. "He lets us call him that. His real name is in his skin, and I can't understand it."

Whatever the dodecapod's name was, he was flouncing gently from side to side, recovered from his amazement and obviously anxious to go on.

Subtle trembled in awe before the death city of the Changing People. All other creatures descended, at life's end, into the mouth of the abyss. Their flesh returned to the greatlife; their bones dropped out of sight into the unending night. Only the Changing People had known the secret of transforming their bones to eternal stone.

Subtle longed for time to dance the smooth, cool stone; the empty eyes; the shadowed valleys the Changing People guarded even in death. Without a dancing time, his tales would be the sketchiest of symbols, scratched on a mere potsherd of memory.

But the water was thick with the signature of godbits, as thick as summer tide red with tiny swimmers. Godbits must visit this reef in great numbers, every day.

How could that be? All Subtle's senses were stressed to the brink of overloading. He could think of nothing but hurrying, hurrying to the call of god. He danced in agitation for the strangers:

*Driven to go, I stay; to stay, I go; god's scent, stronger than mating scent, has seized me: Speed, speed is my breath; I suffocate when I am still. Yet the stranger of familiar scent is godmarked; by it I must stay. Come, friend, speed with me, fly; relieve my suffering; let me breathe again.*

As usual, his heartfelt summons went unheeded. *How thick their skins must be,* he thought. *They feel nothing.* They might be stone like the dead ones. Only the little one felt something. That one attempted to share its skin water with Subtle, and wafted motes in his direction. The motes tasted chiefly of confusion, but at least it was water over the skin—better than nothing. The little one gestured to the others with its awkward limbs, and at last they began to swim with Subtle.

The slope before them formed one shoulder of a vast cone, rising toward the surface. Its smooth contour was hidden beneath a forest meadow of organisms, and Subtle wondered at the richness of the reef. He had never seen such lush and varied growths, such variously tinted herds of fish, shimmering like fragments of brightwarm from the sky edge. All this treasure, yet no predators came to harvest it.

He spun continually, seeking danger scents, but all scent messages were muted by the overpowering signature of the godbits. The strength and complexity of that signature intensified till, in his confusion, he finally realized that such power could not possibly emanate from godbits. It could only be the direct exhalation of god itself.

Subtle swam on in a trance of terror and exaltation. As they ascended into the layer of warm, light water, danger scents at last became evident, powerful enough to penetrate through the godcall.

So many sound and skin vibrations hit Subtle at once that he panicked. It seemed as though every predator in the sea was converging on the same destination. A swarm of enemies must be just beyond the curve of the slope.

It was agony to pause, even though he knew he might be torn to pieces if he continued. But he fought the summons, and stopped to warn his companions.

* * *

"It's like a garden," Bey signed, as they drifted over the coral-terraced slope.

Per looked down and witnessed the colors of the reef that stretched fathoms below his feet, as he hung in the clear water like a fly in amber. Normally he didn't feel vertigo in the water, but dizziness seized him, as if he could feel the whole world spinning, and he had to focus tightly on Bey's face to make it stop.

He tried looking up, but the light stabbed into his eyes and awakened the pain in his head. Squinting, he tried another look down.

Bey was right; the reef flora normally grew in a patchwork, like the plants in a wild meadow. Here, it was as if something had told the organisms how and where to grow.

Automatically, he began to formulate hypotheses. Perhaps there was some distinction in the underlying stone, or in the reef itself, that attracted certain organisms to certain places. There might be mineral deposits or other nutrients that had built up in those patterns. Something nagged at him; something was missing.

Tangleweed! He hadn't seen tangleweed. Probably this environment was unsuitable for some reason.

Then again, perhaps the reef looked like a garden because it *was* a garden, and the tangleweed had been rooted out by a planter who didn't like it any more than Per did.

Dilani tugged insistently on his arm, then slapped the side of his mask in exasperation. She must have been tugging for some time.

"Look at Twelve," she signed, right up against his mask to make sure she had his attention. "I think he is trying to tell us about danger."

"He usually turns purple and white," Per signed. The dodecapod showed some splotches of alarm colors, but they kept disappearing, merged back into rippling indigo. It looked to Per as if Twelve felt as he did—too amazed for fear.

Whatever the warning, Twelve kept going, and the humans cautiously followed. The growths beneath them changed to a uniform carpet of green tendrils that hid the rock below and trailed up through the water, to brush against Per's feet as he swam. Thinking of tangleweed, and of vipergrass and sea-nettles and half a dozen other stinging and clinging growths, Per instinctively drew back his feet to escape their touch. But the touch was pleasant. The long tendrils slid easily past, without entangling them, and they felt dry and soft, like moss. As one long blade of the grassy stuff brushed his wrist, he took a closer look and observed that it wasn't smooth-surfaced like a leaf, but had many small interstices, through which tiny organisms swam in and out.

Suddenly Twelve's tentacles lashed about in alarm, and returned Per's attention to the way ahead. The upward slope had ended, but the mountain had no top. They swam across a sharp edge, and the ground dropped away below them into a crater so wide that the far side disappeared into blue shadows. Shafts of sunlight probed downward into the crater, but couldn't penetrate to the floor because a thick screen of moving bodies covered the opening.

Every kind of creature Per had ever seen in the sea was there—and many he had never seen. Grazers flashed by in schools and streamers—in agitated, glittering cascades—while predators arrowed through their midst, alone or in flights of two or three, plowing an empty furrow that soon filled in again with the living. The crater looked like a boiling caldron for some unholy feast; it was one great feeding frenzy from rim to rim.

Per backpaddled on the lip of the crater.

"Get away," he signed frantically. "Go back!" He felt his heart slam into high gear, burning off the last of his energy.

He felt betrayed. He had trusted Twelve; he had learned to trust him. *How stupid can I be?* he thought. *There's no question of trust with another species. I can't know what he's thinking. I thought he was searching for refuge, like us, and he brought us to a mass suicide.*

Per tugged hard on Dilani's arm, but she still moved forward, resisting him. Bey got his attention and pointed back, in the direction Per wanted them to go.

From all directions, more creatures approached. A pack of

ketos sped by, so close their armored skin nearly grazed Per's arms. Something small and bright darted after the ketos, passing so quickly that it was gone before Per realized that it was a projectile, not a fish. The sound of a whistle made him jerk his head around again. Half a dozen of the White Killers shot past, in hot pursuit of the ketos. The sound of their hunting whistles lingered like a contrail.

The Killers had almost passed out of sight when the last in line turned around. Per saw the pale, snake-pupiled eyes widen. As the Killer turned toward them, Twelve furled himself like an umbrella and dove into the crater, pulling the humans with him.

As they passed through a gap in the stew of bodies, it immediately closed up behind them. The sea churned, bringing up bubbles, strange rumbles, grunts, and squeaks. The water made everything sound close at hand, so the noises brought only alarm and cacophony. Light still penetrated, but it was a clear blue half-light in which the swift swimmers appeared out of nowhere and vanished abruptly into shadows.

Through this chaos Subtle darted, finding a twisting path, and Per followed for dear life as Bey and Dilani tried to move in slightly different directions. They needed to swim freely, but if they got lost, he didn't know how they would ever find each other.

Twelve still worked his way downward, and suddenly they burst out of the crowd of organisms as if emerging from a cloud layer. As Twelve released them, Per looked up and saw the shining underbellies of fish moving restlessly, like wind-blown vapor. Below them, the bone-white, streamlined bodies of a host of White Ones jockeyed for position, like swarms of glittering flies—or like flights of attack fighters, holding formation around their target.

As that image formed in his mind, a cold needle seemed to pierce Per's skull. Where had he seen this—a vision of gleaming little ships, stark against a dark background? But this was neither the time nor the place.

"What are they doing?" he signed to Twelve. The dodecapod paid no attention. Per had to catch up with him, in a burst of exertion that left him gasping and fighting the pain in his chest. He grasped the edge of Twelve's mantle. Twelve whirled, tentacles whipping angrily, but subsided when he realized who had grabbed him.

"What are they doing?" Per insisted. Twelve's colors exploded briefly in strobing alarm patterns, but the orderly progression broke up into a chaotic pulsing that interrupted the outline of his body so that he almost seemed to disappear. Per didn't understand what Twelve was signing, but he thought he understood the colors. Twelve looked terrified.

Dilani leaned close to Per, and he heard the gurgle of her laughter inside her mask. She was afraid, he knew.

"Kill god," she signed. "The White Ones want to kill god. And we have to stop them. That's what he says."

Per shook his head violently, and regretted it. Pain seemed to split his skull, and waves of dizziness reverberated long after he stopped moving.

"No," he signed. "No more Twelve. He's crazy. We're leaving."

He started to swim away, up, but Dilani pulled him back with surprising strength. Twelve danced in agitation, stretching his palping limbs toward them like an appeal.

"Stop," Dilani signed. "Twelve says you have to find god. You, especially you. He says the little pieces of god have tasted you many times, and he thinks you are sick. Some big special kind of sickness. I don't know what. The sign is like the sign for the people in the wall. Sickness that goes with them. He says if you don't find god, you will die."

"Little pieces of god?" Per echoed. "He's crazy."

Then he remembered the jellies that had stung him so many times. Could that be what Twelve meant?

"Where is it?" he signed. "Ask him where this god is."

Dilani shrugged. "Can't. I can't make the sign for *god*. You need more than two arms."

Per turned to the dodecapod.

"Where? Where?" he demanded.

Even though he couldn't imitate Twelve's sign for *god*, the dodecapod seemed to have no trouble understanding what

Per meant. Twelve pointed himself like an arrow toward the very center of the White Ones' array. "Go there," he signed.

*If I were alone,* Per thought, *I might do it.* He had no idea how Twelve had guessed that he was sick, but ever since their descent, the weakness had continued slowly gathering upon him, like sediment encrusting an abandoned shell. Somewhere deep within his cells, error messages were piling up, protein syntheses breaking down in a sludge of static. It might be better to fire himself into the midst of the enemy and take his chances than to feel himself slowly dissipate like a burst of hopelessly corrupt data. But he wasn't alone.

He kicked upward toward the surface, and the young ones followed behind him. Somehow they had to escape from the caldron; if he died after that, they might still have a chance to reach safety.

Then something light and clinging settled on his wrist, and for a moment he thought the decision would be taken out of his hands. The jellies were back—the "little pieces of god"—and he felt the stinging kiss as they penetrated his skin. No euphoria followed. He remained in control, for the time being, but the sense of internal slippage intensified. He felt as if the jellies had injected him with a powerful solvent, and walls were dissolving. Not just in his cells, but in his mind.

He glanced back and saw that Bey was following him, but Dilani was still gesturing to Twelve. Per turned and signed "Get her" to Bey. When he corkscrewed to face front again, he looked straight into a mouth big enough to swallow his head.

It was rimmed with needle-shaped teeth as long as his finger. Behind that mouth, a long flattened streamer of body whipped back and forth like a flag in the wind. Per's hand slapped his thigh in quest for the knife that had gone to the bottom when they met the White Ones. A separate part of his mind said calmly, *Allfather, a ribbonfish. I had no idea they ever grew that big.*

He doubled and tried to dodge out of its way, but the frilled, snaky head darted into his path and wove back and forth. It feinted toward him; for a moment he looked straight down its throat as it turned to face him again.

Memory exploded in his head. *The sinue!* His mind, confused, told him the sinue had come back for him. *It was real!* He remembered the touch of its cold flank, bunched muscles working beneath the slick skin; he remembered the glaring, inhuman eyes, and the grotesque size of the thing, big enough to swallow him alive. For a moment his aging body took on its younger self again: thinner, smaller, but just as naked, just as desperate.

He feinted to the left to make the ribbonfish turn its head, and then jammed his right arm past the teeth, through the gap at the back of the jaw, and rammed his stiffened knuckles as hard as he could against the back of its throat. A cartilaginous cord ran down its back at that point, defended from the outside by the spiny back-frill, but vulnerable within.

The fish convulsed, biting down till the rows of needle teeth meshed, with a sound like gears engaging. The needles raked against Per's arm, drawing precise parallel lines of fire through his skin. The fish's tail lashed wildly until it encountered Per's leg; then it coiled around him, cutting him with the spines of its frill.

The sensation of being squeezed, the sight of teeth inches from his face, sent Per into a frenzy. He tore at the back of the creature's throat with his pinioned hand, beating its face with the other. There was plenty of air in his mask, but he couldn't draw it into his lungs. Suffocating, bursting with fear and loathing, he struggled against the tightening coils.

Suddenly, the mouth opened, the clenched muscles of the tail loosened and let him drift free. The ribbonfish wavered off, listing slightly. A cluster of jellies rose from the back of its head and hung in the water near Per as he gasped for breath. For some reason, it had let him go. Had the jellies drugged it? Or was it their presence that had incited it to attack in the first place? Or had he lost all judgment, imagining that the venom of so tiny an organism could affect the behavior of a fish bigger than he was? He couldn't even guess at the right answer.

He floated in a thickening cloud of his own blood. He felt Bey and Dilani grasp his arms, and tried to push them away. Per had become a hunk of bait; every predator in the crater would soon be speeding toward him. His darkened mind roiled with monsters: not just the various grinding and slashing teeth of Typhon's sea, but the creatures of his ship nightmares.

"Get *away*," he mumbled, thrusting at them as hard as he could. His eyes fell on his weakened arms. The jellies had returned, and brought friends with them. Clusters like frog spawn built up along his wrists. He struggled to scrape them off, but Dilani and Bey still held his arms. He writhed in their grip, but couldn't reach the jellies. He was sick of them; slimy, clinging, clutching things, alien and incomprehensible. They gathered at the edges of the wounds, and he thought they were there to sip the blood that misted away into the water.

Instead of feeling a sting, his skin numbed where they clung, and the pain of his cuts vanished. The jellies crept along the cut surfaces, leaving behind something sticky that sealed off the wound. The extras lifted off his arms and formed a globe a few feet away. The cuts had closed as neatly as if a doctor had dressed and glued them. But his hands—his hands—the fingers were longer, he could swear, and the fingernails were growing. Since they had begun their flight, his nails had grown into two-inch talons, vicious as the claws of the White Killers.

He stared uselessly at his hands, while Dilani and Bey swam hard, pulling him away from the blood cloud.

But they were dragging him downward, back toward the deadly ring of Killers. Per tried to struggle, but he couldn't break their grip. Bey pointed up with his free hand and shook his head vigorously.

Per looked up; above them the water looked like a solid silver ceiling until he realized that the silver was in constant motion. He saw clingfish and stinging combs, and another ribbonfish, bigger than the first. In the place they had just left, a knot of predators slashed at each other in an expanding blood cloud. Per stopped fighting. Bey was right. They couldn't leave the crater. Their only hope was to follow Twelve's directions, to try to evade the White Killers and escape into the depths.

When Bey and Dilani realized he was no longer struggling, they let him go. He looked down at the ring of White Ones.

*They'll tear me apart,* he thought. *I have no chance.* He felt sorry for Bey and Dilani, who would have to watch. The godbit gauntlets itched and burned fiercely. He rubbed one arm across the other, but couldn't even feel the skin beneath the jellies, much less scratch away the irritation.

"Wait here," he signed. "I'm going to dive past them, get their attention. Maybe they'll forget you, leave a hole where you can get through. Stay with Twelve."

He floated, looking at them for a moment longer. He felt as if he should find something else to say, but no words would improve the situation. Dilani stared at his hands as if she expected him to sign again. Then she pointed, insistently.

He tried to curl his fingers under, to hide the long, curved nails.

Subtle curled his tentacles in a rapid little pattern.

"Changing," Dilani signed. "He says you have the changing sickness. You must go to god quickly."

The bitter unfairness of having to leave, with so many questions left unanswered, strangled Per. *This is too fast,* he thought. *I never told the kids the things they need to know. I never found out where the ketos went. I'm not ready yet.*

There was one more thing he had to do; he barely remembered it in time.

"Take this and be very careful," he signed. "Promise!"

He loosed the notebook's strap from his arm and fastened it to Dilani's, pulling it tight. It cost him a pang to let go of it. That fist-sized chunk of plastic held his life. He might get it back, but it wasn't likely.

He could see movement on the edge of the ring of Killers. He must not give them a chance to launch an attack.

"Luck," he signed.

Then he kicked away from them, plunging downward as fast as he could, toward the White Ones outlined in the blue light from below.

## ꧁11꧂

*I don't have a gun; I don't have a knife,* he thought. *This is insanity.* But he stroked forcefully, gaining as much speed as he could before oxygen debt caught up with him. The White Ones swelled in his vision; one by one, the skull-like faces turned toward him. He saw the nearest one raise some kind of weapon to its shoulders, and a dart shot past him. He felt the vortex brush his cheek in its wake. More darts soared up toward him. He twisted jerkily to change course, losing momentum. He was falling toward his enemies; just one of those darts would end him, yet he did not feel afraid. An artificial clarity surged through him.

*About time those damned jellies did something nice for me,* he thought. *At least I'll feel good for the last few minutes. Till the Killers bite into me, I suppose.*

The dive reminded him of something: flying through a long, blue-lit corridor with projectiles racing toward him. He had been weightless then, too. That had been on the ship, he thought. He had learned to fly on the ship, and he had flown the corridors with people shooting at him. His body remembered a skill learned long ago. He shifted back and forth, fast, using his momentum to twist in the water. Shiny darts hummed past him.

He closed on the Killers; he tried to dodge them, to dive under the ring, but they came to meet him. They let go the crossbowlike weapons—Per saw from the corner of his eye how they floated on cords, still available—and launched themselves toward him with arms extended, blades in their hands. Per had no defense.

228

He grabbed at the nearest attacker's wrist, but the knife in the White One's hand slid along his arm, ripping through the jellies, into suit and flesh. The jellies along the cut flushed darkly, absorbing and containing his blood. They set to work again, sealing the wound, but the searing pain remained.

Per thrust his other hand into the Killer's face. Talons he had never had before slashed into the tough flesh. The White One clawed at him and struggled, but now the assailant was trying to get away. The pain in Per's injured arm faded, and he found he was able to use it again, in an awkward, club-like way.

He sank his fingers into the White One's wrist. He could feel his talons cutting through skin and grating against flat bone. He twisted the White One's arm, planting a foot against its chest to give him leverage, and the knife dropped from its grasp. Per tried to seize it, but it tumbled out of reach.

Others closed in on him. Per twirled and thrashed like a ribbonfish in a frenzy, holding them away by slashing fiercely with his clawed hands, using each contact as leverage to turn himself in the water. It was as if a younger self, one still strong and lithe, had taken over his body. That self knew exactly how to use his opponents' strength against them, how to use mass without weight. He could feel the talons slicing flesh, but the Killers bled very little, and the blood looked pale in the blue light.

*They were right about me,* he thought. *I am a killer.* In his final desolation, he thought, *I never wanted to know this.* But the memories were set free, and his body continued to fight. He stabbed his fingers at a White One's throat, saw vapor trails of blood stream out, and turned to face the next.

But his chest hurt already, and his breath was coming hard and fast. The mask couldn't keep up with his need for oxygen. Soon his arms would weaken.

He couldn't look back to see if the others had succeeded in slipping through the line. The next White One lunged toward him with a barbed spear. He turned to let it glide past him, seized the shaft, and twisted it away from its owner. With its long shaft, he could parry their attacks and keep them away a little longer. He jabbed and turned, and jabbed again.

The White Ones' whistling filled his head. They were all around him; he turned and twisted in a cage of bewildering sound, fighting for his life. Their weapons jabbed at him now from every direction. He fended off the lethal blows, but each time at a price. Sharp edges hacked and nipped him like a hundred teeth eating him alive. The jellies along his arms were bruise-dark gauntlets; in undiluted light, they would have been scarlet.

He could not win, but he could last as long as possible. Each moment they tormented him was a moment kept for Bey and Dilani. His vision darkened around the edges, and he panted faster.

Then he heard another sound in the water. It seemed more familiar as it came closer. Suddenly a huge, muscular body knocked him sideways and tumbled the White Ones away from him. The rough contact left a rent in his skinsuit and tore the skin beneath. Even as Per somersaulted under the impact, he recognized the silver-and-black projectile that had sent him spinning. It was Slowbolt.

The rest of the pod was with him. The White Ones' formation broke up under their onslaught, and the eerie chorus of hunting whistles changed to alarm cries.

Per raised his hands to guard himself, and looked for more enemies. The White Ones he had been fighting floated in the water, jerking feebly as they drifted downward. He saw no wounds from Slowbolt's teeth; the keto had simply brushed them aside. Per could hardly believe that the cuts and scratches he had inflicted had been enough to kill such tough adversaries. He stared at the jellies clustered at his fingertips, wondering if they had exuded some poison that reached the White Ones when he slashed them.

He tried to jerk his head upright, but found that he wasn't sure which way was up. His vision had narrowed to a bright circle surrounded by haze. He could feel his wounds throbbing beneath the superficial numbness induced by the jellies. He needed to swim, to fight, but he could only scull weakly.

*The blade must have been poisoned,* he thought slowly and with difficulty. *Or maybe it's because of the jellies. Or because of the changing sickness.*

He looked for Bey and Dilani, but something like a moving wall passed before his eyes. It was a leviathan, too big, too close, for him to grasp its shape; he could only see the details of the great flank as it went by. There was more than one. Fragments of their song boomed and squealed and reverberated through his bones. They fell like slow-moving meteors through the ranks of the White Killers gathered in combat around the keto pod. Shrill whistles fell silent. The skeletal, fragile-seeming frames of the White Ones scattered like broken toys.

The great creatures plunged, spiraling around each other and carrying a vortex of water with them, like sinking ships. Per felt himself drawn in and spinning downward. Pressure went like a spear through his head, and then there was darkness.

Dilani saw Per swimming toward the White Killers. He had always warned them to be careful, so she believed he must have some plan that could keep him safe. But as she saw the White Ones turn toward him, and saw how many of them there were, all armed, she was convinced they were going to kill him.

Her mouth stretched wide in shock and betrayal. Without bothering to signal Bey or Twelve, she launched herself after Per, fingers spread as if she could grab him even at that distance. She was dragged to an abrupt halt by a tentacle that snapped around her waist. She hammered furiously at Twelve's limb, thrashing her whole body in protest. Despair and rage brought tears to her eyes. How could they be so stupid? Didn't they understand? If only she could make the mouth shapes, maybe she could force them to pay attention. But she could not, and she was too enraged to sign, except with clenched fists and flailing arms.

Bey moved in front of her, signing.

"Stay here! He told us to stay!"

*Bey always does what he is told, even when it is wrong,* she thought furiously—but Twelve was strong. *He* should do something to help. Instead he was holding her back—while Per died. At that moment she hated both of them.

From the corner of her eye, she could see that Twelve was moving his other limbs, though she could not make out his sign.

"Yes, now," Bey signed, apparently agreeing. Dilani stopped fighting so hard, distracted by curiosity. Twelve pushed forward; his limb still clasped her, but as a support, not a restraint. She couldn't see where they were going, but at least they were moving.

Ketos caught up with them. Twelve seized a passing fin, and they were jerked into rapid motion. Ketos were all around them, and she felt the vibrations through her body that told her they were "talking" to each other. She tried to look ahead, but the ketos roiled the water till she could see nothing.

Some peeled off from the group, and she could feel concussions in the water, as if they had slammed into something— probably other moving bodies. They passed through occasional cloudy streaks that Dilani guessed were blood, but they were moving so fast that they quickly left the bloody trails behind. Dilani felt pain in her ears and swallowed hard; the pressure was increasing, so they must be diving.

At last she got a clear look ahead. Only a few scattered Killers still swam along with them, and as she watched, more members of the keto pod swooped down on those. Some of the ketos bore gashes, but a thick layer of slime had formed on their skins, stopping the bleeding.

The White Ones gathered to make a last defense. They swam in formation, a star-shaped bristle of spears. The ketos circled them, but before the attack could begin, something dark and immense shouldered up from the depths, bringing a swirl of bitterly cold water with it. A mountainous body rolled past just below them, and a deep, powerful vibration went through Dilani's bones from head to foot. A mouth opened, big enough to drown in, fringed with rows of pale teeth, and a powerful current sucked the Killers toward it. The formation of White Killers was tumbled apart by the pull. With a concussion Dilani could feel all through the water, the great mouth closed. The dark form receded and vanished, and the White Killers were gone.

Dilani could not see Per. Had they left him behind? Or was he falling through the dark waters below them? She leaned out from Twelve's arm and glimpsed a flash of bone white. Two stragglers from the Killer band still swam desperately ahead of them, chasing some object that drifted far below. In the next moment, she recognized the object as human.

It was Per. He made no effort to swim; his arms and legs dangled aimlessly. She drummed her heels against the keto's sides and dug her fingers into Twelve's arm, trying to get their attention.

But Slowbolt had already seen. His body arched like a bow as he put on more speed. The White Ones raised their weapons—a spear and a dart shooter. Slowbolt swooped on them like a bird of prey from the world above. As the keto sped past and turned to face them, Dilani kicked out and struck the nearest Killer in the shoulder. The White One's dart flew wild.

Bey hammered the other Killer with the hand light from his belt, the closest thing he had to a weapon. Dilani saw the Killer turn on him, its narrow-lipped mouth snarling. But before the White One could strike, Slowbolt completed his maneuver. The keto seemed to smile ferociously as his jaw stretched wide. One snap left only drifting fragments of the White One. Dilani saw the muscles of Slowbolt's throat flex as he gulped.

She too swallowed hard, a burning taste of bile from her empty stomach rising in her throat. She wanted the White Ones dead, but it wasn't pleasant to watch. A casual thrust of Slowbolt's tail pushed the remaining Killer out of the way. The keto twisted like a corkscrew and made another pass. This time Slowbolt didn't need to swallow. A single slash of teeth raked the Killer's torso and left it tumbling, like an envelope slit open, life leaking from the rent.

Flexing powerfully, Slowbolt made for Per, who had remained motionless through the whole engagement. Dilani leaned from the keto's back and grabbed his arm. He didn't clutch at her hand; he remained limp. Slowbolt nosed up beneath Per so Dilani could pull him closer.

She did not know what to do for someone who was unconscious underwater. She shook his arm and tapped on his mask. She couldn't tell if he was still breathing or not. She wanted to feel his wrist for a pulse, but his hands were covered entirely with slick bubbles of godbits. More godbits covered a slash that cut deep into his arm. It wasn't bleeding, but the pale, ragged edges were ugly and dead looking.

"What's wrong with him?" she signed to Bey, but he only shook his head.

Dilani turned to Twelve, but Twelve's eyes were not seeing her. His colors were iridescent, and his limbs tremulously shaped a sign Dilani had seen often enough to recognize it at once.

"Go to god," he signed.

Momentum still carried them toward the bottom of the crater's far side. The blue light was most intense there, and the slope was broken by irregular rounded shapes that stood out from the rock. Dilani thought at first that the shapes were raised mounds. As they came closer, she realized the convex mounds were actually concave holes, openings pierced through the rock. The blue light streamed through them, and fleshy, luminous growths like curious fingers stirred at their fringes.

They floated slowly toward the largest of the openings. It widened within and became a vast, round cavern, like a bubble inside the solid rock. In the center of the bubble hung the most beautiful thing Dilani had ever seen. She hung as motionless as Per and stared. Suddenly she understood Twelve's sign. He was mimicking the globe that floated before their eyes.

They were looking at Twelve's god.

Dilani clutched Per tighter, to make sure he couldn't float away while the others bobbed around with their mouths hanging open. She refused to be impressed. She did not care how beautiful or strange this thing was. She only cared about Per. If the god would fix him, it was good. If it tried to hurt him, it was bad, and she would tear it apart if necessary. *Don't care, don't care, don't care!* She pictured the signing in her own mind, though her hands remained locked on Per's shoulders. *Not afraid!* She shook her head vigorously. *Not, not.* But she knew she was afraid.

The god was a transparent sphere; it looked at first like a globe of glass. Then she realized that the sphere wasn't simple. It was built from layer on layer of smaller spheres, and glowing veins of blue, green, and red built branching patterns within the architecture of spheres. At the top of the globe, a fan of crestlike ridges arched down from its pole, like the mountains of Skandia she had seen on the hospital computer. Long tendrils stirred about those ridges, ceaselessly sweeping the water.

Dilani stared at the giant globe, her eyes caught in the pattern within the pattern of glowing spheres. As she stared, she saw that colored fluid, or maybe a fluidlike procession of tiny things—like beads pouring through a glass tube—pulsed through veins that linked the spheres. At least the fluid *seemed* to pulse, but in a different rhythm in different parts of the globe. Dilani began to feel confused. Her eyes darted from point to point but couldn't grasp everything she saw. Then she realized that the entire globe was slowly spinning, and the patterns changed as they passed from her right to her left.

The rotating patterns held her attention; at first she hardly noticed a stream of godbits that spun off from the giant globe. But soon the bits clustered around her so thickly that they obscured her vision, like a flock of glowmoths or a bubble blizzard.

She looked down, and saw that more bits were gathering around Per. They had joined together with the godbits already on his hands. They seemed to be covering him with something like a second skinsuit.

Dilani gripped him fiercely, and the godbits began to

spread over her hands, too. Then something stung her. She snatched her hand back involuntarily, and the bubbles flowed together where her fingers had been. She tried to grasp Per again, but the jellies had already joined into a single membrane. It looked fragile, but it felt tough.

She scratched it and hammered on it, but could make no impression. She clawed frantically at the bubbles gathering over Per's face, but they had covered him completely— almost before she could think. He didn't move. She wasn't sure he was still breathing.

She looked around for help. The black-and-silver swimmer with his sharp teeth might slash the membrane. But she didn't know how to ask a keto for his help. Bey was already trying, like her, to tear away the jellies that coated Per, but he wasn't succeeding. She turned to look for Twelve.

Twelve seemed to be in a trance. His limbs floated free. Dilani saw that a ring of godbits circled his head like a crown. She grasped a limb, squeezed it and shook it to get his attention.

"Help!" she signed frantically. "Get him out!"

Twelve twirled in negation. Dilani saw him make the "changing sickness" sign again, and she thought he was signing "god" and "help," but beyond that she understood little. Twelve's awestruck alabaster pallor changed to bars of reddish purple. He was frustrated, maybe even angry.

Dilani snatched at his mantle, trying to reach the pouches on his belt. Maybe there was a sharp instrument there, something she could use to free Per. But Twelve held her firmly away. Definite red speckles appeared on his skin.

She turned back to Per, but her renewed scratching at the jellies left no mark. In desperation, she was about to try biting at them when Twelve pulled her away, using enough force to squeeze her ribs.

"Die," he signed emphatically with his other limbs—or was it "death," or "dead"? Did he mean Per, or her?

A bubble formed around Per. Tiny filaments, like the limbs of a flowermouth, grew out of the godbit clusters, piercing his skin and binding him to the membrane that had enclosed him. The edges of his skinsuit had begun to ravel and fray; something was dissolving or eating the suit away even as she watched. Dilani felt her chest and throat vibrating, and there was wetness in her mask; tears streamed down.

She struck her fists together in anguish, shaking her head. This horror was Twelve's fault. She tried to bite his tentacle, but the grip was too tight.

"Kill Twelve!" she signed to Bey, but Bey wasn't looking. The jellies had woven bracelets for his wrists and a crown for his head. His hands floated loose, and his eyes were unseeing. She felt the jellies sting her wrists, felt herself slide into their poisoned tranquility. Her mind struggled for a brief time after her body had gone limp.

Per drifted away. Distantly, she could feel Twelve still clasping her, then motion. The keto leapt upward with them. The last thing she saw was the bright bubble that had once been Per, passing out of sight into the blue light below.

## ❧12❧❧❧❧❧❧

Per came slowly back to consciousness. He vaguely remembered fighting with the Killers, but mostly he remembered the leviathans rising from the Deep and carrying him down in their wake.

He felt as if he were still falling, into an abyss of pain. The pain had become all-encompassing. It was a medium in which he was floating, or drowning, like the blue light whose source seemed everywhere.

He was poisoned and cut, and he thought he had pressure sickness, but there was something far more radically wrong inside. He could feel himself failing, sinking, like a frond of weed falling toward the forgotten floor of the abyss. Even breathing hurt. He thought it would feel good to take the mask off, and let the cool water rush into him like the blue light. It would stop the pain.

But he couldn't do it. He remembered Dilani's small, tough hands clinging to his shoulders, refusing to let go. And Bey, who had trusted him completely.

He raged silently. What use was it to be a shiptroll, bred to kill, when he couldn't even move his arms and legs?

It wasn't his body that had betrayed him, he thought. It was the godbits. Twelve's god had forced him to fight, and now it expected him to die without a struggle.

*You made me remember what I am,* he thought. *I'm not going to forget that fast.*

Then there was a swirl of water, and a black-and-silver form nudged under him, supporting him. It was Slowbolt again, and Dilani and Bey with him, clinging to his fin.

Dilani stretched toward Per. Twelve twined a tentacle around her, supporting her in an automatic, companionable gesture as she leaned out and grabbed Per's wrist.

*They're friends,* Per thought. *She didn't make friends with most humans, but Twelve is her friend.*

Dilani brought her masked face close to his. At close range, he could see her habitual scowl, and a pair of worried eyes. She shook him and signed to him, but he couldn't reply. It seemed to take all his strength just to keep his eyes open.

*It's no good,* he thought. *I'm going to betray you. I'm going to die. I can't help it.*

Dilani gripped him so tightly that her fingers sank into his arm. At first it hurt, then the pain diminished. It seemed easier to breathe, too. He felt as if he were floating on something soft and buoyant, like an inflatable rescue raft. That confused him. There was no raft. Had help arrived?

Bey and Dilani were still wearing their masks, so he knew they were still underwater. Dilani seemed very distressed. She kept stretching out her hands as if she was trying to get to him, but Twelve kept her away. Per knew she was upset because he had been so sick. He wanted to tell her he felt a little better, but he still could not speak. He made a great effort and turned his head a little. He seemed to be surrounded by a clear cover. Then he looked down at his own arm.

Tiny filaments extruded from the clear wall of the flotation device. Their tips had penetrated his skin. They grew as he watched, seeking out the vessels in his wrist and the crook of his elbow. Blood flushed the first segment of the clear probe, and then some other fluid washed away the blood. The jellies no longer coated his hands. It wasn't necessary—he was inside them. In violent revulsion, he tried to sit up, to tear his way out, but he couldn't move. He had a horrified vision of the jelly filaments knitting themselves into his back while he lay floating. *I've been swallowed,* he thought. *Now I'm being digested.*

One arm was still free. At last he was able to drag the hand up to his chest and sign, fumbling.

"Go! Go! Please go!"

Twelve was dragging Dilani away, out of his field of vision. That was good. Per didn't care whether or why Twelve had betrayed them. If only the dodecapod would lead them away before they, too, were trapped.

He made a last-ditch effort to focus on Dilani, for as long as he could still see her. The color of her hair and the precise shade of her skin didn't matter any more. Her deafness did not matter either. He remembered when she had first signed "Teach me, teach me." He hadn't been able to teach her then, because he hadn't learned the most important thing himself.

He understood now, just as he was about to lose sight of them forever. He summoned his strength for one more sign, not knowing if they would even see it.

"I love you," he signed. "I'm sorry."

Then he fell into the endless blue.

With an internal slam, like a door being flung open, strange thoughts began to flood Per's conveniently emptied mind. New awareness dawned. They had only been setting him up. The jelly creatures planned to use him for something more than food, and he couldn't stop them. He could only listen and watch as hallucinations swarmed his mind like godbits gathering in his head.

Again, as when the godbits had first claimed him, he experienced the sensation of being a book whose pages were being rapidly riffled. He knew that information was being extracted from him, but didn't understand how. Then the clear membrane above his face began to change, and he realized that this was not a hallucination. The membrane puffed out in selected spots, like hives on human skin. The edges of the puffed spots grew more definite, and they took on color, making them easier to see. The membrane was replicating shapes Per had seen on the ruined wall.

One shape appeared larger than the others and stayed longer, without changing. Per recognized the bipedal, fin-footed organism whose bones he had seen cemented into the reef. The bipedal shape changed; it shrank and bent until it went on all fours, and grew a tail, but the shape remained familiar. Per remembered that the tall bipeds in the wall had been accompanied by smaller, four-footed skeletons. This shape could have been one of those.

The four-footed creature sank back on its haunches, stretching its front feet out in front of its face, and the knobby ends of the front legs changed. Extensions like fingers appeared. Then the "hands" grew disproportionately large, as if for emphasis, and they stretched toward a small round shape. Small dots appeared around the round shape, and it grew.

Then the four-legger began to change again. Small dots came from the now-huge roundness, and surrounded the four-legger, and it straightened till it was once again a biped.

The membrane rippled, and the figures disappeared. Another one formed: This one was also a biped, but it had a strange growth around its head. Suddenly, Per realized that it was meant to be a human—perhaps himself—wearing a mask. Dots surrounded the human, too, but when they did, the shape wavered and became grotesque. It sprouted strange excrescences; the lower limbs stretched, then disappeared.

Again the figures changed. The human shape reappeared, but it was surrounded by a circular outline. Dots came from the inner edge of the surrounding circle, and touched the human. Gradually the human shape dissolved, till there was nothing left but a round shape. Then a human form reappeared outside the circle. Dots came from the circle, and the human form changed again till it again looked human— but fin-footed like the biped in the first sequence. The final shape replicated itself triumphantly into a crowd.

Just when Per thought the demonstration was over, the membrane formed more shapes: one human with mask, as before; one human with mask and filaments streaming from beneath the mask—this one was a little smaller than the other; one with no lower limbs; and last, a shape with tentacles. The larger human separated from the rest and merged with the circle again. Dots emerged, and the others began to change again. Another shape appeared, finned and streamlined—a keto, Per guessed. It carried the others away, toward a truncated cone that might be meant for an island.

The membrane smoothed out, and Per lay still.

He thought he understood, though in the visionary way one understands things in a dream. It seemed the bipeds had at one time gone on all fours. Somehow they had created the god, and it had changed them. That might have been an accident, but the iconography seemed to indicate that it was their tool, that they had made it on purpose to change themselves.

If his logic was correct, the god was still alive and working. It had started to change the humans, but the method was incorrect; the changes were destructive. The second sequence of images had shown him the god's intent. It had no plan to return the humans to their original state. Change was inevitable, but it was meant to transform, not to destroy.

That brought him to the part of the sequence that he did not want to confront. It showed Per himself selected by the god globe to be absorbed or disassembled. It wanted him for research purposes—that was the only interpretation that made sense to him. Somehow this would help the globe proceed with its task, changing the remaining humans into a form that fit this world.

The last sequence was the most immediately urgent. It seemed to show that while Per was absorbed, the ketos—and Twelve—would take Dilani and Bey to a safe place. Or so he hoped. For himself, there would be no escape.

Absorbed. But was that really so bad? he asked himself. After all, what were his alternatives? He couldn't see any way to resist the process. Somehow, the membrane was now his life support. Even if he could force it to withdraw from him, most likely he would die. And where would that leave Bey and Dilani? They would be alone in the open sea, surrounded by enemies, still bearing within themselves—if his guess was correct—the seeds of their destruction. The thought of this transformation horrified him—or would have, if the godbits hadn't taken away his ability to fear—but it was their only chance to live.

One thing he didn't understand: Why had it been necessary to show him all this? Communication implied intelligence, though he couldn't guess at what kind of intelligence. For some reason, Twelve's god wanted his understanding and his consent. He did not know how to signify either, yet he somehow knew his permission was needed.

Subtle had time to writhe his remaining unencumbered limbs to record a brief thought of how amazingly strange his position had become—one limb around a member of the Teeth, others embracing creatures from the world beyond the Dry. The Teeth had killed many of his people; yet this pack of Teeth had saved his life. Strange things happened during the truce of god, so he had been told, but he had never imagined anything like this.

Now that he was close to both of them, he tasted a certain faint similarity in the skin water of the Teeth and the Dry creatures, and he wondered if the Teeth had acted at the command of god, or because of some bond that made Teeth and strangers smell the same. He regretted that he might never know.

More bitterly, he regretted the relentless pace of events, and the constant need to use his limbs. He had not found any time to weave a dance, however sketchy. Events still boiled through his consciousness and shimmered on his skin, but unless he could dance them soon, they would be forgotten, remaining as lusterless fragments of memory. Godbits could penetrate him and retrieve those fragments, and reconstitute them for the memory of god, but the full truth would be forever lost to the Round People. To live through the calling of god and be unable to remember it afterward would be the ultimate cruelty. The astringent, inky skin water around his mantle flavored the sea with whispers of his thought.

Subtle found it unpleasant in the extreme to touch the strangers now, but he forced himself to hold on to them. Their skin traces screamed of wounding and disintegration, of agonies and wrongness within. They brought back memories of flayed flesh shaken in voracious jaws. The strangers' bodies broadcast the message that they were being destroyed.

Normally Subtle would have fled in prudent haste from the merest hint of such disaster. He could taste numbing, calming motes emanating from the godbits, but beneath the calming motes were others that terrified him. He was no longer jealous of the strangers. The touch of god seemed a severe and dreadful gift.

But he had been chosen, designated as the messenger and protector for their journey. His reckless adventuring had led him into the jaws of death, but he would not turn back now, though he tasted his own dissolution in the blue-lit water.

Per was gone. Dilani had never imagined that happening. She had never believed that anyone as strong and smart as Per could die.

For the first time in all their days at sea, she felt in her bones how deep and dark and heavy the ocean was, and knew she was in it on her own. He had left them alone, and she hated him for it. But her hatred was a feeble flame, not nearly hot enough to keep away the eternal cold of the Deep.

*Tired, angry, scared,* she thought, but her fingers barely twitched. She was still under the spell of the godbit poison. Twelve's arm pressed her to the keto's back, and Slowbolt swam as if he had somewhere to go. No one had asked her permission. Per at least explained things to her. Now there was no one. A piercing ache wound through every part of her, as if pain were the cord that held her together and she was nothing but a collection of beads hanging on that string.

Her arm was crushed uncomfortably against something hard, but she couldn't move. She remembered that Per had strapped his notebook to her. She felt a very slight stirring of curiosity to know what Per had written. Inside the notebook, there were still words from him she had not seen—it was almost as if she could look forward to talking to him again. Maybe in the notebook he had explained.

Thinking of Per, she remembered being on dry land, seeing the sun and feeling the wind. She wanted air; she wanted light. She wanted to go up. No! She wanted to go back and get Per. But she had no choice. She went where the ketos carried her.

The ascent took a very long time. Per's armband with its gauges had disappeared with him, but Slowbolt seemed to understand the danger. The keto paused many times on the way up. Dilani hoped he was doing it right; Per had told her often how bad it would feel to come up at the wrong time. She didn't think she could stand to feel any worse.

The pauses seemed to take forever. During one of them, Slowbolt and Twelve took turns hunting for food. Each of them, in his own way, tried to share with the humans. Slowbolt brought a fish, held with comic daintiness between his lethal teeth, and butted them under the chin, trying to get them to open their mouths and take it. When at last he realized that they weren't going to accept the gift, he performed a twist in the water that reminded Dilani of a shrug, and swallowed it himself.

Twelve offered a fish too, but more tentatively, signing "Fish—eat," with a questioning mien as he did so. He examined their masks with one tentacle tip, but accepted it when they pushed his limb away. He tucked the fish neatly into his own hidden mouth, with a discreet hitch of his mantle, like a human hiking up a sagging pair of pants.

Dilani felt the saliva rush into her mouth when she saw the firm-fleshed silver fish. If she could have pushed it through her mask, she would have bolted it ravenously. But the flash of hunger was rapidly followed by a surge of nausea that made her gulp uneasily. Her mouth stayed dry no matter how often she sipped from the water tube, and there was a strange taste on her tongue. The piercing pain continued to stitch its way through her insides, growing spiky inside her head. While Slowbolt and Twelve finished their meal, she signed to Bey, "I feel sick."

Instead of the response she expected—"It's nothing," or some other comforting fiction—Bey signed brusquely, "Me too. Worse than you." She was astonished. Bey never complained. He was always cheerful. She watched him carefully when they moved on again; his movements had taken on a halting, disconnected quality. Perhaps Twelve was counting wrong; perhaps they were going up too quickly. Perhaps Bey, too, would die.

He stopped signing and curled up, with his arms clutching

his belly. Gradually he bobbed farther and farther away from them, till Twelve pulled him back. Bey's arms came untucked and drifted wide. Dilani peered into his mask; his eyes were half shut, his mouth half open. She shook his arms, but they stayed limp. She turned to Twelve for help, but he made the side-to-side motion she took for not knowing, or not caring, or not being able to decide.

Dilani tried to push her hand through Bey's belt, to keep him from drifting off again. Her fingers felt funny—sore and awkward. They looked wrong; they were too long and thin, and a pale, patchy color, not short and brown as they always had been. She blinked and stared. It must be fog on the mask, or a trick of the dim light. Those were not her hands. She pushed closer to Twelve's slick, dense skin. He was her only safety now. She closed her eyes and rocked herself to and fro against the pain. It hurt as much as ever, but between the sharpest stabs, she drifted in and out of sleep. She was uncontrollably tired.

Dreams came to her in sharp, vivid flashes. Some were the always-dreams of fire and black water, but some of them she would have liked to keep. Those were the dreams of someone with warm arms, dry arms like a human, not cool wet ones like Twelve. That was the person whose eyes stayed on hers and whose hands danced with hers—maybe her mother? And there was another face that bent close to her with bright, seeking eyes. This face looked at her through a trembling of ripples that broke the face into a thousand pieces that reformed and then broke up again so fast she could not recognize it, though it seemed familiar.

She tried to seize it, but her hands would not clasp, and then she was awake again, her mouth so dry it hurt, in the black water with unconscious Bey.

The dream had been wrong. She woke up weak and sick, but able to use her hands. Only now there was nothing to use them for. She could cling to the keto, but that was all.

Hours must have passed; Twelve was moving them again, up, but so slowly. At last she saw cloudy falls of light sifting down toward them, and beyond that, the crumpled-foil underside of the surface. Then she remembered that there had been another sky, a sky of fish. It was gone now. The great schools and their predators had melted away.

Stragglers still haunted the crater's mouth and made it a rich hunting ground. Slowbolt tore through the nearest school with hungry joy, but Twelve declined the fish that he brought back. The dodecapod's color was uncertain; he had lost his azure clarity and taken on a muddy tinge, darker in the hollows of his body, as if he couldn't spend the energy to make himself bright.

"Where are we going?" Dilani signed. But the answer was impossible to understand. "Where god tells the keto," she thought he signed. But she had no idea what he meant.

At last they were high enough to cross the rim of the crater. Once that was done, there were no more pauses. Slowbolt hunched his muscled back and began to swim in a dogged rhythm that never slowed. He stayed deep, but he cut the water like a spear without changing direction. Clinging to his fin, Dilani, Bey, and the discolored Twelve flapped on the keto's back like dark, tattered rags stuck to the stick of the spear.

*Well, this is it,* Per thought. *This is the last time. Or the first time. My one and only death.* The jellies still maintained him in a state of calm, so he couldn't really feel afraid. He grasped a passing thought—that he wasn't behaving very heroically. He should be struggling to the end, trying one doomed ploy after another to get himself out of the inevitable. That was what the heroes in stories always did, and they always won. Well, almost always.

The mask fell from Per's face, and he watched the clear wall bulge out, enclose it, and pass it neatly through the membrane that enclosed him. There was a momentary stab of fear, and instinctively he held his breath: Now he would drown. But drowning was a familiar fear, easy to face compared to being swallowed alive by curious jellyfish. It wouldn't take long; then this cluttered and wearying dream could end.

When he could not hold his breath any more, he gasped.

But instead of cold, heavy, pressurized water, his lungs filled with air. It was cool and had a strange, faintly sweet scent that seemed richly delightful after the chemical taint of the mask.

Per remembered his fear. If he couldn't die, he couldn't escape from whatever horrors lay in store.

Breathing was very enjoyable. With each breath, a little of his pain was stolen away, until it was all gone. Gradually, it began to seem funny that he kept forgetting to be afraid. It felt so good to feel nothing. He could move his eyelids, and his lips and tongue, but the rest of his body no longer responded to any of his suggestions. He wondered if he might be dead now, in which case it seemed all right for the jellies to eat his body.

Because he could do nothing to save himself, he didn't have to struggle or be afraid. He could relax and observe this unique, unrepeatable event. *I was always best as an observer, anyway,* he thought.

People sometimes thought of their mothers when they were dying, he knew. But if he had ever had one, he still did not remember her.

People sometimes prayed. Twelve's god had turned out to be a simple fact, though it didn't seem to have done Twelve much good. Still, it was theoretically possible there might be a power out there that was listening to him. But when he tried to think what to ask, his mind stayed blank. He'd ask for Dilani and Bey to be safe, but he wasn't sure any more what "safe" would be.

When he thought about praying for himself, he still couldn't think of anything. He'd done what he had to do, on the small chance that it would keep the kids alive. He couldn't take that back. He was definitely afraid of pain, but nothing hurt right now, and if it started hurting, it probably wouldn't last long. He wished he could change some things, but he'd had Sofron, if only for a little while. He'd had Typhon and its oceans, and all the beautiful and dangerous beings he had touched and seen.

*Just make sure you use me up,* he said to the hypothetical god. *Recycle me. I don't want to be wasted. I don't know if I worked out the way you wanted, but thanks anyway. I liked being alive.*

The last feeling faded from his face; his lips went numb, and his sight bled away to gray. *Sofron,* he thought, and it was something like a prayer.

# ᐳᑲ13ᑊᑋᔐᑊᑋᔐᑊᑋᔐ

Dilani came back from the dark and fiery dreams when the incessant rocking of those dark waters changed to scraping and bumping. The springy surface beneath her heaved and bucked as if trying to shake her off. She tried to cling, but her hands felt as if they were on fire.

She fell off into shallow water, and the waves dragged her along the bottom. Her skin burned in agony as the rough sand scraped it. She was on the beach, and there was a keto with her, but she could not remember why. Her mask thumped against the solid shore, and its edges dug into her face and hurt.

Something terrible assaulted her ears. It was like the vibrations from keto talk, but a hundred times closer and more powerful. It overwhelmed her. It was unendurable. It seemed to drill through her head. She tried to tear the mask off, but she couldn't make her fingers work. Where was Per? She signed for him, but he did not come.

Melicar was dozing half-upright, leaning against one post of her hastily built shelter, when she was startled awake by a shrill, broken whistling and warbling just offshore. She thought she had been dreaming it, but she staggered upright anyway and tried to rub her eyes back into focus.

There was something tumbling to and fro in the shallow water. Probably the tides had returned another body. She was tempted not to go. She had seen too many drowned and sodden remnants of the storm. But someone had to keep track of who was dead and who was living. She took a last deep breath of untainted air and staggered down the beach to look.

At first, she could make no sense of the shape. Then it started to break apart. It had tentacles, fins—arms and legs! She felt nauseated. The thing looked like a pile of dismembered limbs.

But then a hand pushed out of the water. Something rose up in deliberate movement. It was alive. She put on a breathless burst of speed. She saw dark hair, unmistakably human hair, floating in the water, and grabbed for it.

The skin beneath the hair was dark and rubbery, and she nearly let go in disgust. Then she realized that the face was covered by a mask. She used the strap to tow the body ashore, and ran back for the next.

She saw only one other human body, and at first she thought it must be dead. It had no legs. She dragged it up the beach anyway. When it was laid out on the sand, she saw that there were legs; they were short and misshapen, but unwounded. She pulled the mask open. Skin flaked off as she tugged the seal open, leaving raw patches on neck and cheeks. Nevertheless she recognized the face.

"Bey Sayid," she said, amazed. The boy did not answer. "*Bey!* Is it you?" she said, louder. There was something odd about his face: not just the saltburn and the unnatural pallor beneath the mask, but a strangeness about the shape of the ears and the half-closed eyes. She felt the pulse at his neck. His heart was beating very fast, and his skin was hot.

She pulled the mask from the other body. Its eyes fluttered. They seemed curiously cloudy, as if the membrane over the eyeball had thickened. It raised a fist to its face. The fingers were grotesquely long, and webbed together with inflamed-looking tissue, so the fist did not clench well, but Melicar recognized the gesture. It was a name sign. She was looking at Dilani Ru.

They had been sucked out to sea on the first day of the storm. Now the Deep was spitting them back, alive. But there was something very wrong.

She considered taking off their skinsuits, then thought

better of it. The suits would at least stabilize their body temperature until she figured out what was wrong with them. She glanced wearily toward the shelter. It would take a large part of her remaining strength to drag them up there, but it had to be done, so she might as well get started.

But something still thrashed in the surf. The doctor blinked and looked again. She thought she had seen tentacles. They were still there. Whatever the thing was, it seemed to be drifting in toward the beach. Behind it, pursuing or nudging it, she saw the sleek, alarming black and silver of a keto. She had never seen one so close to shore. It would beach itself if it came much closer. It took her a minute to realize that the shrill warbling that had never stopped was coming from the keto.

Dilani's hand fumbled toward her face. She was signing again.

"Pink . . . man . . ." Melicar read. *Pinkman.* That was the name Dilani had given Per. Sushan's heart turned over. Had Per been with them? Was he out there in the water? She shook Dilani furiously, but the girl's eyes would not open, so she couldn't see Sushan's pleading gestures.

"Look at me!" the doctor cried, though she knew Dilani could not hear her.

"Hurts," Dilani signed, and tried to cover her ears. Then her head flopped sideways. She was obviously unconscious again.

Bey reached up and feebly grasped Melicar's wrist. His hand, too, seemed deformed.

"Please—can't see you," he croaked. "Who are—?"

"Sushan Melicar," she said. "And you're Bey Sayid."

"Yes . . . where are we? Back at Refuge?"

"Yes. How did you survive? How did you get back here?"

"Drifted . . . the storm . . . Twelve and the keto brought us."

She thought he was talking nonsense, and took his face between her palms to keep his attention. He flinched.

"Hurts. Everything hurts. We're changing," he said. "The changing sickness."

She snatched her hands away, urgently, and then felt

ashamed. But what had she done? Had she brought a new plague ashore?

"Listen!" she said. "You must tell me. Dilani signed 'Per.' Per Langstaff—was he with you?"

"Yes, he saved us from the water. We had the lifeskip, till ... those white things. They fought us, and then— Twelve's god. Twelve said it would help. Per said it was all right, but—it swallowed him. And the keto took us away."

His puffy, discolored face twisted with grief or pain.

"It swallowed him? You mean, he's dead?"

"I don't know!" Bey sobbed. "He's gone. It hurts; it hurts."

Sushan pushed back her own grief and swallowed her questions. There was something immediate that needed doing, as always.

"Where does it hurt?" she asked. "Are you sick?"

"The godbits stung us," he said. "Twelve said we would change. Where's Twelve? You have to get him. He knows."

"What is Twelve? Bey! Wake up! You have to tell me!"

"Twelve, he has . . . the long arms. You know. Tentacles. He signs. He helped us. Get him!"

Bey moaned, and tried to curl up into a fetal position. As he did, Sushan saw a raw, pinkish growth on the back of his neck. She groaned aloud in despair. Even these castaways had not escaped.

Bey had seemed sure that the thing with tentacles could help. She looked out to sea. The tangle of bluish arms had come much closer, tumbling helplessly in the surf. The keto still whistled and called, muscling its way back and forth through the waves insistently.

"All right, I'll get the damned octopus," she muttered in the keto's direction. Then she turned. "But first I'll get you people out of the water."

Again she started to drag the castaways up the beach. As she pulled Bey and Dilani up to the dry sand, they thrashed and moaned. As soon as her grip loosened, they rolled blindly back toward the water. They flattened themselves into the sand so she could not move them, and somehow they writhed and slid down the sloping beach until they lay within reach of the waves again. It didn't seem to bother them that the water washed over their faces.

Sushan cursed bitterly. If she left them in the water without their masks, they would drown. If she left them on the sand with their masks closed, they might suffocate. And they wouldn't stay put. Finally she left them at the water's edge for a few minutes while she limped back to the shelter as fast as she could to get a net and a rope.

The cephalopod was still floating just out of reach when she returned. She launched herself into the water, cautiously up-current of the thrashing tentacles.

She planned to cast the net around the cephalopod's body, but by the time she reached him, she was out of her depth. She couldn't throw the heavy net and tread water at the same time. She had to swim in among the writhing tentacles to position the net.

The cold, limber arms wrapped around her, and for one terrifying moment she was dragged underwater in an unbreakable grip. Through a swirl of froth and stirred sand, she confronted a staring golden eye. She was close enough to see the iridescent pigments of the iris eddying around the total blackness of the pupil. Then she was thrust back to the surface with painful force.

The cephalopod zigzagged violently, but its limbs were entangled with the meshes of the net, and it couldn't pull free. Sushan swam shoreward till she could find a purchase with her feet, and hauled on the rope. The waves pushed the creature up the beach. She strained at the rope to keep the backwash from carrying it out again, and with the next breaking wave, the creature tumbled ashore like a tangled clump of weed.

It was big—the body about the same size as a human torso, and the limbs curled in an untidy snarl at least as long as she was tall. Out of water, it was heavy. She hauled on the net rope and succeeded in dragging the creature a foot or so through the sand. Its flaccid body shuddered, and the limbs lashed out in a sudden convulsion.

She could see that the rough cord of the net dug into the

cephalopod's skin, and gritty sand ground into its delicate coating of slime. Clearly, she was hurting it, so she stopped. She didn't know how long it could survive out of water. Bey and Dilani still rolled to and fro in the waves like driftwood. Somehow she had to get them to safety, as well.

*Damn it,* she thought, *they don't want to come ashore. They seem determined to stay in the water.*

She sat down in the wet sand, nursing her rope-burned hands. Doubletide was coming in. She'd been wasting her energy. The water would float them up to the tide pool near Per's ledge, where she had built her shelter. All she had to do was watch to make sure they didn't drown in the meantime. Then maybe she could slide them over the edge into the pool.

She watched them anxiously as the water rose. At doubletide, she was able to get them over the rocks into the pool with a minimum of damage. She snagged their skinsuits in several places, but she was no longer worried about that.

Once in the pool, the cephalopod floated so limply that Sushan wondered if it was dead until she noticed that the mantle still pulsed rhythmically. It seemed to have too many tentacles; she counted them and got twelve, not eight. Maybe that was what Bey had meant; maybe *Twelve* was the name he had given this creature. But he had said "Ask Twelve; he knows"—not "it," but "he." Either Bey was hallucinating, or he thought the creature could communicate. It certainly wasn't trying to communicate now.

Sushan touched their exposed skin and felt feverish heat, intense enough to warm the water around them. She examined the children's hands again. The fingers had lengthened, and the skin between them had overgrown into a kind of slack webbing. The nails were longer and thicker, almost talonlike. The pinkish growth around Bey's neck was more extensive than she had thought at first, and Dilani's neck and throat seemed to be affected, too. The growth extended like a fleshy fungus. She rubbed her hands in the sand after touching it, though she knew that if their illness was contagious, it wouldn't help.

"I've already screwed up here, as far as quarantine goes,"

she muttered. "I touched them. Whatever they've got, if it comes through skin contact, I've got it all over me. Well, I had no choice. It can't be much worse than what we've already got."

She returned to the shelter and made a quick check of her other patients. Most of them were the newgens who had survived the storm. Lila had disappeared during the evacuation, along with Kee Benksen. She could only suppose that they had both been swept out to sea. Their bodies had not returned. Dilani and Bey had gone from the beach, along with Per, and had been presumed dead.

The others had made it uphill to the grove of trees that marked the island's highest point. The adults had lashed the newgens and themselves as best they could to the trees and any floatable items. The storm waves had risen until even the trees were awash. The colonists had scrambled desperately to climb beyond the rising water and to salvage irreplaceable equipment.

At some point Selma had lost her grip and had been carried away into the churning sea. Melicar thought that probably Selma's weakened heart had stopped under the stress, and that she had been unconscious or even dead when the waves tore her from her parents' grasp. It could have happened any time. That was what she had told Selma's grieving parents, anyway.

They had lost some of the adults, too. Dilmun had been too crippled to stay above water. Melicar missed her every day. She still blamed herself, feeling that if she had seen Dilmun in trouble, she might have been able to save her. She secretly wondered if none of the others had considered Dilmun valuable enough to fight for.

Piping Melu and Bon Skanderup had died when the tree they were clinging to had toppled, crushing them. And there were more—too long a list.

After the winds had faded, they'd assumed the worst was over. They had crept back to the beach, buried the bodies they found, salvaged what they could, licked their wounds, and started to rebuild. Stubs of the posts of the longhouse still showed in the sand. They had lashed sticks and mats and a thatch of reeds to those remnants and had created a shelter from which they could rebuild the settlement.

Then the sickness had come. At first she had thought it was just a minor infectious virus of some kind, understandable after the prolonged exposure and stress. But the fever and lethargy didn't go away. Metabolic disturbances intensified; soon those who were affected sank into coma or experienced hallucinations, and refused to eat or speak. Tumorlike growths appeared and worsened.

Whitman blamed it on something brought in from the sea during the storm. He insisted that Melicar establish a quarantine and take the infected ones away. She noticed that the newgens fell sick faster and progressed more rapidly. They were the ones who were the first to be expelled from the longhouse. But adults also suffered.

Melicar had chosen to build an emergency shelter up on the point where Per's house had been. There was easy access to water and to food from the tide pools. And she didn't feel quite so alone there. She tended the sick as best she could, and returned to the longhouse every day to pick up new victims. Lately, Whitman hadn't allowed her to enter the building. She found the sick dumped on the sand outside.

Whitman wouldn't let her in to examine the others, nor would he let her use any of the remaining supplies. Based on their brief exchanges, through closed doors, she had begun to wonder if he was still sane.

Meanwhile, she made the rounds of the colony's remnants, who tossed uneasily on pallets or hung limp in hammocks in her crowded shelter. She gave them water when they were conscious enough to drink, and sedated them with tangleweed juice when they convulsed or flung themselves from their beds in pain.

Allowing herself a brief moment of self-pity, she bowed her head into her hands and admitted to herself that she wished Bey and Dilani had not come back. She didn't want to watch them die.

Then she splashed her face with cold water to drive back the fatigue. It was time to check her fish traps and prepare food.

Bader Puntherong sprawled in a makeshift hammock. By the harsh, even rasp of his breath, she could tell that he had finally fallen asleep, but she had to wake him up. She needed someone to watch over the others while she foraged, and he was the only one of her patients still functional enough to help.

"Bader!" she whispered close to his ear. "Bader, get up. I need you."

He made a brief, painful noise, opened his eyes momentarily, and then shut them again. He breathed heavily for another minute, and finally raised his head and looked at her.

"Bader, I have to go find something to eat. Keep an eye on Torker. He's been asking for water. If he wakes up again, give him a drink, but yell for me if he tries to get out of bed.

"And keep an eye on the tide pool. I found survivors on the beach, but they won't come out of the water. I parked them in the pool."

He came fully awake. "You're kidding," he said. She had spent so much time with him that she now found it much easier to interpret his garbled speech.

"No, I'm not. They're friends of yours. Bey Sayid and Dilani Ru. I don't know how they lived through it. They're not in good shape. We have to try to help them."

He untangled himself from the hammock so fast he nearly fell.

"Take it easy," she cautioned. "If you fall on me, we're both going down."

She helped him to the edge of Per's ledge, where he could watch both the pool and the shelter, and then made her way cautiously down the rocks to search for food.

The traps held only a handful of prizes. Since the storm, fish had been scarce. She cleaned the raw fish, chopped them in a flat, empty shell, and squeezed green giling juice over them to make them palatable. There was little edible ripe fruit to eat; most of it had been torn away or spoiled by the storm.

She climbed back into the tide pool, letting the wooden bowl of food float beside her. She opened Dilani's mask first. Only a short time had passed, but Sushan hardly recognized her. The discoloration of Dilani's skin had intensified. Thin membranes seemed to be growing over her eyes and nostrils, and the frills of flesh around her neck had grown so much that the straps of the mask cut into them. Sushan tentatively tugged at the membranes round the nostrils, but Dilani grimaced and arched her neck as if the touch were painful. The growths did not seem to be interfering with her breathing. Sushan decided to leave them alone.

The water tube was still full, but Dilani's lips seemed dry. Sushan patiently dripped fresh water across the girl's mouth till she swallowed and licked her lips. Then she tried to spoon in some fish. Dilani turned her head away. Nothing Sushan could do would make her eat.

Sushan fastened her mask again and turned to Bey. He groaned and pawed at his mask.

"I can't see," he said. His voice sounded strangely husky and sibilant. Sushan wondered if the growths were proliferating inside his throat.

"Leave your eyes alone; give them a chance to heal," Sushan said. She doubted that they ever would heal, but she hoped the authority in her voice would have some calming effect.

"Get it off; get it off," he said. When she tried to restrain him, his claws scratched at her. Deep, angry-red grooves had appeared in his neck, and as he struggled in distress, his breath whistled shrilly—a bizarre, inhuman sound.

Dilani suddenly roused enough to clutch her ears and sign again, "It hurts, it hurts!"

Sushan shoved Bey's mask shut and moved away until his thrashing subsided. His feet seemed to be undergoing the same transformation as his hands, and fleshy growths similar to those on his neck were bulging around his ankles. Sushan looked again and frowned. His legs seemed longer than she remembered. She supposed they had been tucked under him and were now floating free, making them appear longer.

She hesitated before trying to feed the dodecapod. But Bey seemed to think that the creature had information they needed, so she tried. Recalling that octopi had their mouths underneath, she felt among the tentacles and discovered an opening. Sushan dipped out a handful of chopped fish and tried to thrust it into the mouth. The creature refused to eat. It did not want food. Yet it kept clutching at her legs. Trying not to panic, she moved backward a step at a time, toward the edge of the pool.

She bumped into Dilani. The creature immediately let go of her legs and twined one tentacle around her arm. She tried to jerk away and realized just how strong the cephalopod was, even in its illness. It tugged on her arm insistently, wrapping another of its limbs around Dilani. It almost seemed as if the creature wanted the doctor to examine Dilani again.

Sushan ran her hands over the girl's unconscious body.

"Is this what you wanted?" she said. "Am I missing something?"

She touched Dilani's arm where the tentacle lingered and found a hard, rubbery lump. Her fingers recognized the shape of the battered object even before she got a good look at it. It was Per's field notebook. She unfastened the strap with trembling hands.

"Thank you," she said to the blue cephalopod. But it was no longer interested in her and let her go. It reached for Dilani instead and floated quietly next to her.

Cradling the notebook against her body, she stumbled out of the pool. She saw Bader limping across the sand toward her.

"I thought something was wrong," he said painfully. "What happened?"

"They brought back Per's notebook," she said.

Bader settled into the sand, his eyes intent on the water that held his friends.

"You go back and rest," he said. "Read. I wi' watch."

Sushan could hardly wait until she reached the shelter to unfold the tiny screen. She paged greedily to the last entry. But it told her nothing of the newgens and their plight, nothing of Per's fate. It was a brief note, obviously entered in haste:

*The lifeskip is gone. White Killers took it? We are alone in mid-ocean. Follow Twelve?*

She began paging back through the remaining notes for any information she could glean. She was already prepared for disappointment. She knew now that Bey had spoken the truth. Per had outlived the storm. But he was probably dead now, as they all would be soon. And yet . . . it had never been safe to assume.

*He was down to the last froth of oxygenated blood draining from his brain like foam disappearing into sand, and when that was gone—* But it did not end. The gray began to modulate, to waver, to break up into lights and darks. He *felt* again—a sense of pressure, a chilling, a prickling like many needles. And then a cold rush that awakened, like taking a deep breath of chilled air. But he felt no lungs or throat, and there was no air.

The paler shades of gray brightened and shifted. He saw distinct patches that differed not only in the amount of light, but in the quality of it. It felt like seeing color. It was seeing color, but he had no eyes. The colors came at him from all directions, constantly changing. The command that once would have closed his eyes had no effect. He could not shut off the assault of perception. He must be hallucinating. This must be what happened as consciousness broke down—but he wanted it to stop.

The sense of pressure and movement came at him from all sides, too; he felt ripplings, shivers, slow swells, crossing each other, setting up resonances and diffractions. Something touched him everywhere.

The sensations did not fade. They grew and spread, like dawn. He felt a kind of strength surging through him. It wasn't heartbeat or blood or breath, but it filled all those functions. There was no more pain. But suddenly, everywhere, there was the feeling the jellies had kept from him.

He was afraid.

He was terrified.

He was still alive.

Something within him contracted and flung itself violently outward, like a scream. There was no scream, but there was sound.

Suddenly he occupied the center of a ring of resonances. He felt their beautiful, proportionate patterns with his whole self. He sent out the sound again, this time not violently, but in long, sustained wonder. He perceived the pattern as exquisite pleasure. For a moment the confusion of brightness and pressure ceased to threaten him.

He knew exactly where he was, though he could not name the place. The ocean was touching him; his new self-surface understood each variation of pressure, each movement, as communication. He felt the sea floor beneath him, reflecting the pulses he sent out to it; every detail of its contour would become perceptible, if he chose to focus there.

He sensed the long roll of waters rebounding from coastlines far away, and he sensed the nearer islands, though he had no name for the measure of their distance and shape. He felt the myriad complexities of temperature, salinity, and current in the water, and all the lives in it touched him through the traces they left in their wake.

All his senses had come on again, doubly bright and strong. He had been rebooted, but not with the original program. He wanted to stop and think about what he was and how this had happened, but he couldn't find a way to ignore the messages that reached him from every side. He wondered if this was what it felt like to be a baby—to receive input from everywhere and to be unable to control it, or to find the channels that would lead to physical response.

He cast about in the random, uncontrolled way that babies wriggle. Sometimes he found himself struggling in confusion; sometimes he encountered whole new dimensions of pattern and signal, more information than he could possibly process. There might be more to his mind than there had been when he was a human. But he had no hands and no eyes.

One thing he searched for and could not find was a sign of the human children. He remembered what they looked like. He could hold that picture in whatever he used now as a mind. His memories were still with him. But he couldn't find a match to that picture anywhere in the present.

Searching, he plunged through the surface of some barrier and touched a self that flew. It was like plunging for the first time into Typhon's waters. For a moment he thought he was that self. Then he heard it singing, and knew it was outside himself, though he was carried in its wake. Where had he heard that song before? Where had he touched such joyful speed?

Then he knew. That swift, bright spearhead with its wake of music was a keto. He heard its song, and for the first time understood. He had been right; the ketos were intelligent.

Packed, multilayered stanzas hit him like the stutter of waves against a rocky shore. He felt a rueful twinge when he thought of his efforts to communicate; this resembled human speech so little. Syllable by syllable, word by word, laboriously constructing a single message—the ketos would never have the patience to slow down that far.

Most of the information would not even be comprehensible to humans, if it could be translated. Per found that some part of himself, that he did not consciously control, was sorting that portion of the data: constant reports on water conditions, news of who and what swam alongside, locator signals that changed as the keto moved.

There was a note of desperate urgency in the keto's communication. Per picked out the top line of the song, leaving behind the water messages. He was surprised at how succinctly practical the keto sounded. He had expected poetics, and got something more like code bursts.

### ** Name * location ** name * location **

The location-frequency changed by a tiny fraction each time it sounded.

| g | Pair of splitfin strangers | g |
| o | (not for eating) | o |
| d | carried by this-name swimmer | d |
| s | Single stickylimb | s |
| i | (not for eating) | i |
| c | carried by this-name swimmer | c |
| k | Trio carried: godbitten | k |
| | Trio carried: thingmakers | |

** Destination: nearest Dry edge **
**?Destination: coordinates follow **
Not for eating *GODBITTEN* Not for eating
Help help * Need thingmakers * Help help
Help help ?? Where where ?? Help help
Emergency ** Seek me People seek me ** Emergency

**Name * location ** name * location **

The message kept repeating, with minor variations, while all around it wove the useful information, and around that, the keto's personal observations. It wasn't necessary for the keto to vocalize his weariness; the form of his comment and the tone of his song communicated that.

For a long time, Per could hear nothing else. He was stunned with hope. It must be Slowbolt. What other keto could be carrying "godbitten strangers"? Per was amazed and humbled to recognize that, although the keto called them "strangers," the intonation he used nevertheless informed all listeners that these strangers "tasted of his pack." The rescue call was the same that would be used for an injured keto. Slowbolt was trying to take them to safety.

But how was it possible to see and hear all this? Suddenly he doubted his own perceptions. He wanted to believe they were safe. He wanted Slowbolt to be intelligent. He might be dreaming the whole thing.

Maybe he was unconscious, still in his body, in sensory deprivation in sunless waters, and he would never again be able to tell what was real. That frightened him badly. Fear-triggered chemical responses surged through him, uncontrollably.

In his fear, he fell out of contact with the keto and back into confusion. The pure joy he felt with its song ebbed away from him. He twisted and turned within his own mind, searching for some certainty, thrashing in random panic like a terror-stricken child. *Don't leave me here; don't leave me alone,* his mind screamed.

The silent faces of the bone people gleamed toward him from the dark reef. That memory was insistent: It was his and not his. The long, skeletal fingers reached toward him, and he tried to withdraw.

As the gleaming bones penetrated his space, they shifted form. He was still facing a skeleton. It was enclosed in a clear membrane, somewhere in the water. It gleamed like the other one, picked and polished clean. But it was different; the fingers were shorter, the toes mere stubs. The delicate neck spines were missing, and the skull seemed misshapen compared to the other. It was a human skeleton. Two finger bones bore thickened ridges where they had once been broken. One toe was missing a joint. The skeleton was his own.

And at last there was peace. He found himself in a cool green-lit place that felt calm and spacious. Ferny, dew-wet plants surrounded a shallow bath shaped like a spiral shell, built of tiles carved with the shapes of sea creatures. He recognized the shape of the bath. He had seen those shapes in the ruined underwater city. Now he knew what they were.

He also knew that this was not a real place. It was a memory of home, from the mind of another.

*Is anyone there?* he thought. *Hello?*

An inquiry went out along some pathway in the being he now inhabited. He sensed no response, yet there was a feeling of watchfulness.

He approached the bath. The water, or something that looked like water, invited him. As he imagined stepping into it, he pictured looking down at his feet. He half expected to see bones, or if not, then the familiar pink-white human skin. That would convince him he was hallucinating.

Instead he saw nothing at all. The water shivered as if he had stepped into it, but it gave back no reflection. He could feel the ripples urging him, drawing him deeper into the pool, but he was invisible. He moved with the ripples, feeling warmth rise around his insubstantial self until he was immersed.

*Welcome.* It wasn't a voice, but it was a communication, a feeling that would have expressed itself as *welcome* in any of the languages Per spoke. The feeling of a silent presence strengthened until he had to look. He knew he wasn't really looking with physical eyes, but his attention sharpened, and as if in answer to his focus, a shape appeared.

It sat on the other side of the pool, with its feet in the water: long-boned, finny feet—the smooth, froglike skin fresh and healthy—swirled with markings of rose and orange. His gaze traveled up the body to the long skull framed in its spiny frills. Here was the shape he had seen in the coral wall. But that one had been enameled bone, and this was alive and complete. He was looking at one of the Changing People.

Questions tumbled into his mind, but the creature moved its long hands languidly in a sculling gesture: *Wait.*

It slid into the pool without a splash, and approached him. It was a frightening sensation; he still could not see himself, but the tall being swam into the space that he occupied, and seemed to mingle with him like sugar molecules poured into water.

Suddenly the feeling of being shuffled, riffled, read, that he had experienced when the godbits sampled him, returned in overdrive. Images flashed by faster than he could recognize them. But this time the sampling was reciprocal; for each bit snatched from him, another slid into place, till an equilibrium was achieved.

*Now we can communicate,* said the Changing Person.

*How did you do that?* Per questioned.

*Biochemically stimulated memory formation,* the other answered. There was a pause, a hint of uncertainty. *Did that make sense? Right words?*

Per assented; not in words so much as in a flavor of the waters around him.

*It is a capacity built into me for storage of memories. I am a historian as well as ...* the thought died in confusion. *Sorry. We are not yet fully integrated. I think you have no word for what I am. I will try to show you.*

The Changing Person showed him an image carved on the wall, one he had not noticed before. The shape was four-limbed and tailed. It was shown horizontal, on all fours, its neck ruff lying flat along its back.

*This was the beginning of our journey. We lived in shallow water; we breathed both water and air.*

The image filled in with color, and moved through the changes as Per's guide spoke. Around it, the structures of a city grew up on the shore.

Per was awed at the culture they had built on the brackish margins of Typhon's seas, even before the Change. Living in water, with their soft damp skins, they found the development of metal technology difficult and slow. Instead, they had become ingenious manipulators of the biological diversity at the water's edge. Over the course of thousands of years, they had gained the ability to manipulate their own genetic processes, and they had decided to transform themselves: to create a form that could walk erect and survive away from the water.

*We began as swimmers, and when our first life was complete, we changed into air breathers who could walk on land.*

Per nearly lost himself in the tantalizing details of the process. Every aspect of the Change had been carefully recorded and stored within the god, for those who might come after. Per watched as the webbed and gilled swimmers approached the first of the gods. As scientists of the People watched, jellies clustered around volunteers and injected them with the tiny messengers of transformation.

Fascinated, Per watched as the changes began. He found that, if he chose, he could look below the surface and see the results in every system. The People's reconstruction of their own cells took place in carefully timed stages. Peripheral changes took place first: The fragile, finlike feet toughened and stabilized; the finger webs shrank to increase mobility and dexterity; the eye sockets grew protective bony ridges, and the membranes of the eyes themselves thickened to block out the extra ultraviolet they would receive in the Dry. The porous, water-absorbing skin thickened and darkened.

Respiratory and circulatory innovations were the most crucial, and came last. They had to occur in orderly progression, but quickly enough that the organism would not choke and die during the changeover. Sometimes the delicate balance was destroyed, and the subject died before completing the Change. All through the process, subjects had to be monitored and supported, lest a body's reactions to this invasion overwhelm it before the changes were safely incorporated.

The watchers performed operations designed to regulate raging fevers, to support runaway metabolic rates, and to keep oxygen flowing through vital organs. Again, if this support was lacking, the subject might die.

The first generation to receive the Change had become the Great Ones, the heroes to whom the Changing People looked with religious awe and pride, the first to stand upright on Typhon's surface. Most of their offspring had the new genes for the Change built in, triggered when the transformation from nymph to adult began. Some did not, and some grew malformed by errors in transcription. They were taken to the god; some of them were repaired, and some died. But the Changing People survived, and began their long exploration of the world above the sky edge.

Per wondered where they had gone, in the end. Had they all perished when the edges of their continents were drowned? He felt paths for exploration opening before him, but he turned forcibly away from them. That was not what he needed to know now.

The god had been designed as a living storehouse for the carefully tailored viruses that triggered the Great Ones' metamorphosis. Over time, more organisms were added to the treasury: biological adversaries to fight parasites or disease; more mutated viruses, yielding other effects or other species; colony organisms that formed neural networks to carry memories or perform simple tasks. Samples of all these lived in the giant globe, along with the processes that would activate them.

*What about you?* Per queried. *What are you? Where did you come from?*

Unlike his other questions, this one did not trigger automatic retrieval. Instead, the flow of information slowed and stopped, and he found himself again in the pool with the image of the Changing Person.

# ⊚14⊚⊚⊚⊚⊚⊚

*I came here by the same way as you,* the Changing Person said slowly. *The god was all that. But it could do nothing by itself. It had no mind, only tricks and memories. The Great People had to trigger every action. It could not feed or protect itself. Like you, I was disassembled by the god and rebuilt as an analog inside it. This is how I looked, before. Of course, this body no longer exists in the now.*

With startling vividness, Per saw his own skeleton again, in the waters of the pool. He reached for it without thinking, but touched nothing.

*It is in the water with my messengers,* the guide said. *I have sent it to the wall to be entombed with the bones of the Great People. We do you that honor.*

"*. . . of his bones are corals made,*" Per thought. "*Nothing of him that doth fade,/but doth suffer a seachange/into something rich and strange.*"

There was a pause, as if the god persona was still processing. *What is that?* it said. *What are you saying?*

*It's poetry,* Per said. He was relieved that the concept translated.

*I hope you have stored much of the Deepsong of your people,* the Changing Person said. *Of course I hear the Deepsong here. But still, it has been sometimes lonely.*

Per still could not read feeling in the soundless voice of the god. But he thought he detected a trace of curiosity, or yearning, perhaps even wistfulness in the waters that bathed him.

*Do you have a name?* he asked.

Ripples jumped in the water, as if something had been startled.

*A long time ago, I was called*—Per heard the memory of a sound, but it was not a human sound. The closest his human mind could come was *Kitkitdildil*. At the same time he heard the words in his own language, and saw the picture they called up: a thicket of reeds at the margin of a marshy inlet.

*It was an ordinary name. The meaning was "Flower of Rushes." In the spring, in the long-ago before the People changed, there was mating among the rushes. It was a spring name. My family lived in the spring part of the city.*

In Per's mind's eye, the rushes stirred, releasing a fragrance that he seemed to feel with his skin as well as his nose.

Suddenly the image vanished.

*This is what happens,* the Changing Person said, without any hint of emotion. *So many changing seasons of memories, and so long a time unchanging here below, the passing of tides and the dancing of the moons—it is a weight of much water flowing over me. I begin to think and lose myself in what might be done. I forget to act.*

*That is why you.*

*Why me what?* Per said.

*I was left here to be the guardian of the god and to take care of this world for the Great Ones, till they return. The time was so long. I entered a waiting sleep, with certain signals planted to awaken me. When I felt your people enter the water, I woke up, thinking it was my own come back. When no one came to me, I sent messengers to look for you. After many changing seasons, the messengers came back, and I knew that you were strangers.*

*Did you infect us?* Per demanded. *Was that your doing?*

There was a pause. *In a way. The change motes live in the water now. We sent out so many that they live by themselves, seeking a place to do their work. They found such a place in you. But they have no minds. They do as they were built. They did not know that you were different, so instead of changing you, they only made you sick. That was not my wish.*

*I mean well to you, because I need you. I am old. The White*

*Killers grow strong. Strange new creatures grow in the Great Ones' gardens. The Laughing Teeth and the Round Folk serve me, but I need help from beings born with hands. So I sent the Round One to bring you here. I need new memories, new thoughts. And I needed to take you apart so I could see how the change motes should deal with you to keep you living.*

Per caught at Kitkit's words. *I heard the ketos singing,* he said. *I did, didn't I? Yes, I thought so. Where are they going? Where are they taking my people? What have you done with them?*

There was another pause. Instead of providing him with the information, the Changing Person seemed to withdraw.

*Look, and find out,* he said.

Per would have exploded with anger, but he did not know how to do it in his new form. He experienced extreme agitation and impatience, and the flavor of those things permeated the water around him, inciting action.

*Where are they? How do I find them?*

*They are with the Laughing Teeth,* the god said, and then fell silent. Per received the impression that it was waiting, daring him to find an answer.

He had found the ketos once; he knew he could find them again. He discovered that if he focused tightly on ketos, more and more information flooded toward him along that path. The keto images unfolded and showed him everything about them: the special heat-exchange system that made their blood warm; the gills that sucked oxygen from the water; the modified swim bladder that used air to supercharge the blood for swift sprints and for battle; and the sensing organs that gave them instant orientation. *So that's how they do it,* Per thought.

He had been right: the ketos carried viral inclusions in their genes. The Changing People had changed the ketos, too. He found fascinating records of discussion. The ketos had been offered a chance to receive hands, and had only showed their teeth in bright, deadly laughter. Willingly, they had agreed to be faster, smarter, more deadly, in return for serving as messengers to the god. Their new organ systems only improved on what they already enjoyed. They had refused to come in from the Deep, to be tied to things made by hands.

Impatiently, he pushed aside all other information to seek out the answer to one immediate question: How could he communicate with them? From his new perspective, he knew keto songs reached him through a series of relays. The message passed from keto to keto. Visual and sensory information came more slowly, passed through chains of godbits his predecessor had already sent out.

The god's records held a collection of individual sound signatures, tied to the feeding range, genetic relationships, and color patterns of the ketos. Obviously they were important; the god had taken great interest in them. Resonance organs in Per's "skin" sorted the incoming matrix of sounds and located the keto whose broadcast he had picked up before. It was Slowbolt, still close enough that most of his song was coming through unaided.

Additional messengers showed Per that other ketos from Slowbolt's pack were trying to catch up, but none of them were close. He wondered what the nearest Dry edge could be. *Surely I must have access to geographical information,* he thought. He tried to recall it, but got a review of his own position instead. How had Kitkitdildil managed his array of knowledge?

He knew the chamber in which they sat was not to be taken literally, but he looked around anyway, wondering if the artifacts he saw there might help him. He placed his hands on the tiled edge of the bath. It felt like running a sim, back on Skandia: Each action segment felt real, but a part of his mind stayed outside, manipulating, and knew that it wasn't completely real. It made him nervous, too. Running a sim had always made him nervous. It made him fear that other things, lurking in the back of his mind, might come out.

He was about to step up out of the water when his hand brushed against something, and the scene before him blurred and trembled. He performed a clearing operation—if he had still had eyes, he would have said he blinked—and the chamber solidified again.

His hand rested on a decorative tile, carved with a green triangle. He noticed that a band of carved tiles ran around the spiral margin of the bath. Each of them bore a different symbol, and some of the symbols looked like the glyphs he had seen carved on the drowned wall. He ran his fingertip around the raised triangle.

The water shivered around him. Its pearly sheen coalesced into tiny beads. Under his finger, the smooth ceramic turned to a webbing of small spheres strung on limber stems or wires. He ran his hands across them and found that he could read the arrangement as a map of ocean currents. Larger nubs at certain nexuses marked the presence of islands. As he touched them, he drew on stored information.

The location data he had received from the ketos fell into place among the bead maps. He knew where he was. And Slowbolt was halfway to Refuge. At the moment his course was carrying him on a tangent to the island.

As Per cast about, no information from Refuge came to him. The god's news-gathering network seemed to have been disrupted by the storm. What was the term Slowbolt had used? *Thing makers.* He looked for any news of thing makers in the island net.

The water trembled around him again. Vertigo assailed him as his frame of reference flip-flopped. Suddenly he was in shallow water, looking up. Fragmented by the shifting planes of the surface, he saw a monstrous vision looming: flat and mottled brown; divided by fleshy openings, one lined with flat white teeth; holding two flat, smallish eyes, both on the same side of the face. It was a human being, seen through Typhonese perception.

Once he recognized that, he was able to shift back to a human point of view. Immediately, the face became familiar. *Sofron.*

He wanted to cry out her name, but it turned to a knot of underwater vibrations that Sofron could not have recognized. A wild excitement shook him, and he tasted/felt his own agitation in the water. Throughout the near ocean, god messengers hesitated, confused by this outburst, awaiting a change in mission.

Per wasn't able to pinpoint how recent the image might be. He still had only a vague understanding of the god's time frame. But it tasted fresh to him; it was easy to restimulate the memory in the nearest godbits. Definitely, the picture was associated with a shoreline whose map analog he could call up. There was a feel of distance, but in space, not in time. Sofron had been alive there—probably was still alive.

For all their skill, Per thought, the Changing People had failed in building the god. They had left it without equipment to weep, to curse, or to exult. He had found Sofron again, only when he could never go to her. But she was alive—she was still alive.

The form of Kitkitdildil, sitting in shadow by the edge of the pool, raised his head and looked at Per with eyes that shifted around their pupils like indigo smoke.

*This was a female of your family?* he asked.

Per suspected that the god persona had full access to all his memories, but he could at least avoid discussing them. *Yes,* he said. He left his emotions unspoken, for the god to read if it could.

*Have you thought what you are sending them?* the god asked.

*What do you mean?* Per said, baffled by the abrupt change of direction. But he had felt the knowledge fall into his grasp before he finished asking.

"Changing sickness"—that was what Twelve had called it. They were all infected. And he had sent them back to Refuge, to Sushan and the others, who would not know.

*Can't you cure them? Put them back the way they were?*

The colors of the god remained dark, and the water felt cold to Per.

*The water itself will reinfect them,* the Changing Person said. *I was made to change the children of the Deep. I do not have the power to stop the Deep from changing.*

*Can't you do something?* Per demanded, with a force that echoed in the waters like a shout.

*I have already done what I can,* said the god. *I have shown you how the changes were made. Your people have the changing sickness already. If it continues on its ancient path, the way that was not made for humans, they will die. Only if you help me to complete the transformation can they survive.*

*You wondered why I did not let you die. This is the reason. I need not only the knowledge of your shape but the cooperation of your mind. You can let them all die now, if death seems better to you than the changing. You see what can be done. Now you must choose.*

Its form withdrew into the shadows. It left Per alone to learn how a god feels loneliness and grief, to contemplate what he had already done to his people and what he was about to do.

*Show me,* Per said at last. The god turned its storm-cloud eyes upon him, and he was drawn into the ancient vision.

Dilani couldn't even put a name to what was happening to her. She could only sign "Big pain, big pain" over and over. Everything in her body hurt, but she could name those things: her head, her legs, her hands, her chest. The godbit sting was making them different, horribly strange and ugly, but it didn't matter if only the hurting would stop.

But the big pain was something else. It seemed to come from all around her, from outside, yet it was inside her, too. When she opened her mouth in protest, it seemed to leap inside her head and pierce her skull. It went right through her ears.

Someone came when she was in the water, bringing her food. She could not eat. Her body demanded nourishment, but even a sip of water felt like swallowing fire. Her body floated, wreathed in fever and pain, as if the bad dreams had come back for her, and she was in the black water again, and the water was on fire.

Her mind curled into a tiny bubble and tried to float away. The pain was like a tether that would not let her go. She bobbed at the end of the tether, willing herself to snap the string and disappear.

* * *

Sushan woke up suddenly. Bader was calling her, a garbled shout that had syllables in it. He was trying to tell her something, but she couldn't understand him. Shielding her eyes against the dazzle of the early sun, she tried to figure out what he was doing.

He was waist-deep in the water below the ledge, near the tide pool. Alarmed, Sushan hurried down the rocks after him. He had hardly been out of his hammock for days. She didn't think he was strong enough to stand up to the waves.

As she approached, she realized that he was shouting "Ketos!" a word that was hard for him to form with his crooked mouth. She scanned the waves beyond the surf for the black-and-silver fins, but the water was blank. Then she gasped. In a burst of spray, a long, muscular body sprang free of the water an arm's length in front of her. There were more of them in the surf. It looked like a whole pack, whistling and smacking the water like a rowdy waterball team.

Then the one who had come closest arched its body like a bow and sprang nearly over her head into the pool where Bey and Dilani floated. Bader had followed before Sushan could reach them. There was hardly room in the pool for the keto and five more bodies. The keto's tail thrashed the water into foam, and Sushan could hardly stand up. She couldn't see who or what the keto had bitten.

"Get out, get out!" she yelled furiously. "We're not snacks, damn it! Go away!"

Water splashed into her mouth, and she choked, staggered, and sat down. As she fell, she found herself face-to-face with the keto. It shone with vigor. It shook its head gaily and opened its great mouth, full of teeth as blindingly clean as surgical instruments. But the teeth didn't flash forward to catch her. The mouth clashed shut, and the keto flipped itself free of the pool, negotiated the shallows with effortless dexterity, and disappeared into the Deep.

As it went, it shed something like a gleaming skin. But it dissolved as it entered the water. It broke up into a foam of bubbles. Sushan thought her eyes must be playing tricks on her. But the bubbles did not break. They formed sticky clumps in the water. They gathered around Bey and Dilani and the blue creature.

*They must be some organism from the Deep, stirred up by the storm,* Sushan thought. *They were riding on the keto. Perhaps it jumped into the shallows to get rid of them. They might be parasites.* She tried to brush them away from Dilani. For a moment they clung to her hands, with a soft, insinuating touch. Then they stung her. They dropped away as she staggered to the edge of the pool, wringing her hands in pain. The shock dizzied her. She had to sit down.

After a dazed moment, she remembered Bader. He sprawled on the sand, panting. "Ow," he said. He lowered his head and lay still.

*It's not fair,* Sushan thought. *Volcano, storm, ketos, jellies, viruses—enemies without and within. How many ways does this world want to kill us? One would be enough.* She realized too late that these could be the same jellies Per had described as stinging him, shortly before his journal entries ended. Was this what had killed him?

She tried to get up and see if Bey and Dilani were all right, but she couldn't move. The sting left a kind of lethargy in its wake that was better than tangleweed. She thought of the few words Bey had said when he first came ashore: *godbits stung us. Twelve said we would change.*

After a long time of agony and blindness, when Dilani had forgotten that anything else existed, something touched her. It eased the tight covering from her body. At first she thought it was ripping away her skin; the water scalded, and she tried to jerk away.

Then the water changed; there was a new, soft touch that washed gently over her, soothing and cooling. The cruel bindings that cut around her neck were loosed and fell away, and a rush of delicious coolness swept through her chest. With the coolness came a sudden taste as visible as a word. The water spoke to her skin and spoke in her mouth and the passages around her neck where she could taste it.

The water whispered with flavors of hope and body-soothing comfort. Its soft touch drew her back toward her body, lured her into that now-strange and unfamiliar form.

There were others in the water with her. Now she could taste them. There was the bitter musky smell that made her think of danger and help at the same time. Then there was a friend taste. She had forgotten the word for it, but the message went in her mind with a smooth yet nubbly feeling, and a flavor of blue. She could rest in water that tasted of friends.

"Allfather," Sushan breathed. The sting had worn off, leaving her with a headache, but able to move again. She stared down at the faces beneath the now-quiet water.

Somehow, the masks had been taken from them.

The masks were not all that was missing. As she reached to pull their heads above water, she saw that the skinsuits were gone as well. They hadn't been removed and left in the pool. They were simply not there.

*They're probably dead; they probably drowned while I was passed out from the sting,* Sushan thought desperately. She grabbed Dilani by the hair and tried to prop her head out of water, even while she reached for Bey.

She grasped Bey's throat to tip his head back so she could try to clear his airway. Most of his neck and face was coated with something clear and slick, like the bubble jellies. This time nothing stung her, but she couldn't tear it away. As her hands closed around his throat, she felt a pulse: not a faint or rapid pulse, but a strong, regular beat. His mouth was shut, and his nostrils were covered by the membranous growth. She nearly dropped him back in the water in shock when he moved, turning his head irritably to get away from her grasp.

She looked more closely. The reddened grooves on his neck had deepened, and their puffy edges had turned to delicate frills of flesh. The slits pulsed rhythmically.

Sushan pulled his head up out of water and tried to pinch his mouth open. He reacted violently. He arched his back like a fish flapping out of water, and twisted from her grasp to immerse himself again.

While Sushan had been busy with Bey, Dilani had quietly slipped back into the water. Like Bey, she floated beneath the surface. The fleshy frills around her neck seemed to waver softly back and forth inside the bubble that enclosed her face.

"They're breathing underwater," Sushan muttered.

She let them float free while she examined them. The fleshy frills around their necks extended six inches or more, and they were discolored like multihued bruises. Their noses were flattened, the eyes still sealed by translucent pinkish membranes. The skin of their bodies seemed translucent, too, and it drew tight over bones whose placement and shape no longer seemed quite human. Dilani's ankles had budded into fleshy growths like Bey's, and her feet, too, seemed to be elongating into taloned flippers.

She looked down at them fearfully, and met the cephalopod's yellow eye looking back. Was there knowledge behind the gold that flowed like shifting sands? Its skin color had darkened from a delicate azure to a dull, dark indigo. She would have sworn it was in pain.

She frowned. She thought she remembered that earlier, she had only been able to see one eye at a time. The eyes had been fixed on opposite sides of the head. She could see both eyes now, one of them just visible beyond the curve of the head. Its limbs no longer looked entirely separate. Several of them seemed to be fusing together. Twelve—if this was Twelve— was changing, too.

She scrubbed her fingers in the sand again. A faint, aromatic, bitter yet musky smell clung to her hands. It was not unpleasant, exactly, but it startled her each time she noticed it. It was different. Not right. Not human.

"Oh, Per," she said wearily. "Why in hell's kingdom aren't you here? They're not just sick. They're changing into something that isn't even human. I don't know what it is. A contagious cancer? Bey is growing legs, Per, I swear. How is that possible? You must have had some idea what was happening. Why didn't you come back to tell me?"

She sat with her head hanging, as if waiting for an answer. Finally she took a deep breath.

"All right. All right, I know," she said. "I'm not stupid either. I must have some idea, even if I don't have all the data. Bey is the key. Something stopped his legs from growing. A genetic defect? No, that wasn't the cause. That was the mechanism. Now something else has turned the mechanism on again.

"Maybe the same thing that made them short is making them grow again. Not just a mutation—something that *causes* mutations. It happens to the natives, too, because it's happening to the octopus thing. So we know for sure that it wasn't radiation in transit."

She had read all of Per's notebook now, and nothing explained this. It seemed there would be no further message from Per. The children were the only message he had sent. She wondered how long she had to figure it out before she, too, began to change.

With the coming of the new godbits, Subtle returned to some form of consciousness. He tried to dance his shape, to examine himself and see what damage he had suffered.

*I, Subtle . . . I, Subtle . . .* That was as far as he could get. His body would no longer shape the familiar signs. When he tried to sign *I am of the Round Folk,* his limbs refused to budge, as if they were bound by tangleweed. His eyes no longer brought him the round world; his sight had narrowed to a wedge, and the rest was darkness. With deep and bitter sorrow, he realized that he was no longer of the Round Folk. He could no longer shape that name. Even his own name was a mere shadow of itself. Perhaps that, too, would fade, and he would be left without language.

Despair tainted the water all around him. He had to have clean water, but he found himself unable to swim. He could only thrash his stiffened body in convulsive jerks that battered him against the stone confinement of the pool. The Dry creature who had put him here was trying to keep him safe, but it was killing him to be imprisoned with the poison of his own sickness.

He longed for the familiar embrace of the Deep. In his maimed condition, he might well be killed before he reached the reef, but he did not care. Let the Deep swallow him; let his blood fume in the water, bearing his dying curse back to a cruel god. Staining the rocks with the ink of his pain, Subtle dragged himself up over the edge of the pool to seek the sea.

A trickle of water from the incoming tide sustained him as he wallowed over the rocks and sand. His tender under-skin seemed to have toughened. The grit no longer hurt him as he crawled. But when he tried to stretch his limbs, he found them missing. Only two of his front-side arms responded. He saw them when they came within his new, restricted field of vision, and at first he thought they must belong to some other being. They were straight, and broken in the middle, and re-pellently smooth, without any grasping pores. They ended in the strange cluster of little forelimbs that deformed the arms of the Dry creatures. He rolled and tried to whip his tentacles about him to turn away, but the strange limbs moved with him. They were his own. He felt a dead weight dragging behind him on syphon-side, but his new, limited vision could not tell him what that was.

Gasping, he dragged himself to the surf and gratefully felt the water enclose him. He tried to jet away from the shore—but he could not. His syphon and mantle no longer functioned. He bent the ungainly new arms and slapped himself, and found that his body had turned to a strange cylindrical thing, with a frame of bones beneath a thin, tough skin. He felt along the sides. Unless the new skin lied to him, there were only two limbs there, opposite his head, for a total of four. He tried to imagine what he might look like, and could visualize only a memory of the White Killers, grinning.

In his horror, he allowed the waves to pound him into the sand and cast him back upon the shore. He had stubbornly believed that if only he could get back to the water, he would be all right—he could swim away and escape. To find himself helpless even in the sea was the final shock. He gave up trying to save himself. The circle of his life was broken. He could no longer dance his memories; he could not even swim. He had gone to his god in grief, begging for transformation, and his prayer had been answered. He had become a monster.

When Dilani woke up, her eyes were unstuck. She could see again. Outlines and colors were clear and bright, but they wavered as if seen through a transparent distortion. She tried to sit up, and floundered. She wasn't lying in a bed; she was floating in water. She bobbed around until she finally got her feet under her.

She stood up; water streamed off her. As she tried to take a breath, she felt an unfamiliar movement in her chest. The air seemed to catch in her throat; she gagged, and a rush of warm seawater streamed from her mouth and down the sides of her neck. It felt as if water were coming out of her ears. Frightened, she put her hands over her ears, and found that the water trickled from newly grown slits in the side of her neck. She had holes in her neck!

She stared in horror at her hands, but the warm salt water on them was clear with no tinge of blood, and her neck had stopped hurting. She wasn't wounded. She coughed and gasped. The slits in her neck pressed together like lips, and she was breathing air again.

Something touched her shoulders—delicately, like a scarf. It felt like a kind of frill with spines that shaded and protected those strange openings in her neck. She tugged on it. It wouldn't come loose, and force hurt; it was attached to her. It was part of her. The spines suddenly stiffened and extended, shooting the frill open like an umbrella at the back of her neck, as if her fear had caused the reaction.

And then the big pain stabbed through her head again. It was awful, unendurable, a sensation she had never experienced. Her mouth opened in the grimace of protest she had always used, and the pain intensified. Her chest was completely empty of air. She gasped, and the pain stopped for an instant. She was so startled that she closed her mouth and took another breath.

The pain had stopped, but there was still something happening in her head that had never happened before. It wasn't intense and terrifying, but it was all-pervasive. When she moved through the water, it seemed to move with her. Could it be possible that she was causing the pain herself? She held still, but the sensation didn't stop completely. It came from all around.

Now that she was awake, she remembered the flavor of the water. Her body could taste the water now, and told her it was the flavor of Twelve. She looked around for him, but he wasn't there. Then she saw the position of the moons, and their fullness, and felt the steady incoming stream of cool, oxygen-rich water from the sea. The tide was coming in, and her body also seemed to know that.

To her new eyes, the moonslight was nearly as clear as day. She saw a shape dragging itself through the shallow water below the pool. She thought it was Twelve, though there was something wrong with the way he looked and moved. Impressions from her strange new sense grew more intense. Twelve and the others were moving their mouths, and the results hurt her head. As he splashed through disturbed water that glistened white in the moonslight, Dilani felt other perceptions, too, but less intense. The feelings seemed to grow and shrink with the rise and fall of the water, as if the waves were causing sensations similar to those that resulted from the mouth actions. Dilani did not see how that could be; water had no mouth.

The new sense helped her follow Twelve's progress as he slid through the shallow water. She tried to catch up with him, but he was moving fast. He floundered out into the surf before she could get to him. Then all the fight seemed to go out of him. He let the surf carry him back to shore. Dilani rolled him over, afraid that he had become unconscious.

He was so misshapen she could hardly recognize him. His head and torso no longer formed a smooth, rounded whole, but were separated by a thin, unnatural-looking stalk. Some of his limbs seemed to have fused together, and others had vanished, unless they were wrapped around that ungainly trunk.

Suddenly Dilani felt as if yet another inner eyelid had opened, clearing her sight. Twelve now possessed two legs and two arms. His compact body had separated into a trunk and a head. He no longer looked like a deformed cephalopod. Instead, he was beginning to resemble a deformed biped.

Golden eyes stared blindly up at her. The hands moved jerkily, at random. Dilani looked in vain for the strong, supple arms that had woven a language of beauty and freedom in the round world of the Deep. The god had changed Subtle, too. Dilani saw her own pain and anger mirrored in his helpless struggle.

The human-shaped mouth opened, letting out that sensation of piercing strangeness. For the first time, Dilani found a meaning in this assault on her senses. Unable to sign, to communicate, Subtle called to her in the only way he had left. Sound could be painful to the heart, not just the ears; Dilani heard his confusion and loneliness. She didn't know how to answer him. She touched her skin to his and cried with him for the bitterness of change, and for the graceful dancer he had been and would never be again. The sounds were harsh and ugly, but they were shared.

She stayed with him as the water deepened and the sky changed colors and the moons moved around the world. She could feel it all spinning, but that feeling stayed at the back of her mind while she concentrated on Twelve.

She wondered how she would talk to him if he could no longer sign. The waves broke over her, submerging her head, and it seemed natural to inhale instead of holding her breath. Again she had a feeling of movement within her chest; a noisy, prolonged burp rumbled out of her, and then the cooling water flowed easily over the slits in her neck. As soon as she was immersed beside Twelve, the water began telling her things. She tasted the dark bitterness of his pain and confusion. Along the narrowing in his trunk, what looked like the remnants of his mantle twitched and convulsed in distress.

Dilani stretched out and floated as close to him as she

could. Carefully, she rubbed her hand across the skin near the mantle in a light, soothing motion that came to her automatically. She felt a warmth around her wrist, diffusing out around her hand. She did not know what it was, but something moved from her skin to his, something that made the water taste warm and comfortable. The trembling of his mantle slowed. She could feel the taste of his skin improving.

*Now maybe I can learn his real name,* she thought. Patterns of color followed her hand as she stroked him. Forgetting the other humans, she floated close to Twelve, happily speaking the skin language at last.

She realized that he was very confused. The changes in her own body were nothing compared to the change from round to long, from twelve limbs to four. She felt a great need in his skin motes, something like thirst or hunger, or a craving for painkilling medicine. She wasn't sure what he needed, but she could clearly perceive that he wanted to go deeper into the water. She decided to take him there.

She disentangled herself and sat up, and saw a stranger in the water. Dilani's mouth opened, and another stab of the strange pain went through her. The stranger splashed and floundered. A spiny frill grew from its neck, and the frill suddenly shot open when the stranger saw Dilani. Its mouth opened, and again the pain shot through Dilani. The stranger lunged at her, and she leapt backward; for a moment they wallowed underwater, clutching at each other with long, slender hands that were webbed and clawed. When they shot up into the air again, the stranger retreated, holding its hands palm out, scrambling backward on its knees. Its frill opened and closed uncertainly. Then its mouth moved, but no pain followed. It was making a mouth shape at her. Unbelievably, the mouth shape was familiar. It was saying her name.

Then, with those misshapen hands, it signed to her.

"I'm Bey," it said. It made the *B* sign, followed, for emphasis, by the hand's edge chopping off legs. But she shook her head.

"Yes, yes, it's true," the creature signed.

"Bey has no legs," Dilani signed.

"The legs grew," the creature signed. "I am very surprised, and I'm very happy. I can't make them work right. I fall down all the time. But I will walk!"

It bounced up and down experimentally, and its mouth made something like a smile. Thin, bloodless lips stretched wide over teeth that were sharper and more numerous than they had been.

"You don't look like Bey," Dilani signed. "You look terrible, weird. Bey is handsome."

"Thank you," the creature signed. It made a little mock bow, extending its hand from the lips in the same gesture Bey had always used.

"You look fine," it continued. "Dilani was too pale and pasty. You're beautiful colors now."

She held out those unfamiliar, clawed hands, then touched her face very carefully. She did not want to hurt herself with her talons. It was frightening to be so different. But inside she did not feel different. She was only stuck in a different kind of shell. Still, she glared at him.

"Joke, joke," the stranger added hastily. "Dilani is beautiful."

It patted her shoulders and looked at her anxiously, with its head on one side. It was Bey. It had to be Bey. No one else paid so much attention when she was sad or frightened.

"Dilani," the mouth shaped, but this time she flinched. Somehow Bey was creating pain.

"Stop, it hurts," she signed, trying to push him away.

He shook his head. "Not pain. You're hearing. The god of change put my legs back, and it made you hear."

Dilani clapped her hands over her ears and shook her head, but strange things happened inside her ears, flutterings and vibrations, an assault on everything that had once made sense.

"Dilani," he said again.

It was true that he could make things happen to her when he moved his mouth. But still she signed, "No, no, no."

And being Bey, the strange, frilled, many-colored creature did not argue, but let his hand stay kindly on her shoulder.

Bey's hand had been warm. Now it felt cool and slick, like Twelve's skin.

When that thought soaked in, it finally took Dilani's attention from what had happened to her.

"Twelve," she signed. "We have to help him. He's worse than us. He can't move, can't sign."

Bey shrugged. Dilani would always be Dilani, whatever shape she came in. She had a one-track mind. Twelve mattered to her. She would brush everything else aside until she got her own way.

"What can I do?" he asked.

Dilani tried to scowl, but the expression fit badly. The forehead of her new face would not wrinkle in the old lines. She grimaced again, this time drawing her mouth out long and thin, and raising the points of her neck-frill wickedly.

"Make him swim," she signed at last, decisively.

She pulled at one of Twelve's limp arms, and dragged the unmoving body a little deeper, far enough that Twelve's head submerged. Twelve began to make strange gargling noises as his respiratory system tried to decide between air and water.

"I don't think this is a good idea," Bey signed in alarm, but Dilani wasn't looking at him. He punched her on the shoulder to get her attention, but she just kept pulling at the heavy body.

"Damn!" he yelled. "You're drowning him."

For the first time ever, Dilani turned to look at the sound of his voice.

She didn't take time to sign, just smacked the water with one peremptory palm.

*Get him in the water,* Bey interpreted, and found he had repeated it aloud to himself.

"W'rrahw," Dilani said, showing her teeth at him.

"Are you talking to me?" Bey said, astonished. She glared at him. He couldn't tell if she had tried to repeat his words, or if she was only growling. One thing was certain: she had discovered sound, and was using it against him as a weapon.

He helped her drag Twelve seaward. The water made it easier to stand up, and less painful to fall down.

Dilani let go of Twelve's arm long enough to sign again.

"He needs—more—something," she signed sketchily. "More. We are finished. He isn't. He is changing more."

Before Bey had time to ponder this, he saw the blue nodes in the water, flocking slowly together with the characteristic bobbing, dancing motion of godbits. They gathered around Twelve's head and spine, but this time they did not cover his face. The first time Bey had seen godbits, they had frightened him with their mindless, inescapable swarming. This time they seemed to touch Twelve almost gently, choosing their spots with delicate precision.

Dilani floated next to Twelve for a minute. Her face smoothed out and she relaxed. Bey wondered if she had gone to sleep, but before he could try to rouse her, she emerged from the water of her own accord.

"Now he feels good," she signed. "His skin is good. The water tastes better."

Twelve drifted slowly deeper.

"Will he be all right?" Bey signed. As he did, there was a splash just beyond Twelve. A keto fin broke the surface and smoothly vanished again. They were still on watch, apparently. They would certainly make better guardians than any human, or ex-human.

Dilani turned toward the beach, and a real human appeared. It was the doctor. Her mouth and eyes widened. Dilani cringed, but too late. The strange, stabbing feeling needled through her once again. It seemed to be the first thing humans did when they met each other.

The doctor and Bey waved their arms at each other and flapped their mouths, and the feeling battered away at Dilani. It no longer terrified her; apparently it could go on and on without harming her. Gradually she realized that Bey was right: it wasn't exactly pain. It was like being shoved under a waterfall, or tickled when she didn't want to be. It was an overload of meaningless sensation, an assault she could not escape.

Finally Bey remembered his manners.

"I'm telling her we are really us," he signed rapidly. "And what happened. I told her about Twelve's god. She is telling about the storm. Selma is dead, she says. And other people, too."

Sushan turned to Dilani. "Sorry," she signed belatedly. She returned to the mouth noises, but more slowly, and accompanied with her clumsy sign.

"Please do sit down," she signed, with a little sarcastic twist of her mouth. Dilani thought she, too, looked a little different, but decided that it was just the difference in her own eyes. The doctor sat down in the sand. She moved slowly and awkwardly. Dilani could see that she was tired.

"And Per . . . ?" Sushan signed.

She looked at them very sadly, without finishing the question.

"The storm did not kill him," Dilani signed. "The storm took us into the water, far away. And then, there was a thing—"

Her hands made a globe for the god, but she did not know how to continue, how to explain. She faltered, dropped her hands, and let Bey tell the story. As his mouth moved, she watched, and felt the new sensation. It wasn't all of a piece; it altered from big to small, and in other directions, too. She supposed that was how they could tell one "sound" from another—by the little changes. It no longer hurt her to hear, if they didn't make the sound too big, but it was an ugly, graceless feeling.

She felt cheated and angry. They had always acted as if she was missing so much, as if they had some precious thing she could not know about. If this was hearing, hearing was stupid. She didn't understand how they could put all their thoughts and feelings into a series of mouth noises.

Dilani saw a few tears roll down Sushan's face, but Sushan brushed them quickly away. She thought Sushan must be sad for Per. Dilani could tell by the way she held her shoulders that there was a lot of crying inside her, but she wasn't going to cry now.

Sushan spoke more mouth noises to Bey, but she paused to sign, as well.

"This can't be a sickness," she said. "It has a plan. It shaped you too perfectly. A virus could interfere with your DNA, but only for its own benefit. It would not make legs grow or repair ears. This is engineering—a tailored program of some kind that uses viruses to get inside human cells in a very, very complicated way. Allfather! If I could get a look at this 'god'—if I could find out what it is—"

Dilani had some trouble understanding her. There was a lot of spelling in her speech, and the kinds of words Per had used. But Dilani could see the frustration in Sushan's movements.

Bey waved his hands, interrupting her.

"My father!" he signed. "Is my father alive? What about the other newgens?"

The doctor rubbed her neck irritably, as if it was itching. She scratched her wrist; then she forced her hands to be quiet.

"Sorry," she signed. Dilani thought everyone seemed sorry this day.

"Yes, yes, your father is alive. All the newgens lived but Lila and Selma. But there is a problem. Come with me."

She took them back to the shelter above the pool. Dilani had not noticed it before, when she was underwater. Now it made her angry and sad. This was the place where Per's house had been. No shack full of sick people should be here. No storm should have carried away Per's house. Someone should have stopped it.

She took one horrified look at the people inside, and turned her back. If she looked at the waves washing across the stone ledges, she could pretend that Per's house stood behind her, as always.

She had seen Bey's new colors pale when he saw the humans lying on their beds inside.

# ⊚⦿15⦿⦿⦿⦿⦿⦿

"My father—he isn't like that, is he?" he whispered. He started automatically to sign. Then he noticed Dilani's turned back and let his hands drop.

"Bey, I'm sorry, but Whitman, your dad that is, has not taken this well."

"But he's alive, isn't he? He's all right?" Bey asked quickly.

"He's alive. And he's not as sick as some. But he's not what you'd call all right.

"During the storm, when you and Per disappeared, we lost seventeen more people, and we were stripped of nearly everything. My medical supplies were float packed, but most of them were carried out to sea.

"Before Per left, we'd discussed the possibility that degeneration was accelerating in all the colonists—not just the newgens, but the adults too seemed to be slipping. As if we were all infected by something I couldn't quite put a finger on. After the storm, it became obvious. I can't diagnose it now, of course. All I can do is note the symptoms. But there's a progressive breakdown of the immune system and metabolic functions. Tumors, liver and kidney failure—it's ugly, and there's nothing I can do. Literally nothing. I bring them drinks of water."

"My father," Bey interrupted. "Is he sick?"

The doctor shrugged.

"He's one of the better off, as far as that goes. But he just wouldn't believe that we were all infected. He insisted it was something in the water. He stays away from the sea. He won't touch fish. He's been surviving somehow on the meager supply of fruit and things out of the woods. Lately he has barricaded himself in the longhouse with a few others who listen to him. He threatens me with a fish spear when I try to contact him. He seems to think I'm poisoning the patients. He's been raving about trolls and gene bombs."

She paused, as if realizing that she wasn't talking to herself anymore. She touched Bey's arm.

"He's not responsible, Bey. I think it's affecting his mind. But if he sees all of you, I don't know what he'll do. I think you should stay out of sight for awhile."

Bey shook his head. Sushan noticed that when he tried to look determined, teeth gleamed at the corners of his mouth.

"No, I need to talk to him now. Don't you see? When he knows what the changes can do, when he sees that I'm fine and I can walk, then he'll understand and he'll stop all this. I'll go to him now."

He turned eagerly to go, then turned back again.

"Bader—is he—"

"He watched the pool for hours. He fell asleep last night. He's still sleeping."

"Then I'll go to see my father," Bey said. "But if he wakes up, be sure to tell him we're all right, and we'll be back."

He collected Dilani, who was happy to go with him.

"Come on. We'll swim," Bey signed exuberantly. The next minute he tripped and sprawled on his face in the sand. Bey couldn't get used to being so tall. He was taller than the doctor. He kept feeling that he was about to fall. He had known how to use his legs when they were bowed stubs, so he knew how to take steps, one after the other, but when he did, his whole body swayed above the ground, and he had to fling out his hands for balance. He staggered joyfully down to the beach, and floated out into the current.

The water was wonderful, too, but fearsome. So many teeth lived in the Deep, teeth who would find him succulent prey. A shadow crossed the edge of his vision. He turned, with the fear taste in his mouth and on his skin. In the Deep he was naked. In the Deep, there was nowhere to hide, no protective buildings, no humans to call for help. In the Dry, the other living things were small, and few of them could threaten him. In the Deep, the hungry mouths were many, and the only defenses were speed and sharper teeth.

He needed weapons and a skill for violence; having neither, he felt as naked as a baby. Even as those thoughts tightened his skin, the lips drew back involuntarily from his teeth, and his fingers stiffened, presenting talons.

He wasn't completely unarmed. He signed to Dilani that he would hunt on the way down the shore. He was ravenous for the first time in days.

Hunting cheered him, too. He rejoiced in the agility and speed of his new body. He plunged through bright schools of little fish, amusing himself by trying to catch them in his teeth. His taloned hands were quick; he no longer needed a knife or spear to seize his prey. Nothing ever tasted as fresh and delicious as their cool, salty juice and their yielding flesh, mingled with the tender crunchiness of bones.

He enjoyed their panic flight, and only when he was sated did he realize he had actually been able to taste their fear, and had savored it like an extra spice. It bothered him that he enjoyed their small deaths, but when he thought of the dead things that humans ate, he felt nothing but distaste. Live food was so much better.

It was strange to come ashore at the familiar beach and find no boats, no fish pens. The once-familiar cluster of buildings was gone, too. Only a ramshackle collection of post-and-matting shelters stood near the longhouse. As he approached the shelters, he saw remnants of two or three boats smashed and half buried in the sand. He concentrated on walking with his best balance, with long, even strides that showed off his new height.

Dilani grimaced as they reached the shelters.

"Bad smell," she signed.

Bey's spines rose uneasily, but he told himself it was just some rotting storm wrack somewhere.

"Papan!" he called. "It's me, Bey! I survived. I'm all right. And look, my legs are healed."

He thought he heard movement inside, but there was no answer.

"Papan?" He reached for the door. Maybe they couldn't hear him distinctly. He might as well go inside.

In the next moment, there was a ragged rip in the matting next to his hand. He felt a sudden swift flight of air brush his skin. It took him another breath or two to realize that someone had fired on him from inside the hut. A shrill whistle of alarm burst from his lips, and he clapped his hand to his mouth.

He had to try again before he could form a shout instead of a whistle. "Hey in there! Don't shoot! It's me, Bey Sayid! Where's my father?"

This time there was an answer.

"Get away, freak! You have no father here!"

The voice was unmistakably Whitman's, but Bey had never heard his father so agitated.

"Papan, honestly, it's me," he said. "I know I look different, but if you'd just come out—"

He put his hand to the door again. This time he felt a sting like that of a flying insect. The next thing he knew, he was rolling on the sand, clutching his bleeding hand to his chest. Not far away, the butt end of a harpoon bolt stuck out of the sand. It had ripped his hand as it went past.

"Take your troll plague somewhere else, or you will be killed," said his father's voice.

Dilani had not understood one word, but stood bolt upright, fists clenched.

Bey whistled and rolled, knocking her to the sand beside him, as another dart shot through the place where she had been standing.

"Come on, " he gestured.

"But your father—" she began to sign.

Bey shook his head and scrambled for the water.

* * *

The doctor looked up as they trudged back to her shelter.

"He shot at me," Bey said.

"Oh, Bey, I'm sorry," Sushan said. "He's not himself. I doubt he even knew it was you."

"He knew," Bey said. "He'd rather see me dead than like this."

He sat in the sun and watched the dark water restlessly turning and turning beneath its sunny surface. Safe as he was now, he could understand how lonely and dangerous their journey had been. He hadn't let himself think about it while it was happening. There had been no hope for a long time. Now, in the warmth of the sun, he shivered and felt cold, looking inward toward the dark waters they had traveled. *They expected us to die,* he thought. *They always expected us to die. And we almost did. No one can tell me if these changes are good or bad. I only know that I can live this way, and I want to live.*

Dilani helped Melicar turn and wash her patients, and held their heads up while the doctor gave them water. The people made noises, but they did not disturb Dilani any more than the grunting and squeaking of fish.

At the back of the shelter, they came to an empty bed. The doctor said something. Dilani was beginning to know the sound "no." Then the doctor signed "No, not again," and the name sign that meant Torker, the fish boss.

The big man had rolled from his bed. They found him wallowing in the sand just a few feet from the shelter. He churned with dogged determination toward the sea. Melicar put her arms around his shoulders and tried to turn him around, but even now his strength was so great that she could barely restrain him, and could not drag him back.

He had no shirt on. Dilani saw veiny, purple knots of flesh standing out on his naked back like growths on a felled log. He raised his head blindly. His eyes flashed white, as if a membrane had grown across the pupil inside. He dropped his head for another effort, and she could hear his breath rasping. Such effort—she felt sorry for him. Since she had learned to hear, she had learned that pain was everywhere. Even breathing could carry the sound of pain.

Dilani pushed Melicar's hands away with a growl.

"Let him go to the water," she signed. "He needs the water."

"No," the doctor signed. "He'll drown himself. He's not in his right mind. They're all doing this. They cry for water constantly. I bring them water to drink, but it's never enough. I find them crawling out of their beds at night. I have to tie them down."

Bey had come looking for them while they were bent over Torker.

"Can I help?" he signed.

Sushan slumped back, looking exhausted. "No. I can't get him back in bed one more time. I just can't do it. Just hand me that cup."

Torker drank, and then his struggles slowed and stopped. Melicar covered him with a piece of plastisheet.

"He can sleep here as well as anywhere. I give them tangleweed juice mixed with water. It's all I can do."

"What is that on his back?" Bey asked.

Melicar shrugged. "I don't know. I've never seen anything like these tumors. They bleed. They get infected. I think he must have some internal tumors too. He writhes in pain. I put tangleweed extract on the exterior ones, but I can't give him enough to numb the internal pain. Not without killing him."

Her eyes said she had thought about it.

"Is my father going to be like that?"

"I don't know." She lowered her head and spoke even lower. "I think so, yes. I think we're all going to end up like that. I think it's the end stage of this thing that's been affecting us all since we arrived on Typhon. Per had some clue to it, before he left. But I don't know enough to stop it now."

Bey looked at Dilani. He had seen her signing "In the water."

Sushan lifted her head and met Bey's eyes. "You're the only ones who have made it. There must be a key somewhere, if we could find it before it's too late for us."

"If we could talk to Twelve," he said. "He knows something we don't."

"Where is he?" Sushan asked.

"In the water," Bey signed. "Come and see."

They looked for Twelve; when they didn't see him, Dilani dipped her hands in the water, and then submerged her head. She felt his presence, and beckoned. Sushan hung back nervously.

"There were some unusual jellies, back when you were unconscious," she said. "They stung Bader and me, and we passed out. It was a strange thing. Watch out for them."

Before they could reply, Twelve found them.

He breached the surface like a keto, rising full length from the water, as if weightless, for one moment before he splashed down. Even Dilani had not expected what they saw.

He had a bipedal body—two arms and two legs—but his torso, in the glimpse they had, was thicker than a human's, and oddly formed. Something wrapped around it from behind and, as he fell, unwrapped and extended. It looked as if he still had two of his old limbs. His skin was Twelve's old colors, patterns of iridescent blue and gray.

He moved jerkily toward the shallow water, sometimes moving arms and legs, sometimes losing patience and jackknifing his whole body like a keto. He flopped onto the sand like a beached fish, and after several tries, rolled over so that he was faceup, and looked at them.

The changes in his body were remarkable, but it was the face that made them gasp. Above the forehead, there were feathery tufts that resembled hair, colored an odd off-white. The eyes were still golden with ever-moving pigment, but except for the color of the eyes, the face was a thin-lipped, blue-skinned version of Per.

"He looks like Per," Bey said.

"Blue-Pinkman," Dilani signed simultaneously. The resemblance was unmistakable.

The creature's mouth moved.

"Hating it," Twelve said.

Bey was so startled that he yelled. Dilani stared at him as if he had lost his mind.

"What?" he stammered.

"Hating it," the creature said again, in a harsh, indistinct growl. "Hating stupid talking."

"How? How can you do that?" Bey said.

"Godbits giving wemem'ering. Peyo-god sending."

Twelve's hand fumbled up over his shoulder to touch the back of his neck, where the godbits had been.

"The godbits gave you memories? Is that what you're saying? Peyo-god? What is that?"

"Pe-yo," Twelve enunciated. "God."

Then his hand came up and unmistakably shaped the name sign: Pinkman. Per.

Even though she could hear, Dilani didn't understand. She began to pummel Bey's arm to demand interpretation.

"Hell's teeth, Dilani, I don't know what's going on any more than you do," he said, shaking her off. "Wait, Doctor. He's trying to explain. Per is god? Is that what you said?"

Twelve made his hand nod: yes.

"Per is dead," Bey said. "Your god ate him."

Twelve hand-nodded again. "Yes. Ating him. He is living now."

"I don't understand," Bey said hopelessly. "You mean, because you remember him?"

"Yes, he is sharing wemem'ering." Twelve tried to move his arms in a sign, but smashed them against the sand in frustration.

"Hating it," he growled in his toneless voice. "Shaping is saying. This I is having no shaping. It being bwoken."

"What do you remember about Per?" Bey asked.

"Shaping is saying," Twelve repeated. "This I is all around. Now being only one piece. Shaping is too unsame, there is no saying. Is losing all I-wemem'ering. So Peyo-god is giving saying. Godbits is talking in here."

Again he put his hand on the back of his neck, where the godbits had swarmed.

As Bey tried to interpret for himself, he also tried to help Dilani understand. He turned to her from time to time, his hands moving slowly as he found ways to express the ideas for her.

"You mean, because your shape is different now, the language is too different? That Per gave you some of his memories so you could use our words? And he used the godbits to send memories from him to you?"

Twelve stared at Bey's hands as if for confirmation of the words. Then he nodded his head again.

"Is why godbits. Bwinging little pieces of eve'ybody for god, and then god is ating. Now Peyo is god."

Melicar interrupted. "Wait! You said the god ate Per. When you eat the fish, is the fish still living?"

The gold in Twelve's eyes moved, and his skin hue deepened a shade. Finally he uttered a hiss that Bey thought was an affirmative.

"Fssh being in greatlife, this I in greatlife. Someday this I is living in fssh. But wemem'ering of this I being not in fssh. Wemem'ering of this I is living in Rround People all around. Only god is ating skin shaping and wemem'ering too. God is ating eve'ything but is changing not. But now god is changing, too. Now god is Peyo. Big changing all around."

His accent was thick and indistinct, but improved gradually as he spoke.

"I'm trying to understand," Bey said. "The god ate Per's body, right?"

"Yssss. Is taking and using, making all in bits. Now god is knowing Dry people, is making Dry people changing."

"But is there a part of Per that is still alive?"

Twelve jerked his arms and legs irritably.

"This I is saying. You-I is not sharing saying—why?"

"Guess I'm just stupid," Bey muttered. "Say it again."

"All-around of Peyo is being living now," Twelve said with

harsh emphasis. "Peyo is god. This I is saying! God is re-mem'ering all around. Eve'ything. All knowing of Gweat People. Eve'ything. Now all knowing of Peyo is living in god."

Twelve pawed at his head again.

"What is being this inside-seeing?"

It took Bey a minute to understand the question.

"You mean your brain? Your mind?"

"Ysss. Mine. Min-duh. We-I is ating skin of things. God is ating mind. Fssh-skin is living in this-I skin. Peyo-mind is living in god-mind."

"So the god ate Per, but he isn't dead? His body is gone, but he's still alive."

"Peyo is god," Twelve said with finality. His lips worked and twisted. "You-I is giving-sharing water with this-I," he suggested.

"Huh? Oh, sure." He dipped water with his hands and poured it over Twelve's face.

"This-I is now learning living in the Dry," Twelve said when he was refreshed. "The Great People is learning this in the long-time. Now this-I is not being Round People but still this-I is learning and remembering. Peyo-god is helping with sharing-remembering. If not, this-I is losing thinking in the mind.

"Going crazy, you mean?" Bey said helpfully.

Twelve hissed assent. "But still this-I is hating her."

"Her? Who do you mean?"

"God. This-I is saying."

"Is god a her?" Bey wondered if there would be any end to the strangeness. Had Per become not only the god, but female?

"Is not Dry creatures having two-sides reproduction?" Twelve said. He seemed as puzzled as Bey.

"I think so—if what you mean is that there are two different sexes. But Per is male, not female. Was, anyway."

"Is females not being bigger?" Twelve said.

"No, not usually. I'm male. Per is male. Dilani is female. This one here—" He indicated the doctor. "—is female, too."

Twelve hissed thoughtfully. "This-I is having broken thinking."

"You mean you made a mistake?"

"Ysss. This-I is now hating him-god."

"He was my friend," Bey signed. He would have liked to stop and think about this information for awhile, but there was no chance.

"I don't understand," Melicar said. "What is he saying? Explain!"

"I think he means—" Bey tried to think how to sign it for Dilani, too. "—he means that the god—that's a creature, Doctor, not a myth. They call it something we can't say, so we call it god. We all saw it, too—even Per. Anyway, Twelve says the god has some kind of way to store memories. It stored Per's memories, and I guess the godbits—those jelly things—can transfer those memories. They gave Twelve some of them."

Melicar rubbed the back of her hand across her nose and sniffed noisily. "It makes sense," she said. She had regained her businesslike doctor's voice. "If you can believe it at all, that is. You can't have a functioning body without the synaptic connections in the brain that control that body. If your friend didn't have time to build those connections, they would have to be installed for him. Otherwise, he'd have no control, no feedback. Look at Dilani. She has hearing now, but it makes no sense to her. She isn't wired for it. Maybe it will come in time."

She paused and coughed.

Twelve twisted his head from side to side, peering up at Melicar. He reached wet blue fingers and rubbed her neck, then touched the hand to his own gills.

"Is changing," he said with finality.

Melicar's uniform tan wasn't very informative, but Bey could see that she paled.

"I can't," she said. "I have to be here to take care of them. I cannot be sick."

"That's just it," Bey said. "If you want to be here, you have to change. Otherwise you will die. Once they sting you, they can't take it back."

"What is it?" Sushan said. "Why is this happening to me?"

A pained expression crossed Subtle's face. He hummed to himself, but found no words. Finally he spoke.

"Is still not finding words for me inside-seeing. In the water is better sharing-telling. In the water is better."

"Tough! Tell now!" Dilani signed impatiently.

"Great People is making selves, long in the long-time. Great Deep is making Great People, but they is wanting Dry, too. They is changing selves to coming out there, for making many made things, for finding metal things, for bringing down the brightness, making the great stinging brightness."

He signed "Fire."

"For changing selves, is making god of changing. God is being everything in one thing, all the little things in the big thing. People is making god, god is making People. Is always changing back and forth until People is leaving. From Deep to sky edge, into Dry. Dry, too, is having sky edge."

He lifted his hands toward the sun.

"Great People is always passing through all edges. Therefore is calling Great. Because for them, no edges. Long in the long-time they is going, but god still is living, and Great People is living in god. All in the water all around is still being little made things, alive like godbits, made for changing the People.

"Then you is coming here, and little god-spit things is having no mind. Is just made things, for making."

He paused to search for the word.

"Tools, they is. They is just only working. Is working on you, but you is being not People, so making is all around wrong for you and you is dying with no one to eat you. Is sad sad dark stupid. God is getting old old, is not changing any more. Who can make god young again?

"Is looking for more mind, is finding you. Not Great People, but close enough. God is eating Per to make plan for you. Then is changing you right way. Now like Great People you is living on all sides of sky edge. New People. And god is having new thinking from Per, is having new mind. God is subtle. Now this-I is seeing inside, all around changing."

He lowered his head, and his colors were subdued with dejection.

"Once in the long-time, this-I was great dancing. You would be sharing-knowing, in the dancing. Now this-I is not dancing. From this-I to you-I, there is no telling."

"Someone did this to us on purpose?" Sushan said. "Is that what he's saying?"

Dilani watched and listened with great attention, trying to absorb every drop of meaning from their words and signs. Now that she could hear them talking, she could no longer tune out their mouth flapping as she had when it hadn't affected her. Then, she had been able to tell herself it had nothing to do with her. Now, she could see how much she had missed. Whenever Bey or Per had not been there to sign for her, information had passed by her like dust on the breeze. She didn't want to miss any more words that might be important for her life.

"Not exactly," Bey said to Sushan. "We got mixed up in a plan that wasn't made for us, I think that's what he means. There were people here before us—we saw their bones, Per and Dilani and I. They made the viruses or whatever it is in the godbits. That's what made us sick. But Per, or the god, or whichever it is now, could only cure us by finishing the job. It was too late to go back."

Dilani watched his sign carefully as he translated for her, checking it against his words. The signing seemed subdued and gloomy. Bey was unsure of himself. The low and listless sounds in his voice must have a similar implication.

"Per did this to us," Sushan said. "Oh, hell. They always said he was a reversion—too smart for his own good or ours, willing to play games with other people's lives. He raised the stakes too high this time."

Turning to Twelve, she finally lost control. "Why did they have to make you look like him?" she gasped. "Why his face?

Why send a gargoyle of Per to haunt me when my human life has ended?"

"They-all is having faces already," Subtle said in his painful, broken growl. "Only this-I is having none. God is using the face he is knowing. Peyo-god is sharing face with this-I. Now you-I is hating. This-I is hating, too."

Dilani remembered how Per's ravaged face had looked when she had last seen it. Hot, angry feelings boiled inside her, and she sent out a sharp whistle of wrath that made the others wince.

"You should be glad," she signed furiously. "Per did not play tricks. He died, and the jelly thing—" She refused to call it god. "—took away his body. He knew he would die. He wanted to save us, and he did save us. You are still alive. You stop being human when you're dead. Human means alive, right?"

She stopped. She couldn't make them understand, and even if she'd had plenty of spoken words, she wasn't sure she could say what she wanted to say. She could still see Per's face, and she was full of love and grief.

*If they could see what I see,* she thought, *they would understand. But no one can ever know what I know. No one can ever be Dilani but me, and I am still Dilani. Why can't they understand?*

"I'm sorry," Sushan said, rubbing gritty hands across her face. "Many times I imagined that we'd somehow find a way to save ourselves. I never imagined this." A last bark of laughter escaped her. "Per always had a gift for picturing things no one else could imagine."

Dilani moved a hand through the air impatiently, to brush away conversation that no doubt missed the point, as far as she was concerned.

"Why are you still sad?" she signed. "It is time to get well. Put them in the water now."

Sushan looked uphill to Per's ledge.

"Hell's teeth, I forgot Torker's medicine. He'll be wandering again."

The humans followed her. Bey saw how she limped, how

one arm trailed, how the red welts showed on her face and neck. The godbits had stung her—the new, improved godbits that had come for Twelve.

Twelve stayed in the water, watching them with eyes of bitter gold.

Torker was already struggling toward the water again, like a giant turtle migrating to the sea. Dilani hissed at the doctor when she tried to restrain him. Dilani had once wanted to hit Torker with a stick, but then he had been tall and threatening. Now he reminded her of a mutilated animal. She didn't want to hear the pain sounds of his breath.

"In the water," she signed fiercely.

"Doctor Melicar," Bey said with his best winning respect, "is there anything more you can do for him? Will he get well?"

Melicar opened her mouth as if to argue, but thought better of it. "No."

"Then let him go. I think the godbits will help. Anyway it can't get worse."

"I don't like to see him crawling like that."

She spread the plastisheet in such a way that Torker would crawl onto it. Then Bey and Dilani took a corner each and helped her drag Torker to the sea.

They were knee-deep, then waist-deep, and nothing happened. They had to hold his head above water to keep him from choking. Bey wondered if he had been wrong, if the godbits had rejected the other humans for some reason.

Dilani uttered a whistle of recognition just as Bey's skin twitched with a feeling he did not understand at first. A flavor came to him through his skin, a flavor that was familiar, terrifying, and seductive—the taste of godbits. The deeper water beyond them twinkled with sparks of light, spiraling toward them as thick as stars on a clear night. Godbits laced the water in swarms and clusters, so many Bey couldn't move without brushing them, yet they ignored him.

Instead, they clustered around Torker until he was visibly outlined in ghostly blue dots of light. They began to merge and spread across his face, as they had done with Per. Torker floated away from them, motionless. Bey and Dilani laid hands on Melicar, gently restraining her from trying to stop him.

Then the godbits were swarming around Sushan's own knees, gathering at her wrists where her hands trailed in the water. She floundered for the shore, gasping "No! No! Not now!" Her eyes were glassy, and she constantly rubbed her wrists, which had become puffy and mottled.

"Stay with her," Bey signed. "I'll check on Torker."

The big man was now floating in water ten feet deep, still the center of a godbit galaxy. The pulse points were covered, but Bey laid a hand flat on Torker's chest, and could feel his heart pulsing beneath the godbit membrane.

"He looks more peaceful," Bey reported to Melicar. "And his heart is still beating."

He saw the doubt in her eyes. She must be wondering if he was merely reassuring her, so she would not oppose him as he quietly drowned her patients. That was the disadvantage of being his father's son. People expected the same ability to smooth out ugly truths.

"Send Dilani if you want," he said stiffly. "She wouldn't bother to lie."

"No, I believe you," she said. "But how can he look peaceful? You and Dilani were in pain. Don't you remember?"

"You kep' us from the wa'er," Twelve interrupted. "We needed to go in wa'er, find godbits. Godbits is feeding, is making skin water good. Peyo-god has sent more godbits, is special for humans. No more pain."

Bey ignored the handful of other adults who lay together in the back end of the shelter, and went straight to the newgens. Their pallets were pushed together in a huddle, so they could get comfort from each other's nearness.

Dilani had not thought she had missed any of the others, but when she saw Bader's face, something hurt inside her chest.

When Bey touched him, Bader looked up and rubbed his face fretfully.

"Who is it?" he mumbled. "I can't see."

Dilani could tell that his mouth sounds were garbled and indistinct. His mouth made him speak badly, even worse than Twelve. She had not known that before.

As if he had never been away, Bey dropped back into the sketchy whisper the newgens used for secrets.

"It's me, Bey. And Dilani. We were lost in the storm, but we're back."

"I saw you," Bader mouthed. "I waited by the pool a long time, but you didn't wake up until too late. I can't see any more. Sure you're not dead? We're getting pretty close now. Maybe I'm hearing you from the other edge."

"No, I'm kicking, but different. Feel." He moved Bader's hand over his face and neck.

"That's taking newgen to an extreme," Bader whispered.

"Think you could live like this?"

Bader traced Bey's lip with his finger, pausing to test the sharpness of his teeth.

"Nice teeth," he commented. "You got a mouth. You can speak. So be ugly, I don't care."

"There's more," Bey said. "I went to the water, and the jellies stung me. I thought I was dead, but when I woke up, I was like this, and they had given me my legs back, too. If you could go in the water and be drowned, and then come back to life and be well again, would you go? Tell truth, cause I can make it happen."

"With a face?" Bader mumbled.

"Yes, sure. Like new. As good as mine, anyway. Only with fins, too."

There was a gurgling sound: Bader's mutilated laugh.

"I'm hurting, Brother. Put me in the water. Fins and all."

"What about the others?" Bey asked. "Can any of them still talk?"

"I don't think so," Bader said. "Amina, maybe. But I listened to them for days. Crying for the water. Trying to crawl there. Melicar had to tie them up. I think they want to go. I vote *go* on behalf of my discussion group."

He clutched at the edge of the cot.

"I'm so hot," he whispered. "Burning up. Can't swallow. It hurts. Get me to the cool blue. Please."

"All right, Brother. Easy; we'll help." Bey turned to Dilani, who had permitted him a private conversation with unusual patience. "He votes to go in the water," he signed.

They pulled Bader to a sitting position and slid him off the cot. Bey pulled another piece of sheeting off the shelter roof and laid him down on it.

"The doctor won't need this any more," he signed to Dilani behind Melicar's back.

"We do the pulling," he said to Melicar. "I'll get Twelve to help. You aren't strong enough."

Most of the adults were unconscious, too, but a few of them were alert enough to notice what was happening. Dilani heard their weak cries of alarm and looked curiously in at their pale, frightened faces. A woman screamed.

"Help! Trolls are stealing the children!"

She half fell from her bed and floundered away from the shelter, calling for Whitman Sayid. There were more cries, and Melicar's voice sounded. Dilani hung back a little, wondering what they were saying.

"Keep going," Bey said shortly. "Ignore them."

"What hurry?" Dilani complained, briefly letting go the edge of the sheet.

"I'll tell you what hurry." Bey stopped to sign, breathing hard from the effort of pulling Bader's weight. "These are my people—us, the newgens. I don't want any of us left behind because the oldgens are arguing again. You saw us tied to the beds in there. They decide what to do with us, what risks we can take. They decide if we're human or not. Makes me sick. *No!* Not any more. We're all going in the water. Let's see them catch us then. You understand?"

Dilani nodded. She understood well enough.

Bader's cramped limbs relaxed as the water lifted him. Dilani held his head up carefully as they swam with him, out where the godbits could reach him.

"Don't be afraid," Bey said. "You'll feel them sting, but then you won't be afraid any more."

"Like going to the doctor," Bader panted, trying to smile. Water splashed over his face, and Dilani wiped his eyes.

The small lights gathered like flower garlands around his wrists, and the fear washed away from his face.

"It's better," he whispered. "Oh, blue—"

They let him slide into the arms of the sea.

Bey floated silently for a minute, watching the godbits gather around their friend, then swam quickly back to complete his task. The unconscious patients went in quickly, since there was no need to assuage their fear. Still, Bey supervised each one with fierce care. He left the adults to Twelve and the doctor.

Melicar ventured as far out as she dared, to watch the godbits tranquilizing and enclosing her patients. She looked long into their calm faces, until they drifted slowly away.

"Believe, Doctor. They're all right now."

Bey stretched out a hand to her, drew her farther into the water than she realized.

"Even if they—even if they die," Melicar said, "it's better this way. The suffering—I could do nothing for them. Nothing. They aren't hurting now."

"It's time for you to join them now," Bey said.

Melicar stretched her head toward the sky, gasping.

"I can't. I'm sorry, I can't. I'm too scared."

"It won't hurt," Bey said.

"Feels great to swim forever," Dilani signed helpfully. "Not hungry, not tired. Like flying."

A first scattering of godbits tasted Melicar. She thrashed briefly, gulped water, and choked.

"I live with pain," she wheezed. "Just can't—go under. Like suicide."

She was hyperventilating.

Bey held her eyes. Twelve swam carefully behind her, and Melicar began to relax, against her own will. Twelve was calming her somehow.

"If you ever want to know what happened to Per, this is the

only way," Bey said. "It's what he did. Are you coming or not?"

She took a last breath and nodded. She didn't struggle as Twelve gently pulled her down.

Then there was nothing to do but wait.

## ༄16༄༄༄༄

Bey spent several days of boredom and anxiety, following Dilani and Twelve up and down the beach as Twelve tried to gain control of his new body. He tried to teach Dilani to use a few words, starting with her name. She couldn't run away from his constant repetitions, so she learned eventually to call herself "Ni," Bey "Ba," and Twelve something like "Dwo." She seemed to take the position that one syllable was enough for any word.

"Leave me alone," she signed irritably, when he tried to continue with more lessons. "This is ugly. It gets into my mind and makes me confused." In imitation of Twelve, she signed, "I hate this stupid talking."

"But think about this," he signed. "If you learn speech, you can understand everyone, not just me."

"Don't want to understand them," she replied. "They are stupid."

Her stubbornness made him want to jolt her out of her blinkered viewpoint. Did she think he'd be happy to spend the rest of his short life jumping like a frog whenever she wanted an interpreter?

"What if I die?" he signed. "Think about that. You'd have no one to talk to."

He was sorry as soon as he said it. Total panic swept across her face. The inner eyelids snapped shut over her eyes, and her neck frill shot erect in threatening spikes. Her skin blanched till she almost resembled one of the White Killers. Her fingers stiffened, showing the talons, as if she would claw

Bey, but she thought better of it. She threw herself down on the sand and dug into it with her fists. A loud, wailing sob escaped her involuntarily. She paused, startled, and then repeated the effect.

"Sorry, sorry," Bey signed hastily, but she wasn't looking. Twelve dragged himself over to her and rubbed his wrists against the soft membrane beneath her frill. That seemed to calm her after a few minutes. She sat up and gave Bey a hateful look, loudly sniffing back tears.

"Mean, bad," she signed.

"Agreed, all right," he acquiesced. "But I spoke the truth."

"Teach me," she signed reluctantly.

So, while Twelve crawled and walked and crawled again, up and down the beach, Bey tried to teach Dilani about the sounds that humans called words.

Once he was well into the task, he began to see her point of view. Nothing seems more stupid than a word mouthed twenty times over. Signs were quick and graceful, and often bore some resemblance to the things they meant. By the time Dilani had learned a halting imitation of a word, Bey no longer wanted to hear it. He could understand why she preferred to retreat into restful silence.

She liked some aspects of speech. When she found that she could talk to someone without looking at him, she would put her hands over her own eyes and try to guess what Bey was saying, or hide and call to him, popping out the next minute to see if he had heard her. She drove him to extreme irritation by shouting his name every five minutes just to make him jump, all through one afternoon. Then she disappeared for so long that he went looking for her.

He found her in a narrow gorge where rocks made a triangular corner bisected by a rivulet of water. She didn't notice his arrival for several minutes, and he silently watched what she was doing. She turned her head slowly back and forth, sometimes shifting her whole body, and then returning to her original position. Occasionally she uttered short cries, in varying pitches. He moved his head like hers, trying to discover her game, and found that the voice of the falling water changed, reverberating at different angles from the echoing rocks. She was playing with the sounds.

When she turned and saw him, he was afraid she would be angry, but she was too engrossed in her discoveries.

"It changes," she signed to him. "I can't see it, but it moves. Look, the little rocks go like this—" She rippled her hand. "—and the noise goes like this, too. Sometimes noise is like a sign about the shape of things."

She made the grimace that had replaced frowning.

"It's pretty," she concluded. "But talking is still stupid."

Subtle had nearly lost his life in his quest to enter the Dry. Now he sometimes felt that he would die if he had to stay in the Dry a moment longer. He rested by visiting the Deep. He listened to the currents and rose at times to the surface to feel the pattern of the swells. It was hard to hear the Deep in his new body, as if he was wrapped in a thick blanket of someone else's skin, but he learned.

The Laughing Teeth still cruised the lagoon, guarding the Dry creatures who were undergoing change. It was a wonder and a terror for him to swim with the Laughing Teeth, unbitten. He tasted of them now. He had their musky scent all over his skin, disturbing and thrilling. He tried to recall his memory dances from the time of his round body. The dances themselves seemed to him like lost gems, packed with crystalline layers of irrecoverable memories, gleaming and beckoning as they tumbled from his grasp into the long abyss of forgetting. He sorrowed for his lost body, and yet, at the same time, he mourned the fact that he could no longer truly wish it back.

He listened and learned to hear the talk of the Teeth, their laughing, multilevel chat, full of fierce ironies and joke flashes that passed in an instant. They called others in the water "slow life." Though Subtle painfully longed for the kindness and the deep, full thoughts of the Round Folk, the joke bit; it was true.

He could remember those long, slow days in the twilight, on the edge of the abyss. He could remember those days, but he could no longer live them. His blood moved to a different rhythm. He no longer lived in welcome solitude, grooming his thoughts till they formed a stately structure, to be viewed by a scant few. He knew now what it was like to live in a school. The Round Folk had scorned such promiscuous gathering; it was the way of lesser folk.

True, the multitude of sensations darting in from every side distracted him. They were painful and startling; but they were all so new. He wasn't happy, and yet, he felt as if he danced in a rain of treasures. He swam fast; he spoke fast, with the brief, flickering gestures of the once-Dry folk. Yet no one lived as fast as the Teeth. He could never keep up with them, but he could not stop following them. He hated them, and they troubled him, and he loved them.

The young Dry creature they called Dilani followed him around as he followed the Laughing Teeth. He found her easier to talk to than the others, because she spoke with her body, as if she, too, had once been a Round Person. She heard the Deepsong better than the others, as well, though at times she seemed curiously ignorant about things Subtle wanted to know about the Dry.

Since he had learned that she was a female, he tried not to spend too much time in her presence. He didn't know how breeding would occur in the new shapes. He was afraid the interaction of their skin motes might trigger the kind of catastrophe that had robbed him of Redheart.

But she wouldn't leave him alone. She was always pushing through the edge of his scent sphere. He wasn't sure how she made him feel. If he could have given her a Round Folk name, a name with meaning, he would have called her Disquiet, or Troubling the Waters. She was always restless and edgy, like an object with many points that couldn't be comfortably grasped.

"Stop following this-I," he signed to her. "Be swimming with others."

"You don't like me," she signed. Her skin scent immediately turned bitter and dark.

"When two-I are much together, mating happens," he signed. "Liking, not-liking, is not important. There is no choice. This-I is not wanting mating with you-I."

She showed her teeth at him.

"Mating!" she signed with extreme disgust. "Who said anything about mating? Not me! You-all talk about mating all the time. I never asked!"

"I only want—" he began. He couldn't think of the way to express *protect* with his new limbs. "Want you to be safe. Not die."

"Who dies from mating?" she signed scornfully. "You're telling lies."

She was making him angry. The motes between them certainly did not resemble any mating signals he had ever encountered. Nevertheless, he was anxious.

"We do. Round People. The female makes eggs and dies. I don't want you to die."

"How do you know?" she signed. "Have you done this?"

"Of course," he answered with gloomy dignity. "I am an adult. And you?"

"Not exactly," she signed. "But I know how it works! Nobody dies!"

Subtle considered his body. He knew there was no mating arm. Perhaps there would be no eggs, either. This was what he had gone to seek from the god: a life that did not require death as the price of continuing. But it seemed the ultimate indignity not even to know how he could reproduce.

"I don't know how it works," he signed. "Neither do you. These bodies are different."

They had drifted closer together as they spoke. Her scent was not unpleasant, though it was still disturbing. She smelled of the Laughing Teeth, but so did he. There were overtones of wariness in her scent motes, but no hostility. He detected curiosity, an invitation to approach, and in the colors of her skin he read a tentative friendliness.

He thought painfully of Redheart. He would never touch

her skin again, and now he would never again dance her memory.

*I have always sought the friendship of females,* he thought. *Look where that has taken me!*

"I don't know anything," he signed. "Better you swim elsewhere."

The female didn't seem to realize that he meant her to go away.

"They do this," she signed, touching her lips and the side of her face. He did not recognize the sign. Before he knew what she was doing, she approached him and touched her lips to his. He thought she meant to bite him and recoiled. But the water became soft and very pleasant. His fright washed swiftly away. He wondered vaguely if there were godbits around. He seemed to have lost all caution, as he did when the godbits stung.

Her lips did not feel very pleasant; they were too thin and firm. But where her neck rubbed against his, the delicate gill covers touched, and the warm outbreathing from her gills mingled with his. A sudden complex burst of chemical messages sent a shiver through him.

*Oh no, it's happening again,* he thought, struggling to keep a grip on his fears. His mind sent useless messages to tentacles he no longer had. He had noticed that the Dry folk also twined their arms around each other, though they only had two. The pressure of her skin against his intensified the sweetness of the water. When she had first touched him, as a Dry creature, he had hardly been able to stand it. Her skin had been so thin and dry, so unresponsive. Since the transformation, it was sleek and springy, more like real skin. He felt an absurd desire to press his teeth against her smooth shoulder.

He panicked. Had he become something that would eat its mate?

He unwrapped his arms from hers and backpaddled several feet, where the motes in the water were less powerful. His head cleared a little. Then he realized that he wasn't in the grip of irresistible madness. It was not the same as it had been with Redheart.

"Your skin feels good," Dilani signed.

"Swim," he signed. "We should stay nearer to the shore."

He swam ahead of her, through cold water, feeling his heart slow down.

He had to admit that, in that moment, her colors had been very beautiful, like shadows of the brightwarm as it dipped below calm water, like none he had seen before. He wondered what would have happened if they had been at home in shallow water. He had no idea what was supposed to happen next.

He glanced back to be sure she was still following, and met the huge eye of one of the Laughing Teeth. It sparkled with secret laughter. The Laughing Person rolled in the water to offer him a fin; as he caught it, a voice in his mind said *Skin is truth*. We are of the same skin now, he thought. Not Round, not Dry, and not the Great People over again. We are still changing, and what we will be when it ends, maybe even god can only guess.

No thoughts of mating remained when he saw that the Laughing Teeth were carrying them to the place where the Dry creatures awaited transformation.

The ketos churned the water, perforating the surface in leaps of alarm or exultation. Through an explosion of bubbles, Dilani glimpsed Bey, also swimming, signing "broken, open, out." Dilani dodged around the floating forms of the other newgens, each dreaming in its silver bubble. She didn't know what Bey meant. Nothing had changed.

She caught up with him just below the surface, struggling with a goggle-eyed, bipedal form she didn't recognize at first. Dilani heard strangling noises. She couldn't tell if the unknown person was clutching Bey, or trying to escape. She darted over to help him.

The other person was frantically trying to reach the surface, eyes bulging with panic. Dilani tried to boost the figure upward, but Bey shook his head at her, hard. She saw that he was trying to drag the person downward. It looked as if he were trying to drown the other. Its struggles weakened, and

Bey succeeded in pulling it deeper down. It hung limp for a minute. The choking sounds ceased. Then it turned a blind, wondering stare toward Dilani, through its luminous eyes.

Bey loosened his grip. Its hands fluttered upward toward its neck and hovered over the gills, the neck frill. It felt its head and face, and stared in amazement at its own hands.

Awkwardly, it flexed the webbed fingers. Dilani realized that it was trying to sign.

"Sushan," it signed.

It no longer looked like Sushan. A feathery mat, like Dilani's but lighter, protected the top of the head and made a V shape down the back of the neck. The rose-colored hue of Sushan's skin deepened toward scarlet under the intensity of the moment, and was dotted with freckles that ranged from gold to purplish brown. The skin of her face was smooth and delicately colored. No scars showed anywhere.

"You've changed," Dilani signed.

"I know. How much?"

"Quite a lot," Dilani signed.

Sushan fingered her neck again.

"You pulled me under," she accused Bey. "Why?"

"You panicked," he signed. "You can breathe in water or in air, but if you panic, you choke. I had to pull you under so your body could change to breathing water."

"I was very frightened," Sushan signed. "I still am."

"Come up," Dilani beckoned. "Don't be afraid!"

Sushan choked and wheezed again when she made the transition back to air, but she began to gain confidence in the water.

Bey had moved on to another hatchling. Bader, too, had emerged from his cocoon. Bader had no fear. He was laughing before he got his head above water. His colors were rich and deep, and he ran his hand over his face again and again.

"This is amazing!" he shouted to the sun. His words were smooth and round. "This is my birthday! I just hatched out!"

"What about the others?" Melicar said. "Where is Torker? Why haven't they come out?"

"Godbits is tasting you first," Twelve said. "Others come later."

They came ashore at the old beach, and their joyful mood evaporated at the sight and smell of the longhouse.

"What have you done about them?" Melicar asked. "How long has it been?"

"Seven days," Bey said. "We tried to bring them food and water, but they throw slingstones at us. I guess they've run out of harpoon bolts. They scream if they see us. We left them alone the last couple of days."

"Well, we have to try to help them now," Melicar said. "When they see the changes . . ." She let the sentence trail away.

"That's what I said." If Bey had been swimming, the motes of irony would have darkened the water. "Now I think we should leave them alone. Don't go near them. We have to think of our own safety first."

"We can't just leave them like this."

"Just wait until they have to come out for food; then catch them and put them in the water."

Sushan's neck frill rose uneasily. "Don't you think we should give them some choice?" she said. "What if they prefer not to be treated? We still need to help them."

Bey's normally friendly face grew cold, and his colors darkened ominously. He looked very alien at that moment.

"No. They're dangerous to themselves as they are, and dangerous to us, which is more important. You can do what you want, but I'm not giving them a choice. No one gave me a choice. They were all for voting on how to run my life, when I was the one who was lacking. Some of them would have voted to end me. They thought I didn't know that. Now this is my world, and I'm doing what I think best. I won't have a handful of hysterical oldgens living on this rock as scavengers, still thinking themselves more human than the rest of us because of the shape they're in. They can sink or swim, like me."

He looked at Bader, who nodded. The two of them dove

back into the water, followed by Dilani and Twelve. When they reemerged, Bey was smiling and calm again.

"We exchanged motes," Twelve said to Melicar. He looked pleased.

One by one, Bey and Bader chased down and netted the stragglers, and dragged them into the water. Twelve helped, with his great strength. In the end, Sushan helped too; she gave them tangleweed juice to help sedate the sick adults. It seemed best to get it over with. The colonists could protest later, if they survived. It helped that they refused to recognize her, and wouldn't call her by name.

Dilani stayed in the water with the ketos. The remaining adults weren't people she cared about one way or the other.

Whitman was the last to go. He had been hiding under mats in a storage area, and finally made a break for the trees. Bader tripped him up with a cast of the net, and Twelve enveloped him with his extra limbs.

When they had him waist-deep in the waves, the ketos came to push him farther out. They whistled gleefully. To them it seemed to be a game. He continued to struggle. Toward the end he looked toward Bey as if he recognized him at last.

"Bey, help me," he shouted. "Don't let them do this. Son, help me!"

Bey's mouth gaped, and his tongue flickered in distressful motion, but he looked steadily at his father.

"I am helping you," he said. "Believe me, Papan. It's the only way. I'm doing what has to be done, the way you always taught me."

"You're not my son!" Whitman screamed, in the last struggle to keep his head above water. "Troll! Monster! You never were my son!"

Slowbolt's blunt nose bulldozed him under. In a moment, the water showed no trace of his passing.

"Don't be sad," Dilani signed to Bey. She wanted to rub her

wrist against his neck as she had seen Subtle do, but she could taste her own skin water, and it was almost as distressful as Bey's.

"Don't mind him. You are not a monster." She could almost mimic the word. "When he is well, he will stop telling lies."

"Not all lies," Bey signed. "I am a son of Typhon. We always were Typhon's children. Monsters, to him. A father gives more than a shape for the body. A shape for the life is important, too. He never liked my shape."

Twelve joined them, breathing hard. Lines of godbit bubbles clung to the long scratches in his arms where Whitman had clawed at him.

"That-I is all right," he said. "Godbits is calming. That-I sleeps now till all is changing."

"Maybe he won't make it," Bey said. "Maybe I've killed him."

Subtle hissed thoughtfully.

"This world is killing all the humans," he said. "Not you. You-I is not killing. You is only making that-I live different, and for this he is hating. This-I is understanding hating. This-I is thinking you-all monsters, too, but now thinking is changing. Maybe that-I is changing thinking too, when new eyes is coming."

Subtle bent so his gills were close to Bey's, and Dilani felt eddies of the calming motes he shared. But Bey kicked away from them.

"Don't. Not now," he said. "Just let me be sad. Sometimes humans want to be sad."

He dove under and swam down deep, and floated in the shadow of the reef, watching the godbits swarm around the colonists' motionless bodies.

A light wind fluttered the flames of their small fire, and rattled the leaves of the tubewood trees. They didn't need the fire; the weather was mild, and their new bodies didn't easily feel cold. But the fire gathered them in a circle of each other's company.

Earlier that day, they had all visited the bubble garden where the humans were floating—all still breathing, their faces empty of pain or fear. Torker's gills seemed nearly grown, inside the bubble. Soon they would face the problem of trying to explain what they had done.

Then they had wandered the island, seeing how much had changed, pointing out to Subtle where various landmarks once had stood. They had burned the makeshift longhouse with its sad detritus; no one would need it again. By mutual unspoken consent, they ended up on the point where Per's house had been. They had left Melicar's shelter standing, though they seldom went there.

Their fire was built on the smooth slab of rock that had formed the first terrace of Per's experimental garden. The storm had swept it clean.

Sushan had already searched long in the sea drift on the shore and in the woods behind the point for something of Per's, but not even a scrap of recognizable wood was left.

"Gone," she said sadly. She lowered herself to the warm stone of the empty terrace, cradling the battered notebook she wore always strapped to her arm. "All gone. Nothing's left of the humans!"

Subtle stretched out his long hands and fingered Sushan's wrists, head on one side, as if deciphering clues written on her skin. His burning golden gaze moved from one of them to another.

"This-I is thinking," he said. "You-all is saying always 'human, human.' When this-I is round, I is dancing always 'round, round.' Now this-I is no more round, but still I lives the inside-seeing that is making the dance. Seeing is making shaping, and shaping is making seeing, like the god makes Changing People and the Changing People makes the god. But when shaping is changing, still the seeing is not dying.

"This-I is thinking, human is not shape. Human is not only made things you could find. Human is love, and remember."

"You're right," Sushan said. "I have his thoughts and

memories in here." She touched the notebook. "But I remember the shape I knew, and I miss it. I hoped to find something else that would remind me of that—something he made and used. That was expecting too much, I guess."

She wiped the thick, gleaming tears from her eyes with her taloned fingers, carefully.

"Wish I knew what was in these," she said absently. "My whole body is an experiment looking for a place to happen. Well. I'll get used to it in time, I suppose."

"There's us," Bey said. "We're left. And we're the last thing he made. Or the first. Subtle says he isn't dead."

Subtle leaned forward, staring into the fire—a never-ceasing wonder to him, a marvel out of legend come to life. The light glowed in his eyes.

"I is still thinking, he is alive," Subtle said. "The god is awake now, and thinking strong because Per-god is living there. In my remembering is a part that is very bright, so that I think the god is wanting this-I to be thinking toward that thing.

"Does you-I remember the fallen cities, deep deep down? There is other cities, on the edge of the greatshore, the island too big to swim around. Is being much danger there, but still the Round People go sometimes. Just to the edge we swim, where shallow water is covering the places of the Great People.

"This-I went to such a place, proving this-I is thinking strong and fast enough to be a scholar. There scholars is finding metal things and bringing back, for making the scholar's knife.

"When the changing ones wake up, we-I is building rafts, for taking all the human madethings that are left, and we-I is going to the dead cities. The Teeth will help us. We-I will be looking there for all the madethings of the Great People. Not only bright metal for knives, but all the things that humans is knowing how to use. I shares remembering from the god, telling me the Great People left many things behind."

He shivered with awe, his skin shimmering momentarily

indigo, at the thought of touching the creations of the Great Ones. He looked up through shifting cloud curtains at the stars—another wonder. Now, beyond the sky edge, he saw the brightness of another boundary waiting to be crossed.

"The Great Ones went beyond the sky, long in the long-time. They is leaving the god here to keep this world for them. But now he is awake, is asking where is they and why they is not returning. Maybe in the dead cities, this learning can be found. Maybe you-I is speaking again to your sky island."

He pushed a stick farther into the fire and watched it flame up—his own fire, to hold in his hand. *Redheart, Redheart, who would believe this?*

"Per-god is telling many stories," he said. "Round People is telling stories, too. Ending of one story, beginning of another. The greatlife is round."

Dilani had drifted away. She wandered down the rock ledges where Per's ocean garden had been planted, hoping she might find something that would make Sushan feel better. It wasn't true that everything was gone. Here and there she noticed a plant or two that she recognized, tough or lucky enough to hang on even after the gardener had left. She reached the edge of the waves and looked up. A brush of movement caught her eye. A bit of blue green waved like a bright feather caught among the gray and white of the rocks. Clinging like a tree frog, she pulled herself up the steep, undercut bluff until she could see what it was.

It wasn't a feather, but a branch of feathery needles on a tiny tree. Gnarled roots gripped a scant clump of dirt caught in a crack between tilted rock layers. The waves must have carried this one from its place on Per's terrace, but they had capriciously replaced it in a spot where it could cling to life.

Very carefully, she rocked the stem and felt the root ball break loose from its nest of rock. She lifted the tree, its roots still gripping the clump of dirt like tiny, many-fingered hands, and tucked it tenderly into the crook of her arm. She felt a kinship for the tree. It was something Per had touched and cared for in his solitary way. It was one more thing he had changed, and left behind, another castaway.

She slithered back to level ground with it and brushed through the group. Their words rolled off her.

"Found this," she signed to Sushan.

The reaction was just as she had hoped; Sushan's eyes lit up, and she dropped what she had been saying in midsentence.

"It's one of Per's trees! His tinkering for salt resistance must have worked better than I thought. I remember the day we argued about this. One tie to the shore!"

Her hands reached greedily to examine it. But Dilani could not make herself let go of it quite yet.

"You know what to do?" she signed. "How to take care of it?"

Sushan's hand bent protectively, possessively, around the artful curve of the branches, but she pulled back to leave signing space.

"You can count on it," she signed. "We'll give it the best place on the raft until we find a better home for it."

Dilani pushed the tree into Sushan's hands, but Sushan shook her head.

"You found it. I'll show you what Per used to do with them, but this one's yours. It's up to you to make it grow."

In Kitkitdildil's memory room, among the ferns, Per turned his thoughts toward the shadowy figure of Typhon's god. He had seen faces, not through the trembling surface this time, but directly visioned in the Deep. They had been hard to recognize. They weren't as he remembered them; but he thought they were people of his own.

*It looks as if you've won,* Per messaged to the old god. They had interlaced their vocabularies over a time that was long in the consciousness of a god. Per had become adept in the use of the god's scent motes and colors. Their communication now was as subtle and as accurate as it could be, between two minds so differently shaped.

Per continued. *You have changed the agents of the Great*

*Ones and made them work for people from a different world. My people have entered the change and lived. This is a great achievement.*

Kitkitdildil stirred the water negligently, releasing an astringent taste of irony.

*Your achievement, not mine.*

*How so?* Per asked, surprised.

*Yours was the knowledge of your people's functioning. I shared only the knowledge of the god's extensionals, so you could build the change motes needed. Your work was delicate and exacting. You are indeed a great scholar. My accomplishment lay elsewhere.*

*And where might that be?* Per was truly curious. And he was playing for time. The god had accomplished what he wanted, for whatever reason he had desired it. Per had never lost sight of the fact that he had no real existence, no body, no control. He was a collection of memories. In any real sense, he was probably already dead.

He tried not to forget that. At any time, the god could terminate this consciousness, even as he had awakened it.

*First, my fortunate choice,* Kitkitdildil said. *My sample was limited, but I chose you. It is hard to imagine better.*

*Thank you.* Irony was on Per's side, this time. *And is there more?* Per was tired of the game. *Or are you going to end it now?*

There was a pause, of sufficient length that Per felt he must have surprised Kitkitdildil.

*End it? No. That is no longer in my power.* He corrected himself. *May no longer be in my power. At any rate, it would no longer be easy or pleasant.*

*What do you mean?* Per thought he had steeled himself against all possibilities, but he felt uneasiness stirring within him and coloring his surroundings.

*Please don't do that, my friend,* said Kitkitdildil, humor softening the sharpness of Per's unease. *It creates an unpleasant flavor. I mean just this: As I allowed you to work with my data and extensionals, I knit you into the structure that is me. I cannot erase you now, without destroying pathways I too must use.*

Per's alarm was sharp and biting. *And I can't leave.*

*No.*

*So you're telling me that I am now your slave? Or a slave of your god? Which is it?* Per deliberately forced bitterness into the waters.

The god neutralized it deftly. *You misunderstand.*

Suddenly, Per felt as if he were weightless in a softly illuminated sphere. Vistas of memory and sensation stretched away in all directions. He saw reed gardens and burning mountains, star maps and gene maps, and the spiral paths that led back into his own history. Somewhere he saw the trembling reflection of Sofron's face, and the traces that might lead back there.

Kitkitdildil had told the truth. Per was meshed with the neural center of the complex organism that formed the god. All the vast storage of its records was open to him, arranged in orderly patterns, like the spiral galleries of a museum, or the chambers of a shell.

Kitkitdildil's voice echoed softly. *Helpers with hands? That was one goal, but a minor one. My first need was new knowledge, new understanding, new strength. There was only one way to find those things, but I think I have succeeded. I have not made you a slave. I have made you a god.*

Anger, fear, loneliness, a desperate search for a way of escape, all churned chaotically through Per's thoughts, leaving a turbulent wake of sensation. Kitkitdildil made no move to still the storm, but let Per rage.

Exhausted, Per let the turbulence fade, and found himself again among the ferns by the pool. The water was calm, faintly tinted with sadness.

Still Kitkitdildil said nothing, but *I am sorry* whispered all around Per.

Finally, tentatively, he searched for the feeling that might have been a laugh. It seemed to him that this configuration had not been used in a long time.

*Yes. You will be sorry,* he said. *Put that in your memory and hold on to it. But—I guess we'd better talk.*

Kitkitdildil's presence brightened joyously.

*Yes,* said the god to its brother. *There is much that you must know.*

# ✎ FREE DRINKS ✎

Take the Del Rey® survey and get a free newsletter! Answer the questions below and we will send you complimentary copies of the DRINK (Del Rey® Ink) newsletter free for one year. Here's where you will find out all about upcoming books, read articles by top authors, artists, and editors, and get the inside scoop on your favorite books.

Age _____  Sex ❑ M ❑ F

Highest education level: ❑ high school ❑ college ❑ graduate degree

Annual income: ❑ $0-30,000 ❑ $30,001-60,000 ❑ over $60,000

Number of books you read per month: ❑ 0-2 ❑ 3-5 ❑ 6 or more

Preference: ❑ fantasy ❑ science fiction ❑ horror ❑ other fiction ❑ nonfiction

I buy books in hardcover: ❑ frequently ❑ sometimes ❑ rarely

I buy books at: ❑ superstores ❑ mall bookstores ❑ independent bookstores ❑ mail order

I read books by new authors: ❑ frequently ❑ sometimes ❑ rarely

I read comic books: ❑ frequently ❑ sometimes ❑ rarely

I watch the Sci-Fi cable TV channel: ❑ frequently ❑ sometimes ❑ rarely

I am interested in collector editions (signed by the author or illustrated): ❑ yes ❑ no ❑ maybe

I read Star Wars novels: ❑ frequently ❑ sometimes ❑ rarely

I read Star Trek novels: ❑ frequently ❑ sometimes ❑ rarely

I read the following newspapers and magazines:

| | | |
|---|---|---|
| ❑ *Analog* | ❑ *Locus* | ❑ *Popular Science* |
| ❑ *Asimov* | ❑ *Wired* | ❑ *USA Today* |
| ❑ *SF Universe* | ❑ *Realms of Fantasy* | ❑ *The New York Times* |

Check the box if you do not want your name and address shared with qualified vendors ❑

Name _____
Address _____
City/State/Zip _____
E-mail _____

anzetti

**PLEASE SEND TO: DEL REY®/The DRINK**
**201 EAST 50TH STREET, NEW YORK, NY 10022 OR FAX TO**
**THE ATTENTION OF DEL REY PUBLICITY 212/572-2676**

# DEL REY® ONLINE!

## The Del Rey Internet Newsletter...

A monthly electronic publication e-mailed to subscribers and posted on the rec.arts.sf.written Usenet newsgroup and on our Del Rey Books Web site (www.randomhouse.com/delrey/). It features hype-free descriptions of books that are new in the stores, a list of our upcoming books, special promotional programs and offers, announcements and news, a signing/reading/convention-attendance calendar for Del Rey authors and editors, "In Depth" essays in which professionals in the field (authors, artists, cover designers, salespeople, etc.) talk about their jobs in science fiction, a question-and-answer section, and more!

Subscribe to the DRIN: send a blank message to
join-drin-dist@list.randomhouse.com

## The Del Rey Books Web Site!

We make a lot of information available on our Web site at
www.randomhouse.com/delrey/

- all back issues and the current issue of the Del Rey Internet Newsletter
- sample chapters of almost every new book
- detailed interactive features for some of our books
- special features on various authors and SF/F worlds
- reader reviews of some upcoming books
- news and announcements
- our Works in Progress report, detailing the doings of our most popular authors
- and more!

## If You're Not on the Web...

You can subscribe to the DRIN via e-mail (send a blank message to join-drin-dist@list.randomhouse.com) or read it on the rec.arts.sf.written Usenet newsgroup the first few days of every month. We also have editors and other representatives who participate in America Online and CompuServe SF/F forums and rec.arts.sf.written, making contact and sharing information with SF/F readers.

## Questions? E-mail us...

at delrey@randomhouse.com (though it sometimes takes us a little while to answer).